SPELLBOUND
BY
SIBELLA

Paul B McNulty

DEDICATION

To Treasa, Dara, Nora and Meabh.

ACKNOWLEDGMENTS

I gratefully acknowledge the support of a writers group, the-corner-table.com whose members reviewed draft copies of chapters of my manuscript; the Inspira Literary Agency, London who described an early draft as "… the best work of historical fiction that we've received …;" the 2012 William Faulkner Novel Competition who chose *Spellbound by Sibella,* as a finalist; and Elaine P Kennedy who edited the penultimate draft of my manuscript.

I have received permission to reproduce specified items in my manuscript as follows:

- extracts from "The Lynch Blosse Papers", *Analecta Hibernica,* 1980, volume 28, pages 113-219 by K W Nicholls, The Irish Manuscripts Commission;
- three quotes from the Thomas H Nally Papers and two quotes from "The spancel of death / by T. H. Nally", courtesy of the National Library of Ireland;
- an inscription on the grave of John Moore, story@hiwaterfordmuseum.ie;
- the third verse of *Eileen Aroon* and the first couplet of the Epitaph of *Gray's Elegy,* The Oxford Book of English Verse: 1250–1900, http://www.bartleby.com/101/663.html;
- the first two lines of a Christmas carol, David Wood, http://www.wfiu.org;
- a quote by St Ruth, http://www.ucc.ie/celt/online/E703001-001/text002.html;
- three prayers from the BCP of the Church of Ireland, biblosweb@aol.com;
- the Extreme Unction prayer, csm@traditio.com;
- the second part of the second verse of *Finnegan's Wake,* rodsmith@rodsmith.org.uk;
- the 1787 portrait of Miss Constable by George Romney, Calouste Gulbenkian Museum, Lisbon.

I have e-mailed copies of my manuscript for comment to Jeremy Ulick Browne, 11th Marquess of Sligo (descendant of Lord Altamont) of Westport, County Mayo; Ivor Hamrock, Mayo County Library; Brian Hoban, local historian, Castlebar, County Mayo; Richard Hely Lynch-Blosse, 17th Baronet of Oxfordshire; Cece Miles of Atlanta, great-great-great-great grandniece of John Moore; and Patrick Sheridan, local historian, Balla, County Mayo.

I also acknowledge the assistance of: Lar Joye, National Museum of Ireland; Captain G E Locker, Fenham Barracks, Newcastle Upon Tyne; Maria Luddy, Professor of History, University of Warwick; Craig Lynch-Blosse, New Zealand; Richard Hely Lynch-Blosse, 17th Baronet, Oxfordshire; K W Nicholls, historian, University College Cork; Dr Brendan Rooney, National Gallery of Ireland; and members of my extended family.

The night is darkening round me,
The wild winds coldly blow;
But a tyrant spell has bound me
And I cannot, cannot go.

(First verse from the poem
Spellbound by Emily Jane Bronte, 1837)

CHAPTER 1

"MAMA, ARE WE REALLY expecting Mr Lynch-Blosse of Balla House this afternoon?" Sibella Cottle asked as she twirled a russet curl.

"Indeed, we are," replied Louisa Moore, the Mistress of Ashbrook, County Mayo as she joined her foster-daughter and niece at the breakfast table.

"Is he the young man with the broken heart?" Sibella asked, all wide-eyed.

Louisa merely nodded in response.

"I have seen him at the Maidenhill Ball surrounded by a bevy of Big House damsels." Sibella's green eyes were twinkling. "They say he's a right womanizing rogue."

"You should not gossip, my dear." Louisa returned to the table with bacon and egg from the chafing dishes.

"Why is he visiting us?"

"He may feel the need to remove from home for a time."

Sibella was intrigued. Unaccountably, she could feel herself blushing. Was it possible that the twenty-four-year-old heir would stay at Ashbrook? If so, she might cast a spell on him, she thought impishly.

"I expect you to be on your best behaviour, young lady," Louisa admonished while buttering her toast.

"May I be excused?" Sibella asked as she gulped down the last of her milk. She was up and away before Louisa could even answer her.

Sibella commenced her welcoming preparations in a welter of excitement. One minute, she was racing upstairs to check her appearance and then down again to inspect the drawing room. The white-panelled room of the modest two-storey house featured a portrait of Sir Thomas More above the fireplace. She softened the stern image by arranging fresh daffodils on the mantelpiece and sideboard. Would Mr Lynch-Blosse notice the subtle shades of yellow, gold and white in the sweet-scented flowers, she wondered?

Later in the day, Sibella was at the window straining her neck to get a better view. "I can see a young man cantering up the hill," she called. Sibella had one last look around the room. She had heard that Mr Lynch-Blosse was a great hunter and rider. He would surely feel at home in a room with hunting, shooting and racing prints even if the daffodils eluded his attention.

1

After the butler escorted him into the drawing room, Louisa Moore extended the hand of friendship. "Mr Lynch-Blosse, welcome to Ashbrook; allow me to introduce my foster-daughter, Miss Cottle."

"You are surely welcome, Mr Lynch-Blosse." Sibella curtsied as her heart began to beat a little faster.

"I am delighted to meet you, Miss Cottle."

Sibella admired the sensuous lips on his rugged face, his blue eyes, and brown hair tied in a queue. How elegant his fine clothes were, she thought, a red riding jacket worn over a dark waistcoat and tight beige breeches.

Doctor Moore, the Master of Ashbrook, joined the company. "Mr Lynch-Blosse, please excuse my late arrival. I was in the stillroom preparing some medicine."

"Not at all, Doctor Moore. What a splendid location you have here, overlooking the Ashbrook River."

"Lady Lynch told me you would like to spend some time away from home," Moore said.

"I need to get away for a while. Grandmamma thought Ashbrook might be the place for me."

"I hope Lady Lynch is keeping well," continued Doctor Moore, sipping his ale. "I shall escort you around the estate after our refreshments. You should become familiar with our modest property before reaching a decision."

"May I ride with you, Papa?" Sibella asked. Anticipating that they might go riding, she wore a full-length maroon habit with a white bow at the neck and black boots.

Moore nodded and then escorted Harry to the stables, accompanied by Sibella.

As they progressed through the fields, Sibella noted how well Harry handled his gelding; that added to his appeal. She wondered if he was showing off to impress her. Perhaps he would teach her some new tricks were he to stay for a while.

At the end of the tour, Harry thanked the Moores while Sibella glanced at her foster-parents. "If Mr Lynch-Blosse comes to stay, mayhap he could give me some riding lessons?"

"Certainly," Harry said. "I have previously given instruction to my younger brother, Francis. I should be delighted to do so if your father were agreeable."

"We shall consider that in due course." Moore raised his eyebrows.

Sibella was disappointed at the cautious response but relieved that Harry appeared unperturbed.

"Thank you again for your hospitality." Harry bowed ever so slightly. "I really must return home."

* * * * *

A FEW DAYS LATER, a letter arrived addressed to Doctor Moore, Ashbrook House, Straide, County Mayo. Sibella could scarcely control her excitement because it bore the embossed seal of the Lynch-Blosses. Could it possibly be from Harry? She followed the footman as he handed the precious document to her foster-father and watched as he opened it. Doctor Moore cast a quick glance at the letter and handed it back. "You may read it now, my dear."

Sibella clutched the letter and bounded up the stairs to her bedroom where she looked at it for ages before opening it. She read it out word for word several times while pacing the floorboards.

Balla House,
Balla,
County Mayo, Ireland
Saturday, 20 February 1773.
Dear Doctor Moore,
I want to sincerely thank you for your kind hospitality during my recent visit. I told Lady Lynch how generous you were towards a poor man with a broken heart! In return, I offered my humble services as a riding coach to a charming young lady.
Grandmother reminded me of her maiden name, Mary Moore, and her distant relationship to you. She has decided to write you seeking permission for me to visit. I hope and pray that you will view her request in a favourable light. In that event, I shall look forward to renewing acquaintance with your charming family.
Yours faithfully,
Harry Lynch-Blosse.

Over the next two weeks, Sibella had only one person on her mind, Mr Lynch-Blosse, an heir to a baronetcy. She dreamt about him every night; in her sleep, he would declare his love for her and kiss her to distraction. Every morning, she came to her senses with a splash of cold water from her bedroom basin. On the other hand, if Harry came to stay at Ashbrook, she might never get another opportunity to attract his attention. Was she crazy to contemplate the possibility of falling in love with him? Sibella, now aged eighteen, felt it was high time she was married.

When Lady Lynch and Harry arrived on a sunny morning in early March, Sibella was waiting in the drawing room, dressed in a green gown over a white petticoat. She wore her red hair tied up with a hanging curl on either side of her pale and delicately freckled complexion.

"You are most welcome, Lady Lynch." Doctor Moore kissed his relative lightly on the cheek. "It is so good to see you after such a long time."

"Goodness me, Doctor Moore, how time flies." Lady Lynch flicked an imaginary piece of fluff off her shoulder. "I'm not inclined to visit or entertain as much as in my younger days."

Louisa poured the tea while the housekeeper passed around the scones. As the china tinkled and the aroma of the freshly baked scones wafted to their noses, Sibella broke the silence. "Perhaps Lady Lynch and Mr Lynch-Blosse would like to see around the house at their convenience?"

"Capital! I should enjoy that, Miss Cottle," Harry said while his grandmother declined.

Louisa smiled. "Sibella, please escort Mr Lynch-Blosse around the house and do not linger overmuch, my dear."

Sibella and Harry walked quietly through the hall featuring a facsimile of the portrait hanging in the drawing room. Harry stopped to admire.

"That is Sir Thomas More," Sibella said.

"He who was beheaded by Henry VIII." Harry nodded.

"Exactly! We claim descent from Sir Thomas. He surely is our inspiration."

"Most interesting, Miss Cottle."

Sibella led Harry through an estate office bedecked with dog collars, firearms, fishing rods, fox brushes and stag horns.

"This house is beginning to feel like home already."

"I am pleased to hear it," Sibella said. "We have four bedrooms upstairs, one for the Master and Mistress, one for me and ..."

"Will I be given my choice?" Harry joked as they climbed the stairs.

"Of course, kind sir, in the event that you receive an invitation to stay." Sibella smiled, revealing her well-formed dainty teeth. "Now for my final exhibit — please follow me to the stillroom!"

Harry laughed as they moved downstairs.

"Actually, it is Doctor Moore's stillroom." Throwing open the door, she cried, "Voila! I am permitted to prepare medicines and cosmetics under supervision."

"What are you making now?"

4

"Mama has requested some lavender water. I must distil some oil from fresh lavender, then add distilled water and a little alcohol. Papa is allowing me to work on my own, this time."

"I am impressed, Miss Cottle. What else can you make?"

"I am going to make a perfume using musk, wild rose and mugwort."

"Splendid!"

"Mama said we might pay a visit to witch Judy in Balla to seek her advice."

"Christ!" Harry blushed. "Please excuse me, Miss Cottle."

After the unexpected profanity, Sibella realized that Harry disapproved of witch Judy and wondered why. As a precaution, she refrained from telling him of her cure for a broken heart — although presumably, that was just what he needed.

Harry lingered in the stillroom, apparently mesmerized by its exotic scents and magical glassware, while Sibella returned to the drawing room.

Quietly entering, she overheard Lady Lynch say, "Poor Harry was completely overthrown when his marriage to Miss Mahon ended. He needs respite from Balla. People there are over-concerned with his private life."

"Perhaps we could send him to my brother in Alicante." Moore laughed as Harry returned.

Sibella scowled. She would not approve unless they sent her to Alicante as well.

"Harry, I have been informing Doctor Moore that you are not in the frame of mind for foreign travel." Lady Lynch clasped her reticule and then cleared her throat. "However, I know you would love to gain experience at Ashbrook: it will be much easier to do so in a tidy compact estate, and then you may apply that experience to the estate you will inherit."

"Would you like to stay here for a while, Harry?" Moore said, steepling his fingers.

Harry nodded.

"We would be delighted to have you … if you do not object to a little work. Your riding skills are top class — I have seen you at the hunt. You could also coach Sibella."

"Thank you, Doctor Moore. If you are agreeable, I shall take up residence in a fortnight."

Sibella was tempted to say that she was surely agreeable but wisely held her counsel.

* * * * *

ON A WILD AND windy morning in late March, Sibella was beside herself with excitement as she waited for Harry to arrive. When she saw an ornate carriage trundling up the steep avenue, her eyes opened wide. Was this regal entrance a figment of her imagination? When Harry alighted, he looked quite dashing sporting a blue frock coat with metallic trim and tight grey breeches over white stockings.

"You are surely welcome, Mr Lynch-Blosse." Sibella flashed a warm smile at him.

"Thank you," Harry replied.

"Once you're settled ..." Sibella hesitated, and then said, "I can't wait for my riding lessons to begin."

"Of course; but I must first commence my routine as prepared by Doctor Moore."

"Thank you, kind sir."

"Tomorrow, I shall ride around the estate with the agent visiting the tenants of Ashbrook. I have to make note of any requirement in fencing, livestock and maintenance. When I have finished, perhaps we may go for a short ride with your groom."

On the following day, Sibella waited impatiently for Harry to finish his work. She wandered through the house, interspersing embroidery in the drawing room with reading in the library. Finally, Harry was ready. She felt a frisson of excitement when Packie Burke lifted her on to her pony. Off they galloped, with the groom leading, into the open fields of the estate. Sibella loved the feel of wind in her face. She pretended not to notice the fleeting glances from Harry as he assessed her capability.

When they stopped for a break, Harry patted his gelding on the neck. "You are a good rider, Miss Cottle."

"Thank you. You will redden my cheek with your flattery."

Harry laughed. "I shall teach you how to jump fences on our next outing."

Sibella enjoyed the contact as the coaching commenced. She got on well with him, although she was cautious about their developing friendship in the light of his failed marriage.

She wondered how he would cope with the formal dinner at Ashbrook which was held weekly. Dinner commenced at eight of the clock sharp on the following Saturday. Doctor Moore sat at the head of the table opposite Louisa, flanked on either side by Sibella and Harry. They discussed estate and house management issues as well as national and international events.

Sibella listened carefully as Doctor Moore opened the conversation during the soup course.

"Harry, did you know that Benjamin Franklin visited Ireland just two years ago?"

"I'm not quite sure who Benjamin Franklin is. I vaguely remember Master Ralph talking about him at the academy in Castlebar."

"You were not paying attention, Mr Lynch-Blosse." Sibella teased as she noted the rush of blood to his face.

Moore lightly touched his lips with a napkin. "He's an American patriot, a scientist and an Enlightenment thinker."

"What did he think of Ireland?" Harry asked.

Sibella was not surprised when Doctor Moore responded with his customary authority.

"Mr Franklin was astounded at the level of poverty in Ireland. He was concerned that America would suffer the same plight if England's exploitation of the colonies continued."

"If he had come to Mayo, he would have seen real poverty among the tenantry and the dispossessed," said Harry while Sibella silently urged him on. "Perhaps we should be seeking independence."

"Exactly, Mr Lynch-Blosse!" Louisa sipped her wine. "From whom did you hear this story, Doctor Moore?"

"I heard it from The Honourable James Cuffe, Member of Parliament — a friend of Harry's father."

The world of politics and intrigue fascinated Sibella. She had much to learn and always listened carefully whenever such topics arose.

After a main dish of garnished venison and a dessert of dried fruit, the connecting doors to the drawing room were opened. The ladies sat by the wood fire in the drawing room while the men enjoyed port at the dining table. Sibella chatted about her youthful hopes and dreams while Harry cocked an ear to their whispered conversations.

When Doctor Moore yawned, he said, "I must retire, Mr Lynch-Blosse. You may wish to join the ladies."

"Thank you, Doctor Moore." Harry walked into the drawing room and sat by the fire.

"I enjoyed the discussion at dinner, Mistress Moore," Harry said, gazing into the glowing embers.

"I am pleased, Mr Lynch-Blosse," Louisa replied as she sat back from the fire. "I shall knit a little before bedtime."

"I hope you did not object to my little intervention." Sibella felt the blood rushing to her cheeks.

"Of course not, I enjoy your banter. It is such a pleasant change from the stifling formality of Balla."

"Doctor Moore was impressed. When you warmed to your subject, you spoke impressively." Sibella gazed into Harry's blue eyes; they had a softness about them that was appealing.

They continued to chat for ages until Louisa began to click her knitting needles more vigorously. Sibella whispered, "I must retire. We may talk again on the morrow."

She departed after lightly kissing her foster-mother on the cheek. As she walked upstairs, her heart was beating fast again. Did Harry really like her as much as he said, or was it just a harmless exchange between two lonely souls? That night she dreamed that he kissed her. It excited her. She wanted more.

After breakfast on the following morning, Louisa rattled her chatelaine. "I think you like Mr Lynch-Blosse."

"He is certainly an interesting man." Sibella sighed as she focused on the type of information that would impress her foster-mother. "He told me how he was born in London — how his parents married — where the name Blosse came from — his father's conversion to —"

Louisa interjected. "Are you falling in love with him, my dear?"

Sibella blushed. "Of course not!"

"Mr Lynch-Blosse is romantically experienced. He could break your heart and destroy your reputation."

"Mama, we are merely friends who enjoy conversing together."

"You are spending far too much time with him." Louisa raised her eyebrows. "Make sure you behave correctly, young lady!"

"There is no need to worry — Mr Lynch-Blosse is a gentleman."

"Gentlemen have their needs too, my dear. Doctor Moore is worried."

"I'm in perfect health, Mama!" Sibella sought to lighten the tone.

"It is your heart which worries him."

"My heart is beating away as strongly as ever."

"Mayhap it is beating too fast, especially in his company." Louisa's tone sharpened.

Sibella paused to embroider a little more and then changed tack. "I told Harry about Cottlestown in Sligo. He said we might visit sometime if you were agreeable. We could ride early on a Saturday and return in time for dinner."

"Certainly not! Harry has a reputation with the female sex. We must protect your good name, my dear," Louisa said. It was clear she was not pleased.

"I have heard about his failed marriage. What else is said of him?" Sibella persisted.

"He may have lost his compass after his mother died at such a young age." Louisa's face reddened.

"How did he lose his compass?"

"None of your business, young lady … goodness me, look at the time! I must have a word with the housekeeper. You may progress with your sewing." Louisa hastily departed.

Sibella was now even more interested in the affairs of Harry. Cottlestown could wait. What did Louisa mean by Harry losing his compass? She had to find out.

CHAPTER 2

IT WAS NOW THREE months since Harry's arrival at Ashbrook. Sibella's friendship with him had flourished. Curiosity about his intentions consumed her mind: should she encourage him to take their feelings to a romantic level?

After yet another riding session, they stopped by the Ashbrook River. Packie Burke tethered their horses while they sat on an elevated rock.

"What mischief did you get up to at Balla?" Sibella whispered.

"Why do you ask?" Harry inquired.

"I asked Mama for permission to ride to Cottlestown with you. She refused in order to protect my reputation."

Harry hesitated.

"Are you sure you want to know?"

Sibella trembled, surprised by her own courage.

"I want to know everything about you."

Harry grasped his riding crop.

"Very well, then," he said.

Sibella wondered if he would conceal his affair with a servant in the Big House. She had heard about it at the Maidenhill Ball and from the housekeeper at Ashbrook. How would she feel if he lied?

"My first love was for Sally Colgan, a pretty servant in the Big House. From time to time, she brought me a chocolate drink in the morning. Overcoming my shyness, I began to talk to her. She was nineteen, two years older than me."

"What happened?" Sibella asked.

"We fell in love. Our secret romance blossomed. Months later, Sally was pregnant. She asked me what we should do. I said I would talk to Sir Robuck, who was furious. He insisted that I break off the affair immediately. In due course, Sally had her baby at home. We named her Ellen. I tried to see Sally again but both families discouraged contact. In the end, I accepted that it was the best thing for both of us and especially for my little girl."

Sibella's heart was pounding when she asked,

"Did you want to marry her?"

"To be honest, no. I accepted that I was too young to marry."

"But did you love her?"

"I was infatuated with her at the time, but not now." Harry blushed.

Sibella wondered if Harry was embarrassed or hurt by the memory of the inevitable questioning and censure at Balla.

"What about your daughter?" she asked.

"Ellen is doing well. She is at home with the Colgans who are anxious to put the affair behind them. They want to give Sally an opportunity to marry a good man of her own class."

Sibella was horrified at the plight of Sally Colgan. The poor girl must be broken-hearted, with her reputation in tatters as well. Nonetheless, she was impressed that Harry had told the truth. He would not have done so unless he wished to win her trust and perhaps her heart. She adjusted her riding hat and then sought to lighten the mood.

"You are quite a rogue, Mr Lynch-Blosse, but thank you for being honest."

"Now it is your turn, Miss Cottle. What mischief have you been guilty of?"

Sibella felt a rush of blood to her face.

"Not much, apart from an incident at the Maidenhill Ball after the Ballinrobe Races." There was a sparkle in her eyes on remembering the excitement of the occasion. "Much to my surprise, my dance-card was full. The country dancing was vigorous and warm. One of my partners invited me outside for a breath of fresh air. He escorted me to an area where young couples kissed and hugged, and were very intimate. I became frightened. I said I must return at once. He clutched me and tried to kiss me. I slapped him across the face and ran back to the hall crying."

"What an ignorant scoundrel!"

"Hush, Harry," Sibella said while Packie Burke returned after watering the horses. She could see that Harry was incensed; that was a bit rich, given the story she had just heard. "I learned my lesson that night. I mistakenly thought that gentlemen behaved like gentlemen."

She concealed the fact that the young buck had hissed, "You red-haired bitch of Ashbrook." That would be her secret until she knew Harry better.

"Tell me his name and I shall whip him."

"It's all right, Harry. I have long since recovered. Please do not tell my family. If they knew, they would never let me go to a dance again. They're even worried about me chatting to you like this." Sibella could see the comment disturbed him somewhat, and wondered what the reaction could mean.

* * * * *

SOMETIME LATER SIBELLA HEARD that Louisa had arranged a meeting with Harry in the drawing room. Curiosity got the better of her.

She left her work in the stillroom and listened to their conversation from the adjoining dining room.

"I think you like my foster-daughter," Louisa said.

Sibella held her breath as Harry spluttered,

"I am very fond of M-Miss Cottle."

"You must restrain your interest or Doctor Moore will not be pleased." Louisa paused. "It must be nice to meet someone so agreeable after —"

"— after my failed marriage," Harry interjected.

Sibella felt her pulse throbbing as Harry told Louisa the story of his marriage.

"After falling in love with Miss Mahon, I became concerned about our different religions. She persuaded the priest that I was about to convert to Catholicism so the wedding could proceed. We married secretly in Galway and honeymooned in London and Suffolk."

"What did your family say to that?" Louisa asked.

"They were horrified. Sir Robuck threatened me with disinheritance. I was devastated. Reluctantly, I agreed to apply for an annulment. I had little choice."

"And how is Mistress Mahon?"

"She was as distraught as I was," Harry said. "She is still grieving. I hope she can forgive me."

Late that night in bed, Sibella wondered if she should pursue her relationship with Harry given his chequered past.

"It will not be easy without antagonising my foster-parents and his family," she realized.

With these thoughts swirling in her mind, she tried to fantasize about him before settling for a sleepless night.

* * * * *

APART FROM RIDING, SIBELLA and Harry often strolled along the bank of the Ashbrook River during the summer warmth. A shrub or tree occasionally concealed them from the watchful eye of Louisa Moore perched on an elevated sun-bench.

"Mama told me the story of your marriage," Sibella said. "It is indeed amazing! Poor Mistress Mahon, will she ever recover?"

"Christ! Shall I ever recover?" Harry said.

Sibella had become accustomed to his occasional profanity. She ignored it and asked,

"Will you marry again?"

Harry paused, and then said,

"I must marry again."

"Why?"

"I am under pressure to father a male heir."

"Has your annulment come through?"

"Uncle Peter is dealing with that," Harry said. "Once I have a suitable bride in mind, he will conclude the business."

"Have you anyone in mind?" Sibella smiled as Louisa waved.

"I do."

Sibella gasped and almost fell into the swirling waters.

"Do I know her?"

"You do. Now, shall we walk home?"

She looked long and deep into his blue eyes, eyes that were alive with sensitivity.

"You must tell me who it is. I promise to keep your secret."

"It is someone who has banished my inner turmoil, someone who has made me strong again, someone who has prepared me for the next great adventure of my life," Harry said, and then departed abruptly leaving Sibella with her mind in a whirl.

Moments later, she joined Louisa on the bench overlooking a landscape dotted with mature meadows.

"You are deep in thought, my dear," Louisa greeted her.

"Mr Lynch-Blosse just told me that he intends to marry again. He has someone particular in mind."

"How exciting. Who is the lucky lady?"

Sibella nervously ran her fingers through her russet curls.

"Someone whom I know," she said.

"Possibly Lady Harriett?"

"I am not acquainted with her."

Sibella was silent as she tried to make sense of Harry's hints.

"Could it be me, Mama?"

"Good heavens, Sibella! I know he likes you, but even if he wished to marry you, his family would oppose it."

"Why should they? Is there something wrong with me?"

"Of course not, my darling daughter," Louisa sighed. "It is merely the way of the world. You are a Catholic and you are —"

"— illegitimate?" Sibella interjected, taking advantage of the opportunity to query her mysterious parentage.

"Sibella, please!" Louisa implored. "You are the lawful daughter of my late sister, Isabel, and your late father, Michael Cottle. You must miss them terribly, even though Doctor Moore and I love you as dearly as our own daughter."

"Thank you, Mama. Please excuse me."

Tears came to her eyes as she rushed to her bedroom. She threw herself on the bed and sobbed. After a while, she turned over on her back with her head on a high pillow. Passing clouds periodically shadowed the midsummer sun. The changes in light complemented her mood, which vacillated from optimism to pessimism. She knew one thing for sure: she had feelings for Harry, and he seemed to have feelings for her. He would probably return to Balla after completion of the harvest. What would she do if he asked her to marry him?

$$* \quad * \quad * \quad * \quad *$$

OVER THE COMING DAYS, Sibella was distracted and confused. Eventually, she opened her heart to her foster-mother while sewing in the drawing room.

"Mama, I think Harry is in love with me. What should I do?"

"I am not surprised. You are a diamond of the first water. You are intelligent, educated and blessed with an engaging personality. Of course he's in love with you, my darling."

"Suppose he wants to marry me? You said his family would oppose it."

"Not only that, Sir Robuck would disinherit him. You would end up in the same sorry mess as Mistress Mahon."

"So if he proposed, we would have to wait until his father died."

"You would — without any guarantee that he would keep his promise."

Changing tack, Sibella asked,

"Did Mistress Mahon become pregnant?"

"Sibella!" Louisa cried. "Not that I'm aware of; but if she did, she would have been sent away to have the baby, and have it fostered."

"Just like me, Mama!" Sibella continued to question the secrets of her past.

"No!" Louisa raised her voice, only part of which could be attributed to pricking her finger with a needle. "Your mother was not sent away. You were born in Sligo, where your parents lived."

"Was my father sent away?"

14

"No! Your father passed away when you were an infant. Your mother said that, on his deathbed, the handsome man cried ever so much when he held you, hugged you and kissed you goodbye. She thought he would never let you go."

This account of the loving farewell of her father brought tears to Sibella's eyes. It was an image, she would cherish forever. Notwithstanding the love of the Moores, she still missed her natural parents. She also missed not having a young female friend with whom to share her dreams and frustrations. Female acquaintances she had aplenty; however, those from the Big Houses looked down on her while those of more modest background were either poorly educated, excessively giddy or both. She was therefore grateful for the opportunity to open her heart to Louisa. As they continued to talk, she began to mature and to prepare herself for the future.

Harry's hint of love haunted Sibella over the summer and into the autumn. What would she do if he made an advance? Fortunately, her mind was distracted by work and by the joy of frequent trips around Mayo. Louisa chaperoned the young couple wherever they went. Castlebar was their most frequent destination, where the ladies shopped and Harry renewed acquaintance with his hunting and gambling associates.

They even crossed the border into Sligo to visit Cottlestown. Sibella knelt for the first time at the burial plot where her parents rested. After placing two red roses on the grave, she prayed for their salvation. She would have stayed there till sundown if Harry had not dragged her away.

During this time, she enjoyed Harry's flirting although he confined it to lingering looks and the lightest of physical contact. She wondered why he behaved so impeccably even when Louisa was absent. She responded by entertaining him with her wicked repartee. Occasionally, she pressed a half-closed fan to her lips, an invitation to him to kiss her, which he ignored.

Towards the end of the summer, Sibella began to wonder if Harry had changed his ways. Louisa's chaperoning became more relaxed and the opportunities for flirting increased, yet he still made no move, not even a hug or a peck on the cheek!

* * * * *

SOMETIME BEFORE THE LEAVES began to turn, Sibella shared her distress with her foster-mother.

"I am still so undecided, Mama."

"What are you talking about, my dear?"

"Mr Lynch-Blosse."

"Good heavens, I thought you had forgotten all about him!"

"I have tried and failed. I have a decided partiality for him. Should he propose to me, I wish to accept, but I am concerned about his previous relationships."

"I understand your fascination with him. He would be quite a catch. I believe he may have up to ten thousand a year when he inherits."

Sibella gathered her thoughts. She could not resist the temptation to remark,

"If Mr Lynch-Blosse is developing a relationship with a Catholic of humble background, he would be jumping from the frying pan into the fire, as Sir Thomas More once said."

Louisa laughed and then asked,

"What will you do, Sibella?"

"I am unsure."

"His family will oppose it."

"I understand that, but it is also a great opportunity. Harry's father is ill. When the poor man passes away, I could become the Mistress of Balla House, one of the most powerful women in Mayo."

She felt like saying, *"Not bad for the red-haired bitch of Ashbrook!"* but wisely refrained.

"Sibella, you are losing the run of yourself, my darling."

Sibella knew she could be making the biggest mistake of her life, but she admitted,

"I am growing very attached to Harry. If he confirms his love for me, I will surely go with him."

"As your foster-mother, I warn you, you must not rush this decision."

"What will Papa think?"

"I regret to say, he will forbid it. But I will always love and cherish you, whatever happens."

"That means the world to me. I love you so much." They embraced as both women shed tears.

Louisa departed, leaving Sibella torn by conflicting emotions.

As evening fell, Harry sauntered into a garden resplendent with the maroon shades of the tree peony surrounded by the whiteness of oriental poppies. Sibella pretended not to notice him as she admired the variety of colour in the romantic setting.

Harry approached her after picking a poppy. "Did I see some tears this morning?"

"Louisa confirmed her love and support as I look to my future. I am such a fortunate girl to have the Moores as foster-parents." Sibella paused, adjusting her petticoat. "Can you bring tears of joy to my eyes with your dreams for the future?"

Her heart began to race when Harry looked deep into her green eyes, and said. "I want to proclaim my love for the most beautiful girl I have ever met. I feel so passionate and yet so relaxed in your company. We would be a remarkable couple."

Sibella was elated, although the cautionary words of Louisa reverberated in her mind.

"How would your family feel?" she asked.

"My father would oppose it, but the poor man is seriously ill. Once he passes away, the road would be clear."

Sibella was unsure. Decision time had arrived. She could banish Harry and stay at Ashbrook. In which case she would marry less favourably, or she could risk a union with the womanizing rogue, carrying with it the prospect of a stellar social elevation. If that failed, she must return humiliated to the Moores: if they would still have her.

CHAPTER 3

THE FIRST CHILL OF autumn air made Sibella more conscious of the passing time. The meadows were dotted with haycocks and the corn was now ripe. She feared that Harry's time at Ashbrook would expire once the harvest was over. Would that signal the end of their romance just as it was beginning to bud?

Her concern lingered until Doctor Moore intervened. When he summoned her to the estate office, her pulse began to throb. She could not help but wonder if she was in trouble.

When she saw Harry there, her anxiety increased. Was her foster-father about to send him home? She glanced at the handsome man from Balla, but Harry remained impassive.

Doctor Moore smiled.

"Sibella, I would like you and Mr Lynch-Blosse to help me with the corn harvest," he began. "Harry, you will stand with the farm workers as they cut the ripe oats. Sibella will stand with the visiting workers as they gather the stems into sheaves. I shall oversee the work."

Sibella was thrilled. She would now have the opportunity to work alongside Harry for the duration of the harvest. The thought made her wonder if Doctor Moore had taken leave of his senses.

After they departed, she whispered,

"I thought he was going to banish you to Balla."

"Once the harvest is complete, I shall be on my way," Harry said.

"Dear Lord," Sibella thought, *"What am I going to do without my handsome Harry?"*

On a sunny morning in September, she banished the thought of separation from her mind to focus on the job in hand. While Harry's crew cut the oats, she lifted the spirits of the visiting workers with her quick wit. They enjoyed bantering with her as they bound the cut stems into upright sheaves to dry in the field. Singing and occasional breaks for food and ale alleviated the tedium of repetitive work. She enjoyed the fresh air of the golden landscape, but kept an eye on Harry who seemed to be enjoying himself.

After finish drying in a kiln, the workers spread the dried sheaves on the wooden floor of the Ashbrook barn. The men threshed the corn using a flail with a free-swinging club.

"Have a go at threshing, Mr Lynch-Blosse!" Sibella said. She suspected that Harry had never handled such an implement. His attempt generated much laughter amongst the farm workers.

"I should confine myself to management," Harry said.

"May I have a go?" Sibella asked.

When Doctor Moore nodded, she rescued the flail and raised it high.

"Show 'em how it's done, Miss Cottle," a farm worker whooped.

"Stand back, boys," Sibella said.

She gave the oats a mighty thump. The result set the crowd roaring with approval.

The threshing continued. When it was completed, the workers brushed the corn kernels and remaining chaff into little mounds that were loaded into a winnowing machine. When Sibella saw the passing air blowing the lighter chaff away, she wondered if her romance with Harry would also fade away with the wind.

The grinding of kernels in a corn mill powered by the Ashbrook River did little to raise her spirits. It was almost as if the end of the harvest was about to grind her love for Harry into smithereens.

Three week later, at the conclusion of the harvest, Doctor Moore said,

"Well done Harry and Sibella. I am proud of you."

After Moore departed, Harry wiped the sweat from his brow.

"With my threshing and your management skill, we would surely form a powerful team," Sibella said.

Harry nodded. Later, they both joined an informal house party to celebrate the conclusion of the harvest. People attended in their work clothes, and ate cold meats and bread washed down with ale. Singing and dancing followed in the open air. Brandy and whiskey flowed freely. Older workers relaxed on the grass in a scene illuminated by a bonfire of turf and wood.

Harry danced with Sibella as the tempo of the music mellowed. A love song penetrated the night air to the accompaniment of a fiddle and a bodhran:

When, like the rising day, Eileen Aroon
Love sends his early ray, Eileen Aroon
What makes his dawning glow
Changeless through joy and woe
Only the constant know, Eileen Aroon.

Later in the night, Sibella sat with Harry in the garden as clouds scudded across a harvest moon. "I want to show you something," he told her.

Sibella felt her heart beginning to beat.

"What are you going to show me?" she asked.

19

"A secret, my dear — hush!" he said, handing her a black velvet box. "I shall leave it with you. Now I must retire."

Harry kissed her lightly on her cheek and then began walking towards his room. Sibella waited for a moment, and then retired to her own room, her mind in a whirl. She sat on the side of the bed ... trying to understand his mysterious behaviour. Finally, she opened the velvet box.

She gasped in astonishment at an exquisite Tara brooch. It was made of gold-plated silver with amber and glass studs. A sparkling diamond adorned the decorative pin. She held it to her bodice. Its image in the mirror complemented her red hair and sensuous white skin. What next, Sibella Cottle, she thought while replacing the brooch in its box. She undressed and put on her nightgown; and then it came to her.

"I will just thank Harry before he goes to sleep and return smartly to my room," she thought.

The idea led her down to his room. She gently opened his door without knocking to keep from disturbing the Moores. She saw him sitting in his nightgown by the bed with a glass of tawny port.

"Harry," she whispered as she held the velvet box aloft. "I just wanted —"

Harry interjected. "Please relax, my darling. I shall pour you a nightcap."

Sibella stood at the end of the bed facing him.

Harry rose and crossed to the mantelpiece where he poured another glass of port. He handed her the drink.

Sibella raised her glass and then said, "Thank you for the beautiful gift."

"Lady Lynch gave it to me after my marriage broke up. She said it would bring me luck. Now it is yours."

"I cannot possibly accept it. It is too valuable."

"Nonsense, my dear; may I pin it to your nightgown?"

Sibella felt a frisson of excitement as Harry fitted the brooch close to her bosom. He then kissed her lightly on the cheek before they sat down to sip their tawny potation under the light of a flickering candle.

When Sibella rose to leave, Harry asked her to dance. As they glided slowly around the room, he kissed her and their tongues entwined. Her body was now on fire. They kissed and hugged again. Sibella succumbed to the temptation. Harry was gentler than the young buck encountered at the Maidenhill Ball. She allowed him to loosen her bodice while she opened his shirt. She could feel his manhood pressing against her. As he drew the bed covers down, she sucked the lobe of his ear. She caressed his lower back and moaned as he gently penetrated her. Her elation was complete when she climaxed shortly after him — would that this pleasure could last forever. Harry relaxed on the high pillow as she laid her hand upon his chest. Both drifted into a deep sleep.

Sibella awoke at sunrise to the music of the dawn chorus. Harry snored on.

"My God," she thought. *"What am I doing in his bed?"*

She gently raised the bedclothes, slipped her feet on to the floor, and immediately retired to her bedroom with her mind in turmoil. Making love was what she had been dreaming about for months. How would the Moores react when they learned of it? The house staff would have a field day if they found out. What would happen if she became pregnant?

Sibella avoided eye contact with Harry during the morning. They talked later that day during their riding jaunt.

"I am in love with you, Sibella Cottle. You are a diamond of the first water."

Sibella smiled while smartening her riding jacket; its black colour, offset by a white shirt, complemented her red hair.

"I love you too, Harry," she said; and then lowered her voice. "But the staff must not find out about last night."

"My lips are sealed, however …"

"What do you mean, 'however'?"

"I must tell the Moores!" Harry said.

"Are you mad? They warned me to be wary of your advances. What if I become pregnant?"

"They would guess it was me. I must tell them even if they whip me out of the house."

"Don't, Harry, I will tell Louisa in my own time. You may come to visit when things have quieted down."

Harry nodded while Sibella feared it could all end in disaster.

* * * * *

NOW THAT THE HARVEST was over, Harry had packed his bags after receiving permission to visit Sibella in a month's time.

Two weeks later, she was overjoyed to receive a letter from him:

Balla House,
County Mayo.
Friday, 15 October 1773
Dear Miss Cottle,

I hope you are all keeping perfectly well. Sir Robuck and Lady Lynch were delighted that I enjoyed my wonderful sojourn at Ashbrook. I now feel renewed and ready for the next great adventure of my life. Please pass on my sincere thanks to the charming Doctor and Mistress Moore for putting up with my melancholic persona for such a long time.

I am looking forward to renewing acquaintance with all of you two weeks hence.

With my very best wishes,

Yours sincerely,

Harry Lynch-Blosse.

Sibella was delighted that Harry had been diplomatic in his carefully crafted words, and yet she yearned for a more romantic letter that she could read again, and again, until he returned. In the intervening period, her mood swung this-way and that-way. Was she going to be the centrepiece of the next great adventure of his life, or was she losing the run of herself, as Louisa would surely say?

Two weeks later, Harry arrived on his black gelding. They sat together in the dining room while the Moores remained nearby in the adjoining drawing room.

"How does your father keep?" Sibella asked.

"Sir Robuck is not in the best of health."

"The poor man. Have you told him about us?"

Harry blushed.

"No, but I told Lady Lynch and Uncle Peter."

Sibella bit her lip. She was faintly conscious of the sound of Louisa's knitting.

"I would imagine they were hardly thrilled," she ventured.

"They shall get used to it. You must not worry," Harry said.

His eyes met hers, then, and lingered as he asked,

"How are you, my dear heart?"

Sibella smiled, thrilled with the way his gaze held hers.

"Nothing has happened yet, although I am overdue."

"You will know when I visit next. Say a prayer for both of us." Harry lightly touched her arm. "I love you with all my heart."

He beamed when Sibella drew her fan close to her heart as an expression of her love for him.

"If I am with child ..."

"You must not worry. I shall look after you."

"How will you look after me?"

"Let me think about it."

"You will need to do so quickly." Sibella pursed her lips.

Harry gently laid his hand on hers.

"I shall, my darling."

"Thank you, Harry."

Sibella continued to hold his eye contact. She was convinced by the way he looked at her, that he would honour his promise, though she did not know how. She yearned to embrace him, to let him know through the contact how much she did believe in him.

The look between them lasted for a brief moment more. Then Harry turned and walked into the drawing room.

"Doctor and Mistress Moore, I am most grateful that you allowed me to visit."

Louisa continued to knit while Doctor Moore stared long and hard at Harry. Harry went forward with what he had to say.

"I should like to visit again in a month if you are agreeable."

Sibella heaved a sigh of relief when Doctor Moore nodded. She walked to the hall door and waved as Harry made haste to Balla.

∗ ∗ ∗ ∗ ∗

ONE MONTH LATER, SIBELLA was pale and nauseous. Once Louisa noticed this, Sibella knew she would have to tell her all of what had happened.

"Mama, I am in love with Harry. I could not resist my feelings for him. After the harvest party, we lay together."

Louisa's face dropped.

"How dare that womanizing rogue — Doctor Moore will be furious! Now I understand why he left so abruptly. What will happen if you are increasing?"

"Harry will take responsibility for the child."

Louisa's attack turned from Harry to Sibella at the explanation.

"I am furious with you," she said. "Oh, Sibella, this relationship will not be an easy one. If you have any doubts, you must end it now. If you are with child — I do not know. I would have to talk to Doctor Moore."

Sibella was dumbstruck. What did Mama mean? Would her foster-parents banish her if she were pregnant?

Eventually she said,

"I am increasing, Mama. I am in l-love with —"

Louisa broke into the explanation before Sibella could finish. Tears came to her eyes when she did.

"Sibella, my dear ... we already suspected. I am sorry ..."

Sibella did not understand why Louisa was sorry.

"What do you mean, Mama?"

Louisa, visibly upset, went on to explain.

"Doctor Moore insists that you go to Waterford to have your baby. You will stay with his sister."

The full meaning of what Louisa was trying to say hit Sibella.

"You want me out!" she exclaimed. "You want to send me away and have my baby adopted."

The idea was more than she could bear. She turned and hurried away. Louisa called after her.

"Sibella, wait ..." but she was gone.

The agitated young woman continued to run until she dashed into her room and flung herself on to her bed where she sobbed for ages.

On his next visit to Ashbrook, Sibella gave Harry the shock of his life.

"I have to leave, Harry," she said. "My foster-parents wish me elsewhere. Their reputation would be ruined if my pregnancy became known."

"Oh, Christ!"

Sibella looked him straight in the eye as his chalky whiteness transformed into a burning red.

"I got an unfavourable reception when I told my family of my love for you," Harry stammered. "Sir Robuck instructed me to break off my relationship with you. Lady Lynch said he would disinherit me unless I complied."

Sibella needed time to absorb the chilling message. Would he now abandon her as he had abandoned Sally Colgan and Mistress Mahon? Would Sibella Cottle become notch number three in his romantic escapades?

"Let's walk in the garden," she suggested.

Harry concurred, and silently led the way to the sculpted area.

The beauty of the walk somehow seemed to give the couple an ease in their heavy mood. As they strolled alongside the fruit-laden trees, Sibella said impishly. "Should I pluck an apple from the tree?"

"Why not, my dear? But shall you take a bite?"

"I thought I already had," Sibella teased, and then gave Harry time to marshal his thoughts. "Did you tell them I was with child?"

"Yes; my poor father was apoplectic, reminding me of my liaisons with —"

24

"They want you to abandon me!"

"I would never do that, Sibella. You are the love of my life."

"The Moores say I must go to Waterford and have my baby there."

Harry dropped his voice.

"I have another idea."

"What is it, Harry?" Sibella's eyes opened wide.

Harry hesitated and then whispered,

"Let us elope, my dear heart!"

"Are you run mad, Harry?" Sibella exclaimed.

"Elopement is not so difficult. I have an annual allowance of one hundred pounds —"

"But where would we live?"

"Sir Robuck has asked me to go to Suffolk to arrange the sale of my late mother's estate."

Sibella looked long and hard into Harry's blue eyes. Then she gazed at a landscape adorned with the autumnal colours of yellow, brown and red. Somehow, the ripe harvest spoke to the seed growing within her, and she had her answer.

"I would surely love to elope with you, Harry Lynch-Blosse."

"Then pack your bags, my darling. I shall call for you this day week at six of the clock in the morning. It will still be dark. You must meet me at the corn mill beside the Ashbrook River. Wrap up well and pray that it does not rain."

Sibella felt a frisson of excitement as she mentally prepared for the biggest adventure of her life.

"I love you, Harry Lynch-Blosse," she said.

They kissed and hugged for a moment, and then he was gone. In bed that night, she tossed and turned.

"Am I heading for disaster or a brave new beginning?" she wondered.

CHAPTER 4

Sibella had secretly prepared her clothes for the great journey. She confined herself to one change including a dress, a bodice, a bonnet, a skirt, a handkerchief and a petticoat. These just fitted into a small bag hidden under her bed. She would survive without her hoops and panniers. As the days passed, she drafted a note of departure. She whispered its contents while pacing her bedroom floor:

Dear Mama and Papa,

I thank you from the bottom of my heart for looking after me from infancy to the present day. You are surely the kindest and most loving foster-parents I could ever have hoped for. I am so sorry for having brought shame on you by my irresponsible behaviour and betraying your trust in me. You kindly offered to settle me in Waterford during my confinement. I would have hated that. When Harry offered to take me to Suffolk, I found that plan infinitely preferable. We are now on our way. Please do not be angry with me. I love you both so much.

Your loving foster-daughter,

Sibella.

P.S. I promise to write once we are settled in Belstead Hall.

At five of the clock on the appointed morning, she arose, washed and dressed. She had kept some bread and milk in the bedroom from the previous day. After leaving the departure note on her freshly made bed, she donned her winter shawl and quietly crept down the stairs. She passed by the kitchen without disturbing the cook and opened the back door. The guard dog wandered over, waving his tail. She stroked his head to keep him quiet. He walked with her to the corn mill where she waited; after what seemed like an eternity, she heard the sound of footsteps. She calmed the dog while Harry approached.

He smiled, and then hugged her.

"Our great adventure is about to start, Miss Cottle. Are you sure, my darling?"

"I am sure, Harry. Let's go." She could now call him by his Christian name since they were effectively betrothed.

They walked to the top of the boreen where Harry had tethered a horse and trap. Soon they were on their way. The guard dog ran after them barking excitedly. The horse cantered as more dogs joined in the din. Sibella could see the house lights magically appearing at Ashbrook.

"We must hurry," she cried while Harry whipped the horse. Soon they were on the road heading south to Castlebar as the chase dissipated.

On arrival in the county town of Mayo, Harry tethered the horse at Lord Lucan's Mall.

"Bernard Moran will collect the trap later. I told him I was travelling alone. Thank God, there are no busybodies around. Now where is that coach?"

Sibella had that sinking feeling that it could all go wrong in spite of Harry's confident air.

"Am I about to embark on the same disastrous journey as Mistress Mahon?" she wondered.

She could not help voicing that concern.

"Are we doing the right thing, Harry? What did Lady Lynch say?"

"On my return to Balla from Ashbrook, I said I would depart for Suffolk next week. Lady Lynch and Uncle Peter were delighted because my father wants to settle my late mother's estate before he passes away."

Sibella reverently made the sign of the cross.

"I will pray for the poor man."

"Lady Lynch reminded me that my father was required by his marriage settlement to live sometimes at Belstead Hall. She wondered if I might find it somewhat lonely."

"She's the clever lady," Sibella said.

"I squirmed in my chair and took a deep breath."

Sibella quivered with excitement.

"I said: 'how could I be lonely in the house of my birth, the house in which I spent the first six years of my life? However, should loneliness strike or should Father deteriorate further, I would return at once'."

"You are a naughty boy, Harry Lynch-Blosse." Sibella smiled and hugged him.

Soon they were on the road to Ballinasloe where they would catch the Galway coach to Dublin. Alone at that early hour, Harry felt free to speak. "This journey reminds me of a letter written by my illustrious ancestor, Henry, the third Baronet." He proudly recited from a tattered document drawn from his jacket as they progressed through the rural landscape:

For the Lady Lynche … at Mace near Galway.
My dear Heart,
Here I safely arrived yesterday about twelve (o') *clock at noon, having spent the first night I parted you at Mr. Mayos at Ballinasloe, the second night at a place called Priests Bridge two miles the other side of*

the Tyrrellspass, the third at Maynooth within ten miles of this city. I performed my journey and arrival here in good health ...
    Your dear Husband, Henry Lynch.
    Dublin, June 30, 1677.

"And here we are, four generations later, on the turnpike road to Dublin with only one overnight stop in Milltownpass."

"What was so illustrious about Henry the third?"

"I shall tell you all about it when we reach Suffolk."

Sibella realized that she had much to learn about the Lynch-Blosse family if she was to become the Mistress of Balla House.

"Mercy, what a challenge!" she thought; *"And me only nineteen!"*

Once they reached Dublin, her anxieties dissipated as she enjoyed the sights and sounds of the capital city.

The hustle and bustle of the city entranced her. She noted especially the difference from it and the quiet of the countryside.

Once they entered their room in The Brazen Head, Harry began to tell her his plans for them.

"I will show you around Dublin when we return from Suffolk. Tomorrow we shall be on the high seas to Liverpool, and from there to London."

"Morning sickness is bad enough but seasickness ..."

"Let us pray for a calm crossing and a safe journey."

Sibella was aware of the hazards of robust travel for pregnant women. She said a silent prayer for the safety of her first child as they drifted off to sleep.

Seven days later, after a stormy sea crossing and bumpy coach-rides, they arrived exhausted at Belstead Hall. Both were now even more worried for the safety of their baby.

"Welcome to Belstead Hall, Mr Lynch-Blosse," the butler said.

"This is my betrothed, Miss Cottle from Ireland. We intend a stay of some length, probably into the summer."

"Very well, sir. Allow me to show you to your rooms. You may be aware that the late Tobias Blosse formerly occupied your room."

"So that's where the Blosse name comes from?" Sibella said while climbing the stone-cantilevered staircase in the central hall.

"My granduncle, Tobias Blosse, left his fortune to my mother, Elizabeth. Her marriage to Sir Robuck was recorded in *The Gentleman's Magazine*, valuing her at fifty thousand pounds."

"Goodness, fifty thousand pounds! What is my value, Harry Lynch-Blosse?"

"Inestimable, my dear heart," Harry said as the butler escorted him into his bedroom.

When they reached it, Sibella looked-in and was enchanted by the sight.

"Your room is beautiful, Harry. Look at the flowers on the ceiling."

"Lady Lynch said they are Tudor roses and fleurs-de-lys in the Ipswich manner."

"And the mantelpiece is a carved-stone Elizabethan work of art," the butler said. "I'll leave you to relax now. Dinner will be served sharp at eight."

After sleeping through the day, Sibella and Harry struggled out of bed in time for dinner. Sibella admired the lozenge and rosette panels on the walls of the dining room adorned with vine leaves.

She had the strange feeling that she was now a lady of the manor.

Not bad for the red-haired bitch of Ashbrook!" she thought; and then turned her mind to the meal. The mushroom soup, followed by roast beef with roast potatoes and carrots was both sumptuous and delicious.

"How does it feel to be the squire of Belstead Hall?" she asked.

"Very nice indeed, Miss Cottle."

"Perhaps we could settle here forever."

Sibella had to conceal her amusement when the remark made the footman almost drop his serving tray with its dessert of mixed fruit.

Sibella abstained from wine with her meal but succumbed to the temptation of a modest after-dinner port. Her lingering nausea reminded her to forego replenishment while relaxing in front of a crackling fire.

She and Harry both mellowed nicely as the evening wore on. Soon it was time for intimacy as the candles flickered in the bedroom. After the pleasures of the night, Sibella lay on a high pillow entranced by the elegant surroundings, wishing that this magic could last forever. As the last candle expired, she quietly returned to her room while Harry snored.

* * * * *

O N THE FOLLOWING MORNING after breakfast, Harry kissed Sibella on the cheek.

"My dear, I have some business to conduct in Ipswich."

"What manner of business, Harry?"

"Matters to do with the sale of the estate."

Sibella laughed. Harry was a transparent liar.

29

"What is the rogue up to?" she wondered.

Would he take action now that she was beginning to show? She prayed for good news but cautioned herself not to expect too much as yet.

He returned late that evening, clutching a document in his hand.

"What is it, Harry?"

"We are free at last!"

"What do you mean?"

Bending down on one knee, he rummaged in his pocket and produced a small velvet box. "Sibella Cottle, will you do me the great honour —?"

Opening the box, he produced a diamond-studded ring.

"Will you marry me, my dear heart?"

Sibella furrowed her brow.

Harry's jaw dropped.

"What's the matter?"

She smiled and jumped for joy.

"Of course I will marry you, my darling. This is the happiest moment of my life."

She kissed and hugged him while Harry called for champagne.

"What's in the document?"

"It is a letter saying I am free to marry, signed by the family solicitor in Ipswich," Harry said.

"When will we marry?"

"I have spoken to Rector Garrood who remembers the marriage of my one-time Catholic father to my Protestant mother all those years ago."

Sibella trembled.

"How will he react to my faith?"

"He said that mixed marriages are now allowed in England." Harry frowned. "He asked me if you had attained the age of one-and-twenty."

"How dare he?" Sibella said. "Why?"

"Because at nineteen, you require the written consent of your parents."

"My parents are dead," Sibella snapped.

"Or your foster-parents."

"How did you answer?"

"I said that a gentleman would never dare to ask a lady her age. However, I believe my betrothed has just reached her majority."

"You are so clever."

Sibella was aware that, while the age of majority was normally one-and-twenty, eighteen sufficed on certain occasions. She could swear to eighteen with a clear conscience.

"Harry, I love you with all my heart. When is the big day to be?"

"On Wednesday, the eighth of December. Garrood has agreed to a quiet wedding in Belstead Hall, witnessed by the butler and the chambermaid."

Sibella smiled, wondering if Harry was aware that the date was the feast of the Immaculate Conception. Was he sending a signal to Rector Garrood underpinning her purity? In any event, she could not wait for the great day to arrive. She commissioned a wedding gown from a dressmaker recommended by the butler.

The days flew by so quickly that soon the good Rector was on the doorstep. The butler escorted him into the drawing room where Sibella and Harry were waiting.

Glancing at Harry, he said,

"I attended here many years ago after the wedding of your father, Sir Robuck, to Miss Barker."

Sibella then saw him glancing at her. Was he worried about her religion or her age, she wondered? To dispel any lingering doubts, she looked him straight in the eye.

"Thank you so much for agreeing to marry us, Rector Garrood. I am a Catholic and have reached my majority."

Garrood raised his hands. "You certainly have retained a remarkable youthfulness. It must be the fresh air of Ireland."

"Thank you, Rector. Please excuse me as I need to don my wedding dress and settle my hair."

Sibella retired to her room to ready herself for her wedding. When all of the attentions were completed, she waited until the butler rang the bell and the chambermaid played a wedding march on the piano. She was thrilled when Harry gasped at her ensemble; a long-flowing green dress adorned with white pansies pinned with Lady Lynch's Tara brooch. Rather than bundle her hair high, she allowed it to hang over her shoulders in beautiful curls. She carried a decorative horseshoe on her wrist for good luck.

Harry wore a dark green jacket with a white shirt and cravat over tight off-white breeches and white stockings.

The butler had displayed vases of winter flowers, incense sticks and scented candles on the dining-room table. Rector Garrood stood in front of the temporary altar while Harry rose to greet her.

Just as Rector Garrood was about to commence the ceremony, Sibella heard the sound of galloping hooves through a partially opened window.

"Please excuse me, Rector," said the butler.

Sibella paled. She had a premonition of bad news.

Harry paced the room, impatiently until the butler returned.

31

"An urgent message for Mr Lynch-Blosse from Ireland," he said.

Now Harry paled. With trembling hand, he opened the letter and quickly scanned its content. He collapsed into his chair with the letter dangling from his left hand.

"Are you quite well, Mr Lynch-Blosse?" Garrood asked.

Harry passed the letter to the rector. "I am so sorry, Sibella."

"What does it say?" Sibella cried.

After quickly scanning its contents, Garrood recited:

For the urgent attention of Mr Lynch-Blosse.

Wednesday, 1 December 1773

Dear Mr Lynch-Blosse,

Further to a request from my colleague in Ipswich, and after consultation with your uncle, Mr Peter Lynch, I greatly regret to say that your application for an annulment of your marriage to Mistress Mahon remains unresolved at this time. However, Mr Lynch is confident that your application for an annulment will succeed in the very near future. In these circumstances, may I respectfully suggest that you postpone your wedding to Miss Cottle until we remove this encumbrance to your union?

Please accept my apologies for this intrusion into your personal affairs.

Yours faithfully,

Andrew Edmondson, Solicitor

Castlebar,

County Mayo, Ireland.

Sibella was distraught and dashed out of the wedding chamber while Harry apologized to Rector Garrood for the inconvenience. She ran straight to her bedroom and threw herself sobbing on to her bed where she remained for hours. When Harry knocked on her door later that day, she ordered him away and kept the door locked. How could Harry have done this to her? How could he have been so careless? Had he not realized that the letter was subject to approval from Castlebar? With these thoughts swirling in her mind she reluctantly removed her beautiful wedding gown. Eventually she retired to suffer a sleepless night.

* * * * *

WINTER SOON PASSED. EMERGING crocuses and daffodils heralded the arrival of spring. After reprimanding and arguing with Harry for weeks, Sibella eventually recovered from the disappointment of the wedding debacle. With reluctance, she accepted his promise that he would marry her the moment he was free to do so.

In the meantime, she helped him with the sale of the estate. While Harry went riding and hunting, Sibella hosted potential purchasers including Sir Robert Harland of nearby Sproughton.

"Allow me to show you the unique features of Belstead Hall, Sir Robert," Sibella said. "The huge chimney stack dates from about 1300. Its stone base is in the cellar and its brick shafts are Elizabethan —"

"Most impressive, Miss Cottle," Harland interjected.

"Thank you, Sir Robert. You may be interested in the moulded and fluted roof-rafters dating from 1500; and, finally, the diamond-scratched Blosse names on the library window dating from 1745. It surely is a historic house."

"Thank you, Miss Cottle. You have provided me with much to ponder. I expect to meet Mr Lynch-Blosse on the hunt soon. I shall discuss the matter with him then."

Apart from marketing Belstead Hall, Sibella walked the gardens with a pet spaniel called Ashbrook, read books in the library and started a diary. Both she and Harry enjoyed the challenge of independent living removed from their intrusive elders. Loneliness sometimes threatened, usually offset by Sibella's increasing girth and more vigorous kicking in her belly.

As summer arrived, she felt as big as a baby bear. While the morning sickness had abated, the discomfort of her condition irritated her nerves. Finally, she felt the onset of contractions. She told Harry,

"I think my little fellow is ready to move."

Harry, who had just returned from the hunt, smiled at the presumption.

"Are you sure it is a boy?"

"Yes, my dear, because it's lying low in the womb," Sibella said.

"I shall ask the butler to alert the midwife."

On St John's Eve, Sibella cried,

"Call the midwife."

Harry rushed to the butler who galloped off to collect his sister.

Sibella's contractions became more regular as she moved around the bedroom trying to control the pain. Suddenly her waters broke.

"Where is the midwife?" she screamed.

"She's on her way, my darling."

Harry wiped her sweating forehead with a damp towel. He held her hand as she grimaced with pain.

"My baby's coming. He's in an awful rush."

"I can hear footsteps —"

The midwife entered the chambers ready and able to take charge.

"All right, Mr Lynch-Blosse, you may leave now," she said.

The imperious tone of her voice brooked no argument.

With Harry out of the room, Sibella could focus on the birth as the pushing started. She could hear Harry pacing the creaking floorboards as she laboured. Eventually the baby arrived and an eerie silence descended. Harry could take it no longer and burst into the room. The boy started to cry as the mucus cleared from his windpipe.

The smiling midwife handed the towel-wrapped baby to its proud father.

"Congratulations, Miss Cottle, you are the mother of a beautiful baby boy."

"Thank you for your expert assistance, madam. We shall show our appreciation in due course," Harry said.

The midwife curtsied in response.

Harry handed the precious cargo to Sibella, thrilled with the safe delivery of their first baby.

"Congratulations, my darling."

She held the baby close and kissed him on the forehead.

"I think he takes after you, Harry. He has your lips."

"If this was Ireland, I would celebrate around a bonfire on this midsummer's night."

"Harry, remember you agreed to call him Michael, after the father I never knew," she reminded him.

"We shall call him Michael Henry," Harry agreed; "And surname him Lynch-Blosse once we're married."

CHAPTER 5

AFTER EXPERIENCING THE JOY AND tribulation of giving birth, Sibella focused on rearing Michael. What would her foster-parents think of her now? She would have written earlier were it not for the wedding debacle. She finally decided not to delay any longer.

> *Belstead Hall,*
> *Belstead,*
> *Ipswich, Suffolk*
> *1 August 1774*
> *Dear Mama and Papa,*
> *Please accept my apologies for not having written sooner. I am delighted to say that Harry has proposed and we shall marry as soon as his annulment comes through. Rector Garrood has agreed to unite us in a mixed marriage ceremony at Belstead Hall, now permissible under English law. I fervently hope and pray that you can be happy for us.*
> *In the meantime, I am the proud mother of a healthy boy, Michael Henry, born midsummer on 21 June. We hope to return to Ireland soon. I cannot wait for you to see your first grandchild.*
> *Harry sends you his best wishes and apologizes for our elopement. We simply did not know what else to do. We are very much in love and looking forward to coming home.*
> *Please accept our best wishes.*
> *Your loving foster-daughter,*
> *Sibella*

Two months later, a letter arrived at Belstead for the "Urgent Attention of Mr Henry Lynch-Blosse."

"What is it, Harry? Could it be from your solicitor at home?" Sibella opened her eyes wide. "Perhaps your annulment has come through."

"Mayhap, although it looks like the hand of Uncle Peter," he said. After finishing his bacon and eggs, he broke the seal and read:

> *Balla House,*
> *Balla, County Mayo*
> *1 October 1774*
> *My dear Harry,*

Your father continues to be seriously ill. It is now only a matter of weeks, according to Doctor Boyd. I thought you should know.

I remain, yours affectionately,
Uncle Peter

"You must go at once, Harry. Michael and I will be fine. It is still autumnal weather; I can wheel him for walks in the garden."

"I think we should all go. Our time in Suffolk is up," Harry said slowly, thinking it out. "I must write home before we leave."

"But where will Michael and I stay?"

"You shall stay with my cousin, Pat Lynch of Clogher, just south-west of Balla."

"I would love to go home," Sibella moved her little baby to her second breast. "Michael won't mind where he is, once he can guzzle on my milk."

They kissed and then made hurried arrangements to depart.

Ten days later, after an exhausting coach and sea journey, Harry knocked on the door of the Lynches of Clogher. Sibella watched while she and baby Michael waited in a carriage outside.

When Pat Lynch appeared, Sibella overheard Harry say, "Patrick, I should be most grateful if you could look after my betrothed, Sibella, and my baby, Michael, for a little while. Sir Robuck is close to death. I must send a message to Balla and then proceed there alone."

"I would be delighted to look after … Miss Cottle and your baby boy."

As Sibella and Michael moved indoors, Harry rode off to Balla at speed.

"Please follow me to the drawing room. I shall arrange for some coffee and scones," Pat Lynch said.

"Please call me Sibella."

"You must be exhausted and famished after your travels, not to speak of little Michael."

Pat was about the same age as Harry, single and remarkably similar to Harry in appearance.

"We have taken no harm from the journey, thank you, Pat."

"After you have partaken, the housekeeper will show you to the guest room and look after any needs you may have."

Sibella was beginning to warm to her host, a handsome young man in his mid-twenties. She understood why Harry trusted him so much. Nonetheless, she could not resist the temptation to say, "You must be growing weary of looking after Harry's lovers."

Pat Lynch laughed so much he nearly caused the footman to drop the serving tray.

"How is Mistress Mahon?" Sibella raised her eyebrows.

"I'm not sure, Sibella."

"Has she married?"

"Not to my knowledge."

"I imagine she is very beautiful," Sibella looked inquiringly at her host.

Pat stirred his coffee while he tossed her mischief back to her.

"Not as beautiful as the redhead from Ashbrook. Your elopement has been the talk of the county."

"You surely know how to flatter a young lady, Patrick Lynch."

"And you know how to attract the attention of we poor menfolk." Pat Lynch smiled.

Now it was Sibella's turn to laugh as she and Michael retired to the guest room and waited anxiously for Harry to return.

* * * * *

SIBELLA'S ANXIETY INCREASED AS one day passed and then another without word from Balla. On the third day, Harry arrived ashen-faced.

"What is it, my dear heart?" Sibella asked, embracing him.

"Let us go inside."

Pat Lynch escorted Harry and Sibella into the drawing room and then made to leave.

"Please stay, Pat." Harry wiped his brow. "Sir Robuck passed away last night."

"Oh, Harry!" Sibella threw her arms around him. "The poor man — thank God you were there to see him off to heaven."

"May he rest in peace," Pat Lynch said.

Harry relaxed with a cup of coffee.

"I nearly gave my father a seizure when I told him of having proposed to Miss Cottle at Belstead. Uncle Peter called for smelling salts as Lady Lynch trembled."

"Rector Garrood was all set to perform the ceremony." Sibella turned to Pat, careful to conceal her happiness out of respect for the departed. "He said that mixed marriages are now permissible in England as long as they are performed before an Anglican minister."

Harry continued.

"Father then asked me if my annulment had come through."

Sibella put down her china cup and asked,

"And has it, Harry?"

"I said that the matter is in the capable hands of Uncle Peter."

Harry paused to munch some freshly baked bread. He then continued:

"I told him I was the proud father of a baby boy, Michael Henry, and that the baby is called after the late father of Miss Cottle and after me. After he had congratulated me, I helped him to swallow a dose of laudanum which would allow him to rest for a while."

"What happened then?" Sibella asked.

"Lady Lynch summoned Uncle Peter and me to the library. After locking the doors, she asked if my marriage to Mistress Mahon had been annulled."

Sibella trembled.

"And what did your uncle Peter say about that?"

"He replied that the matter had not yet been resolved, my darling."

Tears welled in Sibella's eyes as she faced more clearly than before the illegitimacy of her darling son, Michael.

"I should leave you," Pat Lynch said diplomatically.

"Stay where you are. I am nearly finished." Harry looked into the middle distance, then said, "On the following day and with a heavy heart, I sat by Sir Robuck. I held his hand and prayed for his soul. I remained there until the vicar came and blessed him with the last rites."

After buttering some bread, Pat asked,

"When is the funeral to take place?"

"In three days, after service." Harry glanced at Sibella. "I want you to come with me and you also, Pat."

Sibella blushed. The pace of events was becoming unnerving. She would be the centre of attention at the service in a Protestant church, both events completely new experiences for her. What would Lady Lynch and Harry's uncle Peter say? How would they address her? Would her estranged foster-parents attend? Would the young buck who assaulted her at the Maidenhill Ball be present? This was all happening too fast.

Three days later, Sibella, Harry and Pat Lynch travelled by coach to the Church of Ireland in Balla whose tall spire overlooked the village. A large crowd awaited their arrival including the dignitaries, Lady Lynch, Lord Altamont, Lady Harriett and The Honourable James Cuffe, Member of Parliament. Sibella wondered if Mistress Mahon would attend. She was delighted to see her foster-parents among the crowd.

The people gasped when Harry held her hand on exiting the coach in which they had arrived. All eyes focused on her as Harry seated her in the Lynch-Blosse pew along the left wall close to the altar. The palpitations of her heart gradually diminished as people moved into the church and the Archbishop of Tuam, Jemmett Browne, commenced the service.

I am the resurrection and the life, saith the Lord:
he that believeth in me, though he were dead, yet shall he live:
and whosoever liveth and believeth in me shall never die.

The Protestant ambience and opulence entranced Sibella. Conscious of the scrutiny of the congregation, she avoided eye contact with anyone other than those she knew. She made an exception for the archbishop, who made her heart jump every time he glanced at her. What would he think of her as a Catholic with a question mark hanging over the validity of her betrothal to Harry?

During the service, Sibella wondered what Michael Cottle would think of his young daughter now. He would probably be worried and shameful that his darling daughter was the unmarried mother of an illegitimate child by a man who might never marry her. Sibella was still determined to show him that she could survive and that he had no need for concern for her welfare.

Archbishop Browne penetrated her entrancement when he recited from Psalm 23:

Yea, though I walk through the valley of the shadow of death, I will fear
no evil; for thou art with me; thy rod and thy staff comfort me.

Later on, Harry nudged her gently as the archbishop led the procession to the adjoining graveyard. They followed the coffin until they were standing beside the burial location. Sir Robuck was laid to rest alongside his beloved, Elizabeth Barker, in a solemn ceremony:

Forasmuch as it hath pleased Almighty God to take unto himself
the soul of our dear brother Sir Robuck Lynch-Blosse, here departed:
we therefore commit his body to the ground;
earth to earth, ashes to ashes, dust to dust;
in sure and certain hope of the resurrection to eternal life,
through our Lord Jesus Christ.

Before the diggers filled the grave, Lady Lynch threw a red rose on to the coffin. Harry followed the gesture by throwing a rose on to the coffin as well.

Harry had asked Sibella to do the honours, but she had wisely refrained.

✳ ✳ ✳ ✳ ✳

AFTER MOST PEOPLE HAD departed from the graveyard, the Moores approached the couple. Doctor Moore shook Harry's hand.

"Please accept our condolences, Harry."

Harry led the Moore's aside for a private moment as he shook the Doctor's hand.

"You know that Sibella has given birth to a baby boy, Michael Henry."

"Congratulations to both of you," Louisa said. Glancing at Sibella with tears in her eyes, she continued, "We should never have tried to send you away."

"Thank you, Mama. It is so good to see you again and to be home in Ireland."

The two women embraced until Harry interjected.

"Sibella and I would be honoured if you would attend the baptism of Michael Henry."

"Will Lady Lynch attend?" Doctor Moore asked.

Harry played his trump card then, because his grandmother had remained a Catholic.

"I am sure she will."

"Please, Robert ..." Louisa implored.

"If Lady Lynch attends, I shall attend," Doctor Moore replied sternly.

"Thank you, Robert." Louisa sighed with relief and then raised her eyebrows. "Sibella, I would love to see the baby."

Sibella smiled.

"Michael is with Pat Lynch of Clogher. I shall tell Pat to expect you."

At that moment, Lady Lynch limped towards them aided by her blackthorn shillelagh.

"Sibella, my dear, it is good to see you reunited with your foster-parents. I am looking forward to my great-grandchild's baptism, if they will allow a poor Catholic to attend."

It was now time for Doctor Moore to smile.

"If they admit you, Lady Lynch, they might stretch a point and admit Mistress Moore and me as well."

"Capital! Now when am I going to see my great grandson, Michael Henry?"

"Whenever it might suit you, Lady Lynch," Sibella said. "Harry will make the arrangements."

While Sibella chatted with the Moores, she saw Harry approach The Honourable James Cuffe, MP. An animated conversation ensued in which Harry gesticulated and Cuffe winced.

Harry returned as Lady Lynch and the Moores took their departure.

With a touch of sarcasm in her tone, she asked,

"Why did The Honourable James Cuffe wince?"

"I was explaining that you and I were betrothed and would soon be married."

"Did he ask you about your annulment?"

Harry's complexion darkened.

"I told him that the annulment was being dealt with by Uncle Peter as a matter of urgency."

Sibella's face dropped.

"Do not worry, my darling," Harry sighed. "Cuffe will have a word with Archbishop Browne. He will explain that you were not required to conform under legislation in England. He expects that the Church of Ireland will approve our marriage once it takes place. The baptism of baby Michael Henry as a Protestant will help the process along. The archbishop will explain the position to the vicar."

One week later, the vicar was still unhappy, but followed the direction of his archbishop. He instructed the parents and godparents to encourage Michael in the life and faith of the Christian Community. He made a sign of the cross on Michael's forehead and presented a lighted candle to the parents with the words:

You have received the light of Christ;
walk in this light all the days of your life.
Shine as a light in the world to the glory of God the Father.

Following consultation with Uncle Peter, the entry on the baptismal register was sufficiently ambiguous to be open to interpretation:

Michael Henry, son of Sir Henry Lynch-Blosse
of Balla and Sibella. Born 21 June 1774.
Baptized 7 November 1774.
Sponsors: Peter and Patrick Lynch.

Sibella was delighted with the attendance of her foster-parents along with Lady Lynch and James Cuffe, although the Member of Parliament had refused to act as a sponsor.

Following the baptism, Sibella prepared to leave Clogher to take up residence in Balla with baby Michael. She looked forward to another massive challenge in her life with a mixture of elation and trepidation.

CHAPTER 6

SIBELLA HAD TO PINCH herself as she settled into Balla House as the betrothed of Sir Harry.

"Am I really the Mistress of Balla House?" she wondered. *"If only I were married, I would be one of the most powerful women in Mayo."*

Her thoughts then turned to all of the things involved with such power. How should she discharge her duties? How should she use her new authority?

Harry's comments, as he stood in front of the mirror adjusting his wig, only added to her concerns.

"An estate of twenty thousand acres now lies under my control," he said.

Sibella hesitated with her answer, and then decided that, for a moment, it was time to celebrate Harry's elevation to a hereditary title.

"Congratulations, my darling, on becoming the seventh Baronet of Balla. Nothing can stop us now."

The words were barely spoken when the youthful housekeeper, Kate Moran, reputedly Harry's half-sister, entered the dining room.

"An important visitor is waiting for you in the drawing room, Sir Harry."

"Who is it, Kate?"

"The Honourable James Cuffe of Ballinrobe."

"What brings him here?" Sibella wondered. *"Is he a friend or foe?"*

Harry answered her questions as though he was reading her mind.

"My late father asked him to guide me in estate matters as my trustee," he said.

"Then you had better not keep him waiting, my dear."

Shortly after Harry departed, Sibella made her way to the dining room where she cocked an ear to the conversation in the adjoining room through the connecting doors.

She heard the booming voice of the parliamentarian.

"Harry, my boy, the time is ripe. I want you to run in the forthcoming election in the Tuam constituency."

Sibella held her breath waiting for Harry to respond.

"Christ! James, you cannot be serious. I know nothing about politics and am far too young at twenty-six. I would be a hopeless candidate."

"Nonsense, Harry, it's in your blood. Your great-great-grandfather, Sir Henry Lynch, was a Member of Parliament. Not only that, James II appointed him as Baron of the Exchequer."

Sibella wondered if the Baron of the Exchequer was the same Henry the third that Harry had mentioned during their elopement. She had forgotten to ask Harry about him on their arrival in Suffolk.

"You have done your research, James, but I am not qualified to serve in the Irish Parliament. I am not a lawyer like my political predecessors. I have more important issues to deal with. I need to focus on estate management, having learned a lot from the Moores of Ashbrook."

"Harry, my boy, you have lots to ponder on. We shall talk again."

Sibella wondered what other important issues remained for Harry to deal with. Was he referring to the annulment of his failed marriage to Emily Mahon?

After Cuffe departed, Sibella asked,

"Harry, my dear, am I really the Mistress of Balla House?"

Now aged twenty, she looked at him with feigned innocence underpinned by a determination to make progress in the world.

Harry raised his eyebrows.

"Of course you are, my darling. However, the situation is complicated."

"No doubt you shall deal with it."

"You remember that my mother, Elizabeth of Suffolk, passed away when I was only six."

Sibella could not resist the opportunity to tease the seventh Baronet.

"Poor Harry; but my mother died when I was an infant."

Harry went on in spite of the gentle tease.

"The important thing is, Father did not remarry. The position of the Mistress of Balla House remained vacant. Lady Lynch agreed to act as Mistress in a temporary capacity. She has now advised a continuance of her position until you find your feet."

Sibella looked intently into Harry's blue eyes as he shifted in his chair.

"How do you feel about that, Sir Harry?" she asked.

"I told grandmother that I wanted you as Mistress of Balla now rather than later. She was reluctant to burden one so young with such onerous duties. Eventually she agreed once you have demonstrated your capacity for the work."

Sibella heaved a sigh of relief. Lady Lynch was a kind old lady with whom she could work. Their common religion and relationship to the Moores of Ashbrook would help to bond them.

Harry's eyes suddenly lit up.

"Close your eyes, my dear."

Sibella watched him turning the key of the family safe. She closed her eyes and heard the tinkle of metal; her wonder grew.

"Voila!" Harry cried as he whipped a silk cloth from an array of silver items on her dressing table.

Sibella opened her eyes and gasped.

"They are so beautiful, Harry!"

"The silver casket was a wedding present from Sir Robuck to my mother. After I was born, he gave her a silver locket. They are now your engagement presents."

Sibella hugged Harry. She opened the locket to find a portrait of Harry's mother.

"So this is the source of your handsome looks," she said, and rejoiced at being on the brink of fulfilling her stellar ambition.

Not long after, she assumed her duties as Mistress of Balla House with the help and advice of Lady Lynch. These included supervision of house staff, dealing with visitors to the house, responding to correspondence and so on. With that delicate transfer of power completed, Sibella hoped to settle down to a normal family life.

* * * * *

IN THE SPRING OF the following year, Sibella complained of morning sickness again.

"When did this happen?" Harry asked.

"After I weaned Michael; I believe I am about six weeks gone. The morning sickness and nausea is worse this time."

Harry kissed her and held her gently.

"Could it be twins?" he asked; and then reassured her. "You must not worry, my darling. We shall look after you."

At twenty weeks, Sibella tried to relax in the drawing room.

"My belly is lopsided already," she groaned. "I can feel some jostling in the womb. The midwife said it could be twins."

Another ten weeks drifted by. Sibella had conceived in early spring and it was now late summer. Visits to the privy became more frequent. Her mood was volatile except when the nanny brought baby Michael to visit her. He was a healthy boy with blond hair. Sibella loved to play with him as he learned to walk and talk.

As time passed, she found it more difficult to find a comfortable position to sit or lie.

"Harry, my belly button has popped. I feel so big and awkward."

"It must be triplets!" he said jocularly.

She threw her embroidery kit at him, hitting him in the head.

"Twins are bad enough but triplets …!"

Both laughed at the idea; then Sibella said,

"Twins or triplets, I will survive, please God."

Sibella then dozed off while the little ones within her fluttered again.

Towards the end of autumn, Sibella was ready to give birth. She encouraged Harry and then Michael to touch her belly and feel the movement.

"Harry, if they are twins, I would like to call them Cecilia and Mary Anne."

"And if they are boys, or mixed gender?" Harry asked.

"Let us wait and see."

At that moment, a loud knock on the door disturbed their conversation. Kate Moran announced: "Mrs. Holian, midwife, to see Miss Cottle."

Judy Holian, a middle-aged woman with thin features and a sharp nose, entered.

"God bless all here," she said, and removed her shawl to get to work.

Harry departed while the nanny fetched Michael.

"How are you, m'lady?"

Sibella sighed.

"I am not my lady yet, Mrs Holian."

"You will be in no time at all," Judy said.

"I hope so. I cannot wait for the girls to come."

"Let me take a look, alannah." Judy rolled down the blankets.

Sibella felt her slightly calloused hand on her belly.

"Plenty of activity there; they should arrive any day now. Everythin' seems to be in order. I will visit daily to keep an eye on you."

Three days later, in the early morning, Sibella's waters broke.

"Harry, please call Judy Holian."

Harry jumped out of bed and rang the bell. The footman on duty soon arrived.

"Please ask Bernard Moran to collect Mrs Holian at once."

Meanwhile, Sibella's labour had commenced. Her contractions now occurred at regular intervals. The pain was intense, relieved a little by moving around. She was now on her hands and knees.

"Where is the midwife?" she cried. The female servants gathered round, anxious to help.

"The baby is coming!" Sibella screamed.

Kate Moran lifted her nightdress.

"Heavens! The baby's head is visible."

At that moment, Judy Holian rushed in.

"Stand back, everyone, please. It's alright, m'lady. Take a deep breath and push."

"Oh, Judy, this is the most difficult birth ever."

Judy soothed her forehead, now lathered in sweat, with a damp cloth. "Now push again."

"It is of no use, she will not come," Sibella cried.

"Just once more, Sibella. I know she will come on the seventh push."

The seventh push came with Sibella straining every muscle in her body.

"Good girl, she is coming."

Sibella could feel the movement and a sudden feeling of elation.

"I am now holding a baby girl in my arms," Judy said.

"How did you know it would be a girl?" Kate Moran wondered.

Nobody answered as the excitement was intense.

"You must cut the cord, Judy."

"I am waiting for the cord to stop pulsing," Judy Holian said amidst a hushed silence. "The baby is still receiving blood from its mother. The girl's lungs are filling, helping her to breathe,"

Everyone's eyes moved from the baby to Sibella and to the ticking clock. At seven minutes past seven, Judy cut the cord with a knife heated over a bedside candle. Sibella watched as she raised the baby and gave it a gentle thump on its bottom to clear the airways. The baby cried to tumultuous applause.

Sibella was overwhelmed with relief as Harry entered. She saw Judy cleaning the baby, wrapping the gorgeous creature in a white shawl and holding it close to her.

"Congratulations, m'lady and Sir Harry. You are the proud parents of a fine healthy girl."

"We are going to call her Cecilia," Harry said, smiling.

"A lovely name, entirely," Judy said. "Sir Harry, if you will excuse us, we have more work to do. Sibella, you will need to go back on your knees in an upright position so I can watch what is happening. They say it takes seventeen minutes from the first twin to the second."

Sibella looked around as the initial excitement subsided and a silent hush descended. "Something is happening, Judy."

"The second baby is easier because ..." Judy frowned.

"What is it, Judy?" Kate asked while gently rocking baby Cecilia.

"The baby is bottom first."

"Grace be with us!" Sibella cried. "Is that a problem?"

"Hush, alannah! It's more difficult. They call it a breech birth. The bottom comes out first." Judy observed the progress of the birth for a time, and then exclaimed,

"It's comin' now."

Sibella could feel the second baby emerging while Kate and the servants gathered round.

"Her legs are flexed at the hip and extended at the knees. As she comes out, her feet will be near her ears. Then the back of her head appears and finally the face. Let us pray that nothin' goes wrong," Judy said while the servants made the sign of the cross. "Everything should be all right as long as the umbilical cord is not squeezed."

"Why, Judy?" Kate Moran whispered.

"The cord supplies the blood to the baby."

Sibella heard the response. She knew that a disruption of the blood supply could damage the child. It was a time for prayers. Safety rather than gender was uppermost in the minds of those observing the drama.

Finally, Sibella felt a baby arriving.

"Kate, I want you to use a shepherd's purse herb to control the bleeding," Judy said. "I will wait a while before cuttin' the cord."

Those were the longest moments in the life of Sibella. When the baby did arrive, she could see it was a deeper blue than Cecilia had been.

"Please God, help me!" Sibella shouted.

After what seemed like an eternity, the baby cried. Another round of applause hit the rafters. Sibella drank a cup of stinging nettle tea to stimulate the flow of breast milk.

Responding to the applause, Harry entered.

"Congratulations, my darling."

Although exhausted and sore, Sibella could now hold her two babies. She cried with joy.

Harry rang for the footman.

"Everyone is invited to a full breakfast. I want to thank you for your help and cooperation: a special word of thanks to our midwife, Mrs Holian and to Miss Moran who assisted her. They brought us safely through the night and into the early morning. May God bless and protect Cecilia and Mary Anne."

As the servants departed for the basement kitchen, Sibella said, "Thank you so much, Judy. I shall repay you for your skill and kindness."

With tears in her eyes, she embraced Judy without disturbing the two beautiful babies. She marvelled at the extent of drama there was in her life.

*   *   *   *   *

WHILE SIBELLA NURSED HER two baby girls, she raised the issue of religion with Harry.

"My dear, you are aware that girls usually follow the religion of their mother."

"As you wish, my dear heart." Harry sat at the side of the bed with baby Michael perched on his lap.

Anxious to re-establish good relations with the Moores of Ashbrook, Sibella said,

"Lady Lynch would be thrilled, as would my foster-parents. Once Cecilia and Mary Anne have settled into a routine, I shall set a date for the baptism."

On the great day, Harry and Sibella travelled by coach to the chapel at Balla. Lady Lynch, Uncle Peter, Pat Lynch and the Moores journeyed separately behind them.

Father Nolan was waiting at the entrance door.

"I wish to welcome Cecilia and Mary Anne, and their parents, Sibella and Sir Harry to my church."

Glancing at the parents and godparents, he asked,

"Are you willing to bring up the child as a Christian?" On receipt of a positive response, he continued, "I claim you for Christ our Saviour by the sign of his cross."

The parish priest traced the sign of the cross on the forehead of the girls, a practice repeated by the parents and godparents.

The party then entered the church and stood around the baptismal font. Holding his hands up, Father Nolan issued the exorcism.

"O God, you sent your Son to cast out the power of Satan, set these children free from original sin."

He then anointed Cecilia and Mary Anne on the chest with the oil of catechumens to ward off evil and bring wisdom and strength.

He asked the parents and godparents: "Do you reject Satan? Do you believe in God? Do you believe in Jesus Christ, the son of God? Do you believe in the Holy Ghost?"

Father Nolan looked long and hard at Harry while Sibella nudged him until he blushingly obliged by saying,

"I do."

Sibella moved forward to the font with baby Cecilia wrapped in a white gown. Father Nolan poured water over her head three times. She howled.

"Cecilia, I baptize you in the name of the Father and of the Son and of the Holy Ghost."

Sibella handed Cecilia to Lady Lynch. She then rescued Mary Anne from Harry. Mary Anne also howled when watered.

Father Nolan said,

"I will now anoint the girls with chrism, a holy oil of olive and balsam. This oil will give strength and suppleness to the limbs. The balsam will preserve you from corruption. I have in my hand a baptismal candle for each child."

Sibella accepted the candles while Father Nolan blessed all present. Lady Lynch and Louisa Moore accompanied Father Nolan to the sacristy to enter baptismal entries under the headings of *Child, Father, Mother* and *Sponsors*.

When Lady Lynch returned she pulled Sibella aside. Resting on her shillelagh, she whispered, "I made sure that the word, *Bastard*, would not be entered beside the names of the girls. Father Nolan wrote the following with his quill: *Cecilia*; *Sir Harry Lynch-Blosse*; *Sibella Cottle*; *Lady Lynch, Doctor Moore, £5*. A similar entry applied to Mary Anne except that the sponsors were Louisa Moore and Peter Lynch."

"Thank you so much," Sibella said.

Lady Lynch steadied herself as Father Nolan approached.

"That was a lovely ceremony, Father. You must join us for a reception at Balla House."

"Thank you, Lady Lynch, but unfortunately I have a wedding later in the morning."

Sibella knew that Father Nolan was honoured by the presence of Lady Lynch, but less happy at being pressured to baptize the children of a Protestant father. The generous contributions may have helped to assuage his reluctance.

CHAPTER 7

SIBELLA RECOVERED QUICKLY AFTER the dramatic birth of Cecilia and Mary Anne. Her hands were now full with three children apart from her other duties as Mistress of Balla House. Harry was busy with estate administration now progressing with guidance from his trustee, the astute James Cuffe.

Harry surprised her one morning when he stood at the mirror adjusting his wig.

"What are you doing?" Sibella laughed.

"How would I look in the Irish House of Commons?" he queried.

"A deal better than that schemer Cuffe, with his blotchy red nose."

Sibella pinched herself again. An election as a Member of Parliament would raise Harry's status in the community. It might even help to expedite his application for an annulment.

"He wants me to run in Tuam. I would have the support of Lord Altamont."

"But would you have the support of the Galway voters?" Sibella cautioned, aware of the age-old rivalry between the two western counties.

"Cuffe says that Robert Dillon of Clonbrock, a co-trustee of my estate, would support me."

"Harry, you should run," Sibella said excitedly. "It is surely a great opportunity. I will support you in any way I can."

Armed with her blessing, Harry advised Cuffe and the race was on.

The Honourable Member of Parliament from Ballinrobe delivered on all fronts. The freeholders of Tuam elected Harry to the Irish House of Commons on 18 June 1776. Bonfires greeted the new MP on his return from the election. Sibella was thrilled. The world was at their feet: nothing could stop them now.

After the glow of victory subsided, Harry said,

"Sibella, I have just found out that Tuam may be a rotten borough." He shifted uneasily while tapping the breakfast table.

Sibella told a white lie, fearing that Harry would withdraw from politics as he became aware of its murky nature.

"I have never heard of such a thing."

"A rotten borough is deemed to be in the pocket of its patron."

"I hope you do not pick up the disease, my dear," Sibella said.

Harry paced the breakfast room.

"I am disgusted that Cuffe paid money for my seat."

Sibella was amused at Harry's innocence of the ways of the world.

"I always thought that Cuffe had a sly look about him."

"If Cuffe thinks he has me in his pocket, he will find he is much mistaken."

Despite the flawed nature of the process, Harry's election consolidated Sibella's position in Balla. However, she continued to worry about her unmarried status and Harry's drinking. Against that background, she sent a message to Louisa Moore inviting her to visit. On receipt of a favourable response, Sibella asked Bernard Moran to pick Louisa up in the Balla carriage.

When Louisa arrived, Sibella noticed her greying hair.

"Look at you, Sibella Cottle, in your fine silks and satins," Louisa greeted her. "I am so proud of you. The lady of the manor with three lovely children and …?"

Sibella saw her glancing at her girth. Sibella answered the implied question immediately.

"Number four is on the way. I pray it is not twins again."

Louisa smiled.

"I always remember the day that Harry visited Ashbrook. Your excitement was infectious. I saw the way that Harry looked at you. I felt powerless to prevent you from making the biggest mistake of your life. Was I not sadly mistaken? You followed your heart and here you are — one of the most powerful women in Mayo, to use your own words."

Sibella blushed.

"Was I not lucky to have two such wonderful foster-parents? You gave me the confidence to aspire to the stars."

Tears came to Louisa's eyes.

"I still feel guilty about sending you away when you needed me most."

"In a strange way, it cemented my relationship with Harry," Sibella said. "Elopement with him was the most exciting adventure in my life. It established a bond between us that will last forever, please God."

"Why should it not last?"

Sibella's brow furrowed.

"I am worried, Mama," she admitted. "Harry is ill at ease but he will not tell me what troubles him. He has begun to drink heavily."

"Whatever could it be, my dear? He is master of a large estate, married to a beautiful woman with three healthy children, and blessed with membership of the Irish Parliament."

Sibella whispered, "Let us walk in the garden."

Surrounded by Easter lilies and the drone of busy bees, Sibella opened her heart.

"You say "married", Mama, but we are not and I fear we might never be. I do not know if Harry's annulment will ever come through."

"Doctor Moore was worried about that, too. What will you do?"

"I don't know …"

Sibella began to cry. Louisa tried to console her.

"Your secret doubts are safe with me. I will pray for you, and for Harry and the children," Louisa said. "Now wipe your tears and battle on, my fine girl. You can handle this. I know you can."

Sibella welcomed the bracing words of her foster-mother and prepared to fight for herself and her children if necessary.

Later that year, Sibella safely delivered a baby boy, John, under the watchful eye of Judy Holian.

"We now have two boys and two girls," Harry said. "Whom should we invite to the baptism?"

"Whoever you would like to invite, my dear heart."

"We could invite Altamont, Cuffe, Lady Lynch, Uncle Peter, Pat Lynch of Clogher and …" Harry looked into the middle distance.

Sibella smiled at the antics of her roguish husband.

"And who else, Harry?"

"I imagine the Moores of Ashbrook would feel uncomfortable in a Protestant church," Harry said. "I know that Altamont likes to travel with Lady Harriett …"

"Well then, invite her, you big monkey." Sibella laughed while Harry scowled.

Some days later, Harry returned from the vicarage, his face reddened with anger.

"The vicar has objected to the baptism of John on hearing a rumour that the annulment of my marriage to Mistress Mahon is not forthcoming. I must ride to Westport and seek the advice of Altamont."

Sibella wondered if Altamont would use the opportunity to entice Harry away from her.

On his return from Westport, Harry said,

"Altamont had also heard the annulment rumour — if Cuffe was not the source of the rumour in the first instance."

"The sly old foxes," Sibella said.

"I told Altamont that I was the happy father to a second son but that the vicar was worried about my marital status."

"What did he say?"

Harry frowned.

"He asked if I wanted to continue my relationship with you."

Sibella had that sinking feeling in her belly as her anger grew.

"The old reprobate! What did you say, Harry?"

"He said the Catholic Church would be reluctant to give me an annulment, to which I replied that my annulment is imminent."

"Is it indeed imminent, Harry?"

Harry squirmed in his chair.

"Uncle Peter has assured me that the matter is in hand."

"You have said that before. This time, I am really worried. You must sort this out at once." Sibella stormed out. Harry rang for a double whiskey.

Sibella later found out that Altamont had spoken to Archbishop Browne, who authorized the reluctant vicar to proceed with the baptism.

The wily old fox, Altamont approached them after the baptism of baby John in the Church of Ireland.

"Sir Harry and Miss Cottle, please accept my congratulations on your most recent infant."

"Thank you, Lord Altamont," Sibella said, fixing her eyes on the one of the most powerful men in Mayo.

Altamont continued.

"Miss Cottle, I believe that Harry needs to get about more in his capacity as a parliamentarian. People will expect him to attend various political and social functions in Mayo and further afield."

"I agree, Lord Altamont," Sibella astutely replied.

Altamont's niece, the refined Lady Harriett, drifted by in the churchyard.

"Harriett, my dear, have you met Sir Harry and Miss Cottle?"

"Congratulations on your beautiful son, Sir Harry," Harriett said.

"Thank you, Lady Harriett. I hope you enjoyed the baptism."

"Very much," Lady Harriett said. "Please excuse me, Sir Harry, I must make haste."

Sibella ignored what appeared to be a deliberate snub to her in Harriett's closing remark.

Following Harriett's departure, Altamont said,

"It is only a matter of time before she marries."

Sibella smiled.

"She is an attractive woman, surely. I am surprised she is not already married."

When Altamont grimaced, Sibella diverted to the political arena.

"Harry is interested in the formation of the Volunteers in Ireland. Can you tell him more about it?"

Altamont pursed his lips.

"It all started with the recent Declaration of American Independence. Just before you took your seat, Harry, the landed gentry formed the Volunteers to protect Ireland from invasion and to protect our property."

"What would I have to do?" Harry asked.

"Each landlord needs to establish a militia from the best and most able men in his locality. These Volunteer units will be coordinated at county and national level."

Sibella began to think how Harry could organize such a unit in Balla. She would discuss it with him later.

* * * * *

IN THE MEANTIME, SIBELLA kept her eye on Margaret McDermott, a chambermaid in the Big House. She was furious on hearing that Harry had flirted with her when Sibella was pregnant with baby John. In due course, Margaret began to show and Sibella called her aside. After much to-ing and fro-ing, Margaret conceded pregnancy but refused to name the father. Sibella insisted she leave her service until the baby was born.

News of the incident spread quickly. The Mistress of Balla had laid down a marker. She would not tolerate inappropriate behaviour among her staff notwithstanding any snide remark concerning her own situation.

Sibella now knew she would have to deal with Harry even though she had no evidence of his paternity. She came straight to the point.

"Harry, have you heard about Margaret McDermott?"

"That rascal Bernard Moran was rumour-mongering as usual when driving me to the mail coach to attend Parliament."

"Bernard loves his gossip."

"He mentioned a story about Margaret McDermott."

Sibella raised her eyebrows and stared into Harry's blue eyes.

"Bernard said she was pregnant and you had words with her."

"What else did Bernard say?" Sibella asked.

Harry lowered his voice.

"He said you had dismissed her."

"The scoundrel; that is not quite accurate. I asked her who the father was; she refused to say."

"I suppose she felt the matter was private."

"That may be, but my authority as Mistress of Balla House would be undermined unless I dealt with the situation."

"Absolutely right," Harry said.

Sibella altered the tone of her voice.

"The staff will be curious about the identity of the father."

"What rumours have you heard?"

"There is a list of suspects as long as your arm, including Lord Altamont himself, the poor man."

"Christ!" Harry grimaced.

"It also includes Cousin Patrick, Uncle Peter and …" Sibella stared at Harry who avoided her gaze.

"Not me, Sibella?"

"Well, what do you expect? They have little else to talk about."

Harry flushed.

"Rumours are rumours; there is little to be done about them."

"Except to take action. Incidentally, I did not dismiss her but sent her home to have her baby there."

"You did right, Sibella." Harry hesitated, and then suggested, "How about a little brandy, my dear?"

Sibella held her silence as she sipped her potation before a roaring fire. She did little to conceal her seething resentment. She suspected that Harry was the father, suggesting that he felt he could philander at will. She had made it clear that she would not tolerate such behaviour. It was a high-risk action, taken against the background of her uncertain marital status. On the other hand, she sensed that Harry was grateful for her generous diplomacy and would respond positively. Effectively, she had told him to grow up and face his responsibilities.

∗ ∗ ∗ ∗ ∗

ONE SUCH RESPONSIBILITY SOON emerged.

"Sibella, I am under pressure to ease the rental burden on my tenants."

"That is not surprising. Most of them live in atrocious conditions, sharing their pitiful hovels with pigs, fowl and domestic animals. You should investigate."

"I have just done that," Harry sighed. "I have seen manure heaps at the door of a home possibly rotten with consumption. I saw tenants in bare feet, wearing rags."

"You should reduce the rents."

"The problem, my dear, is that remission of rental is opposed by my bankers and creditors."

Sibella guessed what Altamont would say if Harry complained of financial pressure. He would urge him to marry and marry well.

"You may recall that Altamont advised me to attend social functions in Mayo. I might learn from the experience of others. Will you join me?"

"Harry, my dear, nothing would bore me more than the tittle-tattle of the latest fashion trends. Your female friends would turn their noses up in my presence. I am far too busy with my duties as Mistress. Our three children, and now baby John, need my attention although the nursery-maids and governesses are wonderful. Please extend my apologies as appropriate."

As time passed, Sibella heard that Harry had been seen conversing amicably with Lady Harriett on a number of occasions. People wondered if Harry was on the prowl for a wife. Reacting to this, she suggested that Harry invite Lady Harriett to dinner.

"Capital, my dear heart! I could also invite the handsome bachelor of Clogher, Pat Lynch."

Sibella was unaccustomed to hosting guests at Balla House, a standard two-storey residence with a basement. Although perched on an elevation, its position was secluded. The surrounding landscape was pleasant but not spectacular, apart from barely visible mountains to the west and south.

The challenge energized her. She wondered if Lady Harriett would be intrigued to receive the invitation. What would Altamont think? Would he discourage his cousin from mixing with a Catholic of uncertain origin? On the other hand, Harriett might see it as an opportunity to ease Harry away from her.

On the appointed day, Sibella welcomed the early arrival of Lady Harriett and Pat Lynch. After light refreshments and a little banter, the foursome set off to explore on horseback. On a bright summer's day, the estate looked in fine condition featuring a patchwork quilt of small fields and woods of various hues and colours. The wild rhododendrons were in bloom providing a riot of lavender and purple against the background of the Partry and Galway mountains. The demesne around Balla House swarmed with pheasants, hares and rabbits startled by the pounding hooves.

Sibella noted Harriett's riding skill and the sophisticated comportment which behoved a woman of her class. She saw her glancing at Harry from time to time during an exhilarating ride through the estate. They broke for lunch at a hunting lodge noted for romantic interludes.

After returning to Balla, Sibella relaxed until the dinner gong sounded at eight of the clock sharp. The footman threw the doors open so that the guests could be seated. Sibella had ensured that the menu and the table settings were of the highest standard.

"I am famished after that splendid ride through your lovely estate," Lady Harriett said. "The hunting lodge is very attractive."

Harry responded.

"You can thank Sibella for the invitation and Patrick for the hunting lodge."

Harriet glanced at Sibella.

"Is that where you met Sir Harry?"

Sibella opened her napkin as the footman served the soup.

"I met Harry at Ashbrook where he learned the art of estate management. Even better, he met me!"

Harriett sniffed, her nose in the air.

"I do hope someone will take me to the hunting lodge sometime," she said. "It sounds frightfully romantic."

"I might take you myself," Pat Lynch said.

Sibella was amused when Harriett smiled weakly at the handsome bachelor from Clogher and then looked long and hard at Harry.

He quickly avoided her gaze and offered a toast to lighten the atmosphere.

"To romance in the hunting lodge!" he cried, to which they all drank.

A momentary silence followed while the main course arrived: venison, potatoes and vegetables, with many side dishes of various delicacies, washed down with a white Burgundy.

"How are the children?" Harriett asked.

"They are in excellent health. Michael Henry is three and the twins, Cecilia and Mary Anne, are just over one year old. Baby John is our youngest."

"What lovely names! Who chose them?"

"We both did. Michael Henry is named after my late father and my Harry."

Sibella was pleased when Harry nearly swallowed a cut of venison after hearing the possessive pronoun. "We named Mary Anne after my mother and Cecilia after ... tell her, Harry."

"The first twin, Cecilia, is named after Patrick's mother," Harry said.

"And baby John?" Harriett retorted.

Harry said, "John is named after Patrick's grandfather, a brother of my grandfather Henry, the fifth, if you will excuse the complicated family history."

Sibella decided that Harriett was deliberately calling attention to her uncertain background. She deflected attention by asking Kate Moran to serve dessert, which comprised an assortment of fresh, cooked and dried fruits as well as creams and jellies.

After dinner, brandy and port was served; the conversation was pleasant and the mood mellow. Harriett stayed at Balla House overnight. In the morning, she departed to her home at Castlemagarrett.

Sibella now had a clear picture of her potential rival. She was thrilled that her confident handling of a delicate situation had impressed Harry. At the same time, Harriett was attractive and, as Altamont was keen to emphasize should Harry be tempted, a substantial dowry would accrue to ease his financial worries.

CHAPTER 8

SIBELLA HAD LITTLE TIME for relaxation. The pace of events was frenetic. No sooner had she delivered one baby than another was on the way. Fortunately, her four children were thriving. As Mistress of Balla House, she was determined to provide them with the best education and training to sustain them for life.

A further advantage accrued following Harry's election to the Irish Parliament. Now she could develop her interest in promoting the welfare of the less fortunate, by encouraging Harry towards a more liberal approach to governance.

Yet there was a dark side to her life as well. His affair with Margaret McDermott had shaken her. The snide glances of servants had forced her to send a pregnant girl home. The barely-concealed flirting of Lady Harriett with her beloved worried her in the light of Harry's evasiveness with regard to his annulment. His dark moods and heavy drinking were now more prevalent.

Refusing to buckle under these pressures, she set aside her negativity and joined with Harry in his excitement about the Volunteers.

In early spring, she inquired,

"Harry, what will the Volunteers do?"

Harry coughed while pacing the library.

"The Volunteers are a part-time militia whose goal is to defend Ireland against a French invasion. Maintenance of law and order is a secondary purpose: that means protecting our property."

"Protecting it from whom, Harry?"

"From the Whiteboys, I suppose."

Sibella knew that the Whiteboys were a secret organization who used violent tactics to defend the rights of tenant farmers. Their name derived from the white smocks that the members wore in their nightly raids.

Sibella paused to reflect on her conflicting loyalties. Her loyalty to Harry was counter-posed against the rights of the ordinary people espoused by the rebels.

"Are we jumping to the tune of the British?"

Harry's face lit up.

"You are the clever one. Altamont said that the Volunteers are loyal to the British crown. However, the Irish Parliament opposes the restrictions imposed on trade. The matter is being discussed with passion by my parliamentary colleagues."

Sibella was amused that her relentless questioning had almost rendered Harry speechless.

60

"How would Benjamin Franklin respond?" she persisted.

Harry ignored the reference to Franklin and gave her his own thoughts instead.

"I must establish my own corps of Volunteers, following the example of Lord Lucan. My Volunteers shall wear splendid uniforms if we can afford them."

"You do look elegant yourself, Harry."

"How do you like my wig?"

Sibella's eyes twinkled.

"It looks as if it's growing out of your head. I like the double row of curls at the bottom."

"That feature is favoured by military and naval figures."

"Is it comfortable?"

Harry chuckled.

"It better be comfortable, or I shall have to speak to Lord Altamont."

"Or you could speak to Lady Harriett!" Sibella taunted.

"Now, now, we shall have none of that. What think you of my red jacket?"

Sibella ran her hand down the front of a jacket edged in black with white epaulets on the shoulder. A decorative shirt protruded at the front under the white cravat around his neck.

"I wonder what the Whiteboys will think of you, with your red jacket."

"You need not worry about the Whiteboys, my dear. That is why we have the muskets."

Sibella's brow knotted. She became even more worried when told of the Act passed against the Whiteboys just before Harry took his seat. Their activities arose from enclosures of commonage, forced labour, unemployment, rack-rents and tithes. Legal redress for these grievances had been set aside. The legislative introduction of coercion resulted in a spirit of non-cooperation among the rural population. People were more inclined to obey the local Whiteboy code than the law of the land.

"Harry, you must win people over by addressing their grievances rather than coercing them. They will be less likely to attack you if you are seen to be progressive."

"You're right, my dear," Harry's pallor deepened. "I shall talk to Cuffe and Altamont."

Sibella was not surprised when both men insisted that Parliament would not budge on the Whiteboy issue. If anything, attitudes were hardening in the House. In order to dispel Harry's gloom, she asked,

"How are you going to establish your Volunteer corps?"

"I shall recruit the most capable and trusted men: land agents, bailiffs, stewards, grooms, blacksmiths, tutors, prominent tenants and citizens of Balla."

"Imagine that!" Sibella exclaimed.

Then she wondered if her father, Michael Cottle, would have fitted into one of those categories.

"We shall procure arms, train and hold parades," Harry continued. "I will need to explain the purpose of the militia corps of Balla as best I can."

"What will happen if the French invade?"

Harry's face brightened.

"We shall charm them into submission."

Sibella laughed. She was relieved that Harry had retained his sense of humour as well as coming to grips with the complex world of politics. A repertoire of charm, cunning and sharp wit would not go astray.

"I shall be off to Dublin tomorrow to attend Parliament," he said.

"What is to be discussed there?"

"Luke Gardiner is introducing a relief act permitting Catholics to take long leases and restore inheritance rights. I intend to support it although Cuffe has warned of opposition to it."

"That is wonderful, Harry. We are all behind you."

Sibella kissed him and left him with a long, lingering look as he departed.

* * * * *

ONE WEEK LATER, HARRY returned with darkened eyes and pursed lips.

Sibella observed this with dismay. "What ails you, Harry?" she inquired.

"I am a much wiser man on the vagaries of politics. You would find it difficult to believe what transpired," Harry said. "Gardiner's bill met sustained opposition. Cuffe and Altamont asked me to vote against it. They pressurized me with veiled threats, but I refused to buckle."

Sibella gritted her teeth at the news.

"Well done, Harry, I am proud of you. How could they be so foolish?"

"But that was not the end of it. The man from London explained that extraordinary times required extraordinary measures. The British army is under pressure in America. France has declared war on Britain. The army needs more recruits, including Catholics, in England and Ireland. It is vital, he said, that Catholic relief measures are instituted to assist the war effort."

Sibella waited for Harry to wipe the sweat from his brow. She was breathless with excitement while absentmindedly raking the wood fire.

"What happened next?" she asked.

"The debate went long into the night without resolution. Pressure mounted on the following day with vague promises for those who voted yes. The man from London had a word with me."

Sibella could now see that Harry was evolving as a politician.

"Who was he?" she asked.

"Sir John de Blacquiere, the Chief Secretary. He welcomed me as a new member of parliament. He asked if I was enjoying the debate on the proposed relief act. I told him that I would support it. He smiled and passed on."

"What happened next?"

Harry took a small sip of his whiskey before answering.

"After another long night, the bill was finally passed. Altamont and Cuffe were fuming as they felt the pressure of the London element. I concealed my delight so as not to irritate them."

"Well done Harry, I am most proud of you. The Moores will be delighted. It might even soften the cough of the Whiteboys for a while. Why were Altamont and Cuffe so opposed to Catholic relief?"

"They said that once you give in to a relief measure, there would be no end to popery demands. Heartened by one victory, the Catholic community would eventually reassert their control over Ireland. Our privileged position would be diminished."

Sibella enjoyed the spectacle of Harry in full flight. He was much more interesting when discussing politics rather than his trivial hunting exploits.

"Well, too bad about them; they need to grow up and look to the future."

"Cuffe was particularly annoyed. He reminded me of the role he played in my election." Harry lowered his voice. "Then he made a nasty remark."

"What did he say?"

"He said that you, my dear, have me under your thumb."

Now it was Sibella's turn to experience a momentary speechlessness. Her furrowed brow gradually cleared and her eyes began to twinkle again.

"Well, that is surely a compliment, if a back-handed one. I must show my gratitude the next time he visits."

Sibella relaxed in front of a roaring fire, a glow of self-satisfaction coursing through her body. "You might pour your kind lady a celebratory port," she said.

It was going to be one of those nights.

* * * * *

AFTER THE INITIAL FLURRY of excitement, the normality of life returned. Sibella focused on rearing her four children and in supervising the management of Balla House. Once more with child, she assumed the additional responsibilities of making the acquaintance of Harry's tenants and the local citizens.

To this end, she walked though Balla one day with Michael, now four years old. He was quite a handful as he hopped and skipped along the wide street of the market village.

On entering the local shop, Sibella was surprised when the proprietor welcomed them.

"Lady Lynch-Blosse, 'tis a lovely day surely."

She felt faint and sat down. How strange but pleasing it was that ordinary people assumed that she was married. Even Michael seemed puzzled; he looked around the shop as if in search of the titled person.

"You're not feelin' too well, m'lady?"

"I am perfectly fine, thank you so much. I just felt a little faint," Sibella said. "What a nice shop you have. I must buy some sweets for Michael and for his sisters, Cecilia and Mary Anne."

"We have barley sugar, caramel, gingerbread, marzipan and nougat."

Michael pointed to the marzipan subtleties formed in the shape of rabbits and sheep.

"I would like a rabbit, if you please, Mama," he said.

"I will take one rabbit and two sheep." Sibella smiled and extracted a sovereign from her reticule. She was relieved to get some coinage back and too diplomatic to check the change.

While Michael devoured his rabbit, Sibella showed him the remains of an ancient Round Tower at the edge of the village. It was about fifty feet high and formed a distinguishing feature close to the entrance avenue of the Big House. She had to restrain Michael from climbing to its pinnacle.

A nearby holy well, dedicated to the Blessed Virgin, deflected his attention when she told him that magic occurred there. Sibella enjoyed the spiritual atmosphere of the holy well, known as Lady Well. She prayed for the magic that would secure an annulment for Harry while Michael asked God for another rabbit.

A carving on a stone block behind the altar of the nearby medieval church fascinated her. It was known as the Evil Eye. Sibella was too much in awe of it to form an explanation when Michael asked why it was so called.

As Michael fidgeted, she quickly knelt and prayed for her parents, for Harry, and for Michael, Cecilia, Mary Anne and John. With the help of God, another member of the family would soon join them. That thought flashed through her mind as she carried her unborn, alongside Michael, to the elevated location of the Big House.

Her third daughter, Bridget, was safely delivered shortly afterwards.

"Another girl," said Michael as Cecilia and Mary Anne giggled.

"Congratulations, my darling," Harry said. "Who should we invite to the baptism?"

"As the babe is a girl, we should invite Lady Lynch and the Moores of Ashbrook. We could invite Lady Harriett to the reception afterwards, if you wish."

"Splendid!" Harry beamed. "She has offered to help with my Volunteer work."

After the baptism, Harry, resplendent in his Volunteer regalia, was the centre of attention. Sibella was not the only one to admire his rugged clean-shaven face, sensuous lips and blue eyes.

At the reception, Sibella noted how swiftly Lady Harriett engaged Harry in an extended conversation. She wore a flamboyant hat of striped fabric with pink satin edging, black and white ostrich plumes, and velvet rosettes. Her flirting left Sibella in no doubt of her interest.

"Do you think that Harry and Harriett would make a fine couple?" Sibella asked Pat Lynch of Clogher.

"I thought you wanted me to marry Harriett," Pat laughed. "Are you not the love of Harry's life, Sibella Cottle?"

Sibella blushed and later asked Harry,

"How was Lady Harriett?"

"As forward as ever. So many questions. What is it all about? What would happen if the French came and if they did not come? She exhausted me but I humoured her."

"Why did you humour her?"

"She offered to buy some muskets."

Sibella sharpened her voice.

"Did you accept her offer?"

"Of course I did, my darling. I also invited her to attend the next parade of the Volunteers in Balla."

"Will she wear the same hat?"

"She told me that the tricorn hat of Marie Antoinette was its inspiration."

Sibella remained silent as a little stream of anger bubbled up inside her.

"Actually, I thought her hat was excessively ostentatious. I shall buy you a much finer one in Dublin on my next trip to Parliament."

Sibella smiled as she saw the tussle with Lady Harriett begin to take shape. She wondered why Harriett bothered with Harry, given that he was not free to marry. Was she missing something? Had Harry concealed information from her? Was Cuffe scheming with Altamont to break her influence on the political liberalism of her Harry? These questions chased one another around in her mind.

CHAPTER 9

SIBELLA CONTINUED TO WORRY. Lady Harriett was a formidable woman with all the desirable attributes of a bride fit for a baronet. Her flirting with Harry at the baptism of baby Bridget was an indication of her interest. Sibella wondered if she had discussed the matter with Lord Altamont. If so, she may have told him of her invitation to the parade of the Balla Volunteers. Would Altamont feel that this was a signal of interest from Harry?

Her worst fears were confirmed when Harry received a letter from Dublin marked "Private and Confidential." She saw how flushed he became on reading it, crumpling it in his pocket as he finished breakfast. After Harry had dashed off to catch the mail coach to Dublin, Sibella found the letter under the mattress, and got quite a shock.

Kildare Street Club,
Dublin
21 October 1782
Dear Harry,

I was speaking to Altamont today, and was delighted to learn from him of your interest in Lady Harriett. He hinted at an engagement. I hope it is true, and offer you my most cordial congratulations. She is a woman in a thousand, and the alliance would enable you to clear that mortgage which has been such a source of worry to me, as trustee, for the past ten years.

Your interest in Lady Harriett is timely because you are now free to marry. Altamont and I have used our influence to secure an annulment of your marriage to Mistress Mahon.

In the meantime, I hope you will have no difficulty in disposing of that other person. Her flaunting of herself as the Mistress of Balla to all and sundry does not alter the fact that you are living with her. Indeed, it is high time that the said liaison ceased and that you settled down to the more serious duties of life. However, as your trustee, I should wish to know that you treated Mistress Cottle and her children decently. Give her a reasonable, even a liberal, sum and send them all, out of the country — the farther away the better.

Yours sincerely,
James Cuffe.

"*Dear Lord,*" Sibella thought. "*The Honourable Member of Parliament has issued a challenge.*"

She wondered if her influence in persuading Harry to support the Catholic Relief Bill had motivated Cuffe. A marriage to Lady Harriett would remove her troublesome liberalism from the political arena, an influence that had caused such embarrassment in conservative circles.

Should she challenge Harry or wait? After all, he was now free to marry her. Her five children depended on her. She prayed for intercession or inspiration and then waited in trepidation.

On his return from Dublin, she expected Harry to discuss the letter with her.

"How was Dublin, dear heart?"

"I love Dublin. There is an energy there, an air of excitement about the place. I saw a parade of the Dublin Volunteers, and I now know what we need in Balla."

"That is good. How did your meeting with the bankers go?"

"Not very well. They want me to reduce the mortgage on the estate."

Harry began to pace up and down the drawing room.

"Is that what that letter was about?"

"What letter?" Harry suddenly stopped pacing.

Sibella looked him straight in the eyes.

"The letter that made you so angry at breakfast."

Harry grimaced.

"Oh, that letter … yes, it was from the bankers, highly confidential. They want me to sell off a portion of the estate. I felt like telling them to go to hell. On reflection, I agreed to investigate and report back."

Sibella continued to stare at Harry, much to his discomfort. Her worry intensified because he had never lied before about their relationship. She knew he was under pressure to abandon her. Why would he lie unless he had decided to succumb to that pressure?

Sibella had no close friend nearby with whom to discuss her predicament. Talking to her foster-parents, the Moores of Ashbrook, required writing first and then arranging transport. Embarrassing curiosity and gossip would have followed. Lady Lynch was too close to Harry. The contents of Cuffe's letter would distress her. The same applied to Uncle Peter and Pat Lynch of Clogher. Her natural parents rested peacefully in the graveyard at Cottlestown. She was an only child with no living relatives that she knew of.

"With whom can I talk?" she wondered.

* * * * *

THE ONLY PERSON WHO came to mind was her midwife, Judy Holian: *an bhean feasa,* the woman of knowledge and wisdom. She had first heard of her through the Moores of Ashbrook, who visited her out of curiosity. Judy was reputedly possessed of occult powers. People came from near and far hoping to find a cure for their malady. Whether she ever solved any such problem is open to question. Her fame resided in her detailed knowledge of local history and her colourful rendition of stories to entertain her guests.

Other features of her skills included "tossin' the cup" and "cuttin' the cards", means by which the future was forecast. Sibella wondered if she should order a love-draught, which would lead to renewed love if drunk by a favoured person. It would cost a few shillings because it required some:

> *king-eel's blood, and the black sow's milk, and the Spanish midges.*

When Judy cast a spell, her subject was expected to respond in the desired fashion. Some labelled her a witch.

Sibella knew that Father Nolan was critical of her activities and had denounced her from the altar. Her superstitious practices, which challenged the orthodoxy of the church, were anathema to him. Sibella also knew that Harry's father had transported her husband, Sean, to America for stealing a sheep. He may have ended up on a plantation as an indentured servant.

When Sibella first moved from Suffolk to Balla, she was of a mind to pay a visit to Judy Holian. It had been five years ago when Sibella had knocked on the door of the modest residence, and Judy appeared with a quizzical look.

"Good morning, Mrs Holian," Sibella said nervously. "I am Sibella Cottle from the Big House."

"I know who you are."

Sibella wondered how much Judy Holian knew.

"I would like to visit at some time that would suit."

"Certainly. Come in for a few minutes now, if you like, and we can have a little chat."

Sibella sat down on a worn-out chair by the hearth.

"Mrs Holian, I would dearly like to know what the future holds for me."

"Well now, I cannot toss the cup as we have no tea and cannot afford to buy it. We can try cuttin' the cards instead."

Judy placed the cards on the table.

"I want you to cut them into three parts. Next, you must cut two parts into three to make seven parts."

"Why seven parts?" Sibella asked.

"The seven parts are for the seven days of creation, and the seven stars in the Plough and because it is the year seventeen hundred and seventy-seven."

Judy arranged the seven lots of cards into the shape of a cross and mumbled a spell over them in Gaelic. She spread one lot of cards on the table, face upwards and scrutinized them. After a while, she raised her eyes from the table and said,

"There is a dark cloud between you and great riches. Powerful enemies will do their utmost to have you expelled from Balla House."

"How can I get the better of them, Judy?"

"You will be advised soon enough, m'lady."

Sibella wondered if Judy was patronizing her by ascribing to her a title that she did not hold. She told the story to Harry, who laughed.

"I am not surprised at the old witch. She is always up to some mischief."

Sibella looked into the flames of a wood fire.

"But who are my enemies?"

"I presume she refers to my family who expect me to marry a lady of my own class and religion."

After further discussion, Sibella was reassured and put the matter behind her. However, she did take care to send occasional supplies of food and clothes to Judy as a token of her appreciation.

* * * * *

Now, FIVE YEARS LATER, Sibella found herself returning to Judy Holian.

"It has taken you a long time to come back to me, m'lady."

Sibella was pleased that Judy continued to use the title that she aspired to.

"Time does fly by, surely? It only feels like yesterday since we last met."

"Two years, m'lady, since I delivered Bridget. Two years, allanah!"

Sibella enjoyed the banter and continued it.

"It could not be so long a time, could it? Regardless, how are you keeping, Judy Holian?"

"Not the best nor yet the worst. I miss that poor husband of mine, transported for stealin' a sheep."

"I heard about that. Have you heard from him at all?"

Judy smiled grimly.

"Not a word, m'lady. I think I may have to work my magic on him."

"I hope he is doing well in America," Sibella said. "He will surely return to you some day, God willing."

"What brings you to my humble home in your fine silks and satins?"

Sibella understood her mocking tone.

"I am worried about Harry. I have discovered that he got a letter from James Cuffe, urging him to marry Lady Harriett, and throw me and the children out on the road."

"They have been tryin' to marry Sir Harry off for the last ten years and what did he do? He married the right class but the wrong religion. Poor Mistress Mahon, she never knew what hit her."

"Harry was young and foolish then ..."

"And now, not so young and still foolish?"

"I know not, Judy. He has always told me everything until now. He concealed *that* letter he got from Cuffe, and worse still he lied about it. He gets on well with Lady Harriett. I am afraid he may leave me for her."

Judy's reply surprised Sibella, for it seemed like it was not at all on topic.

"I have no time for the Brownes and their leader, Altamont, and the way they try to control everythin' in Mayo."

"What have you against the Brownes?"

Judy stoked the fire.

"We are under threat of eviction from Harry's bailiff. He's in cahoots with the parish priest and the Brownes. We could be out on the road any day now."

Sibella caught the meaning of the interjection now, and moved in to assure her confidant.

"Leave it with me, Judy; I can talk to Harry. I will attend to it this very evening."

"Thank you very much, m'lady. This is why I will do anything in my power to prevent Sir Harry marryin' that Browne bitch."

"But what can you do, Judy?"

"There's only one thing for it, the spancel of death."

"What in the name of God is that?"

"It is a serious matter. You must think on it carefully. It will cost you a bit of money."

"Money is not a problem as yet; but what is this spancel?"

"The spancel is a love charm that is attached to the person whose love is sought while they are sleepin'."

"How is it made?"

Judy lowered her voice.

"It is made of a piece of skin from a freshly-buried corpse."

Sibella gasped in horror.

"Dear Lord! You cannot be serious."

"I am deadly serious. You need to think long and hard before you go down this road."

"I will think about it, Judy. Do not fret about the eviction. I will fix it."

Sibella returned to Balla and spoke to Harry about the proposed eviction of the Holians, reminding him of how the midwife had helped her through the difficult breech birth of Mary Anne. He agreed to postpone it. She asked him if he had any news.

"Nothing, apart from the organization of the Volunteer parade in Balla."

"Have we received any exciting letters from Dublin?"

"If only we did," Harry said. "All I receive is dreary letters about mortgages, debtors and creditors."

So there it was. Harry was not going to tell her about that letter. Perhaps he wanted to protect her from its appalling contents. She hoped so. He had nothing further to say, apart from confirming a long-term postponement of the proposed eviction.

In the meantime, Sibella enjoyed recalling the midwifery dramatics of Judy Holian. Her assistance in the birth of the twins, Cecilia and Mary Anne was a source of gossip in the Big House. Now her spells and love charms were what fascinated Sibella. Could Judy help to preserve Harry's love for her? She was sceptical but gave the midwife permission to proceed with the spancel. It was more out of curiosity than out of any sense that it could be effective against her rival, Lady Harriett.

Judy frowned. "As I told you before, you need to think long and hard before you go down this road."

"I understand Judy," Sibella replied. "I can always pull out, should I change my mind."

"Very well then," Judy said. "I will need ten pounds to get the silk, the wax candles and the black chasuble. And another ten pounds to get the corpse."

"Judy Holian, you are an expensive lady. I will give you ten pounds for it all."

"Maybe I could manage with ten pounds ..."

Sibella opened her reticule and handed over ten sovereigns.

"If it works, I might give you a bonus, as well as another consignment of tea."

Judy smiled.

"Go home now and do not come near me again for seven days and seven nights. On the seventh night, you must return with a gold wedding band and seven hairs from Harry's head."

After Sibella returned, she found Harry busy with the preparations for the Volunteer parade in Balla. She insisted he needed a haircut.

"Your wig will be more comfortable if I thin out your lovely brown hair."

"All right, my dear."

On the following morning, Sibella sat him down with his back facing the window of their bedroom.

"Harry, I have some bad news. I can see some grey hairs in the sunlight."

"Nonsense, woman; I am far too young for grey hairs."

Sibella adjusted the towel around his neck and pulled out a hair.

"Ouch!"

"You poor baby! There is the proof."

She showed him the long thin hair.

"I cannot tell what colour that hair is, you rascal."

"Trust me, there are only a few. I shall have them plucked in no time."

Sibella resumed her search and plucked six more hairs.

"It is a strange circumstance how things seem to happen in sevens," she said.

The seven offending hairs were carefully set aside. She now insisted on removing Sir Robuck's gold wedding band for cleaning. Sibella had persuaded Harry to wear it after his father passed away as an indication of his commitment to marry her.

Later that day, Sibella attended the funeral of Ellen Colgan in Balla churchyard. The tragic death of Harry's daughter at the age of fifteen had attracted a large crowd, including many of his tenants. Dressed in mourning black, she stood close to him and prayed with him. She saw him shed a tear when Father Nolan captured the sombre mood on that chilly winter's day. Standing among the yew trees near the Round Tower, he recited:

Here rests her head upon the lap of earth,
a youth to fortune and to fame unknown.

Approving glances were directed at the well-educated priest who had borrowed a couplet from *Gray's Elegy* with the gender altered to suit the occasion.

As the coffin was lowered into the grave, Sibella glanced around at the gravestones of the departed. She wondered where Judy Holian would find a corpse if she was serious about that part of the spell. It had never occurred to her until now that a body might have to be exhumed from the graveyard. She shivered at the thought.

Sibella then saw Judy Holian staring at Harry with a knowing look. Other people looked him at him too, including old man Colgan. Were they expressing revulsion at the folly of his first romance? When Harry approached Colgan, she saw the old man stand his ground. She was relieved when Harry talked with him and shook his hand.

As they left the graveyard, she hoped that the great parade of Harry's Volunteers would soothe his bruised ego. It would distract people's minds and move them on to enjoy the celebrations in the village.

The only problem was that she had miscalculated the day of the seventh night. It was the night of the dinner to celebrate the inaugural parade of the Balla Volunteers. Included among the guests were Lord Altamont, Lady Harriett and James Cuffe. How could she cope with this latest dilemma?

CHAPTER 10

W HEN SIBELLA CALLED ON the seventh night, she saw Judy spinning a bundle of floss silk on the flax wheel. She watched in fascination as Judy embroidered the seven colours of the rainbow on one side of the base fabric.

"Why seven colours?" Sibella asked.

"The colours are for the seven days of creation and the seven years that m'lady will spend in purgatory if she uses the spancel of death."

Sibella turned white.

"Judy Holian, you have caused the hairs to stand on my head. What else have you there?"

"I have a long black cloth with a circular hole in the centre big enough to allow a head to pass through. I have an oak rod, a stone bottle of blood, two pieces of hazel stick bound together with black silk floss to form a cross and seven wax candles. The candles are part of the spell," Judy explained. "You must attach them to the lid of the coffin in the shape of a cross with the blood that I give you."

Sibella squirmed on the rough wooden chair.

"But where is the coffin?"

"Time enough for that, allanah. You must light the candles with this oak twig, reddened in the fire, and then walk aroun' the coffin seven times."

Sibella stood up and paced alongside the open turf fire.

"And whose coffin will it be?"

"It may be that of young Ellen Colgan, may she rest in peace, the poor creature."

"Was she the daughter of my Harry?"

"She was; and if it is her body, that will do the spell no harm."

Sibella paled again as Judy continued.

"We'll not wait long to find out whose corpse it is. My son, Ned, is down at the graveyard with a spade and shovel, and a lantern because there's no moon tonight. They buried young Ellen Colgan ..." Judy crossed herself ". . . near the wall under the trees. Ned will drag the coffin on two planks, over the wall and into the cart."

Sibella clasped her hands.

"What if someone should see him?"

Judy raised her voice.

"Ned Holian is a man of the night. He will not be caught."

Sibella heard a creaking noise at the back of the cabin.

"Hush! That could be him now."

Judy looked through a crack in the back door and then opened it. Sibella watched in horror as Ned brought the coffin in with the help of his brother, Thady, and placed it on the table. They removed the top of the coffin.

"It's young Ellen Colgan. I will take her back when it is done," Ned said as Sibella averted her gaze.

Judy waved her hand dismissively.

"Well done, Ned. Be off with you now."

"Poor Ellen, she looks so vulnerable. Her body is ravaged with consumption."

Sibella spoke slowly as if hypnotized by the surreal atmosphere. Ellen's body was beginning to smell. Her facial muscles had contracted. Sibella quivered when Judy brushed away a maggot on the side of her face.

"We must make haste."

Judy looked at Sibella, who nodded hesitantly.

"Good girl. Now, you light the candles with this oak twig and walk around the coffin seven times. As you're walkin' around the coffin, I will chant the spell and you must repeat those words after me. Every time you make a round of the coffin, you quench a candle with this hazel cross until they're all quenched."

"What happens then?" Sibella asked.

"We lift her out of the coffin and leave her on the straw mat. Then take this black knife, and with one blow drive it into the sole of her left foot. You will then cut the skin off the outside of the leg and continue up the side of her body, over the head and down the other side of the body until you reach the sole of the right foot ..."

"Stop!" Sibella screamed. She turned a ghostly white and slumped into her chair. "I cannot do this."

"You must if you want to spellbind Sir Harry," Judy said. "Take your ease for a little while with a *cupán tae* and let me finish."

"It will take more than a cup of tea to relax me."

Sibella watched as Judy rustled in the bottom of her cupboard and produced a bottle wrapped in paper. She poured some clear liquid into a small glass.

"Drink that, m'lady, to settle your nerves."

Sibella groaned as she put the glass to her lips.

"I hope it's not Holy Water!" she shivered.

The first sip told her it was not.

"Lord; that takes my breath away. It's poteen, is it not?"

"Aye, and a strong one, alannah," Judy said and then continued: "After you reach the right sole, you move the knife up the inside of the left leg and down the inside of the right leg until you reach the point at which you started. You now have a continuous band of skin from which the spancel is made."

Sibella stood up and moved towards the door.

"Well, my nerves may be settled from that fire-water but I am not going to cut the spancel."

"I thought you might feel like that," Judy said. "But there is another way. You can take a strip of skin from the arm and make a small spancel."

Sibella clenched her fists.

"Why did you not say so at the outset?"

"Because they say the full spancel would be more effective."

"My God, give me patience."

Judy paused again.

"Do not be afeared. After you put out the candles, we'll lift her out of the coffin. You take the knife and cut the spancel off her right arm. As you're cuttin', I'll place Sir Harry's wedding band on Ellen's finger while chanting the spell."

Sibella's heart began to pound.

"What will happen if I refuse to do this?"

"You will be the laughing stock of the countryside," Judy said. "Sir Harry will throw you out, and you and your children will be left on the side of the road, beggin' and dying of starvation."

Sibella had a sinking feeling in her belly that told her Judy's words could well be true.

"Go on, then," she said. "What's next?"

"Put the oak rod under the strip of skin and hand it to me without it touchin' the ground. I will cover it in silk with all the colours of the rainbow. Next, I will put Sir Harry's seven hairs and a few drops of blood on the inside. You must wrap it around his left shin while he's sleeping and place the wedding band under his pillow. When the cock crows in the morning, remove the spancel and the wedding band and put them in a safe place."

* * * * *

SIBELLA DEPARTED SOON AFTER with the spancel concealed within her dark cloak. She also carried with her a small bottle of a love-draught that Judy had insisted she should take as well. After arriving back at Balla, she retired to her room. She hid the spancel in her wardrobe and placed the love-draught in her chatelaine bag. After freshening up, she joined Kate Moran in the anteroom.

"Uncle Peter has been looking for you," Kate said. "Shall I tell him you have returned?"

Sibella nodded, fearing that someone had spotted her jaunt to the village.

Shortly afterwards, Peter appeared.

"Where have you been, hmm?"

Sibella felt comfortable in the presence of this warm-hearted, tolerant man but not to the extent of confiding her innermost thoughts.

"I just went to my room for a while to rest."

"Harry went to find you, but you were not there."

"How unfortunate!" Sibella blushed. "I felt in need of some fresh air to clear my head." Sibella opened her fan to cool her face. "How did that troublemaker, Altamont, behave tonight?"

"He took advantage of your absence to sing the praises of Lady Harriett. I saw her glancing at Harry's left hand, hmm. He was not wearing Sir Robuck's wedding band."

"The ring is gone to be cleaned," Sibella said.

"Harry took it all seriously enough, but I do not think he's interested in her."

"But she is beautiful, eligible, wealthy and a Protestant. What more could a man want?"

"Genuine love, I suppose."

"My, oh my, Peter, are you not the romantic! Tell me, seriously, would you be attracted to Lady Harriett?"

"She is an elegant, well-educated woman, but I find her a bit overpowering."

"So who are you attracted to?" Sibella's eyes twinkled.

"None of your business, Sibella Cottle! We had better return to the festivities before Harry starts seeking you once more."

Sibella smiled. She saw Harry flush after she rejoined the banquet, sitting opposite him at the end of the long table. She had heard him calling for attention, asking Altamont to say a few words.

"Ladies and gentlemen, I wish to congratulate Sir Harry on organizing a magnificent parade of the newly-formed Volunteers in Balla. These local militias are crucial to the defence of Ireland and to the maintenance of law and order. On behalf of the guests, I wish to thank Sir Harry and Mistress

Cottle for hosting such a pleasant dinner and providing accommodation for those who have travelled some distance."

The guests applauded and tapped the table. The ladies retired to drink tea, while the gentlemen remained to relieve themselves followed by brandy, cigars and some ribald conversation.

Later on, Sibella told Harry she was fine and would explain her absence in the morning. She kissed him goodnight. Both were exhausted and soon fast asleep. She decided to conceal the spancel affair from him. After all, he had concealed his liaison with Margaret McDermott and the infamous letter from Dublin.

*　*　*　*　*

ON THE FOLLOWING morning, Sibella dashed her face with cold water and sat down by the bedside in her nightgown. When Harry turned over in the bed and looked at her, she opened her heart to him. It had all started, she said, with that mysterious letter from Dublin.

"You were furious on reading it," she reminded him.

Harry furled his brow as he drew himself up on the pillows.

"I could not contain my curiosity. I found the letter under the mattress."

"Christ, Sibella! It was a dreadful letter. I —"

"You lied, Harry," Sibella interjected. "You never lied to me before on such a personal matter."

Harry gazed deep into her eyes.

"I am so sorry, my dear heart. I wanted to protect you."

Sibella raised her voice.

"Do you recall what Cuffe said? 'Give her a reasonable, even a liberal, sum and send her, and them, out of the country, the farther away the better.' Is that your intention, Harry?"

Harry tapped his fingers on the mahogany dressing table.

"I have been under pressure from the trustees to marry a rich lady to shore up the estate. I have resisted that pressure and will continue to do so."

A knock on the bedroom door interrupted their conversation. A housemaid entered.

"Fresh lemonade as ordered by the mistress."

"Thank you," Sibella spoke. "Please leave it on the side-table."

After the housemaid departed, Sibella walked towards the side-table and poured two glasses of the refreshing drink. With her back to Harry, she topped up his glass with a liquid from the bottle in her chatelaine bag. She gave that glass to Harry, who remained in bed.

Sibella sat in the armchair. She set her glass down on a small round table and continued.

"I have read that letter so many times, I can recite it by rote. Cuffe 'was delighted to learn from him of your interest in Lady Harriett. He (Altamont) hinted at an engagement.' Explain that to me, Harry?"

Sibella's heart palpitated. Harry drew a deep breath.

"I cannot explain it. Altamont and Cuffe must have misunderstood one another or were trying to manipulate me. Perhaps Altamont was misled by my invitation to Harriett to help with the Balla Volunteers." Harry paused. "I love you, Sibella, and our wonderful children. I would never do anything to hurt you or them. I hope we can resolve our differences."

Sibella was relieved but wary.

"It is not that simple, Harry, my dear. Once I read that letter, I had to talk to someone who could help me. The only person I could think of was Judy Holian."

Harry scowled.

"I hope you did not discuss our personal affairs with that old witch."

"I would not have done so if you had told me about the letter," Sibella snapped. "I was terrified after reading it."

Harry sat bolt upright in the bed.

"What did the hellion say?"

Sibella was uncomfortable about lying to Harry but felt she had no alternative. She knew Harry must never find out that she had his daughter's body exhumed to make a spancel.

"Judy said that if you married Lady Harriett, you would have to get rid of me." Sibella paused to sip the refreshing drink. "You should drink up, my dear."

Harry gulped down the last of his lemonade. "There is something different about the taste of this lemonade."

"I asked Kate Moran to use a little more lemon-juice." Sibella took another sip. "Hmm, it freshened it up nicely."

"Mayhap! I would still prefer the old recipe." Harry tapped his lips with a handkerchief. "As for Lady Harriett, I have no intention of marrying her."

"If I had known that, I would not have gone next to or near Mrs Holian."

Harry stretched his arms.

"What did she suggest?" he asked.

"A love-draught," Sibella lied. "She said it would lead to renewed love if drunk by a favoured person."

"What is in it?"

"Some secret ingredients; herbs and spices, I suppose. It was a hazy liquid, a bit watery and bitter."

Sibella did not have the heart to tell him that it contained the king-eel's blood, the black sow's milk and the Spanish midges. That would surely have made him retch if he knew about them.

"So you tasted it?"

"Just a little," Sibella smiled. "I had to make sure you would like it."

"Where is it now?"

Sibella struggled to refrain from laughing.

"All gone!"

Harry fingered his empty glass.

"Zounds! I knew there was something different about the taste."

Harry's face darkened at first. He gazed at Sibella long and hard. His countenance gradually melted into a smile.

"Shall we test its power tonight?"

CHAPTER 11

$\mathbf{A}$ FEW DAYS LATER, Harry said at breakfast,

"We need to take stock, my dear"

Sibella surmised that the conspicuous presence of Lady Harriett at the Volunteer's dinner had forced Harry to consider his future. Now that Altamont and Cuffe had secured Harry's annulment, he was free to marry the aristocratic lady. Such a union would ease the financial burden on the mortgaged estate through the accompanying dowry.

"Very well, Sir Harry, let us talk!" Sibella replied.

She helped herself to rashers and egg from the chafing dishes, conscious of Kate Moran's presence in the anteroom.

"First of all, I am not going to pursue Lady Harriett or any other fine Protestant lady."

"Why not?" Sibella taunted.

"You know well why not!"

Sibella knew that Harry was worried about his health although only thirty-three. He had given up hunting; his seven-year period as MP had just expired; he was fatigued, coughing a lot, and drinking too much. His mother had died when only twenty-eight. Perhaps it was in the blood.

"Tell me again," she persisted.

"Because I love you. I want to spend the rest of my life with you."

Sibella heaved a sigh of relief.

"Thank you, Harry, I love you with all my heart."

"There are other matters to discuss," Harry added.

"Go on," Sibella said, her brow wrinkling.

"Let us take a walk in the garden." Harry laid down his napkin and rose.

As they walked among the crocuses and daffodils, Harry said,

"I am concerned about the children."

"The children are fine," Sibella assured him. "They are healthy and receiving a good upbringing and education."

"I know, but there is a problem." Harry spoke with an intensity that alarmed her. "I am worried about the status of our beloved children."

"Do you have an answer to this?" Sibella trembled.

"We must marry."

Sibella jumped into his arms.

"Nothing would please me more than to marry you, my darling. You must name the day."

"But first you must conform,"

"Why should I? Neither Cuffe nor Altamont will push me around," Sibella cried defiantly. "We can marry in England now that your marriage to Mistress Mahon has been annulled."

"That would not remove the stigma of scandal from our living together in sin, especially here in the ancient house of the Lynch-Blosses," Harry said. "A home marriage would restore our tarnished reputations."

"If I were to agree, what date do you have in mind?" Sibella asked.

"As soon as possible," Harry replied cautiously. "Our reputation and that of our children will be secured."

"As will the reputation of our future children, Harry Lynch-Blosse, Commander-in-Chief of the Balla Volunteers!"

"Good Lord! Do you mean to tell me —"

"I have that morning sickness again. You must control yourself," Sibella said. "The nausea is worse than with baby Bridget."

"Ah, that is why you pushed the rashers and egg away at breakfast." Harry raised his eyes. "Twins again?"

Sibella groaned.

"It's just like it was with Cecilia and Mary Anne."

Harry kicked a stone on the gravelled path.

"What does the old witch think?"

"She said it could be twins, although the likelihood of a second set is slight," Sibella said. "I am fearful, Harry. My pregnancy with the twins was a nightmare."

"You must not worry. I shall look after you now that I am finished with politics and the hounds."

Harry stopped and opened his arms. Sibella snuggled into his warm body. Harry kissed and held her gently.

Over the coming days and weeks, Sibella thought about her future as her pregnancy progressed. She had climbed the pinnacle to become the Mistress of Balla House, with standing and influence in Mayo. However, Harry had not yet named the date even though she had reminded him of it on several occasions.

"Is my position still in jeopardy because Harry is free to marry Lady Harriett?" she wondered.

* * * * *

AT TWENTY WEEKS, SIBELLA tried to relax in the drawing room as Harry read some correspondence.

"Have you any further thoughts on our situation?" she asked him.

Harry's face dropped.

"Nothing new, my dear."

"Very well! It is time for me to retire to the land of Nod."

She climbed the cantilevered stairs slowly after kissing him goodnight.

Lying in bed, gazing into the darkness, she continued to worry. Despite Harry's commitment, she knew that Lady Harriett would not abandon her ambition. Was that why Harry continued to vacillate over setting the date for their marriage? All she could do was hope for the best, unless she applied the spancel. She smiled and drifted off to sleep while the little ones within her were waking up.

She had delayed using the spancel because of the story she had heard of its use in Belmullet. A young servant girl had placed a spancel under her pillow and dreamed on it. She hoped that a fellow servant would appear in her dream, but instead her master appeared. His wife died shortly afterwards. She then tied the spancel around the master's arm while sleeping. He fell in love with the servant girl even though she was ugly. He married her. One year and one day later, the spancel was accidently burned in a bedroom fire. The spell was broken. The master now hated his new wife. She confessed and the local community ostracised her. She died half-mad before the year was out.

By the following morning, Sibella had made a decision. After Harry and the servants departed and the children were with their governess and the groom, she opened the secret compartment under the floorboards. She unlocked the silver casket with the key from her locket and removed the spancel. Air-drying and a grain of musk had perfectly preserved it. She looked at it in wonder, caressing its silken surface and then placed it under her pillow alongside Harry's wedding band.

That night, Harry appeared in her dream. He stayed with her all night. No other person intruded. When the cock crew at dawn, she quietly got up while Harry shuffled in bed. She returned the spancel to its hiding place and the key of the casket to her locket. Had Harry noticed?

These thoughts remained with her as the next ten weeks drifted by. She had conceived in early spring, and it was now mid-autumn; she felt as big as a house. Her mood was volatile, except when the children visited.

"Mama," began Michael, now eight years old. He was a handsome boy with long blond hair, probably taking after his grandfather of whom she had no memory. "Will it be a boy or a girl?"

"It could be both a boy and a girl," Sibella said.

"Are you going to have twins?" asked Cecilia, a bright and pretty seven-year-old.

"Maybe," Sibella said. "It feels just like you and Mary Anne."

"Not another two girls!" Michael snorted, supported by an approving glance from his younger brother, John.

"Maybe it will be two boys," Harry interjected as he entered the room.

"Or it could be a boy and a girl," little Bridget suggested, careening across the end of the four-poster bed.

"Then we would have three boys and four girls," said Cecilia.

"After the twins, we would need one more baby boy to make it even," Michael smiled as the girls giggled.

Sibella raised her eyes to heaven as Harry intervened. "Now, boys and girls, your Mama needs plenty of rest to build her strength. The boys will go to the groom for riding lessons. The girls will go to the governess for reading and writing."

"I want to stay with Mama," little Bridget said, sliding head first off the side of the bed.

"Bridget can stay with me. She can help me tidy up."

As they departed, Cecilia and Mary Anne glared at Bridget who smiled in contentment.

* * * * *

TOWARDS THE END OF October, Sibella was ready to give birth. The children came to see her every day. Each put an ear to her expanded belly.

"They are not kicking today," Bridget said.

"I think the little rascals go back to sleep when I wake up, and wake up when I try to sleep," Sibella sighed. "Bridget, tell them to hurry up, please."

The children joined Harry in laughter.

A loud knock on the door signalled the arrival of Kate Moran.

"Mrs. Holian, midwife, to see Mistress Cottle."

Judy followed Kate into the room, removing her shawl.

"God bless all here," she greeted them.

Harry said, "Come along now, children. Mrs. Holian needs to talk to your Mama."

As the children left, Sibella saw Judy glance at Harry long and deep.

"Why did you look so crossly at Harry?"

Judy sat down by the bedside.

"I am a little concerned, m'lady."

"What is the matter?"

85

"I heard just now that Sir Harry is about to travel to Westport."

Sibella suspected what Judy was thinking.

"Dear Lord, is Harry going to ask Altamont for the hand of Harriett?"

"Strange that he did not mention it," she mused.

"I could put a curse on her," Judy said.

"What sort of a curse?"

"One that would stop her scheming."

"No, it is not necessary, Judy. I have a plan," Sibella said. "Now what think you about my babies?"

"It looks like twins again," Judy said.

Sibella winced as she turned over on to her back.

"I cannot wait for them to come."

"Let me look at you."

Judy rolled down the blankets and placed her ear on Sibella's belly.

"Plenty of activity there," she said. "Everything seems to be in order."

"Thank you, Judy. How are you keeping?"

"In fine form, m'lady. Thank you for asking."

After Judy had left, Sibella mused awhile. She knew the time had come to take action. Struggling out of bed, she retrieved the silver casket from under the floorboards. Suddenly, heavy footsteps approached on the staircase, sounding like Harry. She quickly hid the casket under the blankets. The door opened and there he was, soaked to the skin.

"What happened, my dear heart?"

"The heavens opened a few miles out the road. I should have turned back sooner."

A bout of chesty coughing followed.

"Where were you off to, Harry?"

"Nowhere in particular; I just needed some air to clear my head."

"Is there something on your mind?"

Harry scowled and departed.

Sibella now felt justified in applying the spancel. She opened the silver casket and placed the spancel and the wedding band under his pillow.

That night, Harry tossed and turned in bed as if thunderstruck. He rose early and left the room briefly. Sibella retrieved the spancel and wedding band before the cock crew. She had managed to hide them just before he returned.

"Did you have a nightmare, Harry?"

"I had the strangest dream ever. There was only one person in it, a woman."

"Who was she?"

"She was very beautiful and she kissed me."

"Harry!"

"She had red hair, and she was pregnant."

"Did you never dream of me before?"

"Of course I did, but there were always other people around. This one had a rare intensity as if —"

"Exactly, Harry," Sibella interjected. "You are going to be the proud father of twins any day now."

* * * * *

THREE DAYS LATER SIBELLA'S waters broke during the daily visitation of her midwife.

"Let us hope, it'll be less dramatic this time," Judy remarked while ringing the bedroom bell. When the footman arrived she said, "Please call Sir Harry and Kate Moran immediately."

Kate Moran said on arrival, "Sir Harry is on his way to Westport. I will send a rider to call him back."

Sibella gritted her teeth as her labour commenced. Her contractions occurred at regular intervals. The pain was intense, just as it had been with her first set of twins. Before long, she screamed,

"My baby is coming!"

"It'll be fine, m'lady," Judy soothed her. "Now take a deep breath and push. Good girl! The baby's head is now visible."

Sibella was sweating. Kate cooled her forehead with a damp cloth.

"Push again," Judy urged.

Pushing continued. The birth canal gradually widened.

"Just one more push," Judy said.

The seventh push came, Sibella straining every muscle in her body.

"Good girl, here he comes."

Within seconds, Judy Holian held a baby boy in her arms.

Eyes moved from the baby to Sibella and to the ticking clock. It was now six of the clock.

"We cannot wait for the sevens this time, Judy," Kate Moran said.

The servants tried to stifle their laughter.

"We can wait until seven minutes past six, if you have no objection," Judy snapped.

At the appointed time, Judy said, "I will now cut the cord with a knife heated over a bedside candle."

Shortly after, Sibella heard the baby cry.

"Congratulations, m'lady. I will wrap the wee darling in a white shawl."

At that moment Harry arrived, his face flushed.

"Congratulations, Sir Harry," Judy said. "You are the proud parent of a fine healthy boy." Handing baby George to a bamboozled Harry, she resumed her watch at the end of the bed. "Now we have more work to do."

"She is on the move," Sibella said.

"I can see the head," Judy responded. "We are spared the worry of a breech birth on this occasion, thanks be to God."

A baby girl, Barbara, was safely born shortly afterwards. She gave her first cry. Another round of applause hit the rafters. Sibella could now hold her two fine babies. She cried with joy.

As Harry recovered his composure, he rang for the footman.

"Everyone is invited to a celebratory libation. I want to thank you all for your help and cooperation."

As the servants departed for the basement kitchen, Judy sat by Sibella.

With tears in their eyes, the two women embraced.

"Thank you so much, Judy."

Judy then departed and the children rushed in. They were awestruck by the vision of the babies wrapped in their tiny gowns.

"You now have a new brother, George, and a sister, Barbara," Harry announced as the family celebrated the safe arrival of their youngest members.

Sibella stared deeply into the eyes of her beloved.

"I heard you were on your way to Westport."

Harry blushed again.

"I was; and then the strangest thing happened."

"The heavens opened again?"

"No. I stopped at the inn in Belcarra, needing a brandy to steady my nerves. After I remounted, the stupid horse would not budge. I dug my heels in. I turned him left and I turned him right. Nothing! I turned him back and he bolted home as if his life depended on it."

"Goodness me!" Sibella said.

"On the way back, I saw Bernard Moran riding to fetch me. He turned and followed me home. It was like magic. It reminded me of the poem:"

The night is darkening round me,
The wild winds coldly blow;
But a tyrant spell has bound me
And I cannot, cannot go.

Sibella smiled. The spell had worked.

CHAPTER 12

Not long after the birth of their second set of twins, Sibella asked Harry,

"Who should we baptize first?"

"I did not expect a boy and a girl," Harry said.

"Neither did I; my dear heart," Sibella replied as she nursed George and Barbara.

Harry paused while eating his porridge and suggested,

"Should we ask Kate Moran to organize a wet nurse?"

"That bitch is too busy spreading rumours."

Harry grimaced at the reference.

"About what?"

"That I know not. Setting the date for our wedding, mayhap?"

Harry raised his hands in the air.

"Once the baptisms are over, we must move forward," he said.

Sibella knotted her brow. Harry had not only evaded her question but also avoided her gaze.

"After the baptisms, I shall insist on setting the date for our wedding," she thought.

In the meantime, she said,

"As for George and Barbara, I would prefer to nurse them myself." She squirmed in the bed. "Now, for the baptism —"

Harry interjected with his own ideas on that.

"Let us begin with George, as he was born first." Harry paused. "That means we will have … four Catholic and three Protestant children."

"I think seven children is enough." Sibella sighed, gazing absent-mindedly at the pleasure garden.

"Who said there is something special about the number 'seven'?" Harry laughed. "But you are right, seven is enough."

A few days later, Harry said,

"Perhaps we should proceed with the baptism of Barbara first."

Sibella raised her eyebrows in query.

"You've changed your tune."

Harry pursed his lips.

"The vicar is agitated again about baptising children of mixed-religion families. He thought you were going to conform; so did I."

"I wonder where he got that idea."

"God only knows. Even though Lady Lynch is not in the best of health, we should press ahead with Barbara."

Sibella smiled. She always knew when Harry told a white lie. What was wrong with that vicar? Was Harry's influence waning or was the vicar more worried about the illegitimate status of George? Although a similar impediment applied to the baptism of Barbara, it took place after an intervention by Lady Lynch despite the reluctance of Father Nolan.

On the big day, Sibella, Harry and the seven children travelled by coach to the chapel. Lady Lynch, Uncle Peter, Pat Lynch of Clogher and Louisa Moore of Ashbrook travelled separately behind them.

Father Nolan was waiting at the entrance door.

"I wish to welcome Barbara and her parents, Miss Cottle and Sir Harry, to my church."

Sibella was amused when Father Nolan almost choked on having to acknowledge their unmarried status once again.

The party then entered the church and stood around the baptismal font. Sibella held baby Barbara over the font wrapped in a white gown. Father Nolan poured water over her head three times. Barbara cried. Her twin brother, George, also cried with fright even though his baptism would not take place on this day. Their siblings laughed as Father Nolan scowled.

"Barbara, I baptize you in the name of the Father and of the Son and of the Holy Ghost."

Sibella heard nine-year-old Michael whispering to his godmother, Louisa Moore,

"George looks like a girl."

"Little boys are dressed as girls to protect them from the fairies," Louisa said.

"Who is the Holy Ghost?" Cecilia whispered, holding Louisa's hand.

"He is the third person of the Holy Trinity; God the Father, God the Son and God the Holy Ghost."

"Will he frighten us at night?" Michael wondered.

"No; he is there to comfort us in times of trouble," Louisa said.

Sibella interjected,

"Hush, children. Please be quiet."

Father Nolan anointed Barbara with chrism, a holy oil of olive and balsam.

Sibella inhaled the lightly incensed aroma of the chapel air.

"That was a lovely ceremony, Father," she said. "You must join us for a reception at Balla House."

"Unfortunately, I have another baptism later in the morning."

She suspected that Father Nolan was grateful for the invitation but unhappy at having to baptize the children of a mixed marriage; perhaps, though, like the vicar, he was more concerned about the illegitimate status of the children.

∗　∗　∗　∗　∗

Shortly AFTERWARDS, HARRY TOLD Sibella that he had met Lady Harriett at a social function.

"She congratulated me as we were standing in a secluded balcony enjoying the view of Croagh Patrick. I said 'Whatever are you talking about, Harriett?' She snorted something about our twins to which I responded, 'Yes, indeed, twins. George and —' She said she was not interested in their names. I asked her not to be angry and said 'I intend to stand by Sibella'. She said something rude then, which I will not repeat."

"Tell me, Harry."

Harry paused.

"She called you a manipulating hoyden and said you have got me under your thumb."

Sibella pursed her lips.

"No wonder Judy Holian calls her the Browne bitch."

"Now, now, my dear!" Harry frowned. "Harriett finally said you could have me. After calling me a hypocrite and a donkey, she snapped her fan shut and stormed off."

Sibella laughed so loudly that she almost woke the sleeping twins. She controlled her delight, advising Harry to apologize to Harriett if he had misled her, and to express his gratitude for her support of the Balla Volunteers.

With that problem behind her, Sibella now had to look to the future. She prayed that she would not conceive again; her hands were full with the seven children she had.

"I will probably outlive Harry, in the light of his wayward life and the pressure of his leading position in the community," she thought.

Their eldest child, Michael, could not inherit the baronetcy even if Harry married her, now that he was free to marry. That situation came into sharp relief in the following year. Harry's younger brother, Francis, had married and fathered a son, Robert. Harry and Sibella attended his baptism. The family solicitor, Andrew Edmondson, told them that Francis would be the heir apparent, rather than their eldest son, Michael.

Sibella was furious and decided to seek the advice of Judy Holian once again. After settling the children, she walked down the beech-lined avenue to the village of Balla. While there, she could almost sense the curiosity that her presence generated. Was Mistress Cottle visiting witch Judy again? And if so, why?

Ned Holian answered her knock on the cabin door. He wore a slightly cynical smile that irritated her.

"What brings you here, m'lady?"

"Your mother is due a fresh consignment of tea."

Judy called out,

"Come in, m'lady."

Judy was hanging the kettle over the fire as Ned took his leave.

"How are George and Barbara?" she asked Sibella.

"They are very well, Judy. Harry and I are in your debt."

Both women were silent as Judy stoked the fire. The kettle soon began to sing.

"Harry is now free to marry me. He says he's no longer interested in Lady Harriett but he has not set the date for our wedding. What can I do, Judy?"

"You must be strong, alannah. Maybe Sir Harry needs time to sort out his own mind."

Sibella was not sure what that meant. Was Judy referring to the spancel? Was she asking if Harry knew that he had been spellbound?

"You have much to think about, alannah," Judy said. "If you look after Sir Harry and the children, he will look after you. He is a good man, if a weak one. I will pray for you."

Sibella broke down and cried. Drying her tears, she drew solace from the soothing scent and gentle flames of the turf fire.

"Thank you, Judy. I must go."

As Sibella walked home, she decided to visit Lady Lynch. She found her resting in the drawing room, wrapped in a blanket.

"Lady Lynch …" Sibella hesitated while the old woman adjusted her cap. "Something is preying on my mind. When Harry fell in love with me, he made me a gift — "

"Ah, the brooch! He told me about it, the rascal." Her eyes twinkled. "I was surprised you never wore it."

Sibella adjusted the old lady's cap.

"I did not feel brave enough to do so."

"I want you to wear it from now on, in my memory."

Lady Lynch died shortly afterwards from pneumonia. Sibella was heartbroken. Harry's grandmother had supported her at every turn since her move to Balla House seven years ago.

*   *   *   *   *

THERE WAS A HUGE turnout at the funeral of Lady Lynch. Lord Altamont, Lady Harriett, the re-elected James Cuffe MP, Doctor Boyd and Louisa Moore of Ashbrook were among the dignitaries.

Sibella was impressed when Father Nolan paid a fitting tribute.

"I have known Mary Moore before and since her marriage to the late Sir Henry Lynch. That union consolidated the Lynch and Moore estates in southeast Mayo. Both Sir Henry and Lady Lynch were devout Catholics. After Sir Henry passed away more than twenty years ago, Lady Lynch declined an offer of interest accruing to an estate investment. She felt it was inconsistent with her Catholic faith."

Sibella was amused at how Altamont, Lady Harriett and Cuffe scowled at the direction of the homily. She wondered if the clever priest had anticipated the reaction. Could he now deliver an ecumenical blow?

Sibella was not disappointed as Father Nolan continued.

"Despite her commitment to this church, she never complained when her son, Sir Robuck, conformed to the established church. Rather, she supported him at every turn in a spirit of true Christianity. The life of Lady Lynch has been an inspiration to us all, may she rest in peace."

After the burial, Cuffe approached Harry and drew him aside. Sibella drew closer, behind a yew tree, so that she could overhear the conversation.

"Sir Harry, my good man, please accept my sympathies. Your grandmother was a wonderful woman."

"Thank you, James."

"I hope you got my letter," Cuffe said inquiringly.

"I did indeed. I know you have my best interests at heart, but I am in love with Sibella and devoted to our seven lovely children."

Pretending to search for something in her reticule, Sibella was elated to hear these words.

"It is not too late to make your peace with Lady Harriett even though she is furious with you," Cuffe said.

Harry coughed before he answered.

"I regret any misunderstanding that has arisen between us. She is a fine lady. I shall endeavour to renew our friendship, but I am not in love with her and do not intend to marry her."

"How can you possibly love a woman who conspired to secure your love?" Cuffe snapped.

Sibella drew a deep breath. Dear Lord! Had the story of the spancel spread, in spite of her best efforts to maintain secrecy?

"Stop there, James." Harry looked him straight in the eyes. "Unless you immediately withdraw that remark, I shall judge that my honour has been impugned."

Sibella was fascinated. Harry had never challenged anyone to a duel before, even though duelling was common among his gentrified associates. Harry had come of age. He was now his own man. She was so proud of him.

"Harry, I apologize unreservedly. I had no right to speak to you in those terms on the day of your grandmother's funeral." Cuffe paused. "All I was trying to say is that there is more to marriage than love. Lady Harriett would make a good wife and bring a substantial dowry to the table. It would ease your financial problems. As your trustee, I was only acting in your best interests."

"I should not need to remind you, James — you know perfectly well that Sibella and I are engaged to be married."

Sibella looked through the foliage to see the incredulous Cuffe storming off towards Altamont and Lady Harriett, presumably to report what Harry had said.

Meanwhile, Louisa Moore approached her.

"Sibella, it has reached the point where we meet only at baptisms and funerals," her foster-mother remarked sadly.

"Mama, you must visit me at Balla more often now that Papa has passed away."

Sibella referred to the recent demise of Doctor Moore.

"I am so lonely since Robert passed away. I was happy to see you all at his removal, despite the sadness of the occasion." Louisa paused. "Sibella, a rumour is circulating that you put a spell on Harry."

Sibella blushed red and drew her foster-mother out of earshot.

"Harry got a letter from Cuffe urging him to abandon me in favour of Lady Harriett. Judy Holian advised me to spellbind Harry. In desperation, I agreed."

Sibella trembled.

"I did not sleep a wink that night. I felt so guilty but I could not tell Harry what I had done." Tears streamed down her face as Louisa embraced her.

"There is never a dull moment in your life, my darling daughter," Louisa said. "If the situation ever turns sour at Balla, there will always be a welcome for you at Ashbrook."

"Thank you so much, Mama. I could not possibly intrude with my brood of seven."

"Nonsense, Sibella. I have a big house all to myself."

"What about your brother-in-law, George?"

"George and his family hope to return from Alicante but not for some time. In the meantime, you must visit more often and bring the children."

Sibella was thrilled by the invitation. She welcomed the possibility of a safe haven in a time of crisis.

"I will, Mama."

Conscious of the row between Harry and Cuffe, and the subsequent animated conversation between Cuffe and Altamont, Sibella rejoined Harry. As they left the graveyard, they crossed paths with Lady Harriett. Harry thanked her for coming to the funeral; she expressed her sympathies and then stared long and deep at Sibella. Sibella held her nerve.

"Can I now presume that Harriett's interest in Harry is over? Will she now turn her attention elsewhere?" she wondered.

Sibella had much to consider after the burial of Lady Lynch. Her demise signalled the end of an era, the final transformation of the Lynch-Blosse dynasty from Catholic to Protestant. If Harry were to marry her, she would come under pressure to follow suit and conform.

$$* \quad * \quad * \quad * \quad *$$

IN THE FOLLOWING YEAR, Sibella had mixed emotions when Harry scaled back the activities of the Balla Volunteers now that the threat of a French invasion had receded. On the one hand, it gave her more time to weave her charm on him should he renew his contact with Lady Harriett. As time passed, it seemed as if that contact with the cousin of Lord Altamont had diminished, if not terminated. Thus relieved, she now entered a period of relative calm with Harry, enjoying the company of their seven children and giving them the attention they deserved.

That peaceful interlude was soon shattered in springtime when James Cuffe made a surprise visit to Balla House. At least, it was a surprise to Sibella. It was strange that Harry had not forewarned her of the arrival of the trustee of his estate.

After the men retired to the library, her suspicions were aroused when Harry locked the door behind them. Their conversation was so muted that Sibella could not decipher its content. When animated shouting erupted, she presumed that a great argument was in progress.

"Are they talking about me, Lady Harriett, the estate finances or all three bundled together?" she wondered.

Once she heard the door being unlocked, she quickly retired to the drawing room. Harry would surely invite Cuffe to partake of some refreshment before the member-of-parliament returned to Ballinrobe. Instead, through the drawing-room window, she saw Cuffe climbing into his carriage sporting a face even more ruddy than usual.

Normally, Harry would have joined her in the drawing room to update her on the latest news. On this occasion, he walked briskly past the open door and into the estate office, slamming that door behind him.

"Harry is angry!" Sibella thought. *"Whatever did Cuffe say to him?"*

She decided to let him cool down and discuss the situation after dinner.

Harry remained mostly silent during the evening meal featuring a main dish of roast beef. No matter what conversational tactic Sibella tried, he responded with a grunt or a monosyllable. Even, talking of the glowing progress of their children failed to stir his attention. She decided to be patient. When Harry was in a mood, the best time to talk to him was by the fire late at night with a bottle of brandy to hand.

"I suppose you were trying to persuade Cuffe that next autumn would be a good time for us to marry," Sibella said mischievously.

Harry's face clouded over.

"After what I have heard today," he replied sternly. "There will be no wedding."

"Why not?" Sibella cried angrily.

Harry grasped the poker until his knuckles whitened.

"Because you lied to me."

Sibella paled.

"You have a nerve!" she protested. "You lied to me about your affair with Margaret McDermott when I was pregnant with John."

"Cuffe said you engaged in witchcraft with Judy Holian," Harry retorted. "If that is proven, you could end up in gaol."

Sibella trembled, feeling sick in her stomach.

"Do you believe him?" she demanded. "That unscrupulous man has the morals of a goat as you well know."

Harry lowered his voice.

"Cuffe said you made a spancel using the skin from an exhumed corpse."

Sibella felt the blood rushing to her cheeks.

"What did you expect me to do when you rode off to Westport to seek the hand of Lady Harriett while I was heavily pregnant with George and

Barbara? Had I a cocked pistol in my hand, I would have shot you on your return from your traitorous mission."

"He also said that the corpse was that of my daughter, Ellen Colgan."

"No! Absolutely not," Sibella shouted. "I would never have proceeded with the spancel if the corpse was that of your daughter or indeed of any human corpse."

"Jesu-Maria!" Harry exploded. "You should never have engaged in witchcraft."

Harry threw his tumbler at the fireplace smashing it into smithereens.

Sibella turned to silence. Had he continued to interrogate her, she would have reminded him of his second failed journey to Altamont to ask for the hand of Lady Harriett while she was delivering George and Barbara. How would George and Barbara feel if they ever found out about the scurrilous behaviour that had driven her to desperation?

"How did Cuffe find out?" Harry asked calmly.

"I imagine Ned Holian did it for money," Sibella said. "Nobody else knows."

"How can you be so sure?"

"If Cuffe had spread the word about the spancel, Louisa Moore would have heard of it."

"That slimy trustee!" Harry sipped his brandy having fetched another glass. "He thinks he can boss me around."

Recalling the infamous letter that Harry had concealed from her, Sibella felt like telling him that Cuffe did boss him around. The words of Harry's trustee reverberated in her mind: *"Give her a reasonable, even a liberal, sum and send her, and them, out of the country, the farther away the better."*

Harry poured himself another drink.

"Cuffe was thrilled when he found out about the spancel. He knew he could destroy you with it."

"Why not pull the trigger?"

"Aha!" Harry cried. "The old villain realized that it would also destroy me."

"I'm not so sure, Harry." Sibella chose her words carefully. "I do not trust him."

"Indeed!" Harry snorted.

Sibella drew a deep breath.

"So what now, Sir Harry?" she asked.

Harry poked the fire sending an explosion of sparks up the chimney.

"We have both sinned. We are both angry," he said. "Let us go to bed now. We shall talk again in a while. We must work something out."

When Sibella lay on the pillow that night, her mind was in turmoil. The carefully kept secret of the spancel had been broken. The heinous event had been brought to Cuffe's attention in the expectation of a generous consideration.

Cuffe could now use that sacrilegious episode to persuade Harry to abandon her and, instead, marry Lady Harriett, or some other rich Protestant lady. If Harry agreed, Cuffe would keep the spancel a secret to protect Harry's reputation. If Harry baulked, he would not hesitate to dribble out the information in a way that would destroy her if she were the bride; but that would also destroy Harry.

Thus, Cuffe's mission to rescue an impoverished estate through a financially advantageous marriage would end in failure. Cuffe's ambition to acquire an aristocratic title would suffer with his reputation diminished by a botched negotiation. Encouraged by that morsel of speculation, Sibella turned on to her side to join Harry in a deep sleep.

* * * * *

SIBELLA DECIDED NOT TO raise the issue of marriage again until Harry had time to recover from the shock of the spancel story. Instead, she wrote her widowed foster-mother, Louisa Moore, requesting permission to visit with her five older children. On receipt of a positive response, she travelled on a number of occasions with the children to the home of her childhood at Ashbrook. While Sibella chatted with Louisa, the children played in the garden, rode ponies and browsed in the Moore library. Her two-year-old twins, George and Barbara, remained at home with their nanny.

These visits to Ashbrook eased the pressure of Cuffe's threat from her mind. Regaling Harry with the details of each trip made for easy conversation when they relaxed at eventide. She avoided mention of Cuffe and witch Judy to preclude a renewal of Harry's rage over the spancel. Although Harry's trustee visited from time to time, there were no more angry words suggesting that Harry had confirmed to Cuffe that the marriage was off.

As they drifted into the New Year, Harry's mood improved. Sibella had a feeling that he had recovered from the shock of the spancel, and was ready to grapple with their situation. This time, he would have to take the initiative.

One evening after dinner, Harry opened his heart.

"I have thought long and hard about our situation. As I said before, we have both sinned. I am not going to allow Cuffe to push us around. I still love you with all my heart."

Sibella bit her lip. What would Harry say next?

"We need to put the past behind us and focus on the welfare of our beloved children."

Sibella leaned forward in anticipation.

"My dear heart, how can we do that?"

Harry bent down on one knee.

"Please marry me, Sibella Cottle?"

Sibella felt faint.

"Harry! You have taken my breath away. I feared I would never hear those words again. Of course, I shall marry you."

"We must marry, straight away."

Sibella trembled. The initiative had swung back to her.

"Nothing would please me more, my darling. But —"

"But what?" Harry raised his hands.

"In order to keep Cuffe at bay, we should marry in secret."

"Hem!" Harry opened his eyes wide. "I agree, but how can we do that?"

"You could write Rector Garrood in Suffolk to inform him that the impediment to our marriage has been removed."

"Capital!" Harry smiled. "It would be like eloping for a second time."

"By doing so, you would honour the memory of your one-time Catholic father who married your Protestant mother in England. Rector Garrood had fond memories of the reception that followed their wedding at Belstead."

Sibella paused hoping that Harry would succumb to her wish.

"The terms of their marriage settlement required my late father to conform." Harry ruminated.

"Conformance is no longer necessary in England where mixed marriages have been allowed since 1753," Sibella said. "If we married here, I would have to conform because mixed marriages are illegal. I fear that Cuffe would use his influence to delay or spoil my application for conformance."

Harry replied, "Apart from all that humbug, I would like to revisit the home of my infant days at Belstead."

Sibella was elated.

"It would complete our wedding ceremony so cruelly disrupted at the last minute by that letter from Edmondson."

Harry raised his glass.

"That was twelve years ago, he said. "This time Edmondson will write a letter that shall escort us to paradise."

CHAPTER 13

WHEN HARRY BUSIED HIMSELF with estate matters, Sibella presumed that something was on his mind. His increased drinking, punctuated by spells of coughing, was another sign of his discomfiture. On reflection, she wondered if he wanted to marry at home. She could understand that; it would be more convenient. It would demonstrate that he had matured, and was now ready to settle down "to the more serious duties of life" as Cuffe had advised. Most importantly, it would show that he had at last tamed "that woman" with whom he had lived in sin in the Big House, a practise that had scandalized the local community.

Once again, she busied herself with the children and household chores, waiting for Harry to address whatever bothered him. When he started to spend more time away from home, she wondered if he was casting his eye elsewhere. Having discussed the matter with Louisa Moore, she decided to take the initiative again unless Harry had his own secret plan.

She instructed cook to prepare Harry's favourite dishes for a dinner on a Friday evening: mushroom soup, roast partridge and rhubarb tart to be accompanied by a white Bordeaux.

Harry smiled when he sat at the dining table.

"What have I done to deserve such excellent cuisine?"

"Because you are the Master of Balla House, and the wonderful father of our seven children; after dinner, we should relax by the fire in the drawing room."

"Once I am ready, I shall join you there."

As Sibella retired to the lavatory, she figured that Harry would mellow with brandy and open the door to his latest thinking. Having dashed herself with a perfume of musk, wild rose and mugwort that she had perfected at Ashbrook, she joined him at the fire.

"So, what are you scheming, my dear heart?"

Harry grasped his tumbler of brandy.

"You can read me like a book," he said. "Cuffe has driven me crazy. To deflect him, I lied."

Sibella was intrigued.

"Goodness! What did you say?"

Harry sipped his brandy.

"I thanked him for telling me about the spancel. I told him that my plan to marry you was null and void. I said I must now search for a new bride."

Sibella fingered her snifter of brandy.

"Did he believe you?"

Harry shrugged his shoulders.

"I'm not sure."

Sibella smiled.

"I have a plan too. I was thinking of Sunday service,"

"So boring," Harry groaned. "Uncle Peter insists that I attend to fulfil my social obligations."

Sibella took a sip of the fiery liquor to steady her nerve.

"Would you like me to go with you?"

There, she had said it.

"What?" Harry almost dropped his glass of brandy. "Sir Robuck tried to persuade Lady Lynch to accompany him to service after Mama passed away but she refused point blank."

"If Lady Lynch were still alive, I would not offer to accompany you as it would have broken her heart."

Harry gazed deeply into her eyes.

"What would Louisa Moore think?"

Sibella felt a little guilty of betraying the trust of Doctor Moore and Lady Lynch.

"If Papa were still alive, I would not go either."

"So why go to service?"

Sibella steadied her nerve.

"So you can tell Cuffe that I have decided to conform. You need his advice on this matter. I expect that Cuffe will be happy to make sure, with the help of Altamont, that my application for conformance will be indefinitely delayed or rejected."

"Will you really attend at service?"

"Yes, if it will persuade Cuffe of my determination to marry you. It will spur him into action to oppose my application for conformance."

"Zounds!" Harry exclaimed. "That will really set tongues wagging."

"I would dress conservatively; no rouge or perfume. My posture would be meek and humble. I would gaze into the middle distance to avoid the eyes of the local bumpkins …"

"Local bumpkins!" Harry laughed heartily.

His laughter reminded her of how much he had enjoyed the wickedness of her tongue when first he courted her. Sibella took another sip of brandy.

"Attending service with you will be my declaration of subservience to you."

"Hmm," Harry said. "And then?"

"We shall marry secretly in England having diverted Cuffe off the scent."

Sibella watched for Harry's reaction. When she got it, she thought,

"Methinks I have Harry under my spell again."

"How did I ever fall in love with such a clever woman?" Harry smiled. "Let us take it one step at a time. You shall accompany me to service this Sunday and for at least one Sunday every month thereafter. When I am satisfied that Cuffe is off the track, I shall marry you in England next year."

Sibella was thrilled. She hugged and kissed him

"I love you Harry Lynch-Blosse. Is it time for bed?"

She could tell from his warm embrace that he would join her shortly. Because she was still breastfeeding three years after the birth of the twins, she hoped to be spared from another conception. She prayed to the Lord that he would forsake her of pregnancy until the date of their marriage in England was set.

Having perfumed herself again, she hid herself naked under the blankets until he joined her in bed. The memory of their first romantic interlude after the harvest at Ashbrook came back to flood her mind. Her elation was complete when he gently penetrated her; she was now on the brink of realizing her dream.

* * * * *

NOW THAT HARRY HAD agreed to marry her in England, Sibella relaxed to enjoy his company and that of her seven children, now aged from four to fourteen years. Their eldest son, Michael, attended the George Ralph academy in Castlebar. Her remaining children stayed at home under her guidance and tuition, assisted by the governess and their groom. Among them, Michael and Cecilia stood out: Michael for his blond hair, and Cecilia, who fascinated both her mother and governess with her hunger for knowledge.

Harry's health was now a source of increasing concern. Sibella realized that he had lost his energy and lust for life. He suffered from a bloody cough and occasional fever caused by a lung infection. This wasting sickness was known as consumption because it consumed people from within.

Sibella's face was creased with worry when she told him,

"Harry, there is no cure for your sickness, according to Doctor Boyd. He wants you to rest, reduce your work and abstain from wine and spirits."

"It sounds like a death sentence," Harry said, coughing once again.

"Please do not speak so! There must be some physic to treat it. Your hands shake so much, my dear."

Harry laid his hands on the table and steadied them with downward pressure.

"My hands are not shaking are they? My chest is the main problem. Maybe we could try some more magic?" He looked at her, smiling. "Cuffe said that you had spellbound me."

"Harry! That was done to stop you misbehaving."

"By binding us together?"

Sibella dropped her embroidery hoop into her lap.

"What are you talking about?"

"If we were bound together by a spell, you could transfer your good health into my body and banish my bad health."

"And where would your bad health end up?"

They both laughed and then fell silent.

After a while, Harry said,

"Why not have a word with the old witch herself, if only for a bit of devilment? Once she has cured me, we shall marry in England."

"I shall do that, my darling. If the doctor has no cure, no harm can come from asking her."

A week later, Sibella called on Judy with a consignment of food and drink. She was aghast at the state of the cabin. Judy had aged. Her unkempt clothes suggested a loss of interest in grooming herself. Her two sons, Ned and Thady, were even more ragged. Their puckered brows evinced the resentment of the dispossessed in an unjust society.

"M'lady, we haven't seen you in a while," Judy said.

"I have been so busy with the children and all the events in our lives."

"What events would those be?" Judy growled.

"The children growing up; Lady Harriett and the like."

"Sure that was three years ago. As for the Browne bitch, I was happy that Sir Harry gave her the boot. I hear she does her huntin' elsewhere these days."

Sibella sat down on a bare wooden chair.

"She's not as bad as all that, although I am surely glad to see the back of her."

Ned and Thady took their leave while Judy prepared the tea.

"How is Sir Harry?"

"Not the best, Judy. He is coughing up blood and he has the shakes."

"The shakes can be cured by givin' up the drink. The chesty cough is another matter. What has the clever doctor to say about it?"

"He thinks it may be consumption, but there is no cure for it, he says."

"Does he now?" Judy replied. "Well, maybe there's none, but then again, maybe there is!"

Sibella sat up straight.

"Do you know of one?"

"Well, maybe I do and maybe not, m'lady."

"Go on, Judy; what are you trying to say?"

"You know that any person can suffer from nightmares, but especially the sick. In the imagination of a sick person, the little people may persuade them to attend fairy parties at night. The poor invalid is so exhausted that he begins to waste away from the lack of proper rest and sleep."

Sibella raised her eyebrows

"Do you believe that?"

"Well, I do and I don't," Judy replied. "I have also heard that a person can be hag-ridden, changed into a horse by a witch, and forced to attend nightly meetings with the same result."

Sibella directed her gaze at the midwife who had served her well.

"Well, I do declare! But what about a cure?"

"I have heard it said that consumption can be picked up from a recently deceased relative who had the disease, and that the disease is transmitted from the grave to a close relative. The body in the grave acts like a vampire and sucks blood out of the victim, and that is the reason for the bloody cough."

As Sibella listened to these amazing tales, she remembered that Harry's daughter, Ellen Colgan, had died from consumption.

"What about young Ellen?"

"I was thinkin' the same myself. They say the only way to stop the vampire is to exhume the corpse and burn the blood-filled heart or even the whole body."

Sibella felt sick.

"So six years ago, when young Ellen was exhumed, she should have been burned rather than have a spancel made from her skin!"

Sibella was so upset that she had to excuse herself and go home. Her stomach churned at the thought of the ghoulish nature of the exhumation and desecration of the body of the young girl.

"*How could I ever have become involved in that sacrilegious madness?*" she wondered.

More urgently, the gravity of her situation was now clear. If Harry failed to recover, they would have to marry at home. She would swallow her pride and conform for the sake of the children. But how could she do that without alerting Cuffe to her action for he would surely oppose her application?

* * * * *

HARRY'S CONDITION CONTINUED TO decline as the months slipped by. He now spent most of the day in bed. During this time, Sibella decided to visit Ashbrook again and sent a message to Louisa Moore suggesting a date. On receipt of a positive response, Sibella decided to bring only Michael and Cecilia with her, because she needed more time with her mother. She mitigated the disappointment of her younger children by promising them a surprise visit in the near future.

The youthful excitement of blond Michael and auburn Cecilia gave pleasure to Sibella as they set out for Ashbrook. Bernard Moran drove the carriage on a fine, dry, crisp day in the autumn of that year. Sibella inveigled Bernard into supervising riding lessons for the children on the Moore ponies with the help of Packie Burke. Now, she sat alone in the drawing room with Louisa enjoying some ale and cake. After exchanging pleasantries, Sibella came straight to the point.

"Harry is not in the best of health."

"Oh dear; what is the matter with him?" Louisa frowned.

"Doctor Boyd says it's a wasting disease."

"Consumption?" Louisa's sombre tone reflected her concern.

Sibella pursed her lips.

"I fear so."

"Please God, he will recover from it."

Sibella paced around the neat and tidy drawing room.

"He is losing weight and coughing up blood. He also has tremors."

"You must be sick with worry. What will you do if, God forbid, the worst comes to the worst?"

"That is what bothers me. Harry will make provision for us in his will."

"Will you be able to stay on at Balla House?"

"Yes, but only if he marries me." Sibella paused and her eyes began to fill with tears. "If he does not marry me, his family would expect us to move away."

Sibella broke down at this stage as the enormity of the challenge facing her came into sharp relief. Suddenly, she felt the warm embrace of her foster-mother.

"You will survive this challenge, my brave daughter," Louisa said.

Sibella knew she would be welcome at Ashbrook on a temporary basis. It would not be fair to expect a longer-term accommodation. How could a grieving widow accommodate so many young children?

On the long road back to Balla, Sibella was relieved that the children were in high spirits. Michael and Cecilia told her how much they had enjoyed the visit to Ashbrook and the pony riding. Passing through Castlebar was a special treat. Sibella listened to their excited chatter as they responded to the sights and sounds of the county town. She pointed out places of interest including Lord Lucan's cricket pitch as well as the gallows where troublemakers departed to meet their Maker. The eyes of her children opened wide.

As the carriage trundled along the hedge-lined roadway, Sibella was deep in thought. They could stay on at Balla for a while until she found a new home. Accommodation with Louisa Moore at Ashbrook or with the Lynches of Clogher was the most likely possibility. At least she had some pleasant options, while other women in her position often had none. As Balla House loomed into sight, she banished these morose thoughts from her mind and looked forward to enjoying the reunion of the family. She relaxed as Michael and Cecilia regaled their father and siblings with the stories of the day.

As winter set in, Sibella chose to spend Christmas quietly. The children left out a jug of milk and a loaf of bread for Father Christmas in case he was famished. On Christmas Eve, Sibella sang the first verse of a carol from Wexford before the children went to bed:

The darkest midnight in December
No snow, nor hail, nor winter storm
Shall hinder us for to remember
The night that on, this babe was born.

Sibella invited Uncle Peter, still a bachelor, and Louisa Moore to join her family on the festive day. Holly and mistletoe decorated the dining room. After a Christmas dinner of boiled goose and baked ham, Harry retired to bed. Peter wandered off to walk in the snow. After eating their Christmas pies, the children went out to hurl snowballs.

"That was a delicious dinner, Sibella," Louisa told her. "I've been thinking. Should your position here become untenable, you may return to Ashbrook with the children."

Sibella was speechless with gratitude. She could now face the immediate future with greater confidence.

"Thank you so much, Mama. I will need to talk to the children and to Uncle Peter. Peter has been so good to me. I think he knows my days here are numbered."

Louisa relaxed in quiet satisfaction.

"I understand, Sibella. Take all the time you need."

"I am worried about the children. They are full of mischief. They will tear your lovely home to pieces."

Sibella paused and clasped her hands before going on.

"Anyway, how could you afford the expense of eight extra people at Ashbrook?"

Louisa now raised her voice.

"Sibella, my dear, you are my foster-daughter. I would love to have your brood as my foster-grandchildren. I greatly miss the warmth and energy of youth. As for the money, we will get by if everyone pulls their weight."

"Even if we do not marry, Harry has promised to secure our future in his will." Sibella frowned as she recalled the threat involved therein. "Although, I am worried that his bequests will be challenged by the trustees."

"Peter Lynch is a good man and highly respected. He will look after your interests."

Louisa's support and generosity overwhelmed Sibella. A tear of joy trickled down her cheek. She relaxed with her foster-mother in front of a crackling fire with another round of port.

* * * * *

IN THE NEW YEAR, Harry spent even more time in bed. He wondered if the children knew he might not recover in spite of the best efforts of Doctor Boyd. Their daily visits were a source of joy to him, though he missed Michael, who was boarding in Castlebar. When the children recited their little stories, he responded with stories of his own. He loved them so much.

"Sibella, I am still anxious for you and the children," Harry said. "Once I recover, I shall marry you." Harry's voice quivered as his energy and strength ebbed. "Should I fail to recover, I have instructed Uncle Peter to look after you and the children. In the meantime, I must apply to

Archbishop Bourke for a special licence that will allow us to marry, even if you have not conformed.

"Do not worry, my dear," Sibella wept. "Should your application fail, Louisa Moore has offered us accommodation at Ashbrook."

"Excellent! Uncle Peter has agreed to look after the education and careers of the boys."

Harry felt like crying too as he slowly raised himself up in the bed. He had failed his family.

"I will look after the education and training of the girls, with the help of Louisa," Sibella assured him.

"Should anything go wrong at Ashbrook, Pat Lynch of Clogher has agreed to provide assistance."

With their immediate future secured, Harry could lie back and make the most of his last days with Sibella and the children. Apart from making a will, his only immediate problem was the pain of his condition. This he relieved with laudanum. Strict instructions demanded sparing use, but he liked to feel comfortable, and was inclined to use more than he should.

Harry also decided to make peace with those who may have been hurt by his actions or the actions of his relatives. Three women were the offspring of one of the Lynches: namely Kate Moran, Bridget Garvey and Anne Bourke. All were employed in the Big House. Each would receive an annuity of fifty pounds for the rest of their natural lives after he passed away.

Harry had fathered Catherine by Margaret McDermott, also a servant in the Big House. She would receive an annual provision of fifty pounds.

The most difficult case was that of the late Ellen Colgan whom he had also fathered. Cuffe had insisted that Judy Holian had arranged her exhumation to make a spancel for Sibella. That would have shattered the Colgan family had they learnt of it.

"Sibella, could you please invite Mr Colgan to visit."

"Of course!"

Harry was not surprised when Sibella said on her return, "A frosty reception greeted me. I said you would appreciate a visit from a member of the family. The Colgans reluctantly agreed."

A few days later, Ellen's grandfather came to the Big House.

Harry coughed.

"I hope you and your family are keeping well, Mr Colgan."

Old man Colgan looked uncomfortable in the grandiose surroundings of the master's bedroom. He kept his silence and declined the offer of a chair.

Harry raised his hands.

"I was so upset when I heard of the exhumation of your granddaughter, Ellen. I still feel guilty because of my liaison with Ellen's mother, Sally. My behaviour was unacceptable. I hope I can make my peace with you."

Standing tall, old man Colgan said,

"My family was ripped apart by your affair with my daughter and by the desecration of the body of my granddaughter Ellen. I know you are seriously ill, Sir Harry. I am sorry, but I cannot find forgiveness for you. Our wish for your lady and the Holians is that they will roast in hell!"

Harry watched him storm out of the room.

After he departed, Sibella said,

"I have never seen a man so angry."

Harry adjusted his pillow.

"I did my best." He sighed. "We have started a healing process. The Colgans will recover in time."

Sibella shook her head.

"I hope they will not contemplate revenge."

"We should have apologized before," Harry said, almost consumed by a bout of coughing.

"Better late than never."

"I want to make some provision for the Colgans in my will, but with Ellen dead, I am not sure what I can do."

Sibella adjusted his bedcovers and made him more comfortable. Harry felt that he had done as much as he could to determine the proper provision for his loved ones; these provisions now needed incorporation into a will. He wished also to prepare himself to meet his Maker, if such existed, or he could end up in hell. He felt he could escape that fate by expressing remorse for his many sins. Then he would rejoin his mother, Elizabeth, Sir Robuck and Lady Lynch and patiently await his beloved Sibella and their seven children.

CHAPTER 14

Harry RESTED IN BED, having read Sibella's transcription of his inheritance bequests. He expected her to be furious since he had looked after everyone apart from her. When Sibella entered, he asked hesitatingly,

"Are you happy with my bequests?"

"No! Not at all, Harry," she said. "I shall let you talk with Peter first and discuss the issue later."

Harry knew that, although not an attorney, Peter Lynch, was a sensible and experienced man. Inheritance issues were his forte since he had acted as executor of the will of Harry's grandfather, the fifth Baronet.

When Peter arrived, Harry struggled to sit up in the four-poster bed.

"Will you stay awhile, Sibella?"

"I had best be off about my work," Sibella replied, rearranging his blankets.

"Thank you, my dear heart. I need some laudanum before you leave."

Harry enjoyed the nutmeg scent of the reddish-brown liquid as Sibella eased a spoonful through his quivering lips. Its bitter taste made him grimace but its efficacy in killing pain was indisputable.

When Sibella departed, Harry was relieved because both men could talk more openly in her absence.

"Peter, I need your advice in finalizing my will. It would be more straightforward if Sibella and I were married."

"Sibella would have to conform first," Peter said.

"So, if Sibella were to conform, I could marry," Harry said.

"Even if she did not conform, a special license could be procured from the diocese," Peter said.

Harry clenched his fists. He was aware of this but had preferred Sibella's option of a secret wedding in Suffolk. Now that he was unable to travel, he would have to marry at home as soon as possible. By marrying Sibella, his seven wonderful children would be spared the worst aspects of the stigma of illegitimacy. If he failed to do that, it would hurt him deeply.

"How could I have been so stupid in my womanizing exploits?" he wondered.

The thoughts bothered him but he pushed them away. He would now do the best he could for his loved ones.

"Some people would have Sibella and the children out on the road," Harry said. "That is why I must make provision for her and the children in my will."

"That is an admirable thought." Peter sat down by the bedside.

"You have read my mind," Harry said. "I will need your support when I sign my will next week."

"I shall do my best." Peter nodded.

"I have dictated my requirements to Sibella. Will you cast your eye over them?" Harry drew a crumpled paper from under the pillow.

Peter glanced at the requirements. Harry saw his brow furrow.

"Is there a problem?"

"I expect your trustees will object to two items. They will say the legacies to your children are far too generous —"

Harry interjected.

"You can tell that reprobate, Cuffe, I shall stand by my children, to the sword-point if necessary."

"You certainly frightened him at the funeral of Lady Lynch." Peter smiled. "However, your proposal in relation to Sibella is more problematic."

"I want to provide her with a roof over her head."

Peter gently shook his head.

"Legally, that is not possible, because you have willed the house to me and the estate to Robert, your heir apparent; unless …"

"Unless what?"

"Unless you marry her," Peter said.

Harry sighed.

"Let me try one more time, and if I fail to obtain a special license, what then?"

"The trustees are likely to ask me to look after the estate until Robert reaches his majority in seventeen years. In that event, Sibella and the children will be welcome to stay in the house because I will be the only other family member in residence. I would be lonely without them given that Robert and his family reside in Cardiff."

"Thank you, Peter. I am too exhausted to discuss the matter further."

Harry leaned back on the high pillows.

"I shall ask Andrew Edmondson to draw up a draft of the will incorporating your wishes." Peter rolled up the crumpled paper.

"May God bless you; now, I must rest."

Harry slid down under the blankets.

As Peter departed, he said, "I will be here next week to attend the signing of the will. Be careful with the laudanum, hmm. I think it should be used more sparingly."

* * * * *

WHEN HARRY AWOKE LATER that evening, he found Sibella sitting by the bed.

"How are you feeling?" she asked.

"Much better, at first, because I dreamt that we had married. I could see you as the lady of the manor, one of the most powerful women in Mayo. I was so disappointed when I woke up."

"That is a lovely thought," Sibella said.

"How are the children?"

"The boys are out gallivanting. The girls would love to hear a story if you are up to it."

"Send the rascals in."

The four girls, Cecilia, Mary Anne, Bridget and Barbara, rushed in after receiving permission. "Hello, Papa; how do you do today?" asked Cecilia, the thirteen-year-old twin, who was inclined to do most of the talking.

Harry struggled to sit up in bed.

"Much better, girls."

"Will you tell us a story?"

"I shall tell you how your forefathers, the Lynches, came to Galway."

The girls gathered around the bed.

"It was a very long time ago that Dermot MacMurrough was the king of Leinster. He got himself into big trouble and his enemies drove him out of Ireland. King Dermot was not pleased about this and travelled to England. He asked for help there but King Henry was too busy with other matters." Harry coughed.

"Busy with what, Papa?" Cecilia asked.

"Henry was also king of Scotland, Wales and part of France. He was a very busy man. He wrote a letter asking his subjects to help Dermot, after which Dermot met a man called Strongbow in Wales."

"Why was he called Strongbow?" Cecilia gasped with excitement.

His daughter's fascination with history pleased Harry.

"Strongbow was a great man with the bow and arrow. He had reddish hair and freckles just like your Mama. He raised an army and invaded Ireland. First, he captured Wexford and Waterford, and then he marched on Dublin."

"But what about the Lynches?" asked five-year-old Barbara as she crawled across the bottom of the bed.

Harry smiled.

"General Andrew Lynch was one of the invaders. King Henry gave him a big estate in Meath."

"What about Galway?" little Barbara wondered.

"Hold your whist!" Harry coughed again as the older girls laughed. "Some of the later Lynches settled in Galway. Thomas Lynch was made mayor of Galway more than five hundred years ago."

Sibella entered.

"Now, girls, I think it is time to let Papa rest. He can finish the story tomorrow when he is feeling better ..."

"With the help of God," Barbara said, descending headfirst off the bed.

Harry smiled.

"Let me finish this part of the story. All the Lynches of Galway and Mayo are descended from Thomas Lynch, the mayor of Galway. Mayor Thomas is my great-great-great-great-great-great-great-great-great-great-great-great-great-great-grandfather. How many 'greats' is that?"

The girls laughed.

"Say it again, Papa."

Harry took a deep breath. His hands were trembling as he repeated the refrain.

"I think it is fourteen," Cecilia said as she caressed the plait of her auburn hair.

"Well done, Cecilia."

Sibella gently intruded again.

"Very well, girls, time to go."

"Goodnight, Papa."

The girls bumped into their eldest brother, Michael, at the bedroom door.

Harry was amused when blond Michael teased his sisters.

"Were you bored again tonight?"

"No, you silly goose! Did you know that Thomas Lynch from Galway is Papa's great-great-great-great-great-great-great-great-great-great-great-great-great-great-grandfather. How many 'greats' is that?"

"I neither know nor care."

"It is fourteen greats, *amadán mór*!" Cecilia laughed. "You big fool!"

Harry enjoyed the bantering and was thrilled with the progress of the children he loved so much. He was determined that they should know as much as possible about their family background to prepare them for the future. Under no circumstances would he allow the trustees to badger him into reducing their legacies.

* * * * *

THE FOLLOWING WEEK, PETER arrived with a draft of the will prepared by Andrew Edmondson.

"Peter is waiting for you," Sibella said as Harry finished his boiled egg.

Peter sat down holding a rolled-up parchment in his hand.

"How are you today, hmm?"

"Well enough to see the day through, God willing." Harry clutched his chest and grimaced. "I could do with a wee drop of laudanum, my dear."

Sibella fetched the bottle with the reddish-brown liquid.

"You may have a teaspoonful. The dose is to be repeated no more than three times a day."

Harry struggled to sit up as Sibella eased the medicine through his lips.

Peter rustled with the paper in his hand.

"Shall I read it out?"

Harry nodded as Sibella took her leave.

"I will go through it paragraph by paragraph; first, the title and opening paragraph."

Peter read it out slowly.

Copy of the Will and Codicil of Sir Henry Lynch-Blosse, Bart.,
of Balla, Co. Mayo.
All my lawful debts being first paid, I bequeath to my eldest son
Michael Henry Lynch by Sibella Cottle the sum of £10,000 sterling;
to my second son John … £4000; to my third son George … £2000;
to my eldest daughter Cecilia Lynch … £1000;
to my second daughter Mary Anne … £1000;
to my third daughter Bridget … £600;
to my fourth daughter Barbara … an annuity of £200 …

"Splendid!" Harry coughed again, raising a shaky hand to his mouth.

"I wondered about the annuity to Barbara," Peter said.

"I thought she was too young to be bequeathed a dowry like her older sisters."

"Hmm." Peter unrolled the lower part of the parchment.

"Read on Peter." Harry squirmed in the bed to find a more comfortable posture.

"You make provision for annuities of fifty pounds to Kate Moran otherwise Lynch, to Bridget Garvey otherwise Lynch, and to your daughter, Catherine Lynch by Margaret McDermott."

"Very good, Peter. We must look after those women who have been loyal servants of the family. Kate Moran has been with us for years. She will help with the refreshments during the day."

Peter raised his eyes and looked at his nephew.

"Some people will say you are far too generous."

"Maybe so," Harry paused and then changed tack. "We are not certain of Kate's parentage. Many believe …"

"Believe what, Harry?" Peter looked perplexed.

Harry whispered. "Her father may have been Sir Robuck, may the Lord have mercy on his soul!" Harry now drew Peter closer to him. "And the same applies to Bridget Garvey."

"You cannot be sure that is true."

Harry was too diplomatic to repeat the suspicion that Peter had fathered one or more of these women. He paused to recover his energy.

"There is no doubt about Catherine Lynch. She is my daughter by Margaret McDermott. I am duty bound to make provision for her."

Peter cleared his throat and proceeded:

To my uncle Peter Lynch … I bequeath the house and my part
of the demesne of Balla House, my carriage and horses …;
the rest of the stock and household furniture I bequeath
to the said Sibella Cottle…
I devise all my estate in Ireland to the Hon. James Cuffe of Castlegore,
Co. Mayo, and to Robert Dillon of Clonbrock, Co. Galway, Esq…
to hold for … the use of my nephew Robert Lynch-Blosse for life…

Harry cleared his throat. "My late father appointed trustees who would command the respect of the community and the bankers. That is why he selected James Cuffe and Robert Dillon. I am furious that my eldest son, Michael, cannot inherit the title and that it and the estate must go to my nephew, Robert."

Peter nodded. "I think the final paragraph is straightforward."

I have entered into a bond … for £60,000 …
to the said James Cuffe and Robert Dillon,

to secure the payment of the legacies to my sons and daughters …
Henry L. Blosse. 18 February, 1788 …

"That is a fine piece of work," Harry said. "I shall take a nap now and prepare myself for the signing of the will."

Peter left the draft will with Harry and departed.

As he left, Sibella entered.

"Well, my darling, are you content with the draft of your will?"

"Indeed, my dear heart. There may be some revision required. You might cast your eyes over it."

"I surely will," Sibella said.

CHAPTER 15

HARRY STIRRED IN BED after Sibella had opened the shutters. He shielded his eyes from the sunlight.

"I have been dreaming of my ancestors —"

"Not Henry the third again?" Sibella interjected.

"The very man!" Harry adjusted his nightcap. The adventures of Henry Lynch, 3rd Baronet, had always fascinated him. "The bold Henry was attainted of high treason. Now here am I, Henry the seventh, attainted of bad behaviour!"

A bout of chesty coughing smothered his attempted laugh.

"Dream on, my dear," Sibella said.

He felt the warmth of her hand on his forehead.

"I need another drop of — "

"What did Doctor Boyd say, Henry the seventh?"

"In moderation," Harry smiled.

"Exactly, my dear heart."

She fetched the bottle of laudanum from behind the wooden shutter near the bed.

"I shall settle for a small *spoonóg*." Doctor Boyd would be furious with him, but a small comfort would do no great harm.

"The boys would love to see you."

When Harry felt better, he summoned the boys by ringing a hand bell. Michael, John and George trooped into the room. Michael was on leave from school because of his father's illness. He sat by the bed with John while five-year-old George climbed upon the end of the bed.

"Good morning, Papa," said blond-haired Michael.

Harry was pleased with the confidence of his eldest child, now fourteen, who had settled satisfactorily away from home.

"Are you enjoying your break from school?"

"Yes, Papa, I hope it lasts for a long time."

"You want to steer clear of Master Ralph and his fine academy?"

Harry smiled as he gently teased Michael.

"Not really, I like it there," Michael replied happily.

"Capital, my boy. Your education is important. Would John and George like it there, too?"

"I think so. Master Ralph is strict, but he is a fair man," Michael said. "The boys in my class are fine companions."

"Good!"

119

Harry paused and the boys were silent. He suspected that Sibella had warned them not to keep him too long in conversation.

"I wanted to tell you about Henry the third, the father of — "

" — Robert the fourth, the father of Henry the fifth, the father of Robuck the sixth who was my grandfather," Michael interjected, with a smile as charming as that of his mother.

"Exactly! Henry the third was a lawyer who lived in a castle in Galway. He spent a lot of time in Dublin and London. He was appointed Baron of the Exchequer by King James."

"Like a minister of finance?" Michael suggested as his green eyes lit up.

"The Baron of the Exchequer was a judge," Harry said. "He had to settle arguments about money, and ensure that the King received all the taxes due to him."

Young George was fidgeting with the blanket at the end of the bed.

"So he was an important man?"

"He was indeed, but all that was to change."

"What happened?" Michael asked.

"King James started life as a Protestant but became a Catholic when living in Paris. After the death of his Protestant brother, King Charles, James became the last Catholic King of England, Scotland and Ireland, but Protestant England was unhappy with a Catholic King."

"Why were they unhappy?" Michael inquired. "After all, I am a Protestant like John and George, and the girls are Catholic. We are as happy as could be."

"That is a story for another day." Harry held a white handkerchief to his mouth to stifle a cough with his shaky hand. "Poor James was kicked out. His Protestant daughter, Mary, and her Protestant husband, William of Orange, replaced him. James was not happy, and neither were the Catholics of Ireland including Henry the third, your — "

" — great-great-great-grandfather!" the boys interjected in unison.

"So James went back to France to get help. With the support of King Louis, he landed at Kinsale with six thousand French troops armed with swords, bayonets, muskets, pistols and cannon. The Irish Parliament supported James. They wanted to grant religious freedom to all the people of Ireland. However, the Protestants of Ulster supported William of Orange, known to them as King Billy. King Billy defeated King James at the Battle of the Boyne. The following year he marched west and faced the army of James at Aughrim."

Michael's eyes sparkled.

"Tell us about the Battle of Aughrim, Papa."

"King James had an army of 18,000 Irish and French soldiers commanded by St Ruth." Harry smiled, pleased with the undivided attention. "St Ruth landed at Limerick with a fleet, bringing with him arms, clothes and plenty of oats, meal, biscuits, wine and brandy."

Harry paused to catch his breath.

"They were supported by the people of Connaught, including our Henry. King Billy had an army of 20,000 soldiers. They came from the north of Ireland, Holland, Britain and Denmark. Ginkel from Holland was their commander. Ginkel easily captured Athlone, the gateway to the west, because St Ruth was entertaining a lady at that time."

"What strange names they have, Papa!" Michael said as his brothers laughed.

"Strange names indeed, but stranger still was the deciding factor of the battle."

Harry paused to regain sufficient energy to finish the story. He enjoyed the look of rapt attention on the faces of his boys as their eyes shone bright. "At the start, our smaller army was winning and St Ruth declared:

Le jour est à nous, mes enfants.
(The day is our own, my boys.)"

"That is French, Papa?" Michael interjected. "We are learning French with Master Ralph."

Harry nodded.

"Then disaster struck. A cannonball knocked St Ruth's head clean off his shoulders. Having lost their commander, the army of King James fell apart. King Billy moved in quickly and won the day."

"That must have been a mighty battle," Michael said.

"It was the bloodiest battle ever fought in Ireland. Seven thousand soldiers lost their lives. Our Henry accompanied King James to France. He was charged with high treason by King Billy."

"Was he captured, Papa?" Michael asked excitedly.

"No!" replied the yawning Harry. "That is why he never came home. He remained in Brest in the north of France with his twin sons, only two years old; although his eldest son remained in Ireland and became the fourth baronet."

"I think that twins must be a family tradition," Michael said.

"I am a twin," George said proudly as he tried to climb a bedpost.

"Whatever happened to them?" Michael asked.

"That is a mystery. Henry died some years afterwards and was buried there. Maybe the twins settled in Brest or went to Bordeaux to make wine. You will have to solve that mystery on your travels."

Harry was exhausted but pleased that the boys had enjoyed the story. They would know how to answer if anyone called their great-great-great-grandfather a traitor. They might also be inspired to follow a career in the army, something that he needed to discuss with Sibella and Uncle Peter.

* * * * *

AT THAT STAGE, SIBELLA returned.

"Now, boys, your Papa needs to rest."

The boys protested, wanting to hear more tales, but Sibella stood firm. She needed to talk to Harry in private.

After she had rearranged his pillows, Harry asked

"Are you happy with the will, my dear?"

"I am delighted with the generous legacies for the children." Sibella raised her voice. "I am not happy with my provision — "

Harry interjected.

"I understand, my dear heart, but it was the best I could do. I had to leave the house to Uncle Peter."

"Why?" Sibella clenched her fists as she thought about her paltry provision of some stock and furniture.

"I was obliged to do so on foot of a prior commitment by my father to his brother unless I had married." Harry paused. "Peter will allow you and the children to remain in Balla House as long as you like."

Sibella saw the tears welling in Harry's eyes. She felt like saying that he could have done better but was conscious of his frailty.

"Very well, Harry. I know you did your best. You must rest now."

She kissed him on the forehead and departed. Harry needed to focus on the signing of the will in the afternoon. He would be under pressure to disinherit the children.

Sibella checked to see how Andrew Edmondson was proceeding in the library. She found him busy with his quill as he concluded the drafting of the will.

On the afternoon of 18 February 1788, the remaining guests arrived including James Cuffe and Robert Dillon as well as the witnesses. Harry's uncle, Peter Lynch, and his cousin, Pat Lynch of Clogher, were also present.

Sibella instructed Harry's cousin, Kate Moran, to supervise the serving of tea and buns in the living room.

After the guests had settled, Kate said,

"Harry begged me for some laudanum later in the morning. I could not refuse him."

Sibella gritted her teeth.

"You should have called me."

Kate turned on her heel and walked out. There was no love lost between these two women of Balla House. There was an air of mystery about Kate, referred to as "Catherine Moran otherwise Lynch" in Harry's will. Thus, her father was a Lynch, but which one, Sibella wondered.

* * * * *

MEANWHILE, THE GUESTS WERE engaged in robust conversation in the dining room. After Kate departed, Sibella lingered in the anteroom straining to hear the exchanges.

She overheard Cuffe saying he was unhappy with the will. He objected to the generous legacies to Harry's seven illegitimate children by Miss Cottle. Sibella had to restrain herself from entering the fray and verbally attacking the sly old fox. How dare he describe her children as illegitimate? She now understood why Edmondson had named the children "Lynch" rather than "Lynch-Blosse" in the will. In fairness to Harry, a Lynch rather than a Cottle surname would better serve the children.

Sibella composed herself and heard Edmondson insisting that the provisions in the will were the stated requests transmitted to Peter Lynch and confirmed by him. She heard Peter asking if there was a problem, to which Cuffe replied that it was all about money.

"*Is it not always about money?*" she thought.

Cuffe then said that a substantial mortgage accrued to Harry's estate. He and Dillon would have to raise £60,000 to pay for the generous bequests in the will. Dillon wondered if the money was there.

Sibella was now beside herself with excitement. In the silent interlude that followed Dillon's query, she remained motionless so that the conspirators would not detect her presence. She felt a sudden tickling sensation in her nose, just barely controlled by clasping her nostrils. Without surprise, she heard Cuffe say that if Harry had married Lady Harriett, her substantial dowry would have eased the level of debt on the estate.

She was amused when Dillon suggested other ways of relieving the problem such as raising the rents. Cuffe said that such action would encourage the Whiteboys and start a revolution! This time, Sibella did not have to suppress a laugh as the meeting exploded into jollification in response to the exchange.

"So this is what the men actually do at their ever-so-important meetings," Sibella smiled to herself ruefully.

When Dillon suggested selling off some of the 20,000 acres, Cuffe wondered how Sir Harry's heir would react to that on reaching his majority. Peter Lynch reminded those present that Harry's heir, young Robert, was only four years old; the trustees would have to serve for another seventeen years.

Sibella felt like shouting,

"If my Michael inherited, the trustees would have to wait only seven years before he reached his majority!"

The meeting now disintegrated into meaningless gossip. Sibella left the anteroom to check if Harry was ready. On confirming his readiness, she then re-entered having knocked loudly.

"Sir Harry Lynch-Blosse is ready to sign at your convenience, gentlemen."

Sibella stood her ground without flinching as Cuffe stared long and hard at her.

After he nodded, Sibella said,

"Please follow me, gentlemen."

As the visiting party entered the bedroom, Sibella noted how visibly shocked they were at Harry's condition, a young man of thirty-eight. She and Kate helped Harry sit up.

"You are welcome, gentlemen, although I cannot imagine why you are here!" Harry smiled.

"It's great to see you in such good form, Sir Harry, my boy." Cuffe held the will in his right hand. "We are under strict orders not to detain you too long."

"You can stay as long as you wish, although I might drift off." Harry yawned.

"Are you in agreement with the will prepared by Edmondson?" Cuffe asked.

"Andrew has fulfilled his task admirably. I must, however, add a small bequest which Sibella brought to my attention."

The colour of the ruddy cheeks of Cuffe flared at the mention of Sibella's name.

"I wish to add 'to Ann Bourke otherwise Lynch, an annuity of £50 for life'."

"That is fine, Sir Harry," Cuffe said.

Sibella was amused that the trustees hardly raised an eyebrow at the addition of another illegitimate child.

"I can prepare a codicil to that effect," Edmondson said.

"We should ask Harry to sign the will first and get it witnessed." Cuffe's cheeks had recovered their natural colour.

Harry signed the will.

"God bless you, Sir Harry," Cuffe said. "We shall now leave you in peace."

Sibella heaved a sigh of relief. She was pleased that the ordeal was over. Harry had done his best for the children. Her bequest of some stock and furniture was the best he could manage for her, she presumed.

"Dreaming again, Sir Harry?" Sibella smiled.

"I was dreaming that we got married at the last minute," Harry said. "What a furore that would have caused to perfectly complement our stormy relationship!"

Sibella kissed his cheek.

"I love you, Harry Lynch-Blosse. I will let you sleep and do some real dreaming."

She waited while Harry drifted off.

Was he still smarting over the Colgan affair and the spancel? Was he afraid of roasting in hell? Notwithstanding her disappointment with his will, she was determined that Harry would enjoy the pleasurable company of his family while he prepared for the inevitable.

CHAPTER 16

HARRY'S HUNGER FOR FOOD had diminished so much that he had barely touched his breakfast.

After Sibella removed his tray, she said,

"The girls are waiting for you, my dear."

"I have something for you, my darling," Harry said. "Put your hand under the pillow."

Harry saw her eyes light up after a quick scan of the three documents. Tears welled in her eyes as she kissed him.

"I am now the proud holder of three notes for five hundred pounds each, payable to Sibella Cottle. You are a darling. I love you, Harry Lynch-Blosse."

"I love you too, Sibella. And I have a confession to make."

"You will have to wait for the vicar."

Harry ignored the playful jest.

"I want to clear my conscience. You remember the time when George and Barbara were born. I was on my way to Westport to talk to Altamont. I stopped at the inn at Belcarra for a snifter of brandy. Afterwards, my gelding refused to ride forward and I was forced to return home."

"Why did you want to speak to Altamont?"

"I was still upset about the spancel and its link to my daughter, Ellen. In despair, I thought of marrying Lady Harriett. I am ashamed to admit it. Please do not tell the children. I am glad the horse stopped, though I have never understood why. Perhaps it was the curse of the Colgans."

Harry noticed the redness blooming in Sibella's cheeks. He wondered if she had secretly applied the spancel to him. He would understand it, if she had, given his behaviour to her.

"It is of no significance now, Harry. I forgive you. You have looked after the children and me. We all make mistakes; we all have our little secrets."

He noticed Lady Lynch's brooch nestling on her bosom and saw her fingering the silver locket hanging from her neck.

"I have placed your wedding band in your mother's silver casket. It should go to our first daughter to marry for her husband. The key to the casket is in my locket. I shall wear it until I die."

She kissed him and then sat down beside him.

After a while Harry said,

"You can let the girls in now."

As the girls entered, five-year-old Barbara said,

"Papa, you didn't finish your porridge!"

Her sisters tried to stifle their laughter.

"Please behave yourselves." Sibella frowned.

Harry enjoyed bantering with his girls.

"Plenty of time for porridge," he said.

"What will you tell us today, Papa?" asked Cecilia, now thirteen.

"Your Mama shall tell you about the letters."

Sibella walked to the writing cabinet and returned with some yellowed papers fraying at the edges.

"These letters were written by Henry, the third baronet, to his wife, Lady Lynch."

"Were they love-letters, Mama?"

"Well, they were and they were not," Sibella said.

Harry noted their puzzled expressions.

"*My girls are not accustomed to the peculiarities of adult conversation,*" he thought.

Sibella began to read.

"He always started with a loving greeting, 'My sweet heart'."

"And how did he finish?" Cecilia asked.

"With another loving greeting, 'I am yours till death'."

"Ooh …" responded the girls.

Harry could see that Sibella had their undivided attention, apart from that of little Barbara. She was emulating her twin brother, George, by climbing the end posts of the master bed.

Sibella opened the first letter dated October 25, 1672. She read a sentence out-loud:

I see by your silence you are angry but without cause I assure you.

"Why was she angry?"

"She had a toothache." The girls laughed.

For the Lady Mary Lynch,
My dear Heart,
… I believe … your distemper of the toothache do hinder you, which I was sorry to hear of. I would not speak to the Doctor … for they understand nothing of it. When I was in London and troubled with the toothache I never found any good by their prescriptions. Keep yourself warm, eat well and sleep well, that is the best cure. If the pain shall be more constant, you must have that tooth drawn that aches with you.

My blessing to the children. I am yours till death,
Henry Lynch, Galway.

"He did not think much of the doctors," Cecilia said. "But his wife must have been angry about something else, I think."

Her sisters nodded.

"You are right, Cecilia," Sibella said as Harry smiled in contentment.

"Poor Henry had problems with his legal work in Dublin. From time to time, he would run out of money. Four years later, he wrote to his wife seeking help."

Cecilia puckered her brow.

"I thought his wife's money would be his money,"

"Indeed, I often wondered about that," Harry said. "But let me read on."

For the Lady Lynch ... at Mace near Galway
My dear Heart,
I wish you and the children a good new year. I pray send to Galway with all speed the five pounds to Mr. Amory, it being the remains of the thirty pounds payable to Mr. Fryer. If you do not I shall be arrested and more disgraced than if the £30 were due. I beseech you, as you tender my preservation to do this. As soon as this money is paid I will go home to you, which if I perform not, never believe me while I live ...
Your ever dear husband till death,
Henry Lynch, Dublin, January 6, 1676.

"My goodness! Was he arrested?" Cecilia wondered. "What a strange letter to have been written by a man well-in with King James."

The eyes of the girls lit up as Cecilia continued.

"Mayhap he was having an affair, and that is why his wife was so angry with him."

"He was away a lot from home, moving in high company," Sibella said. "Attractive young women would have come to his attention. He may have been tempted. Lady Lynch probably suspected as much."

"You mean he was unfaithful, Mama?" Cecilia frowned.

"I know not, Cecilia, and we should not make inferences without knowledge of the facts," answered Sibella.

Harry wondered if Henry's prolonged absences from home and his financial difficulties were factors in the coolness of Lady Lynch. Apart from her toothache, her health appeared good as she outlived her husband by twenty years.

* * * * *

SIBELLA WAS IMPRESSED THAT these letters, written so many years ago, had made such an impact on her daughters. The proud ancestry of their father would remain with them forever. She was not surprised when they insisted on maintaining a vigil during the day, happy to be in their father's company as his life ebbed away. The boys joined them in the succeeding days.

Shortly afterwards, Sibella almost fainted when the footman announced the arrival of Archbishop Bourke, even though Harry had told her of his invitation to the 3ʳᵈ Earl of Mayo.

"Your Grace," Sibella stammered. "You are most welcome."

"Good morning, Miss Cottle," he said brusquely. "Sir Harry asked me to visit. How is he?"

After recovering from the shock of the episcopal presence, Sibella curtsied.

"Not the best, Your Grace," she said. "The footman will escort you to the drawing room while I inform Sir Harry of your arrival."

As she walked up the cantilevered staircase, Sibella wondered if Harry had invited Archbishop Bourke in relation to a marriage licence. She knocked on the bedroom door to allow Harry time to compose himself. Slowly opening the door, she watched him struggling to sit up in bed with the help of his nurse.

"Archbishop Bourke has arrived, my dear."

When Harry nodded, Sibella rang the bell as a signal to the footman. After a short interval, the footman knocked on the door and announced:

"Archbishop Bourke to see Sir Harry Lynch-Blosse."

"You are most welcome, Your Grace." Harry smiled. "Please take a seat."

As Sibella and the nurse turned to leave, Harry said,

"Sibella, please stay."

Sibella saw the slightest tightening of the facial muscles of the archbishop as if he were uncomfortable in her presence. She sat close to Harry while Bourke sat in the armchair.

"Your Grace, were it not for my illness, Sibella and I would have married at my mother's home in Suffolk," Harry spoke slowly. "Doctor Boyd insisted that I must not travel."

Archbishop Bourke raised his hands.

"And now you wish to marry at home?"

Sibella said,

"I am willing to conform although by doing so I would surely break the heart of my mother and Father Nolan." She looked into the cool blue eyes of Bourke who remained impassive. "But my application to conform has been thwarted at every turn."

Harry nodded.

"That is why I wish to apply for a special license to marry at home."

Sibella felt the pressure of Bourke's gaze interrogating her and then Harry.

"Do either of you have an impediment that would prevent you from marrying?"

Harry coughed.

"I can swear on the bible that I am free to marry, now that my marriage to Emily Mahon has been annulled."

Unaccountably, Sibella felt the blood rushing into her cheeks as if she had something to hide. But her blushing only reflected her delight that at last she was so close to realizing her dream.

"I swear on my heart that I have always been free to marry ever since I reached my majority."

"I must speak frankly," Bourke said.

Sibella trembled but Harry remained outwardly calm.

"Sir Harry, your liaison with Miss Cottle has scandalized the local community."

Bourke stood and walked towards the window. He looked at the landscape, and then turned around slowly.

"Both of you have sinned. My predecessor, the late Archbishop Browne, brought your activities to my attention."

Sibella felt like strangling "Your Grace" and just barely managed to control her tongue.

"However, it is clear to me that despite your colourful escapades, you are in love with one another. I have made inquiries about both of you from reputable sources. You have raised seven fine children who are the clearest expression of that love." Bourke walked towards them. "Your children deserve to have married parents to help them on their way through life. For that reason, I hereby grant you a special license to marry at home on the strict understanding that the ceremony will be private apart from your witnesses. I shall instruct the local vicar accordingly."

Sibella felt like whooping with joy but restrained herself. This time she saw the faintest glimmer in those pale-blue aristocratic eyes.

"May God bless you, Your Grace," Harry said. "You must stay for champagne."

"Thank you, Sir Harry, but my coach awaits me for my next engagement." Bourke nodded. "Miss Cottle."

Sibella stood up and rang the bell. When the footman arrived, she curtsied as the archbishop departed.

Now she could whoop.

"Well done Harry, I am so proud of you." Sibella held his hands and kissed him as he relaxed on the high pillows. "I love you so much. Now where is my wedding dress?"

She retired to her wardrobe to inspect the ensemble she had worn on that day, Wednesday, 8 December 1773, almost fifteen years ago. It had been carefully stored away, awaiting its second coming.

She would soon find out how her figure had survived five pregnancies, seven births and the passage of time. Having un-wrapped the long-flowing green dress, she was thrilled to find that it still fitted her body although somewhat tighter than before. She felt like re-entering the bedroom to parade for Harry's pleasure were it not for the restriction on revealing a wedding gown to the groom. Instead, she donned the red gown she had worn at Michael's baptism and returned with a smile on her face.

"My goodness!" Harry exclaimed. "You look as gorgeous as ever."

"On our big day, I shall adorn my wedding gown with white pansies pinned with Lady Lynch's Tara brooch." Sibella pirouetted on the carpet. "Rather than bundle my hair high, I shall allow it to hang over my shoulders in beautiful curls. I still have the decorative horseshoe to wear on my wrist for good luck."

Sibella prayed that the "good luck" would extend Harry's life for as long as the good Lord would permit.

"How will you keep the wedding secret from the children?"

"For mercy's sake!" Sibella's face lit up. "I shall have to stitch my lips together."

Harry laughed, but a chesty cough intruded on his good humour.

Sibella prayed to the good Lord to allow Harry to recover. The children pestered her with questions arising from the visit of the archbishop. Their curiosity intensified when the family solicitor, Andrew Edmondson, arrived to revise Harry's will to take account of their imminent marriage. Fearful for Harry's health, Sibella kept her secret as best she could so as not to tempt fate.

"You will find out soon enough, my darling children," she told them.

* * * * *

ON THE EVE OF the signing of a revised will and their subsequent union, Sibella continued to conceal the secret of the wedding without exception. That night she sat by Harry's bed with a rosary in her hand and a blanket wrapped around her. During the night, the sound of a horse whinnying and stamping on the cobblestones of the interior courtyard awoke her. A trap was in position there for urgent calls.

Cecilia burst into the room. Sibella brushed the cobwebs from her eyes.

"What is the matter?"

"The courtyard is empty, Mama!" Cecilia shouted as she looked through the window of the bedroom.

"I can hear the tinkle of the cowbell."

Sibella joined Cecilia at the slightly open window overlooking the courtyard. As the tinkle gradually faded, she realized that the horse was galloping away.

"The trap has gone, Mama," Cecilia said.

"But how did it get out? The courtyard is still locked." Sibella was mystified. "Dear Lord! It has gone to fetch Doctor Boyd for Harry."

She rushed back to the bedside to find that Harry had slipped away quietly in his sleep.

"Oh no! oh no." Sibella screamed.

She threw her arms around Cecilia. They both cried inconsolably. The remaining children arrived to join the grief-stricken circle.

"Cecilia, you must send for Uncle Peter at once."

Shortly afterwards, Peter arrived. He gently touched the motionless body of his nephew in farewell and said,

"Please accept my sympathies, Sibella." Peter wrapped his arms around her. "What can I do to help?"

Amidst her tears she said,

"Let us wake him in the dining room."

"I shall stop all the clocks, have the mirrors covered and arrange for a coffin."

"Thank you, Peter," Sibella replied. "I shall ask the women to bathe his body in the bedroom. He will be dressed in white."

The children gathered round the bed in tears.

"Wake up, Papa!" little Barbara cried.

"Papa is on his way to heaven," Sibella said. "He will join his Mama, Sir Robuck and Lady Lynch. We will all meet him there some day in the future."

Peter's men carried the body of Harry downstairs to the dining room. He looked so peaceful when placed on a marble-topped table in the middle of the dark panelled room. She glanced at the opened window, wondering if her spirit could join Harry's on its way to heaven. Nobody walked between the body and the window so as not to impede the spiritual journey. After two hours, Sibella had the window closed and admitted early mourners.

She sat by the wall surrounded by her children, Uncle Peter, and Pat Lynch of Clogher. Kate Moran sat discreetly a short distance away. The landed gentry were the first to call, including Lord Altamont, Lady Harriett, James Cuffe and Louisa Moore. After expressing sympathy, they sat on chairs placed around the coffin at the walls. The footman served tea and sandwiches.

Sibella looked at Lady Harriett, who waved her fan slowly, signalling her marriage to a handsome man in her company. Sibella ignored the taunt and concentrated on her younger children who were beginning to fret amidst the solemn atmosphere.

Peter said, "I will take the children out for refreshment and some fresh air."

"God bless you, Peter."

Later in the evening, the tenantry arrived. The children returned and were at ease within a more relaxed setting. Judy Holian turned up to mourn the man whose father had transported her husband. Sibella was also pleased to note the discreet presence of Catherine Lynch, Harry's daughter by Margaret McDermott. However, the Colgans stayed away, dashing her hope for rapprochement.

As night beckoned, the children retired. Mugs and sturdy plates replaced the china. Poteen and whiskey took precedence over tea. The peasant waking could now begin. After drinking some firewater, Ned Holian contributed a few bars celebrating Harry's elevation to a better place:

(they) rolled him up in a nice clean sheet,
and laid him out upon the bed;
a bottle of whiskey at his feet
and a barrel of porter at his head.

On the following day, a large gathering of the landed gentry attended his funeral mass and burial in Balla graveyard. Male members wore black full-trimmed clothes, plain linen, black swords and buckles. Their female counterparts wore black silk, fringed linen, white gloves, black and white fans and tippets, white necklaces and earrings.

Heartbroken, Sibella allowed Peter to escort her to the graveyard. After the vicar had intoned the last rite, she dropped a daffodil on to his coffin. After the men refilled the grave, an elegant lady stepped forward and dropped a second daffodil on the freshly-turned earth. A gasp of astonishment emanated from the crowd as Sibella fainted into the arms of Peter.

"Who was that woman?" Sibella asked when she had regained her senses.

"She looked familiar. I cannot place her at the moment."

After the gentry had departed, the tenantry arrived to pay their respects thus distracting her attention from the strange incident.

* * * * *

SIBELLA SOON BECAME AWARE of the gap in leadership of the Lynch-Blosse estate. Harry's nephew and heir, young Robert, was only four and living in Cardiff. Under these circumstances, the trustees persuaded Peter Lynch to take over the estate management on an interim basis.

After grieving with her distraught children for some weeks, Sibella approached the new manager.

She sat down, in sombre mood.

"I need your advice, Peter," she began.

"Hmm, what is your concern?" Peter said, surrounded by documents at his table in the estate office.

"I must look to the future. My days here are numbered."

"Nonsense, my dear." Peter leaned back in his chair. "Little Robert is only four. I will be in charge here until he reaches his majority."

Sibella suspected that Peter was under pressure from the trustees to get rid of her and her brood. Being aware of Peter's dilemma, she ploughed another furrow to avoid his embarrassment.

"Thank you, but there are other forces at work to my disadvantage. Kate Moran cannot wait to see the back of me."

Peter affected to seem puzzled, but Sibella was conscious of how well he understood the complex relationships in the Big House.

"I will stand by you, Sibella, no matter what Kate might feel."

"Some people say that her pedigree is superior to mine," Sibella said.

"Even if that were the case, I would still stand by you because of your superior managerial skills," Peter responded.

"You certainly know how to flatter a lady. However, Kate has a strong ally in her husband, Bernard, who is highly regarded by the servants. Together they could make life difficult for me and ultimately for you."

Peter nodded.

"Nevertheless, I urge you to stay here as long as you wish."

"That is a weight off my mind," Sibella said. "Thank you for continuing to serve as a guardian to my children."

Sibella was also under pressure from her older children, who had realized that their future at Balla might be problematic. She sought to reassure them by maintaining contact with Louisa Moore of Ashbrook and Pat Lynch of Clogher, each of whom was concerned for the welfare of herself and her family.

Every month, Bernard Moran drove her and two or three of the children to Ashbrook and Clogher in rotation. These visits helped to accustom the children to a possible change of residence.

On one such arrival at Ashbrook, Louisa Moore greeted her.

"My darling daughter, how are you?"

"Well for the moment, thank you, Mama; but my days at Balla are numbered."

"As I have said before, you are always welcome here at Ashbrook."

"I appreciate your offer but I must not take advantage of it."

"Why ever not, you silly girl!" Louisa scolded.

"My rascals would tear your lovely house asunder." Sibella smiled.

"I have missed the pitter-patter of small feet ever since we fostered you. I have been living here in solitude since Doctor Moore died. Most of all, I have missed your youthful vigour after you left us … how many years ago now?"

"Fifteen years."

"Fifteen years!" Louisa exclaimed. "Anyway, your boys will be away at school in Castlebar. Your baby days are over. Or are they?"

Sibella laughed.

"I certainly hope so."

"I now have an opportunity to refresh my life with the joys and heartbreak of youthful exuberance. I shall not take no for an answer."

Both women shared tears of joy at the thought of their shared future.

After a period of mourning, Sibella informed Peter of her decision to move. When she inquired about the legacies willed to her children, he told her that the trustees were having difficulty raising the money. Despite this difficulty, Sibella confirmed that she and the children would move to Ashbrook. Her three notes of five hundred pounds each would underwrite their welfare for the immediate future.

Before making this announcement, she visited Judy Holian and the Colgans.

"Thank you for attending Harry's funeral," Sibella said.

Judy raked the turf fire, releasing a fresh waft of peaty aroma. She was dismayed that Judy and her modest home were even more unkempt now.

"One must honour the dead, no matter what."

"I know you were not fond of my Harry or his father."

"Why would I be? I lost poor Sean for stealing one miserable sheep," Judy said.

Sibella appreciated that Judy rarely shirked expressing her mind.

"I'm sorry for that; is there any chance he might come back to you?"

"He is probably workin' as a low-grade servant, with no money to come home." Judy poked the fire again. "He cannot read or write. The old fool is too proud to admit it. Otherwise, we might have heard from him."

"If I can ever help ..." Sibella's voice trailed away.

"What has brought this on, m'lady?"

Sibella appreciated that the ordinary people of Balla continued to regard her as the lady of the manor rather than as Harry's mistress.

"You are a clever woman, Judy Holian; you can read me like a book. Apart from the children and Peter, you are the first to know. We are leaving Balla for good. My days as lady of the manor are over."

"Well, glory be! That is unexpected. Why so?"

"We need a new start." Sibella leaned forward to the fire.

"But where will you go, alannah?" Judy's face showed her interest.

"To my foster-mother, Louisa Moore of Ashbrook. I have one final favour to ask."

"And that is?"

"Harry tried to make peace with the Colgans before he passed away." Sibella warmed her hands at the fire. "Old man Colgan told him he could roast in hell — and the same for me and the same for you."

"It was a terrible thing we did, I suppose." Judy frowned.

"I am going to visit old man Colgan and try to make my peace with him. I thought perhaps you might do the same."

Judy blessed herself.

"I should do that, right enough."

"I will let you know how I fare; mayhap the two of us will escape roasting in hell."

Sibella could not resist smiling.

"Go on now, you minx," Judy responded affectionately. "Balla is going to be much less exciting without my red beauty."

Sibella felt much the better after her *tête-à-tête* with Judy Holian. She would now bare her soul to old man Colgan. Shortly afterwards she visited, bringing tea and freshly baked bread as a small gift. "Good morning, Mr Colgan."

"Good mornin', m'lady," Colgan said politely. "What brings you here on this wet and miserable morning?"

"I wanted to have a word with you before I leave Balla."

"Sit yourself down by the fire. Mrs Colgan might wet us some tea."

"I spoke to Judy Holian last week. I told her that making a spancel was a terrible thing to do, and she agreed." Sibella paused. "I was afraid that Harry was going to throw me out. She told me the spancel would secure his love. When I found that Judy would use the skin from a fresh corpse, I was horrified. I am ashamed for not protecting the sanctity of young Ellen's body."

The tears were now streaming down Colgan's cheeks. His wife was so upset that she abruptly absented herself.

After pausing again, Sibella continued:

"I now know that Ellen was fathered by Harry by your late daughter, Sally. Harry was furious with me over the spancel because he knew how much it would hurt you and your family. As he lay on his deathbed, he was anxious to make peace with you. I understand your angry response; we should all roast in hell for subjecting you and your family to this horrible ordeal. I cannot expect you to forgive me, but I wanted to express my apology before I leave Balla."

CHAPTER 17

Prior to her departure from Balla, Sibella received a sealed letter, brought by hand, marked "Private and confidential." The writing looked feminine. Who could it be? She opened it eagerly.

Tuesday, 30 September 1788
Dear Miss Cottle,
Please accept my sympathies on the recent passing of Sir Harry. I would greatly appreciate an opportunity to visit.
Yours faithfully,
Emily Mahon.
Castlegar,
Ahascragh, Co Galway.

Out of curiosity, Sibella told the Mahon footman she would be happy to meet Mistress Mahon.

"What was that all about, hmm?" Peter asked.

"I think you know the identity of this mysterious lady."

"You mean the lady with the daffodil?" Peter scratched his head.

"It's Emily Mahon! You knew all along." Sibella smiled. "She is coming to visit."

"She's a fine lady, Sibella. Is she married?"

"I know little of her — until next Wednesday!"

Sibella turned on her heel and departed with a gleam in her eye.

When Emily Mahon arrived at Balla House, she was still dressed in mourning black. A slim woman of medium height and brown hair, she did not sport a wedding band.

"Miss Cottle, please accept my sympathies on your great loss."

Emily opened her arms and embraced Sibella.

"Thank you, Mistress Mahon."

"Please call me Emily," urged the lady from Galway.

Sibella fingered a russet curl and ignored the request.

"Harry was the love of my life. I had fifteen wonderful years with him and seven children to show for it."

"How are the children?"

"I have three boys and four girls aged fourteen down to five, all in excellent health, thank you," Sibella said. "They miss their father. He told them wonderful stories about his ancestors towards the end."

Sibella paused, not being sure of her visitor's agenda.

138

"How did you become acquainted with Harry?" Emily asked.

Sibella thought the question unsuited to a mourning call.

"He came to visit my foster-parents, the Moores of Ashbrook. I was so excited to make his acquaintance, the handsome son of a baronet. Lady Lynch said that Harry was a man with a broken heart."

"One which healed more speedily than my own when he abandoned me," Emily said caustically. "I beg your pardon, please continue."

"Harry's father was furious with him for eloping with you. Harry needed respite from the poisonous atmosphere at Balla. The Moores, distant relatives of Lady Lynch, agreed to take him on. We fell in love. I increased with Michael and ... the rest you know." Sibella paused. "How did you and he meet?'

"Lady Lynch brought him on a visit to my home when he was a young boy. Years later, I fell in love after we danced at the Maidenhill Ball. I was a Roman Catholic, even though most of my Castlegar cousins had conformed."

Emily raised her hands.

"My family warned me not to marry him but I was young and foolish. Although younger than Harry, I was not averse to taking the initiative. I told the priest that Harry would convert to the religion of his grandmother. On that basis, he agreed to marry us in Castlegar."

Sibella was now three-and-thirty years. She wondered about the age of this woman destined to become her rival. Emily was probably also in her mid-thirties and still eligible.

Emily leaned forward.

"Harry was confused. Lady Lynch and Peter urged caution, because he could lose his inheritance under the Penal Laws."

"Harry told me that part of the story when he started to woo me," Sibella said. "What happened next?"

"After traveling to Castlegar, Harry told the priest how much he admired his grandmother, a devout Catholic. He created the impression that a conversion would follow." Emily paused. "After a low-key ceremony, we were pronounced man and wife, in spite of opposition from Harry's guardian, James Cuffe."

"That scoundrel, Cuffe, wrote to Harry urging him to abandon me in favour of Lady Harriett. I have never forgiven him," Sibella said.

She knew that the antagonism between herself and Lady Harriett was a choice topic of gossip. Was that why Emily regarded her with sympathy rather than surprise?

Emily leaned back in her chair.

"We travelled by mail coach to Dublin and stayed overnight at The Brazen Head. Having enjoyed a delicious meal with copious refreshments we retired for the night and consummated our relationship. It was the happiest moment of my life."

Sibella felt a moment of empathy as Emily gazed at Harry's portrait, savouring the memory of that sacred moment.

"How did you cope with your elopement?"

Emily's face lit up. "We travelled by boat to Liverpool and by coach thereafter. Harry brought me to London to show me his birthplace, and then to Belstead Hall in Suffolk where he had lived for six years."

Sibella interjected.

"Harry also brought me to Suffolk when we ran away. Michael was born in Belstead where we lived for a while before returning to Ireland. I beg your pardon, please go on."

"Our honeymoon passed so quickly. Soon we were on our way back to Balla. The closer we got, the more anxious Harry felt about his family's reception of the news. Lady Lynch and Peter met us on arrival." Emily's complexion darkened. "Lady Lynch explained how her son, Sir Robuck, was dismayed upon hearing of our Catholic ceremony. They advised us to stay awhile with Pat Lynch of Clogher."

Emily sighed.

"Two weeks later, Harry visited Balla but returned with bad news etched on his face. He outlined our options as gently as he could. I was furious. I said 'You are so cowardly not to fight for our marriage. You have betrayed our love and our marriage vows'."

Emily paused while tears welled up in her eyes.

"Annulment was now staring us in the face. We travelled with Peter to Castlegar. My parents were distraught and reluctantly agreed to accept the compensation offered by Sir Robuck."

Emily reached for her handkerchief.

"I was devastated. I needed time to recover."

"The Penal Laws have caused a lot of pain," Sibella said.

Emily paused.

"We applied for an annulment, claiming the marriage was not valid because Harry had failed to convert to Catholicism."

Sibella restrained herself admirably from using an uncomplimentary description of Emily Mahon's conniving ways.

"But you surely knew he would not convert?"

Emily pursed her lips.

"I lived in hope that somehow, some day, we could reunite. I was still in love with Harry. When his father died, I attended the funeral."

Sibella held her hands together and steepled her fingers.

"Harry never told me."

"I was discreet once I saw him in your company. Even though I was still married to Harry at that time, Lady Harriett told me of her determination to wrest Harry from your control. I could not credit her effrontery."

"So Harry had three women in pursuit of him at this stage."

Sibella could not resist laughing. She could almost imagine the seventh baronet looking down from above, intrigued at the scheming of his lovers.

Emily fingered her brown locks.

"I did not have the courage to shake his hand. I wrote to express my condolences."

"Another letter the rascal concealed from me!" Sibella exclaimed. "I have already mentioned that infamous letter written to Harry by James Cuffe."

"My dear Sibella, your fame has spread near and far. I admire your courage and determination." Emily paused. "May I inquire as to your plans for the future?"

So that is why the bitch came, thought Sibella.

"Peter is in charge here — "

A knock at the door interrupted Sibella's response. Kate Moran announced,

"Mr Lynch would like to have a word with Mistress Mahon."

Emily's face reddened.

Sibella nodded.

"Please send him in, Kate."

Peter entered the drawing room, looking coy. Now in his late fifties, the lonely bachelor was remarkably well-preserved. Sibella often wondered why the man had never married.

"It is good to see you again, Emily." Peter flushed. "You are as beautiful as ever."

"Thank you, Peter. Please accept my sympathy on the passing of your nephew, Sir Harry." Emily paused. "You treated me with dignity and respect especially when my marriage ..." she almost choked with emotion "... when my marriage to Harry broke up all those years ago."

"I admired your character and sympathized with your situation," Peter said. "When a decent period of mourning has elapsed, I would like to visit. There are some matters I wish to discuss with you."

"I would be delighted to host you at Castlegar." Emily smiled.

* * * * *

SIBELLA EXCUSED HERSELF SHORTLY afterwards. She was fascinated by the surprising events of the morning: Uncle Peter and Emily Mahon, what a prospect! How would they deal with their respective religious affiliations? Louisa Moore would be fascinated.

Another thought struck Sibella. Had she decided to stay at Balla, would Peter have approached her instead? He had always seemed to admire her. Had he done so, she would have refused because Peter would want to start a family. Had she not told Louisa that her baby days were over?

She wondered if Emily might have a lien on Harry's estate even though their marriage was no longer valid. If so, Sibella would have to tread carefully. So would Peter! Why had she not interrogated Emily more thoroughly? In this thoughtful mood, she wandered absentmindedly around the house, almost tripping over Peter who appeared suddenly with a spring in his step.

"You are deep in thought, Sibella."

"Indeed I am." Lowering her voice, she asked, "Where is your new lady friend?"

Peter reddened again, much to Sibella's amusement.

"I am waiting for her to return from the lavatory. She is not my lady friend, just a … friend."

"She has you in her eye, Peter." Sibella smiled. "You are handsome and eligible and so is she."

"I am far too old to get married. Once you and your lovely children have departed —"

"You will be happy now, to be rid of us?" Sibella said stiffly.

"Of course not. I enjoy your company and that of your lovely children. After your departure, I shall have no one to talk to," Peter said. "When the mourning period is over, I shall rejoin the social circuit. I enjoy the company of women. I hope that Emily will be just one of many female friends. Now I hope you understand!"

Peter turned on his heel, leaving Sibella with her mouth open.

Continuing her wander round the house, Sibella stumbled across Emily Mahon returning from the lavatory. She looked Emily straight in the eyes.

"Thank you for visiting. I have often wondered why you opposed the annulment of your marriage to Harry for such a long time."

Emily blushed and stuttered.

"My family and the priest looked after that matter. I was not involved."

"Nonsense. Of course you were involved!"

"How dare you!" Emily scowled. "Who are you to speak to me like that? Lady Harriett told me a rumour about your mysterious father. She said he raped your poor mother."

Instinctively, Sibella cracked the palm of her hand across Emily's face.

"How dare you speak of my father in such a manner?"

Emily screamed so loudly that the servants' curiosity was aroused. Peter and the children rushed in.

"What on earth is the matter?" asked Peter anxiously.

"That harridan struck me, Peter!" Emily cried and fell sobbing into Peter's arms.

"She has grievously insulted the memory of my father," Sibella said.

Peter glowered at Sibella and escorted Emily away.

Sibella burst into tears as her children circled round her.

"What ails you, Mama?" Michael asked.

Sibella wiped her tears with Cecilia's handkerchief.

"Mistress Mahon and I had a disagreement," she said.

"Were you arguing over Papa?" Cecilia wondered.

"Let us go into the library. I must collect myself."

As Sibella calmed her children, she saw Emily's trap disappearing down the beech-lined avenue on her way home.

"What did she say, Mama?" Michael asked.

"She said that my father had attacked a lady, which is not true. That is why I slapped her." As the children nodded, she said, "Now, off you go and play."

Later that evening, after the children had gone to bed, Sibella pondered on the extraordinary events of the day. She presumed that Emily would have ensured the presence of a priest and two witnesses at her wedding to Harry. A properly constituted marriage was not amenable to annulment unless unconsummated or forced. An application for an annulment would have been as pointless as that of Henry VIII for the dissolution of his Catholic marriage to Catherine of Aragon.

However, since Harry had not converted to Catholicism, the marriage may have been invalid. Sibella wondered if Harry had known the outcome before he received the infamous letter from Cuffe urging him to abandon her. Surely, the trustees would have raised the issue in relation to Harry's will unless the compensation package offered by Sir Robuck carried an exclusion clause. If Emily tabled a claim, the generous legacies to her seven children could be even more problematic; all the more reason to talk to Peter once the heat of battle had subsided.

* * * * *

SOME DAYS LATER, SIBELLA approached Peter in the estate office.

"I must apologize for my intemperance in striking Mistress Mahon, although in my defence, I was provoked."

Peter frowned at her.

"What came over you?"

"She had no right to insult the memory of my father as she did."

"You should not have queried her truthfulness." Peter sighed. "Both of you were in the wrong; both of you are grieving for Harry, as am I. The truth is that Harry, whom I loved dearly as a nephew, has torn my family asunder. Leaving aside his liaisons with Sally Colgan and Margaret McDermott, both of which produced issue, Harry's elopement with Emily Mahon was a disaster for both of them. You are essentially correct; Emily connived to persuade a naive priest that Harry would later convert. Harry, himself an innocent at large, reluctantly acquiesced to a charade that was doomed to failure. I was left to pick up the pieces. I had to eat humble pie with the Mahons of Castlegar and absorb unbelievable abuse."

This unveiling of his tormented heart fascinated Sibella.

"And then the grand entrance of … the redhead from Ashbrook! You are a very beautiful woman, Sibella, blessed with an engaging personality. I could not blame Harry for falling in love with you, but Harry's father was distraught on hearing of this latest liaison. Lady Lynch and I learned to live with it until …"

"Until what?" Sibella said, frowning.

"Until the spancel; that event damaged your reputation irretrievably and that of Harry with it."

Sibella broke down inconsolably. She ran out of the estate office into her bedroom. Throwing herself on the bed, she sobbed until her children joined her and she had to compose herself.

Later that evening, when she joined Peter after dinner in the drawing room, he expressed regret for his plain words.

"I must apologize for speaking so bluntly this morning. It has been building up inside me for years. I have had no one with whom to share the burden of shame since Lady Lynch passed away."

"It is of no account, Peter. You spoke only the truth. I have thought long and hard all afternoon, and am even more decided now that the children and I will depart from this house as soon as we are out of full mourning."

"You will return to your old home?" Peter asked.

"Yes, we will return to my foster-mother at Ashbrook."

"Despite what I said this morning, you are still welcome to stay at Balla until little Robert takes over sixteen years from now."

"What about Mistress Mahon?" Sibella asked.

"What about her?" Peter opened his eyes wide.

"I think you find her attractive."

Peter smiled.

"I shall visit her next year to confirm the exclusion arrangements negotiated with her father in relation to Harry's will."

"She might challenge those arrangements," Sibella said.

"Edmondson has assured me that the arrangements are as secure as the monarchy of Britain."

"You should invite her to the Maidenhill Ball. You deserve a little pleasure after all those years of family torment."

As Peter moved towards the liquor sideboard, Sibella bade him goodnight. She was effectively bidding goodbye to Balla. It was time to move on.

"What will the future hold for me now, and my seven children?" she wondered.

A new chapter in her life beckoned. She tingled in anticipation of the challenges ahead.

CHAPTER 18

O<small>NE</small> YEAR AFTER HARRY died, preparations intensified for the move to Ashbrook. Sibella worried how to explain the situation to her children.

"Mama, why are we leaving Balla?" asked fifteen-year-old Michael.

Sibella sighed as seven pairs of eyes focused on her.

"It's complicated, Michael. Please sit down, my darling children."

They sat down and Sibella opened her heart to them.

"After your beloved father fell in love with me, I began to increase with Michael. Harry had proposed to me, and we ran away to Suffolk where Michael was born. When we returned to Ireland, Uncle Peter said there was a problem."

Sibella paused to silence the children.

"Your father was already married and —"

"What!" interjected Cecilia, now fourteen, while her siblings looked aghast.

"Do you remember Mistress Mahon, who visited here after your father died and caused me to lose my temper? Well, before Harry met me, he had married Miss Mahon, a Catholic from Galway in a Catholic ceremony. She persuaded the priest that Harry would convert to Catholicism. They eloped but, after their return, Sir Robuck persuaded Harry to apply for an annulment to the marriage, as it could have lost him his property under the Penal Laws. Shortly afterwards, Harry spent some time at Ashbrook learning to manage an estate. That is where I met him and we fell in love. Harry tried but failed for many years to obtain an annulment. As a result, although engaged, we could not marry." Tears came to her eyes as she watched their expressions of incredulity.

Michael said,

"If the annulment had come through in time, I would have been the eighth baronet?"

Michael blushed as the girls chanted,

"Sir Michael."

Sibella did not have the courage to tell them about the spancel, as they were far too young to cope with that ghoulish episode.

"If I was wrong to fall in love with Harry, I apologize to all of you whom I love so dearly. I cannot undo —"

"But why do we have to leave Balla, Mama?" Cecilia interjected; her siblings echoed the question.

Now Sibella reddened as the dreaded question required an answer.

"It's complicated. When your beloved father wrote his will, the trustees insisted that he leave me out of it, apart from some furniture and stock. I do not own this house; Uncle Peter does."

"That is terrible, Mama," Michael said.

"He did leave generous legacies to each of you in spite of the trustees. When I complained, he separately gave me three bills each for five hundred pounds. These monies will secure our future."

"I still do not understand why we have to leave Balla," Cecilia said.

"Uncle Peter says we can stay until little Robert takes over."

"Zounds! Who is little Robert?" Michael asked.

Sibella smiled as the story became more and more complicated.

"Little Robert, now six years, is Harry's nephew and the new eighth baronet. He lives in Cardiff, in Wales."

Cecilia's brow now furrowed.

"Mama, do we have to leave Balla because of Mistress Mahon? Is that why you were cross with her?"

Sibella blushed again as the children whispered excitedly.

As she hesitated, Michael interjected

"We know, Mama. It's complicated."

His siblings were beside themselves with excitement, some laughing and others with tears in their eyes.

"Please, children, be quiet," Sibella said. "We do not want the servants to overhear."

When the children were calmer, she continued, "The facts are these. Firstly, Uncle Peter is an aging man. If he died, we would have no friends here. We would have to leave. Secondly, while Peter lives he may start a relationship with Mistress Mahon, whom he admires, now that she is free to marry. She seems to like him also. If she moved into Balla House, she would certainly want us out."

Sibella paused to let the words sink in. She could see that the younger children were confused as they sought guidance from their older siblings. It was just as well she had concealed the story of the spancel.

"Why did Mistress Mahon visit you?" Michael asked.

"Ostensibly to pay a mourning visit, but I suspect she wished to see Peter and look over Balla House. The truth is, we are not wanted here, and it is better for us to leave now of our own volition than wait to be forced out in the future. How lucky we are to have a home to go to at Ashbrook where we are loved and wanted. We can talk more when you have had a chance to think about it. In the meantime, you must finish your packing. We shall be on the road to Ashbrook next week."

After they moved to Ashbrook in the spring, the change in their circumstances was dramatic. From being mistress of a Big House, Sibella was now a guest in more modest accommodation. Her three boys enjoyed the excitement of boarding in the Ralph academy in Castlebar. The four girls missed their father and Uncle Peter, and the more spacious accommodation at Balla.

Later that year, Sibella was proud to celebrate Michael's graduation from the academy. Louisa Moore and Peter Lynch attended a celebratory dinner in Geevy's Hotel in Castlebar, along with Michael's boisterous siblings.

"Have you thought about a career in the army?" Peter asked.

"I have thought of nothing else since Papa recited the story of the Battle of Aughrim," Michael replied. "Yes, that is my wish."

"Sir Harry would be so proud of you. Next year, I shall enrol you in the 58ᵗʰ Regiment as an ensign following advice from James Cuffe."

"What's an ensign?" Cecilia asked.

Peter hesitated.

"A commissioned officer in the infantry."

"Goodness!" Sibella cried. "That means you will be a foot soldier."

"No need to worry. Britain is not at war," Peter said.

"I am not afraid of fighting, Mama."

"That is what your Mama is worried about." Louisa had just finished her apple pie. "I think the children need some air. Should I take them to The Mall to watch the cricket?"

"May we go?" Cecilia asked.

"Of course, but be on your best behaviour."

When they were alone, Sibella frowned at Peter.

"By the time Michael is trained, Britain may well be at war somewhere."

"If his training goes well, I shall apply for his admission to the 13ᵗʰ Light Dragoons." Peter sipped his wine. "They are a light cavalry unit dedicated to scouting and reconnaissance. Their casualty rate is much lower than the infantry."

"That will cost a few pennies," Sibella said, still anxious.

"His first commission will cost a little over five hundred pounds, his regimentals a further fifty to sixty pounds." Peter paused. "Let us worry about the Dragoons in due course."

Sibella felt her cheeks glow red. She was unsure whether Peter knew about her three notes, each for five hundred pounds, now hidden under her mattress.

"Do not worry. I shall take the money out of Harry's legacy to Michael. You should hold on to your three notes as insurance for the future."

Sibella sighed in relief.

Peter fingered his wine glass and hesitantly said,

"There is a sensitive issue on which I would like your advice."

"You are going to propose to me?" Sibella jested. She laughed so infectiously that heads turned at adjoining tables. She noted the disgust on their faces confirming the resilience of her notoriety.

Now Peter blushed and whispered,

"No, I shall not propose even though you are still the red beauty of Mayo."

"My, oh my, Peter Lynch, you have a romantic tongue!" Sibella paused until the curious diners averted their gaze. "How is Mistress Mahon?"

"Never you mind." He leaned forward. "I did visit the Mahon family in Castlegar. When I sought to confirm the exclusion clause on Harry's will, I received another bucketful of abuse." Peter clenched his fist. "Reluctantly, they agreed not to challenge the validity of Emily's exclusion. They knew it was pointless to do so."

"What did Mistress Mahon say?"

"While escorting me to the door she whispered, 'Do not allow my parents to upset you. They are still hurt on my behalf.' That stopped me dead in my tracks. Imagine a man of my age glowing like a youth! She looked at me quizzically." Peter drew in breath. "I composed myself. Suddenly the words tumbled from my lips. I asked her to accompany me to the Maidenhill Ball after the Ballinrobe Races."

Peter arranged his fingers in a steeple on the table.

"Emily paused. Her face dropped; then suddenly she smiled and said I must write to Mr Mahon requesting permission. I now await a reply."

Sibella now realized that the decision to leave Balla was the right one. Emily would surely succeed her as the Mistress of Balla even if Peter did not recognize it yet. She wondered about the "sensitive issue" that Peter had mentioned. Maybe, it was Emily. If not, what could it be?

At that moment, Louisa and the children arrived back. It was time to go home. The sensitive issue would have to wait.

* * * * *

EARLY IN THE FOLLOWING year, Louisa Moore sighed.

"I am feeling unwell."

"I shall call Doctor Boyd," Sibella said.

"Poor Doctor Boyd is not in the best condition himself. Old age is catching up on all of us."

"But not on you, surely?"

"This bitterly cold winter has taken its toll." Louisa looked out through the window at the bare skeletons of the trees. "All I ask is that you look after me in the autumn of my life."

"Of course I will, Mama."

The women hugged and cried.

"My brother-in-law, George Moore, is visiting this afternoon. I want you to meet him."

When George Moore arrived, he entered the drawing room where Louisa and Sibella awaited him.

Louisa said,

"Allow me to introduce my foster-daughter, Miss Cottle."

Sibella nearly fainted at first sight of the incredibly handsome, middle-aged man. He flashed a smile revealing a set of teeth as well formed as hers. His rugged face, high cheekbones and black hair emphasized a well-proportioned body. He shook her hand firmly while his blue eyes and warm embrace entranced her.

Louisa resumed her seat in a needlepoint armchair in the style of Louis XVI.

"George is the younger brother of my late husband, Robert. When I pass away, Ashbrook will fall to George. I have asked him to look after you and your children."

"I should be delighted to do so, Miss Cottle."

Sibella trembled, feeling the imprint of his hands on her arms and a light kiss on either cheek. "Thank you, sir. Gracias." She hesitated. "I would love to hear about Spain."

The great man smiled.

"Please call me George. I went to Spain as a young man of adventure. The wine and spirit trade between Galway and Alicante attracted my attention. I also shipped seaweed from Galway and manufactured iodine there. Fortune was on my side. Some people have accused me of tax evasion and piracy; but such is the lot of successful business men."

This forthright and decisive man fascinated her.

"Why did you settle in Alicante?"

George sat down in a matching armchair.

"I met a wild goose, Catherine Kilkelly. Her ancestors were in the army of King James. They fled Ireland after Sarsfield surrendered at Limerick. We fell in love, married and are now blessed with two sons."

"And I am blessed with three sons and four fine daughters," Sibella laughed. "How like you living in Spain?"

"Spain is greatly to my taste. After establishing myself there, I applied for permission to attend at the Spanish Court. I claimed descent from Sir Thomas More."

Sibella's heart began to palpitate. This man was impressive!

"I was refused permission." George scowled.

"Why was that?" Sibella asked, now hanging on every word.

"I did not possess sufficient documentary evidence." George rose from the armchair. "I temporarily returned to Ireland in 1780 and registered my ancestry in Dublin, in the hope that my claimed descent would then be recognized in Spain."

"What happened?"

"They refused to accept my lineage without further authentication." George clenched his fists. "When I was at home, I reluctantly swore an Oath of Allegiance to George III. That enabled me to lease land under the relaxed provisions of the Penal Laws. The opportunity to settle in Ireland was now a real possibility. That time has come." George glanced at Sibella. "Now I must take my departure. I look forward to renewing your acquaintance."

After his departure, Sibella said,

"He surely has a handsome phiz."

"He is a good man, my dear. He will look after you when I'm gone."

Later that year, Louisa worsened and the doctor confined her to bed. As her condition deteriorated, she said,

"I have been harbouring a little secret that has bothered me for years."

"What is it?" Sibella asked.

"I told you before that your father passed away when you were an infant. That is the truth. Your mother, my sister Isabel, never recovered from the shock. He was a good man, Sibella." Louisa paused to catch her breath. "My sister said she never saw a man cry so much, when on his deathbed, he held you, hugged you and kissed you goodbye. She thought the poor man would never let you go. He left a little velvet box to be presented to you on your wedding day. I should have told you once you fell in love with Harry. You will find it on my dressing table ..."

Her voice trailed off as she passed away peacefully.

Sibella cried and cried. She knelt at her foster-mother's bed for a long time, holding her hand and praying for her soul.

Later on, she opened the velvet box to find a beautiful gold wedding band wrapped in paper. She read the message that accompanied it:

To my dearest Sibella.
This is my mother's wedding band.
I shall miss you so much.
Your loving father, Michael Cottle. 1756. XXX

Sibella was the chief mourner at the funeral mass for Louisa Moore in Straide Abbey because George Moore had returned to Spain. She noted the hostile glance of the parish priest while he fawned over the more distant Moore relatives.

While the tenantry attended in force, many of the landed gentry were absent, not wishing to display any secret remnants of their Catholic faith. Uncle Peter was an exception, as was Mistress Mahon who accompanied him.

✳ ✳ ✳ ✳ ✳

SIBELLA WAS NOW THE temporary mistress of Ashbrook House. This was her first experience of being in charge without the assistance of a male partner. Dealing with the female staff was not a problem; her experience at Balla House stood to her. Dealing with male staff was more problematic because of her lack of experience of dealing with them.

As time passed, her fears diminished through establishing a good rapport with the men, ably assisted by the agent. She was particularly interested in the work of the blacksmith, whose smithy she visited from time to time.

"Good morning, kind sir."

The handsome smith hammered a red-hot horseshoe into shape.

"Good morrow, Mistress Cottle. I could make you somethin' for the house, if you wish."

"What kind of thing had you in mind?"

He shrugged his shoulders.

"Ornamental candleholders, maybe?"

"That sounds excellent. Please do."

The smith nodded as Sibella turned on her heel. Ornamental metalwork would enhance the decor of the house. Master Moore would be impressed if the smith produced quality, but could he be trusted to do so? With these thoughts swirling in her mind, she went about her work.

About a week later, Cecilia called her.

"Mama, please come at once."

"What is wrong, my darling?" Sibella rushed to the drawing room.

Cecilia said, "Do you observe anything different, Mama?"

Sibella scanned the room and there it was — an ornamental candleholder.

"It's beautiful," she exclaimed.

Michael, home on leave from the army, asked,

"Where did it come from?"

"Smith offered to make something for the house." Sibella ran her fingers over his creation. "The man has talent. I shall ask him to make some more. Master Moore will be impressed on his next visit."

Sibella wondered why Michael scowled. Did he distrust the intentions of the artistic blacksmith?

"You like it not, Michael?"

"It's beautiful, Mama," Michael said.

"If Master Moore likes it, I might offer Uncle Peter some," Sibella said. "If they are admired, we might even consider beginning to trade in them."

"That is an excellent thought." Cecilia's face lit up. "I can imagine the title: Sibella's Ornamental Artefacts."

"Is the smith trustworthy?" asked Michael.

Sibella concealed her own uncertainty and noted how much her eldest child had matured.

"Of course."

After the day's work was finished, Sibella walked to the forge to discuss her ideas with the smith.

"No rest for the wicked," she said as she found the handsome artisan still hammering metal. "My children and I greatly admire the candleholder. Could you make some more, please?"

"My pleasure, ma'am. I can show you some designs." The smith paused as Sibella hesitated. "They're in the back."

Sibella followed, making sure not to close the door behind her.

"I have three designs."

Sibella moved into the dimly-lit back room which smelt of scorched metal. Smith had laid out the designs on a rough table. She could feel him moving behind her; he was breathing heavily. Turning round, she said,

"These are beautiful. I will ask Michael and Cecilia to take a look ..."

"You are beautiful too, Mistress Cottle." Smith said.

He was now standing between her and the door as he placed his hand gently on her arm. She could feel the electricity and blushed furiously.

"I must go now."

"Just one little kiss," he pleaded.

"No, no," she cried.

He backed into the door, closing it.

"Just one little kiss before you go."

He quickly put his arms around her and held her tight.

As she struggled to free herself, she could feel his manhood against her as he tried to plant a kiss.

"Let me go at once!" she cried.

He ripped open her blouse and cupped her breast.

She screamed; he tried to cover her mouth. She scraped his face with her fingernails and screamed again, and again.

Having finally covered her mouth, he continued to strip her. Sibella attempted to knee him in the groin. Running steps became audible as the smith frantically tried to consummate the foul deed.

Michael burst the door open and hit the man with the butt of his pistol, knocking him to the ground.

Sibella pulled her torn clothes around her, crying inconsolably.

Cecilia arrived on the scene with a clatter of servants and Sibella fell into her arms. Michael ordered the dazed blacksmith to pack his bags and leave.

Later that evening, Sibella reflected on the horror of the episode while sipping brandy.

"I was so close to being violated by a blacksmith," she lamented. "I was so fortunate that you were here, Michael. You are a man now, well able to protect your Mama and sisters."

Sibella wept again in renewed shock.

"Mama, you have to remember how beautiful you are. Men are always looking at you," Cecilia said with tears in her eyes.

"And men look at you too, my beautiful sister," added Michael. "This episode has been a cautionary one for all of us."

Mother, son and daughter hugged in a circle for a while and then retired. The nightmare was over.

CHAPTER 19

"**M**AMA, THE MOORES HAVE arrived," Cecilia cried as she peered through the drawing room window. "Two handsome men are cantering up the hill."

"Quickly, girls, make yourselves respectable," Sibella said, primping her white gown adorned with a red sash and bow. She knew that her girls were nervous, afraid of losing their rooms, especially when their brothers returned at Easter. Sibella was even more worried that the return of the Moores would herald their eviction.

Sibella greeted their visitors, surrounded by her four excited daughters.

"Welcome to Ashbrook, gentlemen. Please sit down by the fire. We shall have tea and fresh bread shortly."

"Sibella, I want to thank you for looking after Ashbrook since Louisa passed away," said George Moore, the Master of Ashbrook.

Sibella, smiling, curtsied in response.

"Where are your boys?" George asked.

"Michael has a commission in the army. John and George are boarding in Castlebar. They will be home during the Easter break."

George glanced towards his companion.

"Allow me to introduce my son and heir, John."

"A fine young man," Sibella said as her girls sought to stifle their giggles.

John Moore flushed in response. He glanced at Cecilia, now seventeen and at the peak of her beauty. The food and drink was brought in and Sibella poured out the tea.

George stood in front of the wood fire, warming himself.

"John has been studying the law, and will continue his legal studies in London and Dublin."

"Could I also study law?" Cecilia mused, sipping her tea.

"Cecilia!" Sibella cried in mock horror as Cecilia's sisters laughed.

"We live in times of great change," George said, sitting down. "In this democratic era, it is only a matter of time before women are admitted to the professions."

Sibella and her daughters were dumbstruck. They had never heard such radical talk before, not even from Harry or Uncle Peter. Living with the Moores promised to be interesting.

During the Easter break, Sibella was pleased when her children warmed to the stories of Alicante and Paris recited by John Moore. She became aware that Cecilia had begun to look with interest at John, who appeared to have warmed to her attention.

Apart from that potential romance, the girls inquired about the pretty pieces of tapestry brought by the master from Spain.

"The tapestries are splendid," Sibella said.

The handsome man fingered one of his wife's creations.

"They were embroidered by Mistress Moore, who is very skilful. I could arrange for my wife to display her other creations to your daughters."

"They would surely appreciate that," Sibella said and then changed tack. "After you have settled in, would you like to accompany me to Balla House? I need to pay a visit to Peter Lynch."

"I accept with pleasure," replied George.

Sibella sent a message to Peter. On receipt of a positive response, she and George set out for Balla on a sunny morning in April. They travelled with only sporadic conversation, each occupied with their own thoughts.

Soon they were heading up the avenue to Balla House, perched on a secluded elevation above the village. The surrounding landscape was pleasant, featuring barely visible mountains to the west and south.

Kate Moran escorted them to the drawing room and announced,

"Miss Cottle and Master Moore to see Master Lynch."

"It is so good to see you, Sibella," Peter said.

Glancing at George, he stretched out his hand,

"I am Peter Lynch, the uncle of the late Sir Harry Lynch-Blosse."

"I am delighted to meet you. I am George Moore of Alicante and Ashbrook."

"Allow me to introduce Mistress Mahon of Castlegar."

Emily curtsied to George, with a barely civil recognition of Sibella.

Peter asked, "How are you settling at Ashbrook?"

"It is quite a change from the balmy climate of Spain," George said, warming his hands by the log fire. "But I merely jest. I greatly enjoy Ashbrook. It is full of life and enjoyment, if a little short on space."

"I have heard of your success in the merchant trade." Peter leaned back in his chair.

George nodded.

"I have decided to settle in Ireland now that I am older. I am determined to build a mansion in Mayo, but have yet to find an appropriate location."

"Let us hope you find a suitable site and a good architect." Peter paused. "I hear you have two handsome sons. The young ladies of Mayo will be delighted."

"The hint of romance is always uplifting," Sibella said, glancing at a blushing Emily who ignored the remark.

Kate Moran arrived with tea and freshly baked cake just in time to deflect any awkwardness.

After glancing at George, Peter said,

"Emily has kindly offered to show you around after we have refreshed ourselves. Sibella and I have some outstanding matters to discuss."

"Thank you. I love walking the land." George departed with Emily once she had finished her tea.

"Quite a formidable gentleman," Peter said. "How do you find the Moores?"

"Very pleasant. The children love them. They have brought excitement and vitality into our lives." Sibella paused. "Emily Mahon is looking radiant."

Peter's cheeks began to glow.

"We have started to see one another. I mentioned it to Cuffe; he was almost as horrified as he was about your liaison with Harry."

"What ails that man?"

"He says that Emily could wheedle her way into the estate now that I am the effective resident and administrator thereof — at least, until little Robert reaches his majority."

"How could she do that?"

"I have discussed it with Emily. She has denied Cuffe's assertion."

Sibella was fascinated.

"Your secret is safe with me." She now changed course. "Is there something else on your mind?"

"Kate Moran came across a locked silver casket recently. Is it yours?"

Sibella's heart sank.

"Harry gave it to me as an engagement present. I thought it should remain here. The memory of it brings solace to my heart when I think of him. May I leave it here for the moment?"

After telling this little white lie, tears came to her eyes. She had thought about putting the spancel in Harry's coffin or bringing it with her to Ashbrook, but had not liked to do either. The memory of that sacrilegious event still haunted her; she feared the bad luck it might bring to her now or in the future.

At that moment, Emily and George returned in high spirits.

"We have just walked around your beautiful garden," George said breezily at first. "Have I spoken out of turn?"

Sibella wiped her tears.

"I was just remembering the wonderful years I spent here with Harry." She returned her handkerchief to her reticule. "I think we should leave now, George. Thank you, Peter. Good day, Mistress Mahon."

On the way home in the Ashbrook carriage, Sibella asked,

"How did you find Mistress Mahon?"

"She was a charming guide, showing me around the house and through the exotic gardens. She opened her heart to me: her devastation over Harry, her jealousy of you, and her present happiness with Peter Lynch. They seem to be a well-matched couple."

"God be praised."

Sibella retracted into her shell, anxious to avoid any further discussion.

✳ ✳ ✳ ✳ ✳

ON THE FOLLOWING MORNING Sibella's interest peaked when George announced,

"We need a larger house. Our modest accommodation is bursting at the seams. I have my eye on eight hundred acres of rolling hill land on the northern shore of Lough Carra."

"Not as cold as Ashbrook, I hope," John Moore said, presumably missing the warmth of the Mediterranean.

"The site is protected from the Atlantic gales by the Partry mountains. The surrounding woodlands will provide warmth and stillness." George frowned. "However, there is a superstitious curse on the site resulting from the reputed killing of a druid. I have been advised not to build there."

"We should not be deterred by superstition," John said. "What do you think, Mistress Cottle?"

All eyes focused on Sibella, temporarily caught off guard. Quickly recovering her composure, she said,

"I think you should ask Father Nolan to bless the site before building starts."

"An excellent suggestion," George replied. "Although I wonder if that will banish a pagan curse."

Sibella hesitated.

"I could also talk to Judy Holian, who is an expert on these matters."

"Ah, the old witch of Balla; ask her, by all means."

Some weeks later, Sibella was intrigued when George unveiled a draft design proposed by a Waterford architect. Spreading the drawings on the dining table, he said,

"Roberts has suggested a stone-built structure with three levels over a basement, perched on an elevation overlooking Lough Carra."

"That sounds impressive, father," John said.

Sibella's children were agog. Sibella understood their reaction aware that Balla House was impressive; Ashbrook was less so but still substantial. This mansion, however, could play a significant role in the world they lived in.

"How will it differ from any other Big House?" Cecilia asked.

George Moore smiled.

"It shall have a great hall, a chapel and a tunnel at the rear for deliveries."

"How long will it take to build?" Sibella asked.

"At least three years."

The master of Ashbrook sat down, crossed his arms and looked into the middle distance, as if contemplating his ideal home.

Shortly afterwards, John departed to pursue his legal studies while George stayed on to supervise the construction of Moore Hall.

In the following year, France declared war on Britain. Sibella was sick with worry that the front line beckoned for Michael. Fortunately, he survived until Peter purchased a Lieutenancy in the 13th Light Dragoons costing fifteen hundred pounds. Sibella was still worried but relieved that he would enter the safer confines of a cavalry unit. Her cup was full when Michael was transferred to Castlebar, far away from the war zone.

Michael's uniform fascinated Sibella as well as his siblings. The young Lieutenant sported a scarlet jacket over dark blue trousers with gold lace and fittings, a shako hat and a sword.

Sibella's eyes twinkled with excitement.

"Tell us about the Dragoons, Michael."

"Our leader, Major-General Crosbie reviewed us in Castlebar last week. He said our regiment stood at more than four hundred men." Michael tapped his scabbard. "Our average height is five feet six inches. Our weapons include firelocks and carbines, bayonets, pistols and swords."

"What are firelocks and carbines?" Cecilia asked.

"A firelock is a type of musket and a carbine is something between a pistol and a musket."

"Who are you going to fight?" Cecilia wondered.

Michael's face darkened at the memory of their instructions for the forthcoming St Patrick's Day parade. "Uncle Peter knows about the scandal that took place in Castlebar at St Patrick's Day in the past. We must ensure it is not repeated."

All eyes now focused on Peter. He explained:

"Some years ago the Light Dragoons were guilty of bad behaviour on the seventeenth day of March. One was dressed like St Bridget, another like St Patrick, and a third sprinkled mock holy water on startled onlookers from a bucket with a mop."

"Glory be!" Sibella exclaimed as Michael continued to glower.

"They were accompanied by drunken colleagues and their behaviour was deeply resented. Later, the Dragoons damaged property and maltreated citizens, resulting in a riot," Peter said. "One soldier lost his life. The disturbance was eventually quelled by the Mayo Volunteers."

"As an officer, I must prevent any repetition of that shameful episode," Michael added.

"Don't forget your sword, Lieutenant," Cecilia said to laughter that lightened the mood.

$$* \quad * \quad * \quad * \quad *$$

SIBELLA STRUCK UP A good relationship with George Moore as the Moore Hall project progressed. The handsome charmer sometimes looked at her in a way that stirred emotion. Her children would not be happy if anything happened between them. She wondered what Harry would have thought? With the move to Moore Hall imminent, however, it was impossible to avoid his presence.

Setting her emotions aside, she worried about the future once more. The children were excited at the prospect of moving to a new home; Sibella did not have the heart to dampen their expectation. Each had developed an individual personality. The older children were eager to fly the nest, following Michael's example. Sibella insisted that the move to Moore Hall must take precedence over their personal plans. The move was a logistical challenge in which she played a key role. Her organizational talent was appreciated by George; this aided the prospect of her family acquiring tenure at Moore Hall.

When the great day came, a convoy of carriages packed with people and chattels set forth for south Mayo. People stopped to look in wonder as the procession moved through Castlebar. Hours later, Sibella admired a spectacular landscape; water and trees its significant features. The blue line of the Partry Mountains was visible to the west. An ornamented gate heralded their entry to a long ascending avenue, at the crest of which stood the breath-taking mansion.

"Welcome to my home," George Moore proudly proclaimed to Sibella and her family.

She flushed with a mixture of emotion and worry. Why had George said "my home?"

The younger children charged into the mansion, eager to explore. Sibella noted an apex slab in the upper hall bearing the inscription "1795. *Fortis Cadere, Cedere Non Potest.*"

"What does this mean?" Cecilia pointed to the inscription.

"A brave man may fall, but he cannot yield," responded the master of Moore Hall. "It is our family motto."

Sibella entered the great hall, where a large portrait hung. It displayed George as a handsome man in a wig and a vermilion coat with gold lace and buttons, white lace at the collar and cuffs: a Spanish style of garment.

"Your portrait is very like you," she commented. "You should wear that wig more often!"

Before George could respond, Cecilia asked,

"Might I inquire what is contained in the iron chest in the hall?"

George smiled.

"That is where I keep my Spanish gold."

Sibella was stunned. This was another world surely, one of fantasy and fairy-tale.

After settling in, George invited Sibella to sit with him on the front balcony, from time to time, as their friendship flourished. She could almost visualize the pleasures of Alicante while relaxing there of a summer's evening.

"I think the master likes you, Mama," Cecilia said.

"Do not jest, my dear. My romantic days are over. It is your turn now. Besides, he is a married man."

Undeterred, Cecilia continued.

"I have seen the way he looks at you. It reminded me of the wayward glance of the blacksmith at Ashbrook."

Cecilia was right. She also had feelings for the master but was determined to conceal them.

As life settled down at Moore Hall, Sibella and George gradually opened their hearts and shared the memories of their respective adventures.

"You must miss Mistress Moore very much," Sibella remarked, testing the water.

George scowled.

"Catherine and I have had a wonderful marriage. We have two fine sons, all grown up and making their way in the world. In recent years, we grew apart. She did not share my dream of returning to the land of my birth." George paused. "Much to my surprise, she has now grown more enthusiastic about coming to Ireland. Her interest was sparked by her Kilkelly relatives in Mayo."

"The splendour of Moore Hall may be an added attraction," Sibella said.

"Her return complicates matters."

Sibella's heart sank.

"Just as I believed I had found love again, my wife has decided to return to my side."

"May I ask for whom you have developed these feelings?"

The master of Moore Hall looked deeply into Sibella's eyes.

"I have been spellbound by you, Sibella Cottle, since we first met at Ashbrook."

"You are teasing me, George. What would you want with a woman with seven illegitimate children?"

"I am serious. I love you with all my heart, but I must stay with my wife now that she is joining me."

Sibella was overcome.

"I admire and respect you, George. Apart from Harry, you are the finest member of the landed gentry I have met, and the most handsome —"

"Sibella," George interjected. His normally composed face revealed a trace of hesitation. His cheeks reddened slightly.

"What is it?"

George hesitated again.

"I am expecting Catherine to arrive within the month."

"You want us to leave!" Sibella exclaimed.

"I have thought long and hard about this," George replied. "I would like you to continue to look after Ashbrook for me. You will receive half of the estate income for the rest of your natural life. That will secure your future and that of your lovely family."

"The children will be heartbroken. This is a cruel situation."

Sibella abruptly departed to her bedroom. The memory of the spancel came to mind. Had its curse struck again? What could she do to release herself from its haunting power?

Next morning, Sibella sought the advice of Michael and Cecilia. She walked with them through the estate woodland. Sitting on a bench surrounded by majestic beeches, she said,

"Mistress Moore has decided to travel to Ireland and take up residence in Moore Hall."

Michael, home on leave from the dragoons, kicked the base of a tree.

"That means we will be out on the road again."

"He will allow us to remain at Ashbrook."

"I thought he fancied you, Mama," Cecilia said.

"Are you enamoured of him?" Michael asked.

Sibella blushed.

"Of course not."

Cecilia stared into the middle distance as the wind stirred the branches.

"This must affect my relationship with John."

"Soon we must pack our bags and return to Ashbrook. What will the younger children think?" Sibella said. "They will be so disappointed to leave this place."

Michael's face dropped but he recovered quickly.

"Leave the younger ones to us, Mama. Cecilia and I will talk to them. Remember, we are yet fortunate to have such a fine home at Ashbrook."

Sibella reflected on how lucky she was to have such sensible and supportive children. They embraced and hugged amid feelings of trepidation for the uncertain future.

After taking some time to reconcile herself to the change in her circumstances, Sibella approached the master of Moore Hall.

"George, I accept your kind invitation to look after Ashbrook."

"I am glad to hear it, Sibella."

George embraced her for the second time. Her body was electrified; once more, she felt alive.

CHAPTER 20

SHORTLY AFTER SIBELLA RETURNED from Moore Hall to Ashbrook, it was Michael's turn to upset her peace of mind.

"Mama, I have served with the 13th Light Dragoons for two years." Michael paused. "Some of the officers are destined for duty in Jamaica. I am thinking of leaving the army and emigrating there."

Sitting in the drawing room at Ashbrook, Sibella was speechless.

"I can no longer bear army life."

"Merciful heaven, why?" Sibella exclaimed.

Michael avoided his mother's accusing eye.

"You would not understand."

"Try to explain it to me. I need to know. Your brothers want to follow you in your footsteps. They are so proud of you, especially when you wear your regimentals."

"If you really want to know, I will tell you." Michael clenched his fists. "I do not like the army. They are here to put down the Irish. I am Irish and proud of it! I do not want to be part of a force that represses my own people."

Sibella had to be careful not to express her own sympathy with his feelings. Apart from Michael, she had six children who depended on her. Their welfare had to come before any support she might harbour for the rights of the peasantry and the growing mood for revolt.

"They are only trying to maintain law and order," she finally said.

Michael pursed his lips.

"Mama, there are some men in the army who are no better than beasts. The things they say about the ordinary Irish disgust me; and they expect me to agree with them."

"You will always find people like that, wherever you go. You have to learn —"

"I am sorry to interrupt, Mama," Michael broke in. "Sometimes, I know not who I am. Am I gentry or peasant, Irish or British, a Lynch or a Lynch-Blosse, legitimate or illegitimate?"

Sibella understood his anguish and her complicity in its creation. He was a young man of twenty and he must now make his own way in the world. All she could do was to hope and pray that life would work out for him. Whatever happened, she would always love him.

"We must talk to Uncle Peter."

He agreed and some days later they set out for Balla with Michael at the reins. They travelled mostly in silence, both deep in thought. On arrival, they drove up the long avenue to the Big House. Sibella smiled at

Kate Moran who greeted them with an air of polite disdain. They found Peter in the drawing room playing with a little toddler dressed as a girl.

"Is the infant yours, Peter?" asked Sibella.

"I am the proud father of two boys and one girl." Peter blushed. "The youngest boy and girl are with the wet nurse. This little boy has learned to walk."

Sibella had made discreet inquiries about Peter's late flowering but had failed to identify the mother.

"I heard you had been busy! You will end up with more children than I if you are not careful."

"They have brought joy to my heart as yours do to you."

"Indeed! But who is the mother?"

"None of your business, Sibella Cottle." Peter then changed tack. "How did you find Moore Hall?"

"Beyond my wildest dreams; it is a fine place, and George Moore is a fine man. You may have heard that Mistress Moore changed her mind and decided to come to Ireland. George allowed me to stay on at Ashbrook. How could I say no?"

Peter kept one eye on his little one, who crawled towards Sibella and looked up at her with appealing eyes.

"That is wonderful," he said.

Sibella was in no hurry to raise the subject of Michael's altered ambition.

"We came through Castlebar for old time's sake."

"I hope there were no riots there. Nobody would dare take on an officer of His Majesty's army." Peter chuckled. When neither Sibella nor Michael responded, he said, "Is something wrong?"

"Of course not," Sibella responded. "It was very good of you to obtain an army commission for Michael."

"And now there is a problem?" Peter looked quizzically at Michael. "You have been promoted already?"

"No, Peter. The rogue wishes to leave the army!"

"Well, well, well, you are full of surprises, Lieutenant Lynch!" Peter frowned.

Michael faltered in response.

"I want to thank you from the bottom of my heart, but the army does not suit me. I have explained it all to Mama. I need to move on, to create a new life, in a new place."

Sibella noted the intensity of Michael's response.

"You are giving up a promising career, and one that cost a great deal of money," Peter raised his voice, causing his little one to cry.

Sibella was proud when Michael remained firm under Peter's glare.

"Where will you go?" Peter asked, as Sibella picked up the crying child and sat him on her lap.

"There are great opportunities in the West Indies, where some of my friends are bound. I wish to make a life out there."

"As long as you are sure, I shall give you my blessing," Peter said.

"That is a great relief to me." Michael sighed.

"Have you any contacts in the Caribbean?" When Michael shook his head, Peter offered, "I can give you two contacts there, if you wish."

"That would be wonderful," Sibella answered before Michael could say anything inappropriate.

The old man began searching in the concealed drawer of the mahogany writing cabinet.

"You may not like these contacts. Two of our relatives settled in the West Indies, Bartholomew and Catherine Lynch." Peter opened his file. "They were planters and merchants on the island of Montserrat, the Emerald Isle of the Caribbean."

"That sounds wonderful," Michael said. "Why would I not like them?"

"Their plantations are worked by slaves. Bartholomew had fifty slaves and Catherine forty-six."

"It will be good to have someone local who is connected to us," Sibella said while calming Peter's little boy on her lap.

Michael looked askance but gave a hesitant nod.

Sibella realized that her eldest had crossed the point of no return. From now on he would be on his own, preparing to cross the Atlantic to seek adventure in the new world.

Sibella broached a related matter with Peter after Michael departed to walk around the estate of his boyhood.

"I have some business to discuss with you, Peter," she began.

"Nothing as earth-shaking, I hope, Sibella," Peter said. He signalled to the nanny to take his little boy away.

Sibella looked serious.

"I would like to travel to Montserrat with Michael and stay there for a couple of weeks. My agent will look after Ashbrook while I am gone, and the children will be fine with the governess and groom."

Peter looked long and hard at Sibella.

"I need to cash one of my five-hundred-pound notes," Sibella said. "Could you do that for me, please?"

Peter glowered.

Sibella understood. It was bad enough that Michael was throwing away the purchase of his army commission. Now Peter would have to face the wrath of the trustees, who doubted the legitimacy of the three notes Sir Harry had signed on his deathbed.

"Even though your notes are payable on demand, I must advise the trustees of their imminent encashment. I may be able to sell Michael's commission which will help." Peter paused. "Who will travel with you?"

Sibella hesitated.

"Master Moore had intended to accompany me. He thought he would make one last voyage before retiring. However, Mistress Moore is due to arrive from Alicante around the time Michael departs."

"And now you have no companion on your voyage home, when Michael remains behind?"

Sibella looked out at the pleasure garden through the drawing room window, avoiding Peter's intense gaze.

"It would appear not," she said.

Peter paced the floorboards in thought.

"I have never travelled outside of Ireland. I often wondered about my relatives in Montserrat. We have never met. Although I am not pleased with Michael, I understand how volatile youth can be. It might be easier for him in Montserrat if I were to accompany you there."

"You are wonderful, Peter!" Sibella exclaimed, thrilled. "Who will look after your children?"

"Your old friend, Kate Moran." Peter smiled.

Sibella blushed.

At that moment, Michael returned.

"I have great news, Michael. Uncle Peter intends to accompany us to Montserrat."

"That is wonderful!"

* * * * *

SOON IT WAS TIME to depart for the New World. Michael's siblings all wanted to go with him but were doomed to disappointment. The excitement at Ashbrook was intense. Sibella allowed her children to travel to Galway, so that they could bid farewell to the travellers. Amidst the tears of separation, Sibella, Michael and Peter climbed on board the *Rover,* a one-hundred-ton brig, sailing directly to Montserrat. Sibella was grateful to George Moore for using his shipping contacts to reserve three berths. Soon they were on the high seas, on the adventure of a lifetime.

Peter, leaning over the taffrail, was curious about many things on board the ship.

"Why do they call it a brig?" he asked first, his hair dancing wildly around his head.

"Master Moore said that the *Rover* is a private warship known as a privateer brig," Sibella replied. "It is celebrated in song and story since defeating four Spanish warships without casualty."

Come all you jolly sailors, that love the cannon's roar,
A good ship on the wave, your lass and glass ashore,
How Nova Scotia's sons can fight, you ... shall hear,
And of gallant captain Godfrey in the Rover privateer.

"It is also popular with pirates, being fast, manoeuvrable and equipped with cannon."

"Was Master Moore a pirate, Mama?" Michael asked.

"He has been accused of piracy, although I do not credit those rumours." Sibella gathered her shawl around her. "No such accusation can be levelled against the *Rover* now that she is confined to merchant shipping."

Michael glanced at the frenetic activity high on the mast.

"Why do they need a crew of fifty-five?"

"To adjust the sails when moving into the wind or a storm," Sibella replied, exhausting much of the knowledge she had gleaned from George Moore.

Peter, looking pale, asked,

"How long will the journey take? I never thought seasickness would displace my initial excitement."

"About seven weeks if the trade winds are with us." Sibella was not feeling the best either.

"Just as well I am not with child, as I was on my first sea voyage," she thought.

They broke the tedium of the journey by playing cards, telling stories, reading, singing and watching the crew adjust the sails. The graceful surfing of dolphins and the endless squawking of seagulls accompanied them through the splendour of the Atlantic.

After four weeks, Sibella worried about the strengthening wind and darkening skies.

"Is there a storm on the way?"

"I'm afraid so," Peter replied. "The captain has warned me."

Later that evening the storm hit the *Rover* with unaccustomed ferocity. Sibella feared for her life as twenty-foot waves and driving rain pounded the ship over the next two days. She clung to her handrail and bed.

"Do not worry," the captain told her. "The ship will reduce speed by adjusting the sails. Please stay in your cabins until the storm abates."

After two long days and nights, the wind subsided and the sun shone again. The seagulls and dolphins reappeared.

"We are now on the high seas to Montserrrat," Michael said.

He appeared to have tolerated the stormy conditions better than his mother or great-uncle.

Soon they were scanning the horizon for land. A sailor high on the rigging shouted, "Land ahoy!" Pandemonium broke loose at the thought of reaching a safe haven.

"Is it always this warm in Montserrat?" Sibella wondered, baring her shoulders to the sun.

"These are the joys of a subtropical climate," Peter said.

The captain announced,

"Welcome to Plymouth, the capital of Montserrat!"

$$* \quad * \quad * \quad * \quad *$$

THE TRAVELLERS CHECKED INTO the Gingerbread Hill Hotel. Their three single bedrooms, enjoying a common balcony, overlooked the blue Atlantic.

The bold tree colours and the cinnamon fragrance of frangipani overwhelmed Sibella.

"This is close to paradise," she thought.

Having rested during the day, a revitalized Sibella joined her menfolk for dinner.

Over the soup, Michael said,

"Let us try Catherine Lynch's plantation first."

"May we come with you?" Sibella pleaded.

"I would love to see the sugar plantation," Peter said, sipping his coffee.

On the following morning they travelled by coach, traversing the tiny island, ten miles long by seven miles wide. Soon they arrived at the plantation where they found a man of mature years sitting on a swing chair in a sun-splashed veranda.

Blessed with the confidence of youth, Michael approached:

"Good day to you, sir. I am Michael Lynch from Ireland. This is my mother, Sibella, and my great-uncle, Peter Lynch who has a letter for you."

The elderly man broke the seal and quickly scanned the recommendation written by Peter. He glanced at the young man and then read the letter again.

"My name is Neptune Lynch. May I ask you a few questions?"

Sibella listened as Neptune asked him to name his father and mother, his grandparents and former occupation.

When Michael had answered all accurately, Neptune smiled.

"I had to make sure that you really are who you say you are. Please come in."

Sibella looked around the room as a black housekeeper served refreshments.

Neptune motioned his visitors to sit down. He glanced at Michael.

"I inherited this sugar plantation from my late mother, Catherine. My daughter, Annabel, and I would be glad of some help in running it." Neptune paused. "Your education and knowledge of Ireland may be useful in negotiating the export of sugar, rum, arrowroot and cotton. Your army experience would help to control an ill-tempered workforce."

"Can you furnish me with a little background to Montserrat, please?" Michael asked.

Sibella was fascinated by the history that unfolded.

"Montserrat was discovered by Christopher Columbus in 1493. The island came under British control in 1632, at which time a group of Catholic Irish settled here, having fled from a neighbouring island because of anti-Catholic violence."

"Where did Catherine come in?" Peter asked.

"My mother was the only child of one of the Blakes of Galway who acquired this sugar plantation. I am her only child, and my father, one of the Lynches of Galway had predeceased my mother. Annabel is my only child. We now have thirteen hundred acres with a processing plant at the base of a volcanic mountain. The cane fields are higher up the slope. We use African slaves as well as felons and indentured servants from Ireland and Britain."

Sibella was relieved when Michael extended his hand to Neptune's.

"I am happy to accept your offer of employment," he said.

She felt that the prospect of negotiating deals with merchants in Galway would excite him; however, controlling a workforce with good reason to be resentful would be less appealing. She watched as he scanned the list of indentured servants and noted his knotted brow.

"What is it, Michael?" she inquired.

"Listen to the Irish surnames — Blake, Darcy, Farrell, Fogarty, Kirwan, Molyneaux, O'Connor, Riley and Sweeney." Michael reverted to an earlier page. "Do you know who is here? Sean Holian!"

"For goodness sake!" Sibella was almost speechless. "What an amazing coincidence!"

"He must be the transported husband of Judy Holian," Michael said.

"More than likely." Sibella paused. "Neptune, I thank you for your hospitality. It is wonderful that Michael has found employment with a member of our extended family. Peter and I should leave you now and return to our hotel."

Peter added, "Perhaps you might both join us for dinner there, at the Gingerbread Hill Hotel, before we depart for Ireland?"

Neptune glanced at his dark-skinned daughter.

"Annabel and I would be delighted."

Ten days later Neptune, Annabel and Michael joined Peter and Sibella for dinner.

"We have had a wonderful holiday here, even though I sustained severe sunburn," Sibella said, grimacing. "I tried a compress of chamomile and bergamot tea, but to little purpose." Glancing at Neptune, she inquired, "How is Michael getting on?"

"He has settled in well. He's a great worker — a credit to you."

Annabel smiled in agreement as a blushing Michael said,

"I have spoken to Sean Holian. Neptune will give you the background."

"Many years ago, I was asked to take on a man who had stolen a sheep from Sir Robuck Lynch-Blosse of Balla. I understood the robber was married to a witch of a woman. Sure, how could I say no?"

Neptune laughed before raising his knife to the barbequed specialty of stuffed trunkfish.

Sibella reddened at the unexpected revelation.

"How do you find him?"

"He was an angry young man making no secret of his antagonism to slavery. The authorities suspected him of involvement in the slave revolt of 1768 almost thirty years ago. That happened on St Patrick's Day when the Irish were celebrating. They thought we were off our guard, but the plan leaked. The authorities stamped out the revolt, and the ringleaders ended up on the gallows."

"What happened to Sean?" Sibella asked.

She was relieved that Michael had concealed his discomfiture.

"The authorities asked me about him. I said he was a good worker and I had no trouble with him." Neptune paused. "I did not mention his friendship with the slaves. If I had, I would have signed his death warrant."

Sibella could now appreciate that Neptune was a man who understood how the system worked. "What did Sean say when you spoke to him, Michael?"

"He said he was homesick, having been here for nigh on thirty years. With a cynical smile on his wizened face, he said he had not been able to send a message to Judy."

Neptune scowled.

"I would have sent a message for him if he had asked."

Sibella paused, remembering that her son was the grandson of the man who had transported Sean.

"What else did he say, Michael?"

"Sean wants to go home. I said I would help but it would take time. He wept with emotion."

"I would be happy to cooperate in any plan to repatriate him," Neptune said.

"Thank you. I shall tell Judy the good news. May God bless you." Sibella smiled.

"Thank you for a lovely meal. We must return home before darkness falls." Neptune folded his napkin as Michael smiled at Annabel. "I hope you have a pleasant journey home to Ireland."

"I would like to invite both you and Annabel to visit Ireland," Peter interjected. "You could stay at Balla House and make contact with your extended family in Galway and Mayo."

"I would enjoy that very much," Annabel said as she departed with Michael and Neptune into a glorious sunset.

CHAPTER 21

AFTER THE DELIGHTFUL DISTRACTION of Montserrat, Sibella returned to Ashbrook. She was relieved to find that everything was in order, apart from the house that needed a spring-clean.

"Tell us about Montserrat, Mama," Cecilia urged with the enthusiastic support of her siblings.

Sibella described in detail the stormy sea journey, the Gingerbread Hill Hotel, the lush subtropical island, the sugar plantation where Michael now worked and the dark-skinned Annabel Lynch.

"Is Michael in love with her?" Cecilia asked, her sisters giggling in the background.

Sibella enjoyed the story telling which occupied many a night around the log fire.

"We will have to wait and see. What has been happening here?"

"I received a letter from John Moore," Cecilia said. "He wishes to pay us a visit."

"He is more than welcome, my dear."

Shortly afterwards, John Moore arrived on horseback.

John stammered his greeting, his cheeks flushing.

"Thank you, M-Mistress Cottle, for allowing me to visit. I am in love with your beautiful daughter." John paused. "May I ask for her hand, please?"

Delighted, Sibella stepped into the drawing room to allow the couple some privacy, leaving the door ajar.

She heard him say,

"Will you do me the great honour, Miss Lynch? Please marry me."

"Of course I will marry you, Mr Moore," Cecilia said. "This is the happiest moment of my life."

Shortly afterwards, Sibella rejoined the happy couple.

"You do realize that I am unmarried, Mr Moore?" she said quietly.

"Father is aware of that and does not regard it as an impediment. In fact, he has approved an announcement of our engagement which I prepared in the event that Cecilia accepted my proposal."

Sibella nodded.

"That is a relief to my mind. Now we must celebrate in the drawing room with champagne."

No sooner had the footman filled the flutes with the effervescing liquid than John spoke again. "Now that we are betrothed, I would like to visit Dublin with Miss Lynch; but Father objected to the plan."

Sibella's head was spinning. What a forthright young man, she thought, just like his father.

"Father proposed a compromise," John said to banish Cecilia's frown. "He suggested that we meet in Castlebar in a month's time and take the mail coach to Dublin where we shall stay in the Moore town house in Merrion Square."

"What does Mistress Moore think?" Sibella wondered.

"Mother has returned to Alicante for the winter. She has not yet acclimatized to the cold."

"Let me think about it," Sibella said. "Perhaps you and Cecilia would like to go for a ride with Packie Burke in the meantime?"

The two lovers needed no further invitation while Sibella went about her daily tasks of planning the day's requirements with the agent, housekeeper and cook. She tried to conceal her distraction from her daughters, Mary Anne, Bridget and Barbara as she organized their embroidery session. She thought about Cecilia, and how much she would enjoy a trip to Dublin, and she reviewed John's character in the light of his betrothal to Cecilia. Through all of this, she was aware of the excitement that coursed through her veins at the prospect of meeting George again. After lunch, she announced her decision.

"You may tell Master Moore that Cecilia and I will meet you in Castlebar on the appointed day."

Cecilia hugged her mother as John bowed.

"Thank you, Mistress Cottle. Father will be delighted. He has been anxious to visit Dublin for some time. Now I will take my leave, a happy man."

* * * * *

ONE MONTH LATER, THEY were on the road to Dublin. Sibella regaled George with stories of Montserrat while he responded with his past adventures on the high seas. During an overnight in Milltownpass, they spoke privately when walking behind John and Cecilia.

"How do you feel about our lovebirds?" George asked.

"I am plagued with worry."

"You fear the risk of intimacy while we are all living together in Merrion Square?"

"You have it precisely," Sibella said.

"John has come through a difficult period in his life. The French Revolution inspired him when attending the Sorbonne. After returning to the dreary normality of life, he found it difficult to descend from a radical pinnacle. Cecilia has helped to ground him."

"She is now ascending the radical pinnacle through John's involvement in the United Irishmen."

"Allow me to come back to that." George paused to blow his nose. "Concerning their attraction, John is rather old-fashioned. He does not believe in intimacy before marriage."

"Well, that comes as a relief, but will he be able to resist the advances of my affectionate daughter?"

George laughed. He enjoyed the wicked humour of the alluring redhead.

"Do not forget that we will be there with them at Merrion Square. You may keep your eye on your affectionate daughter at all times."

"I am also worried about the spancel," Sibella said.

"You have the advantage of me there."

"This is in strict confidence. After I had borne him five children, Harry was under pressure to abandon me and marry Lady Harriett." Sibella paused. "In desperation, I spoke to Judy Holian who recommended a spancel. I applied it and now I'm worried."

"Why?" George Moore raised his eyebrows.

"They say that if the spancel is burned or destroyed, a curse will fall upon me and my brood. I am thinking of John and Cecilia's welfare."

"I was told that if I built Moore Hall on the shores of Lough Carra, I would be cursed. You advised me to have the site blessed by Father Nolan and now all is well so far."

"I cannot ask Father Nolan to help me because he has named Judy Holian from the altar."

"Leave it with me," George said. "I shall deal with the matter immediately, and I will keep your secret. Where is the spancel now?"

"In Balla House, in a silver casket." Sibella paused. "Thank you. You have taken a load off my mind."

Sibella wondered how George was going to deal with the matter. Was he going to have the spancel blessed and sanctified by Father Nolan? Should she recover the spancel from Balla House?

On the following day, her mind was still in a whirl as they continued on the road to Dublin. Adjusting her tricorn hat, Sibella glanced at John Moore.

"Please tell us about the Sorbonne," she said.

"I was there during the French Revolution of 1789. I embraced the republican mantra of liberty, equality and fraternity."

"Were the women involved?" Cecilia asked.

"Very much so. The Women's March on Versailles forced Louis XVI to move to Paris," John responded. "The formation of the National Assembly was legitimized by the action of seven thousand women."

The recital of these stirring events excited Sibella and Cecilia and deepened their interest.

"What have you planned to do in Dublin?"

"I shall attend a meeting of the United Irishmen. We are inspired by the American Declaration of Independence and the leadership of Wolfe Tone."

"What an interesting man!" Cecilia exclaimed. "He had an affair at one time with Elizabeth Vesey, the wife of Richard Martin, Member of Parliament."

"Who is Elizabeth Vesey?" Sibella wondered, anxious that her articulate and well-educated daughter should be wary of gossiping.

"A Mayo woman from Hollymount, one of the most beautiful and talented women of the day; when 'Humanity Dick,' was away, Elizabeth took a shine to Wolfe Tone, a tutor to the Martins of Connemara."

"You have done your research, Miss Lynch. Our leader has come a long way since then."

John smiled while Sibella noted the liveliness of her daughter.

Having arrived in Dublin quite late in the evening, all four were exhausted and retired early to their separate beds after dinner.

*   *   *   *   *

ON THEIR FIRST MORNING in Dublin, Sibella peered through the window at the opulence of Merrion Square.

"I love listening to the clip-clop of hooves on the cobblestones. It is so different from the quietness of the countryside," she said.

Cecilia added,

"I love the wafting aroma of the brewery. It reminds me of the smell of roasted coffee. What shall we do today, Mama?"

"I would like to visit The Brazen Head, one of the oldest inns in Dublin."

Sibella blushed as George, Cecilia and John stared at her.

"I hope you will not object, George. Harry and I stayed there when we ran away to Suffolk."

"I would love to see the site of your romantic interlude."

"May I come, Mama?"

After glancing at George, Sibella nodded.

John said,

"I am going to Trinity College this morning. I can point you in the right direction if you walk with me."

After a light breakfast, the foursome set off towards College Green, flanking Trinity College and the Irish Parliament.

Pointing to the colonnaded building, Sibella said,

"That is where Harry served as a Member of Parliament for seven years."

Cecilia's blue eyes widened in surprise.

"Really, Mama?"

"How did Sir Harry enjoy the Parliament?" George asked.

"He was so proud of supporting the first Catholic Relief Act, in spite of strong opposition from Lord Altamont and that viper, James Cuffe."

John demonstrated his interest by asking,

"What did the Act achieve?"

"It allowed Catholics to take long leases and obtain and inherit property in the same way as Protestants." Sibella could feel the excitement coursing through her body as she remembered those moments of magic. "Harry was encouraged in his stance by the Chief Secretary, Sir John de Blacquiere."

"Without that Act, Moore Hall would not have been built," George interjected. "Without the support of Sir Harry and his brave colleagues, I would not have met Sibella."

"And I would not have met my United Irishman," Cecilia added.

John blushed.

"The United Irishmen are now seeking greater reform and more autonomy for Ireland."

The foursome sat down on a bench near the Parliament entrance. Looking over his shoulder, John whispered,

"You may know that meetings of the United Irishmen were suspended after France declared war on Britain. We managed to meet discreetly for some time. More recently, we have been forced to go underground as we prepare for rebellion."

"Mayhap you should take a step back," George said, glancing at the House of Parliament.

"Too late, father. I have signed up."

"Dear Lord!" cried Sibella.

"I shall sign up too," Cecilia said.

"It is far too dangerous." John admonished.

"It's just as dangerous for you, John," Cecilia responded.

"Couples have been advised to split; one member only to sign up so that their loved one can provide support without fear of censure."

"You should have discussed that with me before signing up."

Sibella kept her counsel as the enormity of the situation permeated her consciousness.

John's blue eyes now blazed with intensity.

"It does not work like that, my dear heart. My commanding officer looked at me with steel in his eye; either, I consented to go underground or I was out." John paused to draw his breath. "You will be my eyes and ears above the ground. Your activity will be as important as mine."

"Very well; what will happen now?" asked Cecilia.

Sibella was relieved that her daughter had accepted her external role.

John Moore raised his hands.

"The initial strategy aimed at reform. That included voting rights for all men, support for primary education and a further relaxation of the Penal Laws."

"Have you reminded them of the Women's March at Versailles?" Cecilia asked.

John's swarthy face began to redden.

"I shall table that for our next meeting."

"The Penal Laws are a disgrace," Cecilia said.

"How right you are!" John responded. "Catholics are still excluded from parliament, the judiciary and the higher offices of state. However, Protestants have been allowed to marry Catholics since 1792."

Glancing at her mother, Cecilia's eyes lit up.

"Mama! That's only four years after Papa died."

Sibella needed time for this reality to sink in while Cecilia continued.

"If the reform had come four years earlier, Papa could have married you. I would now be the respectable daughter of a baronet's widow rather than —"

"— than what, Cecilia?" Sibella interrupted.

"Forgive me, Mama; I was merely thinking aloud."

George interjected.

"It is not too late to draw back. Retribution will be severe for anyone threatening British rule."

"I shall think about it, Father." John drew his watch from his waistcoat. "Mistress Cottle, could you please excuse Miss Lynch and me for a few moments?"

Sibella nodded and the couple departed hurriedly, leaving their parents in fear and trepidation for their safety.

George said, "You must not worry: it will all blow over as wiser counsel prevails."

George's kind words did little to assuage her fear. Just when everything was falling nicely into place, this rebellion could destroy it all. To lighten the mood, she said,

"That forgetful son of yours left us without directions to The Brazen Head. Anyway … I no longer have the heart for it."

George opened his arms and embraced her: both needed solace.

After a pleasant week in Dublin, Sibella, Cecilia and George returned to Mayo, the ladies to Ashbrook, and the master to Moore Hall. Sibella's worry for Cecilia gradually abated as normal life resumed.

Talk of rebellion faded until late 1796 when John visited Ashbrook.

John whispered in the drawing room.

"The radicals are growing impatient with the pace of reform. Wolfe Tone has been pressing for a French invasion." John paused. "We have just heard that General Hoche will depart with a fleet from Brest. He plans to land at Bantry Bay. You must keep this a secret."

"Tell me everything, John," Cecilia said. "Who is General Hoche?"

"A man of humble origin, he enlisted in the French army as a private when sixteen and rose rapidly through the ranks. He supported the French Revolution and was promoted to the rank of general. Now, at twenty-eight, he has been appointed to lead the invasion of Ireland."

Sibella made the sign of the cross, worried by the threat of imminent war.

Cecilia was beside herself with excitement.

"I never thought I would hear talk of Brest again!" she exclaimed.

Sibella and John Moore looked quizzically at Cecilia. She explained.

"When Papa was dying, he told us that his great-great-grandfather had supported the invasion of Ireland by James II. After their defeat at the Boyne, Sir Henry fled to France with King James. He settled in Brest with his twin baby boys, although his eldest son remained in Ireland."

The memory of Harry coursed through Sibella's mind as Cecilia gazed into the wood fire.

"Is it possible that the descendants of those two baby sons might be part of the invasion force? What do you think, Mama?"

"What concerns me is your welfare. I am going to pray for your safety," Sibella replied. "May the Lord preserve us from all harm."

Over the coming months, John and Cecilia waited patiently for the anticipated invasion. Just before Christmas, John returned to Ashbrook crestfallen.

"What is the matter, John?" Sibella asked.

"The invasion went awry. It began well. General Hoche set sail with a fleet of fifteen thousand men. Wolfe Tone was on board."

Cecilia was almost afraid to pursue the matter further, fearing the worst.

"What went wrong?"

"Having successfully evaded the attention of the Royal Navy with a fleet of forty-three warships carrying 45,000 stands of arms, he approached the Irish coast; but the winter storms scattered the ships far into the Atlantic. Maldita!"

"M-Maldita," Cecilia stammered. "What does that mean?"

John clenched his fists.

"It means 'Damn!' It means this is bad news."

"What transpired?"

John Moore shook his head.

"A curse on them! Only a small number of ships reached Bantry Bay. Even these failed to land, having tossed for some days in the wild weather."

Cecilia frowned.

"That is the worst Christmas present ever. What now?"

"This affects our own plans. Nothing would please me more than to marry you now, my darling." John embraced her and held her tight. "However, if we married now it would endanger your life."

"I do not understand." Cecilia was dismayed.

"The authorities have been instructed to harass the nearest and dearest of our members." John released her and paced the floor of the dining room. "You will have better protection if we live apart until the rebellion is over."

"That could take years!" Cecilia cried.

"I believe it will be over soon." John held her again and looked deeply into her eyes. "Now I must make haste."

John kissed her and then departed with tears in his eyes.

Sibella was furious with him for leaving Cecilia in limbo. She was relieved when Cecilia put her disappointment behind her by convening an informal group of women known as the *Friends of the Enlightenment*, inspired by the Protestant Peggy Munro. Sibella attended their meetings every month in Castlebar where Cecilia unveiled the activities of the United Irish Quiltings in Lisburn. Sibella was fascinated to hear that Peggy

Munro was a sister of the United Irishman, General Henry Munro, a draper in the north of Ireland. Munro's disciples discussed Enlightenment issues from a woman's perspective. As they stitched their quilts, they sought means by which they could align their thoughts with the gospel of the United Irishmen.

Yet time passed slowly. Another Christmas without news left the Enlightenment members impatient. Hope was burning low in Cecilia's heart during the early months of 1798. Sibella trembled on hearing anew that rebellion was imminent. Where was John Moore? Did he yet live?

CHAPTER 22

ONCE NEWS FILTERED THROUGH that the rebellion had begun, both Sibella and Cecilia were sick with worry. They had not heard from John since the outbreak of hostilities. Sibella was relieved when George Moore rode to Ashbrook to share the burden.

"What should we do, George?"

"Leave matters lie for another week or two. John is not a frontline soldier. He would have remained in Dublin in an organizational role."

His response did little to calm Sibella's worry.

"He may have been arrested," she cried.

George lightly touched her arm.

"We shall go to Dublin if we do not hear news of him soon."

The feelings he aroused in her did little to persuade Sibella that remaining at home was the better option. As the weeks rolled by, she became increasingly agitated. Eventually she persuaded a reluctant George to travel to Dublin.

Just as they were about to leave, John arrived to render their journey unnecessary. He was in a state of high excitement.

"What has transpired?" Sibella asked. "We have been heartsick with worry."

"Our ranks were penetrated by an informer last spring. Then the British wounded Lord Edward Fitzgerald while taking him into custody. The wound was not serious, but it was left untreated and he died from infection."

"So that is what happened! Cecilia was surprised when we read of his death. May the Lord have mercy on his soul."

She shuddered as the implications of John's commitment penetrated her consciousness.

"Despite his loss, as you know, the rebellion started in May; most notably in Wexford."

Cecilia said. "I heard that the volunteers seized control of the entire county of Wexford."

"A wonderful achievement! But it did not last." John shook his head ruefully and explained:

"After the British had quashed the rebellion in Wicklow and in Ulster, they moved 20,000 troops into Wexford. The numbers were too much for our brave men."

"So that is how they came to defeat our forces at Vinegar Hill," George Moore said. "But how comes it that you are here?"

"After Vinegar Hill, people thought the rebellion was over. Our forces had been crushed in the southeast and the north of Ireland. But we are not defeated yet; my commanding officer ordered me to return to Mayo." John lowered his voice. "Something is going to happen here soon. You must promise not to say a word. I shall go to Castlebar tomorrow. All of you must go further south to Moore Hall, and wait and pray."

"No!" Cecilia cried. "I have waited long enough. I shall go with you to Castlebar."

Sibella trembled. She knew her determined daughter well enough to know that she could not dissuade her.

"Then you must bring your maid with you, my brave and darling daughter."

On their way south, Sibella saw pike-men on the road heading north wearing corduroy breeches, off-white shirts, green garters, and stockings. Red-coated units of the British Army were also heading north. Having reached Castlebar, Cecilia alighted from the Ashbrook carriage with her maid and John.

Glancing at the groom, John said,

"Please proceed to Moore Hall with Master Moore and Mistress Cottle as quickly as possible."

Cecilia saw tears in her mother's eyes as the carriage departed, generating a cloud of dust in its wake. She could hardly believe that she was re-united with John at last. After a long delay, their romance was progressing at speed.

She saw the firm purpose in his eyes when he said,

"My orders are to wait here in Geevy's Hotel. I am expecting General Humbert to land at Killala in north Mayo with about one thousand men. They plan to capture Ballina and then move south by a secret route, bypassing the British Army."

Cecilia bit her lip, feeling it could all go wrong. The memory of the hopes and dreams of her ladies in the Friends of the Enlightenment came to mind. Their monthly meetings, held in the hotel in which she now resided, had focused on a brave new world that would enhance the rights of men and women. The fact that women had come together to discuss a republican agenda was in itself a step towards greater freedom.

As the minutes and then the hours slipped by, she could feel the tension in the air. When she opened her bedroom window to look out, the normally busy street was almost deserted. Shopkeepers were frantically boarding up their windows. During moments of quietness, she could just about make out the muffled sound of gunfire, clashing swords and the plaintive cries of the wounded.

Did the British know about the secret plan to bypass them, she wondered. If so, their superior force would surely win the day. As her depression deepened, the sound of battle amplified as if entering the town. She heard a commotion on Market Street at its northern end. Looking through her window, she saw members of the British Army running rapidly in retreat.

People shouted,

"Stab them all!"

The Races of Castlebar were in full flight.

The plan had worked. Humbert had *routed the redcoats through old Castlebar*, as recorded by the balladeer.

Forget not the boys of the heather
Who rallied their bravest and best
When Ireland was broken in Wexford
And looked for revenge to the West.

Cecilia was on hand to witness the triumphal march of Humbert into Castlebar. Flushed with the scent of victory, she rushed into the adjoining bedroom.

"Humbert has succeeded, just as you said," she whooped in delight.

"Lock the door behind you, my dear heart," John said slowly and deliberately.

Cecilia suddenly felt pale.

"What is it, John?"

John's brow creased into a frown.

"I need to think before welcoming General Humbert."

Cecilia stared into the brown eyes of her beloved.

"What do you mean?"

"I was chosen for this task because of my experience in France, my linguistic skills and my family mansion at Moore Hall," John said. "I feel poorly qualified to protect those whose lives are now in my hands."

John stopped pacing and looked deep into her eyes.

"What would happen if I were to leave now and return to Moore Hall?"

Cecilia felt faint.

"Your reputation would be destroyed!" she spluttered,

"Would you still love me?"

"I will always love you, John, no matter what."

Suddenly she heard a loud knock on the door. Without waiting for John to respond, the door opened to reveal an Irish officer wearing a green jacket and a bandolier. He bowed ever so slightly and said,

"John Moore, your time has come."

The man withdrew, leaving the bedroom door ajar.

Cecilia understood her beloved's indecision, motivated by the fear of ultimate defeat and bloody reprisals.

"This is your moment of destiny," she encouraged him. "You have been called, and you must answer the call. May God be with you, my darling."

Tears welled in John's eyes.

"Thank you, Cecilia. Your support means the world to me."

He walked downstairs into Market Street before coming face to face with General Humbert, who had completed his triumphal march through the county town of Mayo.

Cecilia was so proud when John raised his voice amidst a crescendo of exultation.

"Bonjour, General Humbert. Congratulations on capturing Castlebar on this day, Monday, 27 August 1798. I have been asked by the United Irishmen to make myself available at your service."

Cecilia held her breath as Humbert looked John Moore straight in the eyes.

"I was expecting you, Citizen Moore. I hereby appoint you as President of the Government of the Province of Connaught within the declared Irish Republic."

Cecilia saw John blushing and bowing in response to loud cheers and the brandishing of pikes and muskets. His appointment was beyond her wildest dreams.

"General Humbert, I am honoured to accept my appointment on behalf of the United Irishmen and the brave people of Mayo." John glanced at Cecilia before continuing, "I hereby invite you and your command to visit my home at Moore Hall tomorrow."

"Thank you, President Moore. We shall depart at nine in the morning."

* * * * *

O N THE FOLLOWING MORNING, Sibella gazed through the window after breakfast while George sat fretting over John's safety. In the distance, she could see a cloud of dust on the horizon to the north.

"George, look! Somebody is on the march."

"Christ! It's a troop of soldiers." George extended his telescope. "The uniforms are blue. They must be French."

Sibella had never before heard George utter a profanity.

"I am frightened. What are they doing here?"

"It is well enough, my dear. John sent me a message last night. He said he would arrive with General Humbert today." George's eyes widened. "Jesu Maria! They are cantering towards Moore Hall. I see a man with a dark green military coat. It's John! And Cecilia is there behind him."

He immediately bolted to spread the news.

Sibella responded quickly. She hastily threw on a flowing green dress and a French tricorn hat. George donned his wig and vermilion coat. They walked with dignity down the three flights of limestone steps as the visiting party approached.

Sibella watched as John Moore alighted from his horse.

"Father, Mistress Cottle, I am proud to introduce General Humbert who yesterday declared the formation of the Irish Republic."

Speaking in French, the Master of Moore Hall bowed.

"Bonjour, General Humbert, you and your officers are most welcome. My groom will look after your horses. Please follow me into the Great Hall."

"Thank you, Master Moore. Our stay will be a short one. President Moore and I have important business awaiting us in Castlebar."

While George Moore remained impassive, Sibella almost fainted at the mention of "President Moore," while John flushed. Fortunately, Cecilia was on hand to prevent her mother's fall and produce her vinaigrette to revive her.

When Sibella recovered, Cecilia said,

"General Humbert has appointed me to the new Government of the Republic."

Feelings of incredulity, pride and trepidation ran riot in Sibella's mind. It was all happening so quickly.

"John will need me in Castlebar."

Cecilia spoke with an intensity that brooked no argument.

"I shall order a valise to be packed," Sibella said, and rushed indoors.

General Humbert shared champagne with Sibella, Cecilia and the Moores. As the visiting party prepared to leave, he said,

"Thank you for your hospitality, Master Moore and Mistress Cottle. Vive la Republique."

Sibella and George watched as the cloud of dust receded on the horizon. They went downstairs to the chapel and prayed for the safety of their children.

Having returned to Castlebar, Cecilia was not surprised to hear that the priority of the new Government was the provision of support for Humbert as he marched eastward across Ireland.

John sighed in his headquarters in Geevy's Hotel.

"Humbert needs eight regiments of infantry, each of twelve hundred men, and four regiments of cavalry, each of six hundred men."

Cecilia remained silent.

"How can we recruit so many at such short notice?"

Cecilia could see the disappointment etched on his face as he struggled to support Humbert in the field.

"You are doing your utmost, John."

Her fears were confirmed when Humbert had little more than two thousand men as he travelled into the eastern province of Ireland. Going into battle at Ballinamuck on 8 September 1798, Humbert was surrounded by the overwhelming force of more than 40,000 British soldiers. Having surrendered after less than an hour of hostilities, the soldiers of the French army were treated as prisoners-of-war. The Irish, however, were shown no mercy. They were treated as traitors and sentenced to death. More than five hundred rank-and-file Irish volunteers were massacred while their officers were hanged.

Cecilia was distraught on hearing that General George Blake of Garracloon, a distant cousin of her late father, was hanged on the battlefield having been found guilty of treason. The rebellion of 1798 was effectively over.

"Our republican dream now lies in ruin," John said, aimlessly shuffling some documents on the table. "You must return to Moore Hall immediately."

"I will stay with you, my darling."

"I shall go underground. The authorities will try to hunt me down. You will be of greater value free than imprisoned with me if I am captured."

"What about your letter of appointment?" she said.

"I shall carry it with me."

"I could stitch it into the lining of your jacket."

"Splendid!" John removed his green jacket and laid it on the table.

Cecilia reached for her sewing kit. She opened the bottom lining of his jacket, inserted the document into the opening, and re-sewed the garment with a matching thread.

As John attempted to escape to Dublin, Cecilia returned to Moore Hall.

"Thank God you are safe, my darling daughter," Sibella said, holding her close.

"Where is John?" George Moore asked.

"He's on the run," Cecilia cried. She fled to her room to weep in private.

"That is what I feared." George trod the floorboards. "He could not have chosen a worse option. They are bound to catch him. The authorities will try him for treason. I must appoint an attorney at once."

"Will he go to gaol, George?"

"They will almost certainly execute him."

"Lord help us!" Sibella cried as the enormity of the situation struck her like a blow. She wondered then if this could be the work of the accursed spancel.

✳ ✳ ✳ ✳ ✳

WHILE WAITING FOR NEWS of John, Cecilia became aware that the British Army was on the march to recapture the western territory Humbert had annexed. Soldiers soon arrived at Moore Hall. They arrested suspected pike-men and seized stock. George Moore insisted that Cecilia hide in a secret room accessible only through a door in the library shelf. Being Catholics, the Moores were always conscious of possible persecution and thought it best to have a bolthole.

After the soldiers departed, Cecilia fell prey to terror that they would capture and torture her beloved.

"The High Sheriff of Mayo, Denis Browne, is collaborating with the British," she cried, as news filtered through of reprisals under his direction.

She felt sick on hearing that soldiers had torched the nearby village of Carnacon, suspected of harbouring rebels. The fact that many a pike-man's door displayed the black ribbon of the deceased reminded her of John's concern for the men under his command.

"What can we do, Mama?"

"We must hope and pray for John's safety," Sibella said forlornly.

Cecilia prayed for him every night in the Moore Hall chapel. Not long afterwards, she saw a rider galloping up the avenue. She rushed to the door as the footman answered.

"An urgent message for the Master of Moore Hall," the breathless man gasped.

Cecilia watched in trepidation as George Moore broke the seal of the letter. She saw his face darken.

"What is it?" she asked.

"John has been arrested at Athlone. He has been driven along the road with other rebels to Castlebar."

"We must visit at once."

Cecilia ran to her room to throw on her warm cloak. As they approached the village of Carnacon, she could see smoke rising, and caught the smell of charred wood and burnt straw. She quivered with anger on seeing women and barefoot children shivering in the autumnal cold while they gazed helplessly at their burning cabins.

On leaving the village, the army stopped their chaise-and-four at a temporary barrier.

"We are on our way to visit my son in Castlebar Gaol," George Moore said.

"Martial law has been declared." The officer in command raised his voice. "We must search you, your drivers and the carriage."

"Why are you burning the cabins of innocent people?" Cecilia asked the army officer. She was furious when the officer directed a withering look at her. "Were it not for the instruction of Sheriff Browne, I would arrest you, Miss Lynch."

After the coach had been permitted to proceed, Cecilia puzzled over the reason that Browne, the brother of Lord Altamont, had decided to let her roam free. Was it because she was the daughter of the late Sir Harry Lynch-Blosse, or, was he responding to the mood of popular support for the rebellion?

Apart from that morsel of encouragement, worse was to follow as they entered Castlebar. Cecilia watched in horror as the army dragged a group of dishevelled men to the triangle and lashed their backs into bloody ribbons. How could they be so merciless? Did they have "to encourage the others" by coating their bodies with tar, and caging them in iron before dispatching them to the gibbet?

Cecilia could feel the tension in the town as George Moore requested permission to visit his son. A jangling of keys heralded their admission to a tiny cell where John sat on a straw bed. Cecilia had to conceal her dismay at the stench and dirt of a room that comprised an earthen floor, an unglazed barred window and a chamber pot.

"My darling!" Cecilia threw her arms around him.

Her spirits rose when she felt the strength of his rugged but cold body.

"What happened?" she said.

"I tried to escape to Dublin, hoping to catch a boat to France or America." John paused. "Everything went well until I was searched in Athlone."

"What did they find?"

"Humbert's letter which you had stitched into my jacket." John shook his head. "I was threatened with decapitation unless I admitted my guilt."

"That is against the law," Cecilia said.

"I proudly handed over my letter of Presidential appointment." John grasped an imaginary document and gestured it towards Cecilia. "I was charged with treason."

"Do not worry overmuch, John. Your father has hired a barrister to defend you," Cecilia smiled. "Were it not for Sheriff Browne, I would have been arrested on our way here."

"You must be more careful, my dear. The authorities are in a vicious mood."

"Perhaps they are afraid of me," she said mischievously.

It was so good to hear John laugh for a change. She continued to chat with him until a knock on the door signalled an intervention by the warder.

"Your time is up."

Cecilia was dismayed. She could have stayed for many hours, exchanging little stories and memories.

"I love you so much." She hugged John one more time. "We must not bend to the foe."

He held her close.

"We shall never bend to the foe."

After returning home, Cecilia focused on the fate of her sweetheart.

George Moore said,

"I have opted for a civil trial in the hope of a more understanding hearing."

"When will we know the outcome?" she asked.

"The court has delayed the trial until next year. The authorities fear a rescue attempt, given the unsettled conditions in Mayo."

Cecilia's face reddened as blood flowed into her cheeks. Why had she not thought of that before? Could she smuggle something into the gaol to aid an escape bid? She was furious when the sub-sheriff refused permission to visit again until the New Year. Well, if she could not visit him, she would write.

Meanwhile, the legal proceedings resulted in John's transference from Castlebar to Athlone, to Dublin, to Ballinrobe and back to Castlebar. Cecilia soon became aware that her lover's health suffered during this traumatic period.

Her worst fears were confirmed when they visited in the New Year to find him in poor condition. Solitary confinement in a cold cell with unpalatable food and deplorable hygiene had dragged him down. His face was as white as chalk except where red with lesions.

"I am so happy to see you," John said. "I kept reading your letter again and again."

"Do you jest, John?" Cecilia sought to cheer her darling. "Nothing would have kept me away, not even the might of the British Empire."

John smiled.

"You know that I love you dearly."

Cecilia blushed. "You are the love of my life, John." She hugged him while their parents maintained a discreet silence.

Relieved of his chains, John bent down shakily on one knee.

"Would you do me the honour, Miss Lynch? Please marry me, my darling."

"I have already agreed to do so," she smiled.

Following her acceptance of his first proposal, she was surprised to receive a second.

"I just wanted to make sure, in the light of our new circumstances."

John continued to kneel.

"I have never been so sure of anything in my life."

She was overjoyed but concealed her emotion, not being sure of his father's reaction.

"You have my blessing, John. I could not think of a finer woman to welcome into my family as a daughter."

Cecilia kissed John lightly on the forehead and raised him to his feet.

"I will marry you, my darling, whenever you wish."

She wrapped her arms around him and held him tightly.

"Thank you, Cecilia. You have made me the happiest man in the world." Glancing at his father, he said, "Could you please ask Father Nolan to marry us as soon as possible?"

Cecilia beamed as George nodded.

"I shall write to your mother in Alicante to tell her the great news."

Sibella wondered if the moody mistress of Moore Hall would return.

News of the proposed prison wedding spread quickly throughout Mayo. Sibella heard that the sheriff, Denis Browne, was apoplectic. She could just imagine him growling in his office as he sought to ban the proposed marriage. The authorities advised that such action would alienate public opinion.

CHAPTER 23

ONE WEEK LATER, SIBELLA, Cecilia and George set off for the county courthouse in Castlebar. Sibella was worried about George. His energy levels had dropped; the long months of obtuse legal manoeuvrings, rough coach journeys and mediocre accommodation had taken their toll.

While travelling through the countryside, the sight of torched villages was a grim reminder of British reprisals. Sibella recited the rosary, pleading for clemency for President John Moore.

As they walked through Castlebar, Sibella averted her gaze from the grisly work of the hangman although his work was thankfully coming to a close.

"What verdict do you expect?" Sibella asked George as they sat to the front of a crowded courtroom.

"He will be found guilty of treason," George whispered. "In normal circumstances, that would mean execution. John's attorney, Alexander McDonnell, is frantically working on a plea for clemency. Not a word to Cecilia. Her hope and his must not be quashed."

"All rise," the clerk of the court cried as the judge took his seat.

A commotion on one side of the courtroom indicated the entry of the accused. Sibella was dismayed at the gaunt appearance of Cecilia's fiancé. Given his weakened condition, the court allowed him to sit in the dock.

The judge raised his gavel.

"John Moore, His Majesty's Government charges you with treason."

"Nonsense," a voice cried from the back of the court to the accompaniment of feet stamping.

The Judge banged his gavel.

"I shall have the courtroom cleared if there is any further commotion."

After swearing-in, John Moore pleaded *Not guilty* to the charge

Following protracted legal proceedings, the prosecution summarized the case for the Crown.

"My Lord, the defendant, John Moore, was arrested by Colonel Crawford shortly after the recapture of Castlebar by the British Army. During interrogation, Moore produced the proclamation signed by General Humbert in which his appointment as President of the Government of the Province of Connaught was announced. By producing this document, he has incriminated himself. Therefore, he is guilty of treason and must face the full rigour of the law."

The counsel retained on behalf of George Moore rose in defence.

"My Lord, John Moore is an honourable man who believes in the humane principles of liberty, equality and fraternity. As a member of the

United Irishmen, he was dedicated to the implementation of these principles in Ireland. The hostility of the British Government to parliamentary reform eventually forced the United Irishmen to adopt radical measures. It is the British Government who should be in the dock here today, and not John Moore. If the defendant is guilty of any offence, it arises from his love of Ireland and his dedication to the basic principles of democracy, and to the rights of man. John Moore is not guilty of treason. He must be found innocent and immediately released."

"Hear, hear!" A man shouted from the rear of the courtroom to the accompaniment of clapping.

Sibella rose and joined in the clapping, as did Cecilia and George Moore. Soon, most people were on their feet apart from the lawyers and members of the landed gentry.

Sibella bit her lip.

"George, how will the verdict go?" she asked.

"The defence counsel has done us proud. He has spoken for the people."

"But will John be found guilty?" Sibella interjected.

Cecilia clutched her rosary beads.

"Let us hope and pray that John will not be found guilty."

Despite the warmth of George's response, Sibella had an uncomfortable feeling that the verdict would break her daughter's heart.

Having re-established order, the Judge went on with the proceedings.

"I am now in a position to announce the verdict, having carefully considered all the evidence." He glanced at the prisoner in the dock. "John Moore of Moore Hall, you have been found guilty of treason."

"Rubbish!" The crowd responded while Sibella embraced a devastated Cecilia.

Sibella dreaded that the Judge would don the black cap sitting prominently on the bench beside him. She waited while the judge composed himself. An audible sigh of relief could be heard when the black cap was left untouched.

"John Moore, I hereby sentence you to transportation to Australia."

"Up the Republic," rang a voice from the rear accompanied by loud cheering.

Sibella, Cecilia and George had mixed emotions about the verdict, but relief predominated. As they left the courthouse, Sibella felt grateful admiration for George Moore's ten-month struggle to defend his son. Even though not completely successful, a sentence of transportation was better than the death penalty.

She saw George come face to face with Denis Browne in the company of Altamont and Lady Harriett. Moore and Browne eyed each other with barely-concealed contempt. Although worn out from efforts to save his son, George still raised his voice to say,

"How dare you prosecute my son, whose only crime was to fight for Irish freedom as your ancestors did at Aughrim?"

Sibella pursed her lips as the High Sheriff scowled. Moore had struck a sensitive blow.

"Circumstances have changed, Master Moore. Your son is guilty of treason. I had no option other than to hunt him down," Browne countered loftily. "If he had been tried in Dublin, he would have hanged on a gibbet."

"You evil man!" Cecilia cried. "His only crime was to love his country."

George tapped his sword in support of her words.

"How dare you authorize the torching of houses on my estates and the seizure of stock?"

Altamont intervened and dragged his brother away to avoid an altercation. An expectant crowd was disappointed as the incident fizzled out.

As they left, Sibella quelled the rage in her heart and retained her dignity, although it was difficult to ignore the contemptuous expression on Lady Harriett's face.

Suddenly, George Moore clutched his chest, staggered and fell on to the stone plinth of the courthouse entrance.

"Please call a doctor at once!" Sibella cried.

Doctor Boyd, who had attended the court case, was quickly found. When he reached Moore, he knelt down and inspected him.

"You must bring him home immediately and let him rest. I shall arrange for a younger colleague to call at Moore Hall tomorrow."

"God bless you, Doctor Boyd."

The Moore Hall carriage soon arrived to ferry George home. With the help of two footmen, Sibella and Cecilia put him to bed and then retired to the chapel to pray for their men.

While George Moore rallied, he was never well enough to leave his bed. The young doctor was unable to help, other than to advise rest and prayer, and pray they did. Every evening in the chapel, Sibella and Cecilia implored the good Lord for his intercession.

Towards late autumn, George spoke to Sibella at his bedside.

"My time has come. Thank you, my dear, for your company over the past seven years. You brought light and comfort to my heart. Cecilia has done the same for John."

Sibella kissed him on the cheek.

"You must rest, George. Your heart is weak."

Sibella wondered why Mistress Moore had not returned to look after her husband and son. She did not trouble George about it. It had given them this last precious time together for which she was grateful.

George said,

"My eyesight is fading but my spirit is strong. I can still see your lovely red hair. Your presence at my bedside keeps me content; but, oh, that we could have kissed more often!"

He stretched out his hand, grasped tenderly by Sibella as she sought vainly to control her tears.

"I want you to contact Father Nolan. I need to prepare my soul for the Almighty. And one last request, I want to be buried at Moore Hall."

George collapsed in exhaustion when he finished speaking. Soon he was fast asleep.

The parish priest of Balla arrived the next day. Sibella knew that the invitation to attend at Moore Hall would please him, although he would probably resent having to renew acquaintance with a woman who had scandalized the village. Her suspicion was confirmed when she met him on arrival. He maintained a discreet silence as she escorted him to George's bedroom.

Sibella instructed the chambermaid to close the shutters and to illuminate the room with wall-mounted candles. She beckoned Father Nolan to the bedside now that the master's eyes were shielded from sunlight.

George whispered,

"You will be sure to marry John and Cecilia before his transportation?"

The priest nodded and then listened to George's confession, anointed him and commended his soul to the Lord.

Sibella was devastated when George passed away in his sleep that night, having lost his sight some hours earlier. After Harry, he was the most remarkable man she had ever met. He had provided her with a roof over her head when her options were limited, and he had not objected to the liaison between his heir, John, and her illegitimate daughter, Cecilia.

Sibella was in love with him, and he with her, she believed. He would have proposed to her had he been free to do so, and she would have accepted, although her children might have objected to the union.

News spread quickly of the passing of George Moore, the master of Moore Hall. Messages of condolence flooded the house, which mourned in private. In accordance with George's wishes, the agent arranged for the burial of his master in a plot at Moore Hall. Father Nolan recited a decade of the rosary at the graveside, attended by George's loved ones and the local community.

∗ ∗ ∗ ∗ ∗

SIBELLA RETURNED TO ASHBROOK, fretting all the while in case the accursed spancel was responsible for the demise of George Moore. Cecilia soon distracted her haunted mind.

"Mama, John is about to be moved to Waterford in preparation for transportation. I must go to Castlebar immediately."

"I will go with you." Sibella donned her cloak. "We can collect Father Nolan on the way. I will send Packie Burke to the sub-sheriff to request preparation of President Moore for his wedding."

Soon they were on the road to Balla. People blessed themselves as the Ashbrook carriage passed by. Sibella collected the priest. People waved in support as they approached the county town of Mayo. Much to their amazement, a sizeable crowd had assembled at the gaol in anticipation of the rebel wedding.

Sibella gasped when a local leader stepped forward, a pike-man by his side.

"Miss Lynch, on behalf of the men and women of '98, please accept a red rose for the bride and one for the groom, President John Moore."

The two men quickly disappeared into the crowd as the sub-sheriff ordered their arrest.

Glancing at the wedding party, the sub-sheriff shouted,

"Please follow me. Make way."

John Moore was waiting in the keeper's room. Still gaunt, he was dressed simply in an open black coat, breeches and shoes complemented by a white shirt and stockings.

"You look wonderful, John," Cecilia said. "The men of '98 asked me to present President Moore with a red rose."

Tears came to the groom's eyes as Father Nolan hurried the ceremony along, conscious of John's limited capacity to stand. Having exchanged marriage vows, Sibella surprised Cecilia by producing two wedding bands.

"Mama, where did you get these?"

"Harry asked me to present his wedding band to his first child to marry."

"It is beautiful."

Cecilia pushed the ring on to the fourth finger of John's left hand.

"The second band was bequeathed to me by my father, Michael Cottle. I always intended to give it to my first daughter to marry."

Sibella handed the ring to John who did the honours.

The sub-sheriff joined in the clapping as Father Nolan announced,

"You may now kiss the bride."

Cecilia walked towards John who was holding his balance with difficulty.

He lifted her veil, kissed and embraced.

"Cecilia, my darling, this is the happiest moment of my life."

The sub-sheriff, happy that the ceremony had gone without a hitch, produced a bottle of champagne and four flutes.

"These have been presented by an anonymous donor. After you have toasted the marriage, I shall leave you in peace for ten minutes; then you must disperse. The prisoner will depart for Waterford early tomorrow morning."

Sibella knew that the next ten minutes would be precious for the newly-weds. She thought of Harry who would have been so proud had he witnessed the marriage of his daughter. His pride would have extended to a fascination with the circumstances of the rebel wedding reminding him of his own controversial life.

Time drifted by so quickly that soon Cecilia rejoined her mother after the groom had returned to his cell. When Cecilia led the wedding party from the gaol, a mighty roar of approval erupted from an even larger crowd.

It was a fitting farewell for a President, Sibella thought as they made their way to Geevy's Hotel to spend the night; and yet so poignant that the young couple could not enjoy even a short honeymoon together.

* * * * *

ON THE FOLLOWING MORNING, Sibella and Cecilia set off on the long and exhausting journey to Waterford. Both women were deep in their own thoughts. Sibella remembered her own abortive wedding to Harry in Suffolk, and how the vicar had eyed her askance, unconvinced that she was one-and-twenty, and could marry without her parents' consent. In any event, her natural parents were dead, but the vicar was right, she was only nineteen and her foster-parents would have refused permission to marry.

When Harry failed to marry her, the stigma of illegitimacy became a burden to her seven children; but she believed that Cecilia, at any rate, had freed herself from that shackle. The honour of her marriage to the former President of the Republic of Connaught would stay with her forever. Sibella prayed that John would return from Australia in due course. She knew her daughter well enough to know that Cecilia would wait for him.

On arrival, Sibella saw two soldiers carrying a man on a canvas sling into the Royal Oak Tavern in Waterford. Later that evening, the commanding officer confirmed her fears; he had detained Moore in the tavern because of his weakened condition, along with two rebel priests, a friar, a farmer and an innkeeper. Sibella and Cecilia visited John in his guarded room after receiving permission to do so.

Tears trickled down Cecilia's cheeks on witnessing his fevered state. She kissed him on his sweating forehead and held his quivering hand.

He smiled in response and his lips silently formed the words, "I love you, Cecilia."

Sibella could feel the tears welling in her eyes when Cecilia said,

"When you married me, you made me the happiest woman in Ireland. I shall not let you go. I will make you recover. While you recuperate, I shall continue to struggle for the ideals you rightly believed in. You will always be in my heart, my darling husband."

Shortly afterwards, the regimental surgeon entered.

"Mr Moore has travelled poorly," he said. "He is suffering from fever. I have bled him regularly in the hope that he might rally. His spirit is strong but his body is weak."

"Thank you, doctor. May we ask one of the rebel priests to honour him with the last rites, just in case?" Cecilia implored.

After the request was granted, a rebel priest anointed the former President of Connaught while Cecilia prayed for him. Her prayers continued late into the night until his pulse slowed.

"Do not leave me now, John," Cecilia cried and cried again. "Do not leave me!"

Her pleas were futile. John passed away peacefully as she prayed. His skin was taut, drawn tightly over the bones of a face adorned with a golden-brown bristle. A relaxed countenance and closed eyes showed the former President at peace.

Sibella was distraught for her devastated daughter. John's death had dashed her hopes for a renewal of their relationship after a period in Australia.

On the following day, the army buried him in the local cemetery at Ballygannon. While preparing his body for burial, Cecilia discovered a crumpled paper in his fist. It was one of her love letters to him.

At the graveside, a United Irishman had secretly posted an inscription pinned to a wooden stake commemorating his death:

Here lies the body of John Moore Esquire
of Ashbrook, Co. Mayo, who died
in Waterford in December 1799 aged 36.

Sibella wondered why John had given his address as Ashbrook: perhaps he had wished to acknowledge the original home of both the Moores and his mother-in-law, where he and Cecilia had met. Both women wept inconsolably. Two great men were dead: a father had predeceased his son by a month, exhausted from his efforts to save him. It was a time for mourning and quiet reflection.

CHAPTER 24

THE PAIN OF GRIEF diminished over the next four years. Life at Ashbrook gradually returned to normality. Sibella's eldest son, Michael, wrote regularly from Montserrat. Up to this time, his letters had avoided mention of romance. Sibella had almost forgotten the expectation she had once cherished that Michael might marry Annabel Lynch, the heir to a sugar plantation. On reading his latest letter, however, she crowed with joy.

Cecilia rushed into the breakfast room.

"What is it, Mama?"

"Call the children. I have great news from Montserrat."

As they seated themselves at the breakfast table, Sibella read:

Galway's Sugar Plantation,
Montserrat, West Indies,
Wednesday, 1 August 1804.
Dear Mama,

I finally took courage in my hands and approached Neptune Lynch for the hand of Annabel. Having proclaimed my love for his daughter, I asked for permission to marry her.

Neptune wondered if I wanted to return to Ireland, which might have posed a problem. I told him my future was in Montserrat. My trips to Galway to sell sugar, rum, arrowroot and cotton would keep me in touch with the country I love. Neptune asked if you would approve of the marriage. I told him you would be overjoyed, Mama.

Shortly afterwards, I proposed to Annabel. She accepted, but wondered if my religion was important to me, as hers was to her. I said that you and my sisters were Catholic, and I would be happy to marry her in a Catholic ceremony. I also said that there were things about me she should know before we married. She smiled and said that her father had already shown her Uncle Peter's letter of introduction, a copy of which is attached.

We plan to marry next St Patrick's Day. I wish you to attend, Mama. You would need to set sail early next year. Your presence would mean the world to me.

My regards to the rascals,
Your loving son,
Michael.

"That is great news, Mama," Cecilia said excitedly. "You must begin to think what to take with you."

Sibella clutched the letter to her.

"Let us think about it over Christmas. Peter may be too old to travel, not to mention all the children he has recently fathered."

"I would love to go there too," Cecilia said. "I could use my inheritance if the Moores were agreeable."

"Let us all go," John and George cried in unison.

"I would surely love that, my darlings, but we simply cannot afford it. You will need to look after Ashbrook. I will ask Mary Anne, Bridget and Barbara to lend a hand although each is busy setting up their new homes with their husbands."

Amid mutterings of discontent, Cecilia glanced at the letter.

"What did Uncle Peter say about Michael in his letter?"

"Let us see."

With their dreams of transatlantic adventure dashed, the possibility of gossip provided some consolation.

"The letter is marked 'Strictly Private and Confidential' from Peter Lynch, Balla House, Co Mayo, 1 May 1795. It reads as follows:"

Michael Henry Lynch is the eldest child of my nephew, the late Sir Harry Lynch-Blosse, 7th Baronet of Balla and Sibella Cottle. Sibella is the only child of Michael Cottle who died shortly after her birth. Her mother, a sister of Mistress Moore of Ashbrook, died when Sibella was three years. She was fostered at Ashbrook, and reared and educated as a young Catholic lady.

In 1773, my nephew, Harry, stayed at Ashbrook after his failed marriage to a Catholic named Emily Mahon. Harry fell in love with Sibella, ran away with her, and not long afterwards, Michael was born.

When Harry's father passed away, Sibella became Mistress of Balla House. Before Harry died in 1788, he made generous provision for their children. Thus, I was able to fund a career for Michael in the 13th Light Dragoons. Eventually, he decided to leave the army and emigrate to the West Indies. As his guardian, I recommended contacting our relatives in Montserrat because I felt you might be inclined to find employment for a family member.

I can vouch for Michael's education and upbringing. His estate and army experience renders him suitable for employment on a sugar plantation or other business of that type, and his contacts would be of assistance to him in any trade between our countries. He is conscientious and an excellent worker. His engaging personality makes it easy for him to work with others. He has my strongest recommendation.

"I never noticed his engaging personality," Cecilia quipped. "Tell us about your father, Mama."

"I never knew him. My foster-mother told me he was very handsome. He was red-haired and freckled, just as I am. She said he hugged me and cried; he would not let me go on his deathbed."

Tears came to her eyes.

"What happened to him?"

Sibella paused as silence prevailed around the breakfast table.

"All I know is that he lies with my mother, Isabel, in the graveyard at Cottlestown in Sligo. We must all go there soon and pray for them."

Sibella tried to control her tears as she realized anew how many loved ones had passed away.

Her children sympathized with her as she composed herself.

"I often wondered about my mother. Where did she meet Michael Cottle? Where did they live? I never found out." Sibella wiped her tears with a white handkerchief. "When my foster-mother was on her deathbed, she gave me my grandmother's wedding band. Because Louisa had no children of her own, she asked me to give it to my daughter who married first. That is why Cecilia is wearing it."

"Goodness," the siblings interjected in unison.

"She was about to say more when she slipped away ..." Sibella paused. "Perhaps she would have told me more about my father. Now I will never know. In any event, we must not wallow in the past but look to the future."

Her children gathered round and embraced her as they took it all in. They did not raise the issue of the spancel much to Sibella's relief. She hoped they knew little of it or had purged it from their minds.

* * * * *

AS HALLOWE'EN APPROACHED, AN invitation to dinner arrived from Uncle Peter, much to their surprise.

"It must be his guilty conscience, Mama; he has been neglecting us," Cecilia opined, reading the invitation.

"There may be something more to it."

"How many children does he have now?" Cecilia asked.

"Seven boys and five girls, I have heard. Quite a family!"

"And nary a wife in sight. Oh, I'm sorry, Mama; I was not thinking."

Cecilia's face reddened.

"I have heard that Emily Mahon thought better of the relationship ..." Sibella's voice trailed away.

"What age is he now?"

"More than seventy years."

"How is the old witch?" Cecilia asked, sipping her milk.

"As fiery as ever. She has given up hope that Michael can repatriate that husband of hers. I must bring her some meat and brandy when we go to Balla."

When Sibella and her children arrived at Balla she found Peter in the company of an unknown young man.

Peter had aged. His hair had thinned and his face had wrinkled.

"Allow me to introduce Mr de Blacquiere," he greeted them.

The stranger bowed.

Sibella curtsied in response.

"That name sounds familiar," she said, looking the young man in the eye. "Are you the son of Sir John?"

The blushing young man nodded.

Peter interjected.

"I wrote to Sir John recently to see if he could recommend an ambitious young man as agent. At my age, I can no longer do the work I used to."

Sibella remarked to de Blacquiere,

"Sir Harry spoke in glowing terms of your father's role in the Irish Parliament."

"Thank you, Mistress Cottle," de Blacquiere said. "I shall convey your kind words to him in the New Year."

Hallowe'en dinner followed with Peter at the head of the table opposite Sibella, flanked on the sides by de Blacquiere, Cecilia, John and George. Carved-out turnips containing lighted candles adorned the side tables.

The footman served roast goose and potato after a starter of vegetable soup. Great excitement erupted when a barmbrack followed but, strangely, no one found the ring. Had someone found the ring, it would have meant certain marriage before the year was out.

After they had eaten, John and George begged to be excused. They departed to watch the older children dancing around the bonfire to expel the evil spirits of ghosts, vampires, werewolves and witches.

After the footman had brought in the port, Sibella said,

"We have good news from Montserrat. Michael is to be married next spring."

"Congratulations, Sibella."

"He has invited me over. Cecilia intends to accompany me." Sibella paused. "All we need is a gentleman to escort us."

"I would have enjoyed it years ago, but I am far too old to travel now." Peter glanced at de Blacquiere who remained impassive. "How long do you intend to stay?"

Now Sibella also gazed at de Blacquiere.

"No more than a couple of weeks."

"I would be honoured to accompany you, but my schedule is far too busy," de Blacquiere said, tapping the table nervously.

"That is so. On the other hand, the marriage of Sir Harry's eldest son is a special occasion. I think you might be spared for such a purpose."

The awkward silence was eventually broken by Sibella.

"I will need to cash the second note Sir Harry gave me in order to cover my expenses. The Moores have agreed to cover Cecilia's expenses from her inheritance."

Uncle Peter grimaced at the thought of approaching the trustees not only for the five hundred pounds but also for de Blacquiere's expenses.

"I shall see what I can do." Directing his gaze to de Blacquiere, Peter said, "Perhaps you could draft a budget for the trip. You could then approach James Cuffe, now Lord Tyrawley, with our proposal."

De Blacquiere's face lit up.

"Should I also reserve a single and a double cabin on the *Rover*?"

"Indeed, my good man. Let us drink to adventure in the Caribbean."

As they drained their glasses, Sibella said,

"I shall write to Michael to tell him the good news."

And write she did, on returning home:

Lieutenant Michael Henry Lynch,
Care of Neptune Lynch Esq,
Galway's Sugar Plantation,
Montserrat, West Indies.
Saturday, 1 December 1804
My dear Michael,
Congratulations to you and Annabel on your engagement. Cecilia and I hope to attend your wedding in Montserrat next spring. The new agent at Balla, Peter Boyle de Blacquiere, has agreed to escort us at the suggestion

*of Uncle Peter. We are looking forward to it and to seeing you again after
your recent visit.*

Best wishes to Annabel and Neptune,
Your loving mother,
Sibella Cottle,
Ashbrook, Co Mayo, Ireland.

Sibella enjoyed Cecilia's excitement as her daughter prepared for her
first transatlantic voyage. Sibella had already undertaken the exhausting
journey, having accompanied Michael on his maiden voyage to
Montserrat. She reflected, as she prepared for the journey, on how the
years were flying by.

In early January, they set sail from Galway amid tearful farewells from
Mary Anne, John, Bridget, George and Barbara. For seven long weeks,
Sibella and Cecilia experienced the harshness of the wild Atlantic gales.
Occasional bouts of seasickness, discomfort, boredom and exhaustion
challenged their morale. De Blacquiere explained that his immunity arose
from his youthful experience in the Royal Navy under Captain Bligh. Now
beginning to feel her age, Sibella heaved a sigh of relief on arrival at
Plymouth port. Michael was there to welcome them.

"Ods bodkins! I have missed you so much," he cried, embracing
Sibella and Cecilia. He warmly shook the hand of de Blacquiere.

"Congratulations on your engagement, Mr Lynch," de Blacquiere said.

"Please call me Michael. Now I must show you our sugar plantation."

As they travelled along the dusty track flanked by exotic palm trees
and scented flowers, Sibella asked, "How is Sean Holian?"

"He cannot wait to get home. I have encountered serious opposition to
his repatriation arising from his misdemeanours." Michael paused. "I
asked my betrothed, Annabel, and her father, Neptune, to accept Sean as
the best man at our wedding. They refused, fearful of the local reaction to
the presence of a rebel among the wedding party."

De Blacquiere raised his eyebrows while Sibella pursed her lips. If
scandal continued to pursue her through life, it seemed that her children,
Michael and Cecilia, were determined to follow suit.

"Why did you describe Mr Holian as a rebel?" de Blacquiere asked.

"Holian was sympathetic to the slave revolt of 1768. He would have
ended up on the gallows were it not for the intervention of Neptune Lynch.
My future father-in-law is no rebel, but he favours reform of conditions for
servants and slaves."

As they came close to Galway's sugar plantation, Sibella looked in
wonderment at the sugar cane plants, now six to nine feet tall.

Michael said,

"Harvesting will start in June. That is when manual labour is most intense as the servants and slaves wield their machetes."

When they arrived, Neptune Lynch was sitting on a swing chair in the veranda.

"It is wonderful to see you again, Sibella."

"Thank you, Neptune. This is my daughter Cecilia and Mr de Blacquiere, the new agent at Balla."

"I can see that Cecilia has inherited the good looks of her mother," Neptune said gallantly. "Please accept my sympathy for your great losses."

"Thank you, Neptune. I can see that Annabel has inherited your fine features."

Both Neptune and his dark-skinned daughter flushed in response.

Over the next few days, Sibella rested while Michael and Annabel guided Cecilia and de Blacquiere around the volcanic island. From time to time, she strolled through the plantation under the watchful eye of Neptune and his agent. In the evening, she joined Neptune in the veranda. Both lonely, they missed their deceased partners and worried about the future of their children.

"Have you ever thought of remarrying?" Sibella asked. "Forgive me, Neptune, I should not have asked."

Neptune laughed.

"I have, but I never found a suitable bride."

*　*　*　*　*

On ST PATRICK'S DAY 1805, Michael and Annabel were married in the Roman Catholic chapel of Plymouth, which nestled at the foot of the Soufriere Hills volcano. Annabel wore a long white dress with matching hat and veil. Her red gloves and shoes underscored a simple elegance. She carried an ingenious handkerchief that, with a few stitches, was transformable into a christening bonnet for their first baby. Sibella and Cecilia were dressed in matching outfits apart from the red accessories.

Michael wore a long, open green coat, an ornamented beige waistcoat and tight dark breeches. Neptune wore a dark broadcloth coat, off-white waistcoat and black breeches.

A piper led the wedding procession as Neptune escorted his daughter and only child to the altar. The ceremony was a simple one, during which the officiating priest wished them well:

May the gracious God hold you both in the palm of His hands.
And, today, may the Spirit of Love find a dwelling place in your hearts.

At the reception in the Gingerbread Hill Hotel, they enjoyed a main course that featured jerk shrimp with rum, cinnamon bananas and cranberry. Then Neptune made a short speech.

"It gives me great pleasure to wish Michael and Annabel every success in the future. Michael has come to us from Ireland. He has been with us for ten years and has settled in seamlessly. He is a credit to his beautiful mother, Sibella, who has made the long journey from Ireland to be with us on this joyous occasion."

Spontaneous clapping broke out as Sibella blushed happily.

Neptune continued.

"Sibella is accompanied by her daughter, the beautiful Cecilia, and by Mr de Blacquiere, an agent representing the extended Lynch family. Cecilia lost her husband, President John Moore, and his father after the 1798 rebellion in Ireland."

Sibella could see that Michael's eyes were tearful with pride at the involvement of his extended family in the struggle for freedom. She also noted how de Blacquiere squirmed uneasily at the mention of rebellion.

"I know that today's union will help to replace grief with the joy of a new beginning."

Neptune sat down to enthusiastic applause as the dessert arrived.

After the speeches, Sean Holian discreetly approached Sibella and introduced himself.

"How is my beloved wife, Judy?"

"She is well," Sibella replied. "She misses you very much, as do Ned and Thady."

"Were they involved in '98?"

"I do not know, but they are alive and well," Sibella said. "When are you coming home to us?"

"I was thinking of stowing away on the *Rover*."

"Does Michael know that?" Sibella asked, intrigued. "What did he say?"

"He laughed first and then warned me off. If I was caught, it would be the end of me."

Sibella was relieved at the mature response of her son.

"What now, Sean?"

"Once things settle down, Michael plans to visit Ireland with Annabel. He hopes to bring me too. Your son is a good man."

He excused himself while tears flowed down his weather-beaten cheeks.

Cecilia rejoined her mother.

"Why was that man crying, Mama?"

"That is Sean Holian, and he is desperate to come home. The poor man has not seen his family since his two sons were babies. Michael is working on it."

After a delightful fortnight in Montserrat, Sibella, Cecilia and de Blacquiere returned to Ireland while Michael and Annabel honeymooned at home in Montserrat.

On their return to Ashbrook, Sibella rested while Cecilia regaled her siblings with stories of the wedding, the Caribbean and the emotional meeting with Sean Holian.

Shortly afterwards, Cecilia began to contemplate the future. "What is going to become of us now, Mama?"

"We will consider that when Michael and Annabel visit. I wouldn't be surprised if Sean Holian travels with them."

CHAPTER 25

IT WAS ALMOST THREE years after the wedding in Montserrat when Sibella received a letter edged in black. Breaking the seal in trepidation, she read its contents to her adult children:

Galway's Sugar Plantation,
Montserrat, West Indies
Friday, 1 January 1808
Dear Mama,
I regret to say that my father-in-law, Neptune Lynch, has passed away. He suffered a sudden heart attack followed by pneumonia but died peacefully. Annabel is distraught. She has buried him in the same grave as his mother, Catherine. We have ordered a Celtic cross from Galway to erect in memoriam.
After a period of mourning, we are preparing to visit Ireland with Sean Holian. He has laid down his machete for the last time. I cannot wait to be home once again. How time flies!
We sail next week on the "Rover" and expect to arrive in March.
Your loving son,
Michael.

Early spring had arrived. Sibella stood on the quay at Galway with John and George. Soon the *Rover* came into view. She was flooded with emotion as she saw Michael, Annabel and Sean Holian standing on the deck. Tears streamed down Holian's face as he rejoiced in a homecoming delayed for over thirty years. After an emotional reunion, the party travelled north by coach through Galway and into Mayo.

As Sibella wiped away her tears of joy, Michael said,

"You look very well, Mama."

"Thank you, Michael. So do you, Annabel."

Annabel flushed at the compliment. They passed into Mayo and she said,

"The scenery is magnificent. It is similar to Montserrat except for the trees and the coolness."

Sibella gazed at the rugged landscape adorned with gorse and heather.

"Those are the Partry mountains to the left overlooking Lough Mask," she said. "We will soon warm you up with turf fires and hot drinks."

Customers stared at Annabel when the group stopped at a tavern in Ballinrobe. It was obvious that they were attracted by the darkness of her skin. Sibella hoped that the attention would not upset her daughter-in-law.

As they moved northward along the eastern shore of Lough Carra, the majestic mansion of Moore Hall came into view.

Sibella pointed towards it.

"That is where Cecilia's husband lived before passing away tragically in 1799."

"Ods bodkins! Stop the coach," Michael said. "Let us pay homage to the memory of the late President John Moore."

"And to the memory of his father, George, who tried so hard to save him," Sibella added.

After an interlude for prayers, the coach continued north through Castlebar and on to Ashbrook.

Sibella was happy to witness the joyful reunion of Michael with his siblings. He entertained them with stories of volcanoes, slave rebellions and the Black Irish. How they longed for foreign travel.

After settling in, Michael raised the issue of his father's bequests.

"I cannot believe that our legacies have not yet been paid, after twenty years."

"I still have one of my three notes for five hundred pounds." Sibella proudly replied. "Your education and army career was sponsored from your father's estate."

"That is only a small fraction, Mama. At least the girls, apart from Cecilia, are married but my brothers have no means to secure careers." Michael scowled.

"Cecilia has generously helped her sisters with dowries from her inheritance," Sibella said.

"It is a blessing that you have Ashbrook now, but what of the future?" Michael wondered.

"Cecilia's marriage to the late President John Moore has strengthened the bond between the families."

"That might not last forever. We must raise the matter with Uncle Peter." Michael paused. "I could provide accommodation and opportunities for John and George in Montserrat."

"That is a lovely idea, Michael; as long as Annabel is agreeable." Sibella changed tack. "Is anything stirring yet?"

"Mama, that is private!" Michael scolded as Annabel blushed.

* * * * *

ON THE FOLLOWING MORNING, Sibella, Michael, Annabel and Sean Holian set off for the village of Balla. They called at the Big House where Kate Moran received them. Harry's nephew, Robert, the eighth Baronet, was away on business, but Peter was there to greet them.

"You are most welcome, Sibella, Michael and guests," Peter's voice trembled now. He was almost eighty and not in the best of health.

As Kate poured the tea, Sibella reintroduced Annabel.

"Peter, you will remember Michael's wife, Annabel. They would never have met were it not for your letter of introduction."

Michael enjoyed being in the familiar surroundings of his boyhood home once more.

Peter said,

"Annabel, you are as beautiful as the day I met you. My congratulations on your marriage. Please accept my sympathy on the passing of your father."

Annabel smiled.

"Thank you, Peter. This is my first visit to Ireland. My late father said I must visit the real Emerald Isle, the home of my ancestors."

"I would like to invite you and Michael to stay with me at Balla House for a while. He can share with you the memories of his youth." Peter paused. "Sibella, would you like to visit also? You may wish to be with your son for a while."

The visiting couple from Montserrat nodded eager assent. Sibella added her own acceptance, and cast her eyes towards Sean Holian who kept shifting his posture on the Irish side chair with ball and claw feet.

Michael responded to the cue.

"This is Sean Holian, the long-lost husband of Judy."

Sibella was relieved that the youthful Sir Robert was away on business as the Holians were not his favourite tenants.

"You are welcome, Mr Holian. I am delighted at the reunion of your family after all these years."

"Thank you, Mr Lynch. It's great to be back in Ireland."

An awkward pause followed. Sibella prayed that Peter would break the silence.

"I know my late brother was responsible for your transportation," Peter said finally. "You stole a sheep, but your punishment was excessive. I want to apologize on behalf of my family."

"Thank you, sir. I am very grateful to Mr and Mrs Lynch for bringin' me home."

Sibella and Michael escorted Sean to the coach yard where Bernard Moran was waiting to drive him in style to his humble abode. She noted the animated conversation between the returned felon and the groom as they departed.

On their return, Michael said,

"Uncle Peter, your goodwill towards Sean Holian is greatly appreciated."

"I must have mellowed in my old age."

Michael paused and his brow furrowed. "I am concerned about the future of my family. What is the situation regarding our inheritance?"

Sibella was proud of Michael's assertiveness.

"It is a long and complicated story. Raising the necessary money is not easy because of the mortgage on the estate. I persuaded the trustees to provide for your education and that of your brothers. I also persuaded them to purchase a Lieutenancy in the Light Dragoons." Peter grimaced. "Beyond that, Sir Robert has been advised by his agent, Peter Boyle de Blacquiere, to challenge the will."

"We always knew that the trustees opposed the will." Michael clenched his fists. "What does de Blacquiere claim?"

"He claims that Sir Harry was not in a fit state to sign the will."

Sibella was shocked.

"You know that is not true."

Michael raised his voice.

"I shall talk to Sir Robert on his return."

Aware that the old man was exhausted, Sibella, Michael and Annabel absented themselves. They walked down the drive and strolled through the village. In the distance, Sibella could see that Sean Holian was receiving a hero's welcome from his poorly clad but energized neighbours. As they moved closer, she saw a man crack his fist against the palm of Sean's hand in admiration while holding a pike.

"You should have been around in '98, Sean. We gave the whores a good run for their money."

The old man retired to the comfort of his cabin after the initial hullaballoo died down.

Sibella saw Judy in the distance.

"Michael, I must greet Judy Holian. Perhaps you could show Annabel around the pleasure garden of Balla House."

As Sibella entered, Sean was regaling Ned and Thady with the stories of his life including the slave revolt in Montserrat in 1768.

"Well, you big fool!" Judy said. "Stealin' sheep is bad enough, but rebellion can lead to the gallows."

Sibella was amused that Judy had not lost her sharpness of tongue.

"What an example to set to your two fine sons. Oh, well you might laugh, Ned and Thady Holian, but you were lucky not to end up on the gallows in '98."

"Were my two sons, rebels on behalf of Ireland?" Sean asked.

"No. Thady has more sense. I fear that Ned is up to the likes of abductin' young ladies, poaching and stealing turnips. If he escapes the gallows, he will likely follow you, and be transported, only this time to Australia."

"You are no angel yourself from what I hear," Sean said.

"You have no right to talk, leaving me with no money and two young men to look after, while you were off stealin' sheep and organizing rebellions." Ned and Thady laughed again while Judy raised her eyebrows. "And what did you mean by that remark?"

"I heard you had the body of young Ellen Colgan dug up out of the ground," Sean said.

Sibella turned white as the memory of her youthful folly came back to haunt her.

"I'm sorry, Sean," she said. "It is my fault. I asked Judy to secure Sir Harry from that harlot, Lady Harriett."

She could see from the startled reaction that the old man was unaware of her involvement.

After recovering his composure, he said,

"I understand now, Mistress Cottle. You needed help and Judy needed the money; but old man Colgan was a good friend of mine. How I can face him I do not know."

"Well, Sean dear, there are worse things in life," Judy snorted. "We were facin' eviction before the spancel. Once the spancel was made, Sibella persuaded Harry to spare us."

"And where is this accursed spancel now?"

"It is still in the Big House," Sibella said.

Ned nodded. She wondered how he knew. She hurriedly took the conversation into another direction.

"That is all old news now; let us forget it. I am delighted that Sean is safely home. I will leave you to your celebrations."

As she left, she was aware that the Holians had fallen silent. Something was amiss.

"It is something to do with the spancel," she thought. *"But what can it be?"*

* * * * *

LATER THAT WEEK, SIBELLA was sitting one evening with Peter, Michael and Annabel in the upstairs living room at Balla House. She noticed how unsettled Michael was, his mind apparently in turmoil. Perhaps he was worried about his failure to father a child with Annabel.

"I should not have mentioned the subject," she thought.

Then she heard a commotion. Was she dreaming? Was someone repeatedly shouting "Fire?" It sounded like Sean Holian.

"Michael! Is the house afire?" she screamed.

Michael jumped to attention. He opened the living room door and saw a flame at the end of the corridor.

"The house is on fire. We must evacuate immediately. Mama, can you help Uncle Peter? Annabel and I will look after the children."

Uncle Peter's twelve children aged from five to nineteen were already awake. The older children quickly directed the frightened younger ones downstairs and into the night.

"We must leave at once," Sibella said to the frightened old man.

Suffering from arthritis, Harry's uncle was slow to move. Sibella helped him to his feet as he grasped his blackthorn stick. She screamed for help as the flames spread rapidly and the heat was almost unbearable.

"Where is Uncle Peter?"

Michael rushed into the blazing house to find Sibella and Peter finally at the bottom of the stairs. A burning beam crashed down beside them as Sibella screamed again.

"Mama, leave!" Michael shouted. "I will carry him out."

As they struggled out of the house, a second beam fell just inches behind them.

Sibella waited in trepidation until Michael finally emerged from the conflagration. Now that everyone was safe, Sibella and Kate Moran looked after Peter while Sean Holian took care of the children. Michael joined with the servants in a frantic effort to quell the fire. Shortage of water and a dry windy night hampered the fire fighters. Flames soon engulfed the timber structure of the Big House, destroying it and its priceless contents. Fascinated tenants watched the flames shooting through the roof, visible for miles around.

Crowds came from the village and surrounding areas to view the scene. Sibella could not believe that the house in which all but one of her children had been born was now a burnt-out shell. All those memories of her tumultuous life with Harry destroyed in a matter of hours, if not minutes.

"What would Harry think, looking down on this sorry mess?" she wondered.

Michael drove Sibella, Peter and Annabel to Ashbrook. The episode had badly shaken the old man. Sibella put him to bed. The residents of Ashbrook stayed up late into the night listening to the story of the great fire.

At one stage, Sibella looked at Michael as only a mother can look at a son. Silently, she was posing the question. He avoided her gaze. Sibella was relieved to hear that at least there were no casualties. Thoughts of the spancel plagued her.

"Could my accursed spell have caused the fire? Could it be the vengeance of a deity against me?"

She shuddered at the thought and prayed that Michael was not involved.

On the following morning, Sibella and Michael returned to the scene. Some of the servants, including Kate Moran, had inspected the damage. Among the debris, Kate found a charred silver casket that had survived the intense heat.

"Do you have the key to this casket, Sibella?" Kate asked.

Sibella denied it and Kate added,

"Mr de Blacquiere has taken a great interest in it. He wants to show it to Sir Robert on his next visit."

"May I see it?" Michael asked.

"You will have to ask Mr de Blacquiere."

Kate hurried away with the box held firmly in her hands.

Sibella whispered, "If you find out where it is hidden, let me know."

"I will have a word with her husband, Bernard. He might be willing to negotiate. Where is the key?"

Sibella blushed and touched her bosom. "It is in my locket — not a word to anyone. Let us sit in the garden."

As they sat amidst the flowering roses, Michael asked,

"What is it, Mama?"

Sibella looked around to ensure the absence of eavesdroppers.

"I noticed that you were somewhat agitated before the fire started, my dear. Is there anything you want to share with me?"

Michael flushed and remained silent. He picked up a stone and passed it from palm to palm.

"You can tell me," said Sibella. "I will not betray your confidence."

"Zounds!" Michael threw the stone into a shrub, causing a rustle of wildlife. "I am embarrassed. Are you certain you want to know?"

Sibella nodded in some trepidation, and he continued.

"When Sean Holian was reunited with his family and had received a hero's welcome, he became overwrought and sought revenge. He approached the old man, Colgan, who readily agreed to participate because of —"

"— the spancel," Sibella finished for him. Her sudden hand movement frightened away a bird in the nearby bush.

"They thought that if they fired the Big House they could destroy the spancel, as well as avenging Sean's many years of exile. Sean believed I might approve of the plan because of my resentment regarding our unpaid inheritance." Michael paused. "It was a perilous undertaking which required careful planning to avoid causing hurt to anyone, and it had to have the appearance of an accident. Together we hatched a plot over a number of days. Colgan was willing to take the risk as his wife had passed away and his remaining family had emigrated."

Sibella was aghast. How could her sensible son, a former army officer and the owner of a sugar plantation, get involved in such a senseless plot?

Glancing over his shoulder, Michael continued.

"We met in the Round Tower at night. Sean said he would accept Bernard Moran's invitation to visit the Big House and tell his stories to the servants. On the appointed evening, I would unlock the storeroom window at the rear. At eleven of the clock, I would go there to view some old documents. At about quarter past the hour, I would leave a lighted candle on the ledge of the window and then rejoin you, Uncle Peter and Annabel in the upstairs living room for a nightcap."

Sibella was beside herself with worry. Her fearful mind could only think,

"What has happened to the fine young man I reared so carefully?"

"You were in the right of it, Mama; I was indeed agitated last night. The more I thought on it, the more I doubted the wisdom of it, especially when I saw the little ones going so cheerfully to bed. I decided not to carry out my part of the plan. Later, Colgan told me he had arrived at the rear of the house under cover of darkness but saw no lighted candle on the window ledge. He calmed the guard dogs and waited. After fifteen minutes, he tried to open the storeroom window but found it locked. He waited a while longer; then he saw a flickering light in an adjoining room. He looked through the window. A burning sod of turf had fallen out of the fireplace and set a rug afire. It was an accident, Mama."

The colour had now drained from Sibella's face. She felt that the cause of the fall of that sod of turf was to be found somewhere in the planning of this elaborate conspiracy. Where was the servant in charge of that room? Was he listening to the stories of Sean Holian?

"Not a word of this shall pass my lips," Sibella assured Michael, trembling, as her distraught son returned to the house.

CHAPTER 26

T HE DESTRUCTION OF BALLA House tormented Sibella. It brought back memories of the fifteen tumultuous years spent with Harry, most of them in that house. It was hard to believe that a fire had destroyed the physical fabric of that experience in one night. She shared her worry with Cecilia, without betraying Michael's secret. "Was the fire at Balla accidental or deliberate?"

"Nobody knows, but speculation is rife." Cecilia looked up from her writing desk. "The name of any person holding a grudge against the Lynch-Blosse family is being mentioned."

"For example?" Sibella sat down in the library.

"The Holians, old man Colgan, Kate Moran and …"

"Are you forgetting someone, my dear?" Sibella looked deep into the eyes of her rebel daughter.

Cecilia blushed and whispered, "Everyone knows you would never do such an evil thing." She fingered her quill. "Do you think that Michael was involved?"

"I looked him straight in the eyes last night. He denied involvement." Sibella stood up. "He is angry with the failure of the trustees to honour your father's bequest, but that does not mean he is guilty."

"Thank God that no one was killed." Cecilia gazed unseeing through the library window.

"If Michael is suspected ..." Sibella burst into tears as the two women embraced.

"Nonsense, Mama. Michael is furious, but burning the house would be counterproductive and the authorities would realize that." Cecilia paused. "Where is he now?"

"Upstairs with Peter; the old man is unwell. The shock has disfigured his right cheek. I must see how he is." Moving upstairs, Sibella entered the patient's bedroom to find him reminiscing about 1798.

"President M-Moore was the brave man!" Peter whispered in a slurred tone. "I sympathized with the rebellion, yet I was too old to involve myself. All I did was claim damages: I was awarded ninety three pounds for missing livestock."

"I am sorry I missed it." Michael sat on the edge of the bed. "They are forever talking about it at Ashbrook."

"I am glad you missed it," Sibella said. "Cecilia lost her husband and I might have lost a son."

"There is something on my mind, Uncle Peter." Michael leaned forward.

"I understand, M-Michael. I should have pushed the trustees to pay out the legacies. I have asked de Blacquiere to raise the matter with Sir Robert."

"Thank you. What can we do for you now?" Michael asked.

Sibella concealed her anger at the thought that Peter might have let matters slide with the trustees. She wondered what favour the old man might request.

Peter glanced at Michael, "I ask only one thing. My c-children are illegitimate: if you can do anything to help them along the road of life, I would be eternally grateful."

"They are with Pat Lynch of Clogher. There was no room for them here at Ashbrook. I will call on them every week." Michael laid his hand on the old man's arm. "I shall ask Sir Robert for his advice on the matter. I will do my best for them; as they are, so was I."

Peter smiled and nodded. Soon afterwards, he passed away without lawful issue. He had signed his will with a mark. Each of his twelve natural children would receive five hundred pounds on reaching maturity. He made bequests for life to Bridget Commins and Judy Kelly, suggesting that one or both may have carried his children.

Despite her anger at Peter's failure to ensure her children's legacies, Sibella still felt much sympathy for the old man. He had lived in the shadow of three baronets: his brother, Sir Robuck, his nephew, Sir Harry and now his grandnephew, Sir Robert. He had served them all well and received little thanks for it. In the autumn of his life, he had fathered twelve children, all surnamed Lynch, knowing he would never enjoy their adult company.

* * * * *

WHEN MICHAEL RETURNED FROM the funeral, Annabel met him with a frown.

"We need to go home to Montserrat," she said.

"As soon as I have dealt with matters here, we will be on our way."

"You have been saying that for weeks." Annabel snorted. "Our sugar plantation will go to rack and ruin."

Michael paced the floor. "Uncle Peter begged me to look after his children and I agreed."

"For goodness' sake! How can you look after twelve children?"

Michael hesitated. "I had not thought it through."

"I have heard enough of this nonsense. I return to Montserrat tomorrow, and I expect you to come with me. If not, our marriage is over." Annabel stormed from the room leaving Michael behind, confused and torn.

Later he pleaded for more time but the lady was adamant. He promised to follow her as soon as things settled down but Annabel was too upset to respond. However, on the following day, she agreed to give him one last chance, as she embarked on the *Rover*.

Michael found it difficult to keep his promise. As soon as he settled one problem, something else cropped up. In order to supplement his plantation income, he offered his services to the reconstruction of Balla House.

At interview, the youthful Sir Robert picked up a document. "After returning to Balla, I offered a reward of one hundred pounds to any man or woman with information about how the fire started." Staring at his impassive first cousin, he sighed. "One person came forward."

Michael evinced interest while trying to retain his composure.

"Unfortunately, there was no evidence to support the allegation." Sir Robert crumpled the reward note. "I have decided to build a two-storey house close to the site of the burnt-out ruin."

Michael wondered if the modest design reflected a gradual disengagement of the Lynch-Blosses from Balla.

"De Blacquiere and I are impressed by your credentials from Montserrat." The new master of Balla raised his hands. "I am happy to offer you a post for six months, to be extended if all goes well."

Michael accepted the offer. He wrote to Annabel informing her of his appointment. Perhaps they could sell the plantation and buy a small estate in Ireland? With his experience in estate management and construction, he could purchase or lease a suitable property. They could try again to have a family. She could renew acquaintance with her long-lost relatives in Galway.

Michael suspected that de Blacquiere was under instruction to keep a close eye on him. Sir Robert had no doubt heard the rumours about the possibility of his involvement in the firing of Balla House.

For that reason, Michael made sure to be an outstanding employee, full of energy and ambition. When de Blacquiere offered an extended contract, he wrote again to Annabel. Almost a year later, she replied indicating her desire to remain in Montserrat. Michael understood her position. He felt guilty about treating her so badly, but his heart was in Ireland.

"You should ask her to reconsider," Sibella advised.

This he did and then waited for a response. In effect, the marriage was in a state of gradual dissolution.

* * * * *

MICHAEL WAS FLATTERED WHEN de Blacquiere sought his opinion after the reconstruction of Balla House. "The demand for grain is rising rapidly as the war between Britain and France intensifies."

Glancing at the lease documentation in the estate office, Michael said, "That will increase the shift from grassland to tillage farming."

"More labour will be required." De Blacquiere tapped his desk. "We are on the brink of a population explosion."

"The tenant farmer will be reduced to a diet of potatoes and milk."

"Exactly, Michael. The land available cannot support the rising level of population. Allow me to read from a letter I have drafted to Sir Robert:"

I have no … hope… that the rents will be paid … as regards a great number of the tenants. All kinds of produce are at the lowest ebb in Mayo …, oats 4s. per barrel of 14 stone, and everything else in proportion. If these prices continue … you will soon find general ruin here amongst … the Irish tenants for as prices now stand it is of little moment what rent a man is bound to pay, great or small he can no more afford to pay one than the other, but I should hope this gloomy picture may mend and that some helping hand may be promptly given to support the landed interest.

Having agreed with the gloomy prognosis, Michael feared he would be required to collude in its resolution. That would mean more evictions.

In the following year, de Blacquiere found more to worry him. "The war is now thankfully over, after the defeat of Napoleon at Waterloo. The population here continues to surge; I have heard estimates of up to six million."

Michael shared his worry. "Fathers are subdividing their land to provide for their sons."

"Landless men are reclaiming mountain and bog as best they can."

"Where is it all going to end?" Michael wondered. "Perhaps I should return to Montserrat and you to Dublin or London."

De Blacquiere shook his head disconsolately. "I shall not desert Sir Robert in his hour of need."

Their worst fears were confirmed when the potato crop failed in 1816. A typhus epidemic aggravated the subsequent famine.

Michael now lived in the reconstructed residence at Balla except when Sir Robert visited. He rode regularly to Ashbrook. "Mama, I am horrified by the suffering of the tenants. I believe the Holians may have contracted the disease. I am going to see them."

"I will come with you." Sibella quickly donned her cloak and shawl. "I must bring some food and provisions."

Soon they were on the road on a bleak day in January. "How do you find de Blacquiere?" asked Sibella.

"He is well enough, if a touch arrogant." Michael urged the horse forward on the pot-holed boreen.

As they entered the village, Michael tethered the trap outside the Holian cabin. When Sean Holian opened the creaking door, Michael had to conceal his horror at the state of the place.

Sean said,

"Our time has come. We have the fever. Not even Judy's magic can save us now."

Michael knew the disease was incurable. Delirium, stupor and sensitivity to light would soon follow, culminating in death.

"I will make you some hot milk with a little drop of brandy." Sibella poured some milk into a saucepan suspended over the turf fire. "How are Ned and Thady?"

"Still healthy, thanks be to God," Judy said quietly. "They're out trying to find a cure but there is none to be found."

Sean added, "They're going to take the boat soon, hopin' for a better life in America. There is nothing left for them here."

Sibella poured the hot drink. She wrapped her shawl around her. "I have left some bread and bacon on the table. We shall leave you in peace now. May God protect you." The Holians crossed themselves for a blessing.

As they departed, Michael said, "I will talk to Ned and Thady in case I may be able to offer them assistance."

When Sibella and Michael visited a few days later, the door displayed two black ribbons. Michael consoled his mother, distressed at the loss of Judy who had been a friend and ally to her. She attended the modest funeral with Michael. Ned and Thady were grateful for their support.

"We sail to America next week," Ned said. "There is nothin' to keep us here now."

Michael understood Ned's desolation. Even though the famine was over, Ned was still grieving the loss of his parents. Ned, and his brother,

Thady, needed a new start. It reminded Michael of his own frustration with army life leading to his emigration to Montserrat.

Michael threw his arms around Ned and Thady.

"I shall pray for your success in America. May God bless you both."

CHAPTER 27

MICHAEL'S MOOD IMPROVED WITH the revival of the potato crop. Green shoots adorned the landscape in the spring of the following year. Even better was the arrival of Charlotte Lynch-Blosse, a beautiful girl of fifteen. Her winning smile, infectious enthusiasm and sharp wit raised his spirits. She reminded him so much of Sibella in her younger days. He admired her auburn hair that stretched to her shoulders in a mass of curls under a straw hat. A daughter of Sir Robert, she had been born and raised in Cardiff. Her father had suggested a trip to the ancestral home. The adventurous Charlotte needed no further encouragement and accompanied him on his next visit to Balla.

Michael befriended his first cousin once removed, showed her around the demesne and gave her riding lessons. He was keenly aware that Sir Robert had instructed the groom, Bernard Moran, to accompany them and had warned his daughter not to become emotionally involved.

When Michael next went to visit Ashbrook, Charlotte begged to go with him as she had heard so much about Sibella. Sir Robert refused permission but relented when Charlotte agreed to the presence of Bernard Moran as chaperone.

During a stop in Ballyvary, she looked at Michael. "Tell me more about your mother, Mr Lynch."

Michael took his ease in The Village Inn while Moran tended the horses. "My mother, Sibella, eloped with my father, your great-uncle, Sir Harry. They were deeply in love but were never able to marry."

"Why?"

Michael was reluctant to reveal the full story. "Before he met Sibella, my father eloped with a Catholic, Emily Mahon. The marriage broke down almost at once but obtaining an annulment was difficult. Then other complications arose because of their different religions and matters of land ownership and inheritance."

"That is amazing." Charlotte's eyes opened wide. "I heard you are married, Mr Lynch?"

"Indeed, I am. My wife, Annabel, lives in Montserrat. I used to live there also but returned home some years ago. Annabel prefers life in the country she grew up in."

"You must take me to Montserrat sometime."

"Let us try Ashbrook first," Michael smiled. He wondered how Sibella would react to his young cousin.

Sibella and Cecilia were there to greet Michael and Charlotte on their arrival. Cecilia offered to show Charlotte around.

"You look very well, Mama."

"Thank you, Michael. You're as handsome as ever and still attracting the young ladies."

"Robert insisted on sending a chaperone with her." Michael waved his hands dismissively.

"I should certainly hope so!"

"Mama! There is nothing between us."

"I saw the way Charlotte looked at you."

"That is merely a young girl's fancy, and I am a married man and much older than Charlotte."

"Indeed you are, you silly boy. Annabel is a lovely woman. And look at you, the owner of a sugar plantation!" Sibella threw her hands up.

"Mama, I know not what to do." Michael paused. "It is true that Annabel is a lovely woman, but my heart and my home lie in Ireland. I begged her to settle with me here. In a strange way, my own feelings about Ireland have made me realize that her heart is in Montserrat." Michael grazed his blond hair.

"Last year I was shaken by the famine and the typhus. The suffering of the tenants was appalling. I did everything I could to help but my efforts were mostly in vain. I felt powerless and useless." Michael shook his head and closed his eyes. "Even when the famine was well over, I thought I might go back to Montserrat. Then I realized I had not seen Annabel for seven years; seven years, Mama! I could not believe it."

Michael could not restrain the flow of his tears.

"And then little Charlotte arrived, full of bubbles, fun, energy and excitement. She had no mind for my woes; she lifted my spirits and I felt alive again, renewed, a new man." Michael stood up and hugged his mother. There was nothing more to say. When Cecilia and Charlotte returned, they were enveloped in the companionable silence.

* * * * *

MICHAEL AND CHARLOTTE CHATTED to their hosts for a while and then departed. On the way home, Michael realized that Charlotte had been fascinated by his sister, Cecilia, as well as by Sibella. These were two strong women who had survived turbulent times. That sense of admiration would do no harm now that Charlotte seemed to have taken a fancy to him. Sir Robert had warned her off him but that might serve to enhance his attractiveness.

Soon she would be on the high seas back to Cardiff, there to mature and complete her education. On the day of her departure, she threw her arms around him much to the chagrin of Sir Robert. No matter how hard he tried, Charlotte continued to occupy his mind over the coming months as winter approached.

In the New Year, de Blacquiere summoned Michael to the estate office. "A letter has arrived from Cardiff."

Michael sat down slowly as de Blacquiere read out the message.

Cardiff, Wales
Thursday, 8 January 1818
Dear Mr de Blacquiere,
Sir Robert passed away suddenly, yesterday. I thought you should know.
Yours faithfully,
Lady Lynch-Blosse.

Michael later found out that Sir Robert had been ill throughout the autumn and early winter. His doctor believed the condition to be a passing malady; however, early in the New Year, his illness took a turn for the worse. He passed away in January, only thirty-four years old. The words of Voltaire came to mind:

Doctors are men who write prescriptions,
of which they know little,
to cure diseases of which they know less...

"What dreadful news. I must make haste to Cardiff." De Blacquiere glanced thoughtfully at Michael.

"I could accompany you, if you wish," Michael said.

"Let me think about it. We must do whatever is best for the family."

Michael knew the stakes were high. De Blacquiere was a paid official whereas he himself was a first cousin of the late Sir Robert, although born on the wrong side of the blanket. Robert's eldest son, Francis, heir to the vast estate, was a mere seventeen. In normal circumstances, de Blacquiere's position as agent to the estate would have been secure. Michael wondered if his interest in Charlotte could be a threat to de Blacquiere's position. Should his relationship with Charlotte flourish, he could be in a position oversee the Lynch-Blosse estate in the same way that the late Peter Lynch had protected the Lynch-Blosse interest in

Ireland. In which case, de Blacquiere would become his servant should he wish to remain at Balla.

Later that afternoon, de Blacquiere announced that Michael should accompany him to Cardiff.

Michael was surprised at this gesture from a man he did not count among his friends. "What about the care of the estate in our absence?"

"Indeed! I need you to draw up a plan to cover its management while we are away. Meanwhile, I shall make the travel arrangements."

When they arrived in Cardiff one week later, Charlotte was still in tears of grief for her father. Michael was pleasantly surprised when her stepmother, Lady Lynch-Blosse, invited him to stay despite her concern over his impaired lineage. Because his demeanour was impeccable, the family gradually warmed to him.

When Michael suggested that Charlotte might visit Balla next summer, her stepmother would not hear of it. Succumbing to Charlotte's pleading, she reluctantly agreed to a summer visit in the future, possibly two years hence.

On the journey home, Michael realized that his feelings for Annabel had diminished. Charlotte now occupied his focus, buoyed by her insistence on returning to Ireland as soon as she could persuade her stepmother to travel. In that context, he enjoyed teasing the upright de Blacquiere.

"Lady Lynch-Blosse may allow Charlotte to visit Balla in the summer of 1820." He smiled as his rival in business rolled his eyes.

"It would be nice if Sir Francis were to accompany her. He could inspect his inheritance." It was de Blacquiere's turn to smile.

The word "inheritance" sparked Michael into action. "I want to raise again the issue of my father's will. Uncle Peter was kind enough to arrange for my education and that of my brothers in Castlebar. He funded my army career from my father's estate." Michael stamped his feet on the coach floor as it rumbled over the bridge at Shannon. "Apart from that, the legacies remain outstanding. My siblings have received nothing."

"I understand your concern. In fact, Sir Robert had asked me to investigate this matter when he reached his majority."

Michael later found out from Kate Moran that de Blacquiere had approached her in relation to Sir Harry's will. She told him slyly that de Blacquiere had found her reminiscences most helpful.

Michael had to control his temper when de Blacquiere said he had sought legal advice in relation to the will. He was even more incensed when the agent allowed him to read a copy of a letter addressed to an attorney, Peter Warren at 47 Henrietta St, Dublin. De Blacquiere had sent the letter when in Paris on estate business.

When Sir Henry Lynch-Blosse was extremely ill and a few days before his death being, by excesses in the way of drinking, altogether enfeebled in mind and body, he gave three notes of £500 each to a certain Sibella Cottle, the mistress of Sir Henry who had got possession of his person and fortune, of which the most complete proof exists in his will which charged his estate with enormous legacies and annuities to this Sib Cottle and her children by Sir Harry. So infamous was this transaction that it would have been immediately set aside if Sir Robert's guardian had done his duty.

Much of the information arose from Catto (Kate) Moran who was in the House when Sir Harry died. She gave the fullest information on the whole business and I learnt enough to convince me that it was more than probable that crime even had been resorted to for the purpose of consummating these vile transactions. One circumstance appeared to corroborate this opinion: she mentions a bottle containing some dark liquid presumed to be laudanum was kept during Sir Harry's illness behind a shutter of the bedroom. She stated to have seen it there immediately previous to the will being signed but having observed Sir Harry to be in a state of torpor, and suspecting all was not right, she looked for the bottle which had disappeared and which she afterwards found empty in the fireplace.

I mention this to show that strong suspicions existed as to the infamy of the conduct of those who surrounded Sir Harry previous to his death, and so strong an impression did the recital make upon me that I submitted it to Sir Robert with an opinion that he could successfully attack the will of Sir Harry but I could never induce him towards investigating the matter further.

Michael now understood why Sibella had warned him to be careful of Kate Moran, mindful of the age-old hostility between the two women. How dare de Blacquiere seek to blacken the reputation of his mother based on nothing but information from Harry's cousin, who clearly disliked the Lynch/Cottle family? Michael also became aware at this time that de Blacquiere had sought information concerning his possible involvement in the alleged arson of Balla House.

* * * * *

WITH THE RECENT FAMINE NOW well over, Michael carefully considered his position while he awaited the return of Charlotte. He could return to Montserrat and seek to renew the relationship with his wife, Annabel, if she would still have him. If she agreed, he would then settle in Montserrat and renew efforts to start a family.

Alternatively, he could pursue his interest in young Charlotte. While seeking to clarify his thoughts, he availed of the opportunity to lease the Ashbrook estate from George Moore Jr. This enabled him to access the second half of the rental hitherto accruing to the Moores while Sibella continued to receive the first half. He had more than sufficient income from his sugar plantation in Montserrat to finance this lease even after allowing for a generous annuity to Annabel for living expenses. By so doing, he established an independence from de Blacquiere as well as securing sufficient income to support a bride should he remarry in Ireland.

In the summer of 1820, Charlotte duly returned to Balla accompanied by her stepmother, Lady Lynch-Blosse and her brother, Sir Francis, now nineteen. A clerical student, he was the ninth Baronet of Balla.

Michael was present when de Blacquiere welcomed the visitors. "Allow me to show you to your room, Sir Francis. Michael will look after Lady Lynch-Blosse and Miss Lynch-Blosse."

As de Blacquiere departed with Sir Francis, Michael showed the ladies to their accommodation. Once Lady Lynch-Blosse and Charlotte were settled in their separate but adjoining rooms, Michael made his way to the staircase.

"Mr Lynch," Charlotte whispered as she opened her door ever so slightly.

Michael tiptoed back. "You are growing more beautiful by the day, Miss Lynch-Blosse." He smiled as Charlotte blushed. "How is your family in Cardiff?"

"They are worried about me!" Charlotte kept an eye for servants within earshot.

"Why is that?"

"My stepmother thinks I'm not safe with you."

Michael had to stifle his laughter as he left the alluring Charlotte to rest and perform her toilette. Their relationship deepened throughout the summer. Both loved horse-riding. Lady Lynch-Blosse had difficulty keeping up with them. Francis joined them from time to time, and kept his stepmother informed. Michael suspected that both were anxious that Charlotte should seek a more suitable partner. He wondered if they had brought her out in London with a view to marrying her off. If so, they had not succeeded as he soon found out.

Michael was now fixated with Charlotte, but he wished to discuss the matter with Sibella. To that end, he arranged a visit to Ashbrook so that Charlotte could be "viewed" again. He understood that Charlotte was more determined than ever to pursue the relationship with him. When Francis informed her of her stepmother's insistence that the liaison must end, she told him, in Michael's hearing, to attend to his own affairs and not hers.

Sibella frowned when Michael repeated his declaration of love for Charlotte. "She is young enough to be your daughter! This is not wise, Michael."

"Look at Uncle Peter, Mama; starting a family when he was past sixty!"

"The silly old fool; who will provide for his twelve children now that the poor man is gone? Particularly when — "

" — they are illegitimate!" Michael finished for her. "Just like your seven, Mama!" He blushed. "Please forgive me. I should not have said that."

Tears streamed down Sibella's cheeks. "It is of no account. I am merely attempting to plan for the future."

"Do not worry about the family. I shall look after them." Michael smiled and the momentary sadness passed. "I may be the one who needs the help."

"Oh, Michael, what are you about, to lead that innocent girl astray?"

"She is eighteen and well able to make decisions." Michael sat down in the drawing room. "She has matured since her first visit three years ago."

"Does she know that you are married?" Sibella closed the book she had been reading.

"She knows."

"And what of your beloved Annabel?" Sibella leaned forward.

"I have to work that out." Michael stood up and paced the floor. "Do not worry overmuch, Mama!"

"I still think she is too young." Sibella knotted her forehead.

"Mama, she reminds me of you. When you fell in love with Papa, you were only eighteen. Look how well you have turned out!"

"You are a rascal, Michael Henry Lynch. Be gone before I poke you with my needle."

Michael left with laughter ringing in his ears. In a strange way, he sensed that Sibella was proud of him. Like herself, he was about to embark on a hazardous course of action but with the possibility of high reward.

* * * * *

"**Y**OU ARE DEEP IN thought." Michael caught Cecilia unawares as he joined her on a bench overlooking the Ashbrook River.

"Sitting here in the evening sun reminds me of Moore Hall and my late husband."

"You must miss him terribly."

Cecilia nodded as the tears welled in her eyes.

"What a brave man! I am sorry I missed 1798. I'm haunted by the thought that you and I could have been on different sides of the barricades. Then I wonder: had I returned from Montserrat, would I have joined you and President Moore? I will never know."

"Well, if you wish to be involved, Michael Henry Lynch, you could do worse than join the movement for Catholic Emancipation."

"Catholic what?" Michael opened his eyes wide.

"Have you heard of Daniel O'Connell?" Michael shook his head. "He is a lawyer from Kerry. You will not believe this!"

"Try me," Michael said.

"He was educated at Douai in northern France, in the same college that John Moore attended!"

"Would they have known one another?" Michael asked.

"I do not think so, because John was ten years older than Daniel. He would not have been pleased with O'Connell, who opposed the rebellion."

"Now I am confused."

"John was a revolutionary and Daniel is a constitutionalist; some people call him O'Connell the Liberator." Cecilia spoke with such enthusiasm that her face lit up.

"What does he hope to liberate us from?" Michael asked, enjoying the conversation.

"Emancipation will lift the remaining restrictions of the Penal Laws. Any Catholic man could become a member of parliament, a cabinet minister or a general, for instance."

"And then what?"

"Eventually he wants to liberate us from the British, which is what John wanted; to have the freedom to run our own country in our own way."

"You are most persuasive, Mrs Moore!" Michael said.

Charlotte and Lady Lynch-Blosse appeared then on their way to the garden; Michael joined them, while Cecilia absented herself.

"Mr Lynch, you must show me around," Charlotte said, her curly hair flying in the wind. Michael offered her his arm and blushed as her stepmother directed a withering glance at him.

They walked through the garden, through the wooded demesne to the east and towards a ruined Catholic chapel to the south. Sitting by the Ashbrook River, they exchanged affectionate looks while Lady Lynch-Blosse was distracted. They rested in the sun for a while until Charlotte inquired about the nearby buildings.

Michael pointed to the corn mill and kiln. "Mama and Papa worked on the corn harvest the year before I was born." The memorable tales of his childhood coursed through his mind. "Let us walk up the hill to the pigeon house."

"What is a pigeon house?" Charlotte asked, all agog.

"It provides a source of winter food. Mama sometimes ordered stuffed pigeons for dinner. They were cooked in a large jug with pieces of celery on top."

"Stuffed pigeons; famous!" Charlotte laughed as they moved indoors.

At dinner that evening, Charlotte inquired of the recipe while glancing at Sibella. "Were they cooked in a jug with … something or other on top?"

"With celery on top." Sibella laughed. "The jug was made airtight with huff paste and then placed in a cauldron of boiling water to a point above the pigeons. After boiling for three hours, cook laid the birds on a heated dish."

"What happened next?" Charlotte asked.

"Gravy was made from the bird juices with butter and flour, and poured over the birds garnished with lemon," Sibella replied.

"I am going to write that down and see if cook can make it at Balla." Charlotte plucked an imaginary quill from the air and pretended to write with it.

After dinner, Michael and Charlotte walked the rose garden accompanied by Lady Lynch-Blosse and Sibella.

"Who was that mysterious man on the wall in the drawing room?" asked Charlotte when Sibella had distracted her stepmother's attention.

"It is Sir Thomas More, who had his head chopped off by Henry VIII." Michael was proud of the association.

"Are you saying that the Moores who fostered Sibella are descended from such a famous man?" Charlotte's jaw dropped.

"That is what they say, although Master Moore was unable to prove it to the Spanish Court."

Charlotte paused. "My brother will be appalled: it will confirm his worst fears. He thinks we are in a den of iniquity surrounded by papists, illegitimates and rebels."

"Jesu Maria!" Michael clenched his fists in annoyance.

"I should not have said that; it escaped my lips before I could prevent it. Francis is studying for the ministry. Being serious and law-abiding, he was embarrassed and begged me not to disclose his feelings," Charlotte said. "But I did not want to hold anything back from you."

"That young man has a lot to learn."

"That is what I told him. If he is going to settle in Balla as master of the Big House, he must cultivate some sensibility; papists, rebels and illegitimates will surround him for the rest of his life."

"Well spoken, Miss Lynch-Blosse." Michael was impressed at her sharpness of mind and growing maturity.

The future now came into sharp focus for Michael. If he started a new life with Charlotte, he would have to curry favour with Sir Francis who controlled the estate and Michael's position within it. Francis would not approve of the relationship with Charlotte because of Michael's illegitimacy and marital status. De Blacquiere would seek to blacken his reputation, with particular emphasis on the spancel used by his mother and the suspicion of arson. However, Charlotte could be an ally if she really loved him.

These thoughts filled his mind as they returned to Balla. Charlotte and Francis chattered away as they traversed the rolling farmland of Mayo. Michael held his silence, all the better to plan the future.

CHAPTER 28

CHARLOTTE LOST NO TIME IN disposing of her rashers and eggs at breakfast on the following morning,

"Mr Lynch, I must tell you what I have been thinking!" Her eyes lit up.

"Problems?"

Michael returned from the sideboard with a bowl of porridge. In the absence of Lady Lynch-Blosse, he was conscious that the aging Kate Moran kept an eye on activities in the dining room. He suspected that de Blacquiere found her reports of dining-room conversation illuminating.

"Not problems, opportunities. Cecilia has been telling me about Daniel O'Connell and Catholic emancipation. It is so exciting."

"I suppose it is, for a Catholic like Mama or Cecilia," Michael said.

"Do you want to know what your sister said?"

"You intend to tell me, anyway."

Michael smiled as her foot lightly grazed his shin.

"Cecilia said it was a ... libertarian issue."

Michael grinned at her careful enunciation.

Charlotte continued,

"She will be supporting Daniel the Liberator. I said I would like to help too." She paused to wipe her lips. "We intend to visit all the Big Houses in Mayo and persuade them to support libertarianism!"

Michael sipped some milk.

"You will meet with a deal of opposition."

Charlotte laid down her fork.

"With my youthful exuberance and her local knowledge, we shall charm them into submission."

At that moment, Sir Francis entered.

"Good morning, brother. Did you not hear the cock crow?" Charlotte asked.

Michael held his tongue until Francis settled with some breakfast. He then sought to curry favour with his new master.

"I can show you around the estate this morning if you wish, Sir Francis."

"Thank you, Michael, but de Blacquiere has already arranged to do that." The young baronet held his nose high. "Indeed, I am already late so I must hurry."

"Finish your porridge, you goose," Charlotte enjoined him.

Michael could scarcely conceal his amusement when Francis blushed in response. Charlotte reminded him so much of his mother in her younger days.

"I have had sufficient," Francis said as he departed.

"You will not find it easy to convert Francis to libertarianism," said Michael.

"But we could practice on him!" Charlotte smiled.

Michael nodded. It now seemed that Charlotte was determined to stay in Ireland. This helped to concentrate his mind. How would Sir Francis and Lady Lynch-Blosse react to her ambition? Not favourably, he imagined; and if so, how would Charlotte respond to the hostility of her family?

"Am I now walking in the hazardous romantic footsteps of my parents?" he wondered.

His attention was distracted on receiving a message from Ashbrook. He frowned when he read it.

"What is it?" Charlotte inquired.

Michael trembled.

"Sibella is not well according to Cecilia. Please excuse me, I must leave at once."

When Michael arrived at Ashbrook, his siblings surrounded Sibella in her bedroom. She was pale and slightly feverish. Michael kissed her forehead and sat down beside her. A quiet calm reigned.

"I am delighted you are here, Michael. Am I not the lucky woman to have my family around me, apart from poor Harry?" Sibella leaned back in her comfortable bed and enjoyed listening to the chat of her adult children. "Lady Harriett and Emily Mahon came to see me this morning."

"What did those hellions want?" Michael said angrily.

"They were here to make their peace with me," Sibella rebuked him gently. "Our old animosities were resolved. Now I want to see your affairs settled, Michael."

Michael knew that decision time had come. He had to choose between living in Ireland or in Montserrat. If Annabel had settled in Ireland, the issue would not have arisen. Michael was now firmly rooted at home. He had implored Annabel to return to Ireland, to no avail. In a way, each had already made their decision without actually dissolving the marriage. Fortunately, perhaps, they had not borne issue.

"I know, Mama, I must choose! I will write to Annabel."

"Thank you, Michael," Sibella whispered. The atmosphere in the room was peaceful, almost spiritual.

Michael kissed her pale hand.

"I will write immediately."

He then retired to the library and began to write. Once finished he rode back to Balla. Cecilia rode with him side-saddle. Cecilia wished to talk to Charlotte as well as revisiting the home of her childhood.

* * * * *

ON ARRIVAL, MICHAEL ESCORTED Cecilia to her room so that she could freshen up.

Before dinner that evening, he chanced upon his sister talking to Charlotte in the drawing room.

Cecilia glanced at Charlotte.

"My dear cousin, being a campaign soldier for Catholic Emancipation will not be easy. Hostile reception will be the order of the day. Doors will be slammed in our faces."

"Michael and I had a fine thought, to try our persuasiveness on my brother to begin with. Even if he disagrees, he would be too embarrassed to say so. With that achieved, we can say to others that Sir Francis Lynch-Blosse of Balla supports emancipation."

"You are the clever one!" Cecilia responded. "We might even consider a visit to grumpy old Altamont in Westport. Persuading him will not be easy, even though relations between the Moores and the Brownes have improved since 1798. Lady Harriett has already visited Mama, her old nemesis, to settle their animosities."

"Who is Lady Harriett?" Charlotte asked.

"Your admirer will tell you all about her," Cecilia said.

"Do I have an admirer?"

Charlotte glanced at Michael. Michael took a deep breath. He maintained his composure with difficulty as he felt the impact of Charlotte's gaze into his blue eyes.

"I am your admirer," he declared.

After Cecilia departed to hunt down a copy of Fanny Burney's novel, *Evelina*, in the library, Michael said,

"Before Lady Lynch-Blosse joins us, could you please glance at this letter that Mama insisted I write."

After Charlotte nodded, Michael handed her the letter, which she quickly read:

Ashbrook House,

Straide,

Castlebar, County Mayo.

Wednesday, 21 June 1820

My dear Annabel,

I hope you have received my last two letters inviting you to rejoin me in Ireland. Having not heard from you for such a long time, I must assume that your future lies in Montserrat. I greatly enjoyed my time in the Emerald Isle of the Caribbean, and was fortunate to have met you and your late father, Neptune. We married for love, Annabel, but I fear that love has faded away. Our marriage has ended in all but name, and I would like to set matters in train for a legal dissolution also. I was very happy when you agreed to come to Ireland — I fervently hoped you would fall in love with the land of your ancestors, but it was not to be. As for myself, my heart is in Ireland and here I shall remain.

You may be interested to know that my first cousin, Robert Lynch-Blosse, the eighth Baronet, has died at home in Cardiff. He was only thirty-four. His heir, Sir Francis, merely nineteen years of age, is now visiting us and will be my new master. His younger sister, Charlotte, and their stepmother, Lady Lynch-Blosse, are also visiting. Charlotte has become involved with Cecilia in the campaign for Catholic emancipation. She wishes to remain in Ireland for the nonce whereas Francis is anxious to return to Cardiff.

Everyone here is in good health apart from Mama, who may not be with us for much longer. We are all praying for her.

I look forward to hearing from you.

Yours affectionately,

Michael.

While Charlotte read the letter, Michael reflected on what was probably the most important decision of his life. Was he insane to turn his back on a sugar plantation in return for the slim chance of a liaison with Charlotte? He waited for Charlotte to read the letter, which she did not once but twice.

"Is it your hope that this letter will put an end to your marriage?" she asked quietly.

"I hope so. I have been as diplomatic as I can," Michael whispered.

"Earlier today, you said you were my admirer."

"I did."

"And when do you intend to start acting as such?" Charlotte asked.

"I thought I had!" Michael replied, mystified. "Perhaps we might take some day trips to Castlebar or further afield? With your stepmother, of course."

Lady Lynch-Blosse, in evening dress, entered the library just in time to catch the last part of the conversation.

"What is that, Mr Lynch?" she snapped. "Please speak up!"

Charlotte smiled.

"Michael has suggested that we visit Castlebar next weekend."

Michael wondered if Charlotte was besotted enough to consider a serious relationship with him. Even if he continued to pursue that course, how could he persuade her stepmother to allow her to stay in Ireland?

$$* \quad * \quad * \quad * \quad *$$

MICHAEL, CHARLOTTE AND LADY Lynch-Blosse set off for Castlebar on a Saturday morning in July in the Lynch-Blosse carriage. The landscape was resplendent with the purple bloom of the wild rhododendron whose beauty raised their spirits, apart from those of Charlotte's stepmother who was tiring of her role as chaperone.

On entering Castlebar, the groom parked the carriage by The Mall where a cricket match was in progress. Michael pointed to the adjacent Ralph Academy, a boxy three-storey building at the top of Castle Street adjacent to the Methodist Church.

"That is where Papa sent me to school."

"You poor boy," Charlotte teased. "Were you very lonely?"

"Not at all; I made good friends here," Michael replied. "We witnessed some weird and wonderful events in our time at the Academy."

"Do tell," Charlotte said.

They were now standing at the Methodist Church. Michael pointed eastwards towards the gaol. "During my schooldays, many a man was hanged there. The most famous was a 'fire-eater', George Robert Fitzgerald."

"A fire-eater! Do you jest?"

Michael suspected that Charlotte would be struck by the tale.

"Fitzgerald was a famous duellist. He once fought 'Humanity Dick' Martin from Connemara. Both men had pistols; each struck flesh but survived."

"Why were they duelling?" Charlotte asked.

"Martin insulted Fitzgerald and Fitzgerald returned the compliment." Michael replied, enjoying her rapt attention.

"What foolish behaviour!" Charlotte laughed. "I trust you have more tales of that ilk."

They walked through the town towards Geevy's Hotel.

"Stirring happenings took place here. Has Cecilia told you of them?"

"No, she has never mentioned Geevy's Hotel."

"After routing the British through Castlebar, General Humbert set up his headquarters here. He appointed Cecilia's husband, John Moore, as the first President of the Republic of Connaught in 1798."

"Gracious!" Charlotte's blue eyes filled with surprise.

"He also appointed Cecilia as a member of the Government of the new Republic. She was fortunate to survive the aftermath of the rebellion."

"I shall scold her roundly for not telling me of these events."

Michael was satisfied that Charlotte now understood the importance of research before gallivanting off to the Big Houses with her message of Catholic emancipation. He continued the tour of Castlebar, visiting the courthouse, the gaol, the army barracks and Lough Lannagh.

Returning to Geevy's Hotel, Michael escorted the ladies into the building. They were served with food and drink after they had tidied themselves and changed their clothes. Lady Lynch-Blosse also took a short rest. After dinner, they retired to bed, Michael to a single room and the ladies to a double.

Michael lay on the bed sipping a glass of port, flanked by flickering wall candles. Just as he was about to retire, the door handle moved. He reached for his pistol but was pleasantly surprised when Charlotte furtively entered. Michael found it difficult to control his heartbeat.

Charlotte placed a finger to her lips and pointed to the room next door. She whispered,

"Before going to bed, I knelt down and recited the rosary. Stepmother asked me what I was mumbling. I said I am now a campaigner for emancipation. She was too exhausted to pursue the matter, and was soon asleep and snoring loudly."

Michael smiled. He arose quietly and shared his glass of port with Charlotte. He noticed how her hand trembled as she sipped the ruby liquid. It was so peaceful and calm together in the room, alone at last. He kissed and embraced her.

"I wish to be with you," she said.

Michael was surprised at how nervous this articulate and confident lady had become. He had to remind himself that Charlotte was only eighteen.

"We must take it slowly, my dear heart."

He kissed her again and began to loosen her bodice. Then he stopped. He paused in internal conflict, feeling her heart pounding with a desire to match his own.

"I cannot do this. It's not fair to you," he exclaimed.

"It is what I want, my darling," she replied.

"My position is too uncertain, Charlotte. We must wait until I can act with honour. I do not want to repeat my father's mistakes."

"I love you, Michael Henry Lynch."

She wiped a tear, composed herself and rejoined her stepmother in the bedroom next door.

When his passion had subsided, Michael wondered what would become of him and Charlotte. Was she really in love with him or merely infatuated? Could he succeed in dissolving his marriage without financial penalty?

"Is this similar to the situation that my father faced when he ran away with Sibella?" With these conflicting emotions swirling in his head, he spent the rest of the night tossing and turning.

Michael wondered if Charlotte was similarly afflicted. He hoped she understood why he had sent her away; that she appreciated how difficult it had been for him. Lady Lynch-Blosse and Sir Francis were strongly opposed to the liaison and he wished to protect Charlotte. He felt sure that her mind, just like his, raged with conflicting emotions. What should they do?

CHAPTER 29

An URGENT MESSAGE AWAITED Michael when he returned to Balla. Sibella had taken a turn for the worse. The priest was on his way.

"Michael, you must go immediately," Charlotte said.

"I want you to come with me … please."

The intensity of Michael's tone and expression convinced Charlotte and Lady Lynch-Blosse to agree.

Each was silent as they headed for Ashbrook in the Lynch-Blosse carriage. Michael was aware that both he and Charlotte were facing a moment of truth. If Sibella passed away, Michael would become head of the family with full responsibility for the welfare of his siblings. Sibella had provided remarkable leadership, but life was never easy for a family born out of wedlock.

Michael was aware of Charlotte's dilemma. Her family could disown her because he was her cousin, already married, illegitimate and without a fortune. Rumours about the spancel and arson did not help his cause. He needed to discuss these matters so that Charlotte could find her moral compass.

After another exhausting trip over the rough road, Ashbrook came into view. Cecilia was there to greet them.

"Thank God you've arrived. Father Nolan is here. Mama wishes to see you; you should go in straight away."

A sombre atmosphere awaited Michael. Although it was midday, the shutters were closed; candles on a chest of drawers and on wall-sconces illuminated the room. A portrait of Sibella's beloved Harry in his Volunteer regalia hung on the wall facing her.

"I'm glad you are here, Michael." Sibella struggled to pass him a document and a small velvet box.

Michael looked at the document. It was a note for five hundred pounds. Inside the box, he found a beautiful Tara brooch with a sparkling diamond embedded in its pin.

"Harry gave me Lady Lynch's brooch before we made love after the harvest party."

"It is beautiful, Mama."

"He also gave me three notes for five hundred pounds each when he found himself unable to provide for me in his will. This is the last one."

"Thank you." Tears streamed down Michael's face. "I will put both to good use for the welfare of the family."

"After I'm gone, I want you to burn the spancel so that its curse may no longer taint this family.

"I shall see that it is done," Michael said.

Cecilia entered. Now all seven children were present with their mother.

"I would like Charlotte to be here too," Sibella said.

"Are you sure?" Michael asked.

Sibella nodded. Michael then went to fetch Charlotte. Sibella turned to the priest and said,

"Please give me the last rites, Father."

"I will, Sibella. Peace to this house, and to all who dwell herein," Father Nolan intoned as the hallway clock chimed twelve. He blessed the holy oil and placed it on a small table covered with a white cloth. Cinnamon, musk and cannabis flavoured the olive-based oil of the infirm, its scent creating a spiritual atmosphere.

"Please kiss the holy cross, Sibella," the priest asked. He then sprinkled Holy Water on her and all present.

"*Asperges me, Domine* … would you like me to hear your confession?"

"I would, Father."

"Confession is a private matter."

Father Nolan glanced at Sibella's children. Responding to the cue, Michael, his siblings and Charlotte took their leave.

"Bless me, Father, for I have sinned. My seven lovely children were born out of wedlock even though I was betrothed to the late Sir Harry Lynch-Blosse."

"Is that all, Sibella?" Father Nolan clasped his prayer book.

"Just one more sin." Sibella grimaced. "I was afraid of losing Harry to Lady Harriett. Judy Holian said Harry would throw me out unless I used the spancel to spellbind him. I did and I hope I can be forgiven."

The priest made the sign of the cross with his right hand.

"I hereby absolve you from the guilt of your sins."

Sibella collapsed in exhaustion as the priest summoned back the family. She was now at peace and could meet her maker with a clear conscience.

Father Nolan chanted, "*Dominus vobiscum.*"

Sibella's daughters responded, "*et cum spiritu tuo.*" They knelt around the bed, their eyes on her frail body.

"You may wish to say a quiet prayer for your mother."

Having allowed time for prayer, Father Nolan extended his right hand over her head and intoned:

In nomine Pa + tris, et Fi + lius, et Spiritus + Sanctus, may all the power of the devil over you be destroyed by the imposition of our hands, and through the invocation of the glorious and holy Virgin Mary, Mother of God, her illustrious spouse, St. Joseph, and all the holy angels, archangels, patriarchs, prophets, apostles, martyrs, confessors, virgins, and all the saints together. Amen.

The ageing priest now anointed Sibella by dipping his right thumb in the holy oil and imprinting her eyes, ears, nose, lips and hands in the form of a cross. "By this holy anointing and his most loving mercy may the Lord forgive you whatever wrong you have done. Amen."

The sacred ceremony of Extreme Unction continued as he commended her soul to the Lord. He left behind the holy water and cross for her use.

Michael followed him and offered refreshment but the poor man refused, anxious to leave at once. Michael summoned his driver and they galloped off to Balla.

* * * * *

SIBELLA WAS NOW AT peace, with one matter only on her mind.

"Charlotte, sit down beside me for a moment or two. I wish to speak with you alone."

Charlotte turned pale as she sat down.

"You remind me of myself when I was your age. I fell in love with Michael's father, Harry. He had such charm: how could I resist?"

Sibella glanced at the portrait of the old rogue, Sir Harry.

"We had fifteen happy years together and seven wonderful children to show for it. Now here you are, a fine young lady with feelings for my illegitimate son who is also married, though separated."

Sibella paused from exhaustion and Charlotte poured her a glass of spring water. She sipped a little when Charlotte held the glass to her lips.

"If you act on those feelings, you will face some of the same challenges that Harry and I met. I strongly advise you not to proceed; but if you are foolish enough to do so, you have my blessing."

"Thank you, Sibella. What you have said means the world to me. Now you must rest."

"One more thing: I am wearing the locket that Harry gave me after Michael was born. It belonged to Harry's mother. It should go to Michael."

"I shall give it to him."

Once Sibella had drifted off to sleep, Charlotte kissed her feverish forehead and left quietly. Michael was waiting outside, pacing the landing.

Charlotte said, "Your wonderful mother has given us her blessing."

Michael breathed a sigh of relief. Cecilia came to bid farewell to her brother.

"We are off to Balla to see Francis before he leaves for Cardiff," he said. "We will be back in the morning."

"You had better make haste," Cecilia replied.

They set off at speed on the bleak and winding road to Balla.

"What did Mama have to say to you?" Michael whispered when Lady Lynch-Blosse had drifted into a doze.

Charlotte spoke with the easy assurance of the young.

"She described the challenges ahead of us."

"How do you feel now?" Michael asked.

"In a strange way, I feel invigorated. If our relationship is destined to be a challenging one, then let us face it together — like Dark Eileen, the aunt of Daniel O'Connell, and Art Ó Laoghaire."

"How will Sir Francis and Lady Lynch-Blosse react?"

"With shock and horror, of course; Francis needs to return to Cardiff and his clerical studies. His head is spinning from his Irish experience."

"Ods bodkins!" exclaimed Michael with a sigh.

Well aware of the difficulties ahead, now he had to face Francis and that blackguard, de Blacquiere, with Charlotte by his side.

Attempting a lighter note, Michael asked,

"Shall I tell you the name some have for Blacquiere?' He paused while Charlotte's blue eyes twinkled in anticipation. "It's 'Queerblack,' his father's nickname, acquired at the time of the Union in 1801."

Both laughed while stepmother smiled having just woken-up.

* * * * *

ON ARRIVAL AT BALLA, Kate Moran asked, "How is Sibella?"

"She has just been anointed," Michael replied.

Kate crossed herself for a blessing, and then escorted them into the estate office where Francis and Blacquiere were deep in discussion.

De Blacquiere motioned towards the chairs.

"How is Sibella?"

Michael paused. He looked de Blacquiere straight in the eye until his rival flushed.

"Not the best. We shall return early in the morning."

"I shall pray for her," Francis said.

"Is there something on your mind?" De Blacquiere asked Michael.

Michael spoke with determination.

"Our inheritance is still unpaid. My mother is on her deathbed, and I will soon bear responsibility for my family. They have need of their bequests, as do I."

De Blacquiere rustled through the rental documentation on his table. "You are aware that the rental money is down. We are in the midst of a population explosion. The tenants do not have the money to pay their rent."

"We are not at starvation point!" Francis interjected. "We could make these payments, spread over a number of years."

De Blacquiere scowled. "The late Peter Lynch made payment before your time, Sir Francis; indeed, before mine. First there was the education of Michael and his two brothers; then an investment was made in an army career for Michael, costing more than two thousand pounds."

Francis looked quizzically at Michael who calmly responded,

"Those early payments are only a fraction of the inheritance of ten thousand pounds which I should have received. My sisters have received nothing."

Francis now turned to de Blacquiere, who tapped the table.

"There is another side to the story. You must understand that the monies bequeathed were extraordinarily generous. I have been advised that Sir Harry was in no fit state to sign his will shortly before he died."

"What do you mean?" Francis asked.

"Sir Harry was in considerable pain towards the end of his life. The late Doctor Boyd prescribed laudanum to relieve the pain. I understand that the prescribed dose was frequently exceeded." De Blacquiere hesitated. "Sibella looked after the medication."

"Who is your witness?" Michael asked.

"I would prefer not to say."

"But you have to say," Charlotte said. "You have made a serious allegation against Michael's mother. You must either substantiate or withdraw it."

Michael was pleased with her intervention. It was now up to her brother to make his first major decision as the new baronet.

Francis glanced at de Blacquiere.

"I suggest that you name the witness, on the understanding of strict confidentiality."

The agent squirmed uncomfortably.

Michael surmised that de Blacquiere had failed to brief Francis on the matter, preferring to focus instead on his family background. Now it was too late. Francis was in a rush to depart for Cardiff, Sibella was dying, and Charlotte was Michael's ally.

"My witness is Kate Moran," de Blacquiere said.

Francis glanced at a portrait of the seventh Baronet.

"Kate, Sir Harry's half-sister?"

De Blacquiere nodded.

"What is her evidence?" Francis asked.

The agent glowered.

"After Sir Harry had passed away, Kate found an empty bottle of laudanum in the bedroom fireplace. That bottle, recently provided by Doctor Boyd, should have been sufficient to last another week. Kate insisted that Sir Harry was in a state of torpor. She believed that Sibella must have plied him with excessive laudanum and then persuaded him to increase the inheritance for each of his seven children by her."

De Blacquiere coughed hesitantly, as though he was uncomfortable with what he had said.

Michael looked at him with incredulity. He could have countered this testimony by saying that Sibella had usurped Kate's pre-eminent position in Balla House, and that Kate had resented this and conceived a strong dislike for Sibella. However, he saw that Francis was settling into a leadership role and trusted him to do the right thing. De Blacquiere was his guardian until Francis reached his majority, but that day was not far in the future. The young baronet now achieved the high moral ground suited to a man intended for the cloth.

"Thank you for that background. Of course, it all happened so very long ago. People's memories become unreliable. It would not be fair to subject an elderly woman to interrogation on the matter."

Francis looked keenly at de Blacquiere, who reluctantly nodded.

"I know you are keeping our perilous financial position under control, and that Michael has assisted you in these difficult times. We are grateful for that." Francis paused. He joined his hands together and steepled his fingers. "I am concerned, however, that not one of Sibella's daughters has received her bequest. Now that Sibella is sadly nearing her last, I suggest that one thousand pounds be set aside to cover her funeral expenses and to erect an appropriate monument to her memory."

Francis glanced at de Blacquiere who nearly swallowed his false teeth before mumbling,

"I will make the necessary arrangements."

Michael had to restrain himself from expressing his delight. Although the bequest would not translate into ready cash, it would save their own money for the funeral expenses. He was astonished at the diplomatic skill of Charlotte's brother. He sensed that Francis was even more surprised as the words had issued unrehearsed from his lips. Michael was glad that Francis had begun to heal the wounds suffered by the Lynch-Blosse family arising from the liaison of Harry and Sibella. On the other hand, his emerging relationship with Charlotte might reignite those tensions. He hoped it would not prove so.

On the following morning, Francis said,

"Michael, please ask Sibella to accept my apologies for failing to visit, as I must return to Cardiff." The young baronet hesitated. "Perhaps Charlotte should accompany me."

Michael tensed on hearing the tone of authority. Resentment of his haughty cousin began to grow in him once more.

Charlotte said forcefully, "I do not wish to travel until Sibella recovers or the worst happens. It would not be right."

"Very well, as long as stepmother is here to chaperone you. However, you must return to Cardiff once matters have settled here."

Charlotte blushed and hesitated before saying, "Yes, Francis."

"I shall pray for Sibella," Francis said.

"Thank you." Michael extended the hand of friendship. "Your kind gesture to my mother will make her happy."

Now it was Michael's turn to hesitate.

"Before you leave, perhaps you might have a word with Kate Moran? Now that she is widowed and advanced in age, it would be good to relieve her of the burden of animosity."

"What would you have me say?"

"That her evidence to de Blacquiere about Papa's will has been carefully considered; that her concern is a testament of her loyalty to the family, or something of that ilk."

Michael took care not to appear patronizing.

Francis looked to Charlotte for her opinion.

"What do you think?"

"It seems a kind thought," Charlotte replied.

Michael watched in fascination as the ninth baronet metamorphised from a boy to a man.

CHAPTER 30

"GOOD MORNING, KATE. WHAT'S for breakfast today?" Michael asked, walking towards the sideboard.

"The usual."

Harry's half-sister pointed towards the porridge, bread, eggs and bacon.

"The porridge is delicious," Charlotte said.

The old woman merely grunted.

Michael helped himself to eggs and bacon from the chafing dishes.

"We are off to Ashbrook after breakfast," he said. "May I have a few words before you leave?"

Kate Moran asked, "What is it?"

"Mama was anointed yesterday." Michael paused. "You and she have not been on the best of terms."

"That is none of your business."

"My mother would like to make her peace with you."

"It's a bit late for that," Kate snorted. "As for you, Michael Lynch, I will give you something your mother left behind — a silver case that survived the fire."

Michael and Charlotte exchanged glances as Kate stormed out of the room.

"What a bitter old woman," Charlotte said on the journey to Ashbrook. "And yet I feel sorry for her. How would I feel if I were the love-child of a gentleman and was displaced, when he died, by his son's lady-love?"

"Dear Lord! We all have our problems. Kate married the groom, the late Bernard Moran and both Sir Harry and Uncle Peter provided for her in their wills."

"Maybe the intervention of Francis will help." Charlotte fingered her auburn curls. "What will you do with the casket?"

Michael wondered if it might contain the spancel.

"I shall tell you later."

"Kate mentioned a fire. What was she referring to?" Charlotte asked.

"As you know, the old house was burned down some years ago."

"Was it accidental?"

Michael nodded.

Each fell silent then as the horses clip-clopped their way to Ashbrook. Cecilia greeted them as soon as they arrived.

"Thank goodness you are here," she exclaimed. "Mama's fever has worsened. You should go in to her immediately."

248

Michael hastened to do what his sister said. He entered Sibella's room and immediately knelt by the bed close to her. His mother opened her eyes and smiled. Michael quickly gave her the news of the day.

"Mama, I spoke to Kate this morning and Sir Francis spoke to her last night. I think she will come around. She returned your silver casket. Charlotte and I will look after it for you."

Sibella tried to speak, but all she could do was form the words, "Thank you, Michael," on her lips.

So many thoughts flashed through her mind then: her tempestuous romance with Harry; her folly in using the witch's spancel to secure his love; her heartbreak on discovering that they could not marry; her good fortune in meeting George Moore who provided a roof over her head after leaving Balla House; her pride in how her seven wonderful children had survived the stigma of illegitimacy; her joy that Harry's great-niece, Charlotte Lynch-Blosse, had integrated so successfully with her family; and finally, her joy at the opportunity to reunite with Harry in heaven.

Michael, his siblings and Charlotte knelt and prayed for her. Shortly afterwards, he gently applied a cool cloth to her perspiring forehead. They prayed while listening to her increasingly laboured breathing. With a mixture of dismay and relief on her behalf, they heard the gurgling sound of the death rattle. She had passed away peacefully.

Her children were distraught. Cries of anguish followed as they hugged one another amongst the tears. Michael found it hard to believe that Sibella had left them. She had been the focus of their lives; how could they cope without her? After a while, they composed themselves and prepared to journey with her to her earthly destination.

* * * * *

"MICHAEL, I'M WORRIED ABOUT the cost of the funeral," Cecilia said. She was in full mourning dress and wore a black tricorn hat.

"Sir Francis has allocated one thousand pounds to cover the funeral expenses and the cost of a monument to Mama." Michael reassured his sister. He appreciated that the money was more than sufficient for the stated purpose; perhaps it was a statement of reconciliation from the new baronet to the extended Lynch-Blosse family.

Sibella had requested burial with her natural parents in Cottlestown. A few days later, after a private waking, the funeral cortege was on the road from Ashbrook to Balla. A simple open carriage led the way followed by a closed carriage with six of her seven children. A smaller closed carriage followed with Michael and Charlotte, accompanied by Lady Lynch-Blosse, who attended only because of her chaperoning duties.

Michael had decreed that Sibella should travel in a plain oak coffin draped with the Green Flag of Ireland that featured a golden harp on a green background. He knew that Harry would have been pleased because the Balla Volunteers used that flag in the 1780s. Cecilia would be delighted as the United Irishmen used a similar flag in the 1790s. Now the Catholic emancipation movement had adopted the Green Flag as its emblem, which pleased Charlotte.

A large crowd assembled including former Volunteers, pike-bearing veterans of 1798 and members of the Catholic emancipation movement. The cortege stopped on the main street at the entrance to Balla House. The parish priest, Father Nolan, had refused permission for removal to the Catholic Church because of Sibella's controversial background. Instead, he recited a decade of the rosary beside the Round Tower in the open air. Michael and his siblings received condolences from the local people who straggled towards them in their own way.

Michael was pleased that the attendance included Lady Harriett, Emily Mahon, Peter Boyle de Blacquiere, Kate Moran and the Moores of Moore Hall. The latter included John Moore's younger brother, George and his wife, Louisa Browne, the niece of Lord Altamont. He was surprised when Sir Francis appeared.

"Please accept my sympathies, Michael. I decided that Cardiff could wait. I wish to honour your mother's memory."

Michael shook his hand while Charlotte opened her arms to her brother. He was pleased that Sir Francis had thought to provide bread and ale from the Big House, as both the waking and the burial were private. The hungry tenantry quickly devoured the refreshments.

After a two-hour stop in Balla, Michael directed the cortege northwards towards Ballina.

He ushered Father Nolan into the carriage.

"Thank you, Father, for making the burial arrangements with your colleagues in Cottlestown. Allow me to introduce Lady Lynch-Blosse of Cardiff and her stepdaughter, Miss Lynch-Blosse. Miss Lynch-Blosse is a sister of Sir Francis who honoured us with his presence today."

The elderly priest smiled at the Lynch-Blosse ladies and said,

"Thank you, Michael. Please accept my sympathies on the death of your mother."

"Miss Lynch-Blosse is a supporter of Daniel O'Connell and Catholic emancipation," Michael said. "She is going to work with Cecilia to garner support from the Big Houses in Mayo."

"I wish you every success. It will not be easy."

Charlotte nodded.

"So I gather," she said ruefully.

After settling himself, Father Nolan raised his voice.

"Is it not strange that I was born in 1749, the same year as your father, Sir Harry? I remember when Sibella came to Balla House not long after my appointment to the parish of Balla, an appointment that is about to expire as retirement beckons."

Father Nolan paused while Michael wondered at the direction of his thought.

"Your mother brought a young boy with her from Suffolk named Michael Henry Lynch."

"I do not remember it." Michael smiled.

"Shortly afterwards, Sibella gave birth to the twins, Cecilia and Mary Anne. It was my first baptismal experience."

"I suppose all baptisms are similar, Father?" Charlotte asked.

Father Nolan frowned.

"Well, it was all a very long time ago, my dear."

Michael understood that the priest had been reluctant to baptize the girls because of their illegitimacy. He also knew that Harry's grandmother, Lady Lynch, had insisted on entering their names on the baptismal register without using the designation "bastard."

"Thank you, Father Nolan," Michael interjected as the priest blushed. "I would like to raise another matter with you later on, perhaps? In the meantime, it's a long journey to Sligo. If you would like to rest or sleep for a while, please do so."

"Thank you." Father Nolan said, and closed his eyes.

He was soon snoring, and remained in a sound sleep until Cottlestown was reached. Charlotte gave the priest a gentle nudge when they entered the town-land.

"Wake up, Father Nolan. We have arrived."

"Where are we?" The confused man tried to orientate himself. "You should have woken me sooner," he said.

"You were sleeping soundly," Charlotte said. "We did not have the heart to disturb you."

* * * * *

MICHAEL RECOGNIZED COTTLESTOWN FROM the central location of O'Dowd's Castle in the locality. The Catholic chapel was located close by to the north, flanked by the River Delvin to the west and the graveyard to the east.

Cecilia and Charlotte distributed funeral *favours*: black hatbands and lambskin gloves for the ladies, and black-edged handkerchiefs and lambskin gloves for the men. Lady Lynch-Blosse reluctantly accepted the favours but remained in the carriage.

Meanwhile, Michael, John and George and the hearse driver had raised the coffin on their shoulders and marched towards the grave. The local priest had identified the location of the burial place of Sibella's parents, Michael and Isabel Cottle.

Charlotte escorted the wobbly Father Nolan, armed with his walking stick, to the graveside. The priest recited a decade of the rosary and then blessed the coffin with Holy Water.

After the menfolk lowered the coffin into the grave, each of Sibella's daughters, Cecilia, Mary Anne, Bridget and Barbara dropped a red rose on her remains. Her sons, armed with spades, covered the coffin with the loose excavated soil. The thud of the falling earth on to the coffin filled Michael's heart with a feeling of desolation. The digging continued until the grave was overflowing.

After a period of silent mourning, Michael raised his head.

"I would like to say a few words before we depart."

He hesitated, unsure of what he wanted to say; then suddenly the words began to flow.

"We have just buried our wonderful mother. She had led a tempestuous life, but her love for each of us has never been in doubt no matter how we behaved. Like us all, she had her moments of fragility and questionable judgment, yet her strength of character and resilience surmounted all the various challenges that would have devastated a lesser person. She has been an inspiration to all of us. Sibella Cottle, we shall always love and treasure you. May you now rest in peace."

Michael could not restrain his flow of tears and had to make use of his handkerchief. He concluded,

"Mama has now joined Papa. We shall leave them happy together in the next world."

Michael and his siblings lingered at the graveside for an age, comforting one another and weeping.

In the meantime, Charlotte escorted the priest back to the carriage to rejoin an impatient Lady Lynch-Blosse.

They travelled in silence on the return journey until Lady Lynch-Blosse closed her eyes and drifted off to sleep. At that stage Father Nolan, who was now quite perky, reminded Michael of his query.

"Thank you, Father, for reminding me. It is the issue of the spancel." Michael leaned forward as the priest winced at the subject he had thought buried with Sibella. "We thought the spancel had gone up in flames when the Big House was burnt to the ground. Afterwards, however, Kate Moran recovered a locked silver casket with an object inside which may be the spancel. She said it belonged to Mama. We need your advice."

The priest squirmed in his seat.

"I am not sure what it has to do with me."

"Perhaps Mama mentioned something in her last hours?"

"That is confidential under the seal of the confessional."

Undeterred, Michael continued to pursue the subject.

"Mayhap we should return the spancel to the grave of young Ellen Colgan?"

"Maybe you should," Father Nolan said. "On the other hand, it might reopen old wounds that are best forgotten."

"I feel uncomfortable having it in my possession." Michael paused. "It rightly belongs to Ellen's grandfather, her only remaining relative in the area. I have not approached him for the reason you mentioned."

"Have you some other solution in mind?" Father Nolan asked.

"Perhaps the spancel could be stored in the church," Michael said. "Her mortal remains could be sanctified and at rest within the Catholic congregation of Balla."

"I would need to think about that," Father Nolan sighed. "I may even have to consult the archbishop. It is a most unusual request."

"Thank you, Father."

Michael leaned back as the coach driver whipped his horses to a greater speed.

"If Charlotte is agreeable, we will look after it until we hear from you."

Charlotte nodded. Michael suspected that she also would want to inspect the mysterious object.

The parish priest was now in a dilemma. The application to make whole the body of Ellen Colgan was a good one if the Colgan family wished it so. If, however, he went to the archbishop, he might have to explain that the application emanated from an illegitimate Protestant possibly living in sin with his own cousin. Father Nolan silently communed with himself: *O tempora, O mores!*

CHAPTER 31

FRANCIS HAD APPROACHED MICHAEL before the funeral cortege departed for Cottlestown.

"I would like to invite the funeral party to dinner at Balla House this evening," he offered.

Michael realized that the young baronet had again delayed his return to Cardiff, aware of the seminal influence of Sibella's demise.

"Thank you, Sir Francis."

"I would like say a few words after dinner, if you are agreeable." Michael nodded and Francis continued, "I would also like to invite Lady Lynch-Blosse, Father Nolan, Kate Moran and Peter de Blacquiere." It was so agreed. "I would have attended the funeral were it not for some unexpected business that I had to deal with before returning to Cardiff."

At the conclusion of the dinner, Francis tinkled his glass and called for attention.

"Ladies and gentlemen, with your kind permission, I would like to say a few words; but first I would like to propose a minute's silence in respect for the soul of Sibella Cottle."

The diners stood to attention solemnly and the great clock tick-tocked through the silence. Francis completed the meditation with, "May she rest in peace."

He then went on to say,

"This is my maiden speech, so I hope you shall not judge me too harshly. I thought I should mark my elevation to the baronetcy of Balla following the demise of my father, Sir Robert. As you know, I am Welsh-Irish although most of my life has been spent in Cardiff. The same is true of my sister, Charlotte. Both of us came to Ireland this summer to spend a second extended period at Balla.

"Neither of us has reached our majority, but I will turn twenty-one in August of next year. Tomorrow, I shall return to Cardiff to continue my clerical studies. I hope to become a man of the cloth like Father Nolan. I want to thank him for giving Sibella the last rites and for making the necessary arrangements for her burial in Cottlestown."

Father Nolan smiled as the guests applauded.

"I am pleased that Charlotte has taken an interest in the campaign for Catholic emancipation. Discrimination against people arising from their religious orientation is intolerable and an insult to the teaching of Jesus Christ. Charlotte has found someone to admire in Sibella's daughter, Cecilia, who has recognized the value of constitutional politics. I hope she will forgive me if I were less enthusiastic about the rebellion of 1798 that visited so much anguish on the people of Mayo. However, I know that she and her husband, the late President John Moore, were inspired by the republican ideal of achieving an independent Ireland and motivated by the North Americans and the French. Please join with me in a minute's silence in respect for the memory of President Moore, who sacrificed his life for the sake of his country."

More applause followed as the mood continued to mellow. Michael was astonished at the maturity of the youthful baronet.

"I am also happy that Mr de Blacquiere and Mrs Moran are with us today. Peter has shown great skill in the administration of the family estate. He had to make some difficult decisions over the years to keep our finances in order. No doubt, he and I will have to make more such decisions together, but that is for the future.

"You all know Mrs Moran. She has served my family with distinction over the years. I know that Kate found it hard when Sir Harry brought Sibella home to be mistress of Balla House. Sibella has now gone to her eternal reward, and I hope that Kate can put her distress behind her in the true spirit of Christianity."

Francis paused. All eyes focused on Harry's half-sister who flushed furiously. She had little option other than to nod assent and smile.

"Thank you, Kate." Francis continued. "Now I come to Sibella's eldest child, Michael. Why does this man crop up in my thoughts?"

Michael blushed, fascinated as to what might follow.

Francis adjusted his dinner jacket.

"It is an odd circumstance that if Sir Harry had married Sibella in Suffolk as planned, Michael would now be the baronet instead of me."

Michael appreciated that his mother's marital situation was now out in the open. Francis had laid it bare, with the courage or foolhardiness of youth.

Francis paused to sip water. The guests whispered excitedly. Michael wondered what would come next.

"Michael has had an extraordinary career, first as a soldier, then owner of a sugar plantation in Montserrat, and now as an estate manager at home. He has settled down to life in Mayo and has attracted the attention of my sister, Charlotte."

De Blacquiere, Kate and Father Nolan looked distinctly uncomfortable while Michael and Charlotte were surprised and pleased.

"I have spoken to both of them at length in the presence of Lady Lynch-Blosse. We have agreed that Charlotte will return to Cardiff tomorrow. She will have time to socialize and consider her future. Next summer, she will return to Balla. In the meantime, Michael has agreed to visit Montserrat once the harvest is complete. He will attempt to resolve his situation with his wife, Annabel, and his ownership of the plantation. Michael has expressed an interest in acquiring partial or full ownership of Ashbrook, Sibella's ancestral home and a property he now leases, and that decision must also be made. When these matters have all been resolved, I hope that Michael and Charlotte will be in a position to make a mature decision next summer in their own best interests and in the best interest of our families."

Francis wiped the sweat from his brow.

"Forgive me for rambling on for so long. Finally, I want to pay tribute to Sibella. She was a truly remarkable woman, of humble origin, orphaned at an early age and fostered by the Moores of Ashbrook. She raised seven wonderful children in challenging circumstances. There was rarely a dull moment in her life. She stood firm even when circumstances conspired to frustrate her marriage to Sir Harry despite her betrothal to him. I hope that I, too, may benefit from her example and stand firm when faced with difficulty."

Michael was dumbfounded but also impressed. The speech was a *tour de force*. Francis had unambiguously established his leadership of the Balla estate. De Blacquiere called for brandy and port. The mood was positive. Catholic Emancipation was on the way, but so too was an imminent population explosion.

Francis had sought to bring closure to the long-running saga of Harry and Sibella's relationship. Even though the young baronet had made some progress, the legacy of the couple would haunt the citizens of Balla for generations to come. On the other hand, if his own romance with Harry's great-niece, Charlotte, had a successful outcome, it could be the key to reconciliation.

* * * * *

A<small>S</small> THE GUESTS BEGAN to disperse, the footman handed Michael a letter edged in black. It was from Montserrat. To preserve his privacy, he walked into the library. He recognized the embossed seal of his plantation. Could it possibly be a message from Annabel? He had not heard from her for ten years. With shaking hands, he broke the seal and recognized the signature of his agent:

Galway's Sugar Plantation,
Montserrat.
Friday, 21 April 1820

Dear Mr Lynch,

I greatly regret to say that you wife, Annabel, has been killed in a tragic accident. In accordance with her wishes, she has been buried with her father, Neptune Lynch, on plantation land.

Please let me know if you wish me to take any further action.

Yours faithfully,

Valentine Blake.

"Oh no!" Michael cried. "No!"

"Poor Annabel," he thought. *"How could I have abandoned her?"*

The memory of his emigration to Montserrat all those years ago came back to flood his mind. How excited he had been by the prospect of a civilian career in the Caribbean far away from the killing fields of Europe.

When he set his eyes on the beautiful dark-skinned Annabel Lynch at Galway's Sugar Plantation, he fell in love. It was his first romance. When he eventually married her in Montserrat, in the company of Sibella, he was the happiest man alive.

When Annabel's father, Neptune Lynch died, Michael became the owner of a sugar plantation. Yet he yearned for Ireland. He had missed the company of his beloved mother and siblings. If he had fathered children of his own, he might not have felt so lonely.

"When I masterminded the repatriation of Sean Holian, I had unintentionally repatriated myself," Michael thought.

He had begged Annabel to stay with him but she never settled in Ireland. The coldness of the climate and the prominence of her skin colour had made her feel uncomfortable. So they parted, never to meet again.

"What a wretch I have been," he sighed within himself.

He was relieved that Sibella had been spared the horror of his news. Earlier that day, he had asked Cecilia and Charlotte to join him in a secluded spot in the pleasure garden after the funeral dinner. He was still in shock when he rejoined them to lead the way with a lantern under cover of darkness. As they entered the walled enclosure, the clouds lifted exposing a full moon.

"What a beautiful night," Cecilia said as a squirrel scampered up a magnolia tree. "Have you a surprise in store for us, Michael?"

"I have, but first the bad news."

"What is it?" Cecilia cried.

Michael felt the blood draining from his cheeks.

"Annabel has died in a tragic accident."

"Oh no! Please accept my sympathies, Michael," Cecilia said.

"And mine too," Charlotte added.

After a silent interlude, Charlotte said,

"May I ask what happened?"

"I do not know, but I feel so guilty."

"Why, Michael?" Cecilia inquired gently.

Michael shook his head.

"Because I abandoned her."

"Or did she abandon you?" Charlotte chimed in.

"Maybe we both abandoned one another," Michael said disconsolately.

Cecilia sat down on the grass by the fire pit and tried to comfort her brother.

"I understand how you feel, but you are not to blame. When John died, I was wracked with guilt. You must keep this a secret, both of you."

Michael sat down. He could never imagine his idealistic sister keeping a secret from her nearest and dearest. He looked at her inquisitively.

"When General Humbert captured Castlebar in 1798, John and I waited for his triumphal entry into the capital town of Mayo. His job was to welcome the victorious Frenchman on behalf of the United Irishmen. As we waited in Geevy's Hotel, John wavered."

Charlotte's mouth opened in wonder.

"How do you mean he wavered?"

"That is a long story for another day. I persuaded him to fulfil his duty," Cecilia replied. "What a silly girl I was! If I had not intervened, he would be alive today."

"But his reputation would have been destroyed!" Michael exclaimed.

"Exactly, Michael," Charlotte said.

"That is what Mama said as she brought me to my senses," Cecilia said with tear-laden eyes.

"That is quite a story, Cecilia. What a secret to keep in your heart!"

Then Michael thought, *"Poor Annabel. I must go to Montserrat at once and pray at her grave. I must stay there for a while and mourn her loss.*

Michael was grateful that both Cecilia and Charlotte respected his desolation. He sat on the grass and peered into the middle distance. All he could see was the image of a happy Annabel linking his arm at their wedding ceremony.

"You need time to grieve," Charlotte said. "We should leave your original surprise for another day?"

Michael was still in subdued mood. He found it difficult to shake the image of Annabel out of his mind.

"You are right, Charlotte. I do need time to grieve. But first, I must complete my duty to Mama. Did you notice the bonfire in the village?"

"Of course; it is St John's Eve," Cecilia said.

"Mama always loved the midsummer festival," Michael continued. "I thought we should remember her at midnight with a tiny bonfire."

Charlotte shivered in the midnight coolness.

"What about your brothers and sisters?"

"We have unfinished business that only the three of us would understand."

* * * * *

MICHAEL OPENED THE LANTERN and set a twig ablaze. He lit a small wood fire in a stone pit out of view of the Big House. They sat around the developing blaze as he placed a silver casket, a velvet box, a dagger and a bottle of olive oil on the grass in front of him.

"Kate Moran gave me the casket a few days ago. She said it belonged to Mama and contained something important."

"Possibly the spancel," Charlotte said.

Cecilia turned pale in the light of the crackling fire.

"Have you the key, Michael?"

"No, but Charlotte may."

Now it was Charlotte who paled.

"Gracious! You think it may be in the locket which Sibella entrusted to me on her deathbed to give to you?"

"I think so. Open it, Charlotte," Michael said.

Charlotte took the locket from her reticule. She shook it. It made a barely audible metallic sound. She opened it slowly.

Michael saw a silver key, a lock of hair and a portrait of a slim-featured young woman.

Against a background of flickering flames, Cecilia said emotionally,

"That is a miniature of Papa's mother, Elizabeth Barker of Suffolk. She died young. Papa must have given the locket to Mama, perhaps when they ran away to Suffolk at the beginning."

"Whose are these hairs?" Charlotte asked, counting the seven strands.

"They must be the seven hairs which Judy Holian required from Papa's head to make the spancel," Michael said.

"And is the spancel in the casket?" Cecilia asked.

Charlotte passed the key to Michael who tried it for size. After a little jiggling, the key entered the tiny keyhole and eventually the lid snapped ajar. Michael lubricated the hinges with olive oil, then prised open the casket to reveal a piece of folded fabric.

Charlotte's eyes widened.

"Is this the spancel?"

"Open it up, Michael!" Cecilia implored.

Michael wondered if the unfurling of the multi-coloured fabric would bring a curse on his love for Charlotte.

"This was made from the skin of Papa's daughter, my half-sister, young Ellen Colgan."

Michael was distraught as the enormity of that sacrilegious deed sank into his mind.

"Poor Mama must have been haunted by the memory of her youthful folly," Cecilia cried.

"She did it to protect her children," Charlotte said.

Each stared at this remnant of history so inextricably linked to their own existence. Silence reigned apart from the crackle of the fire and the rustling sound of wind through the trees.

"Why are we here, Michael?" Cecilia inquired tentatively.

Michael stared into the flames.

"We must decide what to do with the spancel on behalf of our siblings and the Colgan and Lynch-Blosse families. I raised the issue with Father Nolan yesterday. I thought the church might accept the spancel. Father Nolan could sanctify it and return it to the Colgan grave. The parish priest almost had a seizure. He said he would need to consult the archbishop, but I hold out little hope of any action being taken by the clergy. They would like to forget the whole matter."

"Should we burn it?" Cecilia asked, raising her eyebrows.

Michael frowned.

"That is what Mama wanted. However, if we burn it the spell will be broken."

"The spell that linked your parents," Charlotte said. "Now that both are in heaven, an earthly spell cannot affect them."

"But can it affect any one of us?" Cecilia asked.

Michael had decided to be decisive, although not fully convinced of the prudence of his action.

"Mama would never have asked me to burn it, if she thought it would harm any one of us. Mayhap she thought that burning it would release the soul of Ellen Colgan to heaven, as well as releasing the curse into the ether. With your permission, I am going to throw it into the fire."

He paused to await the reaction of his sister. When she nodded after an interval, he looked at Charlotte, who nodded also. Michael threw the spancel into the flames. He grasped the hands of Cecilia and Charlotte as it caught fire and began to disintegrate. Each silently recited a prayer for the souls of Ellen Colgan, Sibella and Sir Harry. As the flames gradually reduced the spancel to ash, Michael joined his hands in prayer.

"Now let Ellen, Papa and Mama finally rest in peace. May I also include Annabel in our prayers."

They gazed into the blazing fire, lost in thought. After a time, Michael picked up the velvet box.

"Mama gave me this on her deathbed. She asked me to give it to you, Cecilia."

Charlotte looked on with interest as Cecilia opened the box.

"It's a Tara brooch!" she exclaimed. "How lovely!"

"Papa gave it to Mama after the harvest at Ashbrook when he knew he wanted to marry her," Michael said.

"It is wondrously beautiful." Charlotte gazed at the precious ornament.

"Lady Lynch gave it to Papa after his marriage to Emily Mahon had broken up. She said it would bring him good fortune. Now it will bring fortune to you, Cecilia."

Tears welled in Cecilia's eyes at the memory of her beloved parents.

"What is it made from?" Charlotte asked.

"She said it was made of silver covered in gold," Michael replied.

Cecilia pinned it on her dress close to her bosom. Charlotte admired its amber and glass studs, stylised animals, spiral patterns and the sparkling diamond embedded in its pin.

*   *   *   *   *

MICHAEL ROUSED HIMSELF FROM his thoughts, picked up the dagger and fingered it absentmindedly. He made a mock slashing movement across his wrist.

"Michael!" Cecilia cried as Charlotte bit her lip.

"Hush, we must not draw attention to ourselves. Do not worry."

"What are you doing, Michael?" Charlotte asked with trepidation.

"I want to swear my love to you forever, my dearest Charlotte."

Michael brandished the dagger in his right hand and nicked his left arm. He pressed a white handkerchief against the burgeoning blood. Shortly afterwards, he removed the pressure to reveal a bright red stain.

"I love you with all my heart," he said.

With her heart pounding, Charlotte blushed.

"Pass me the dagger."

When she received it, she also nicked her left arm until a bloodstain appeared.

Michael pressed his handkerchief on to her bloodied arm and held it firm.

"I love you also, Michael Henry Lynch, with all my heart. I will hold this handkerchief as a symbol of our love until we meet again."

"Then I will marry you on St John's Eve in a ceremony around a bonfire at Ashbrook. Until then, *au revoir*, my darling."

As they lingered before the dying embers, Michael wondered if Sibella and Harry had witnessed the sacred ceremony from above. He hoped that they had done so with unrestrained joy in the happiness of their children.

Paul B McNulty

AUTHOR'S NOTE

The liaison between Sir Harry Lynch-Blosse, 7th Baronet, of Balla, Co Mayo and Sibella Cottle, an orphaned Catholic, is the focus of my work of historical fiction. The baronet's trustees urged him to abandon the alluring redhead and marry a woman of his own class and religion. Sibella countered by commissioning a powerful love charm made from the skin of an exhumed corpse. The local witch, Judy Holian, guaranteed that the spancel would spellbind Harry for life. After Harry died young in 1788, Sibella was in a precarious position notwithstanding the generous provisions made for their seven illegitimate children in his will.

Variants of this story have been published in *Legends of Connacht* by Matthew Archdeacon (1839) and in *The Spancel of Death* by T H Nally (1916), which was critiqued and published by Adele Dalsimer in 1983. Archdeacon portrayed Sibella as uneducated and a "professed woman of pleasure." She was not a peasant, according to Nally, but rather a governess at Moore Hall, the stately mansion of the illustrious Moores of Mayo who moved there from Ashbrook in 1795. I have portrayed Sibella as an orphaned daughter of Michael Cottle and Isabel Kelly, a sister of Louisa Moore of Ashbrook who subsequently fostered her as an infant.

When the Abbey Theatre approved *The Spancel of Death* for staging, William Butler Yeats suggested that the author might use fictional names:

> *lest their retention might cause pain or give offence to*
> *any living descendants of the persons dealt with…*

Nally argued, in response, that the story had been in the public domain since 1839. He also sought advice from Sir Henry Robinson, Vice-President of the Local Government Board of Ireland from 1898 to 1922, who responded:

> *I…think it is the most powerful and dramatic thing I have ever read.*
> *It held me spellbound…my wife (Harriett Lynch-Blosse, 1862-1942,*
> *a great great-grandniece of Sir Harry) doesn't see any reason*
> *why any of her family should object to the play.*

The Abbey Theatre had to cancel its scheduled production of the play on Easter Tuesday 1916 due to the Easter Rising. No theatre has staged the play since then although Sarah Allgood had agreed to play the role of Judy Holian.

These sources, supplemented by "The Lynch-Blosse Papers" by K W Nicholls in 1980 and a report by Craig Lynch-Blosse of Harry's early but unsuccessful marriage to Miss Mahon, form the basis of my novel, which has been extended to 1820, the projected time of Sibella's death. Wherever the documented history runs cold, I have used conjecture to fill the void. The elopement of Harry and Sibella to Suffolk is fictional as is his proposal of marriage. Likewise, Emily Mahon's attendance at Harry's funeral is fictional as well as Sibella's attraction to George Moore after Harry dies.

The fate of Sibella's seven children is largely unknown. Her three boys were educated at the George Ralph Academy in nearby Castlebar. The eldest boy, Michael Lynch joined the British army consistent with Nally's claim that:

> *Some of those children were officers in the Kings Life Guard.*

His subsequent emigration to Montserrat is fictional. Also fictional is Michael's chance encounter with Sean (assumed forename) Holian, the transported husband of witch Judy; his marriage to Annabel Lynch, the sole heir to a sugar plantation; and his later liaison with Charlotte Lynch-Blosse.

The liaison between John Moore, President of the Republic of Connacht in 1798, and Cecilia Lynch, the daughter of Harry and Sibella is fictional. However, if Sibella was a governess at Moore Hall as suggested by T H Nally, then Cecilia could have been a resident of both Ashbrook and Moore Hall in the period leading up to the Rising of 1798 thus providing an opportunity for romance. Thomas Flanagan in *The Year of the French* (1979) also suggested a lover for John Moore, namely, Ellen Treacy of Ballycastle in north Mayo.

I have used some minor license in the interest of clarity. Moate House was the original residence of the titled Lynches, later Lynch-Blosses, in Balla. When destroyed by fire in 1808, a new residence, Athavallie House, replaced it. To avoid confusion, I have used Balla House as a descriptor for both residences.

I have also avoided duplication of first names as far as possible. To this end, I re-christened Lady Mary Browne (cited in *The Spancel of Death)* as Lady Harriett. She was a cousin of Lord Altamont of Westport, a title used as a general descriptor to portray both Peter Browne who died in 1780 and John Denis Browne who died in 1809.

I have used the surnames of Colgan, Cottle and Holian when assured by local historian, Patrick Sheridan of Balla, that local sensitivity is not an issue. Similar comments, supported by surname analysis in Balla, apply to those bearing the surnames of McDermott and Moran.

I would appreciate comments on my novel at paul.mcnulty@ucd.ie.

Paul B McNulty

PARTLY FICTIONALISED PEDIGREE
of SIR HARRY LYNCH-BLOSSE, 7ᵗʰ BARONET

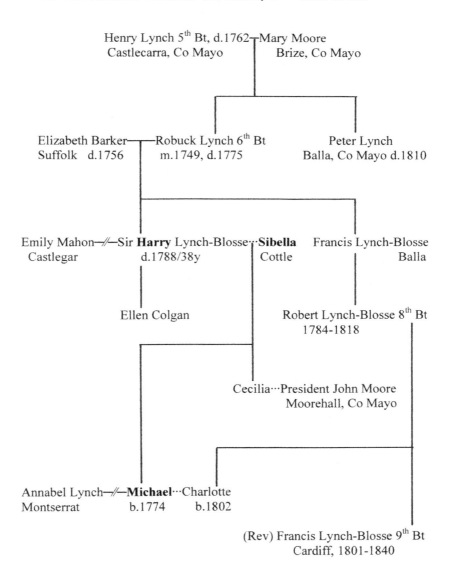

Henry Lynch 5ᵗʰ Bt, d.1762—Mary Moore
Castlecarra, Co Mayo   Brize, Co Mayo

Elizabeth Barker——Robuck Lynch 6ᵗʰ Bt   Peter Lynch
Suffolk   d.1756   m.1749, d.1775   Balla, Co Mayo d.1810

Emily Mahon—//—Sir **Harry** Lynch-Blosse—**Sibella**   Francis Lynch-Blosse
Castlegar   d.1788/38y   Cottle   Balla

Ellen Colgan   Robert Lynch-Blosse 8ᵗʰ Bt
                           1784-1818

Cecilia⋯President John Moore
Moorehall, Co Mayo

Annabel Lynch—//—**Michael**⋯Charlotte
Montserrat   b.1774   b.1802

(Rev) Francis Lynch-Blosse 9ᵗʰ Bt
Cardiff, 1801-1840

ABOUT THE AUTHOR

PAUL B MCNULTY

I write historical novels based on real events in 18th century Ireland. My apprenticeship in writing commenced at University College Dublin where I edited an engineering magazine, *The Anvil*. Afflicted with wanderlust, I travelled west to Ohio State and MIT to continue my studies to master's and doctoral level. While in Boston, my interest in history unfolded through participation in the Committee for Justice in Northern Ireland and in the anti-Vietnam war movement. On return to Ireland, I honed my writing skills, publishing scientific papers as well as writing on food-related issues in the popular media.

Following a career in Biosystems Engineering at UCD, I revisited my historical interest by studying "The genealogy of the Anglo-Norman Lynches who settled in Galway." The consequent discovery of a treasure-trove of forgotten Irish stories inspired me to write *Spellbound by Sibella,* a finalist in the 2012 William Faulkner Novel Competition. My debut novel deals with the turbulent romance between Irish beauty, Sibella Cottle and the rakish Sir Harry Lynch-Blosse of Mayo. Critiques from a writer's group, The Corner Table, of which I am a founding member, guide my writing.

I am at an advanced stage in my second novel, *The Abduction of Anne O'Donel,* a finalist in the 2012 William Faulkner Novel-in-Progress Competition. My third novel, *The Bloody Bodkins,* is at an earlier stage of development. It explores the possibility that a man may have been hanged for a crime he did not commit.

I live in Dublin with my wife, Treasa Ní Chonaola. We have three children, Dara, Nora and Meabh, and a grandchild, Lily Marie. I derive inspiration from the wild splendour of Mayo and Connemara. My website address is http://paul-mcnulty.com.

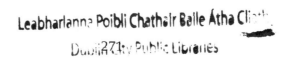

CPSIA information can be obtained
at www.ICGtesting.com
Printed in the USA
LVOW01s1747190516

489053LV00013B/547/P